Everything in the galaxy followed a logical structure.
Legion Dark Operator Kel Turner believed that. To know
the order of battle and how an enemy unit was organized,
was to know its purpose and how to destroy it. That logic
existed down to the smallest scale, down to what made
up life itself. Know a molecule's structure, you knew its
function—they were one and the same. It was no different
for Kel. He was Dark Ops and Dark Ops was him. Down to
his last cell.

But the covert action arm of the Legion was changing.
And so was he. Because if Dark Ops wasn't the same, how
could Kel be Kel?

From fighting a gray war against a cunning adversary
bent on genocide, to slogging through a jungle hell full of
rabid dog-men, Kel wasn't going to stop until the mission
was done. He *was* his mission. But if the day was coming
when there would no longer be a Dark Ops for Kel, then
what would his mission be?

Who would he become?

DOC SPEARS   JASON ANSPACH   NICK COLE

ANGLES OF ATTACK

DARK OPERATOR   BOOK 5

GALAXY'S EDGE

ISBN: 978-1-949731-46-0

Edited by Lauren Moore
Published by Galaxy's Edge Press

Cover Art: Tommaso Renieri
Cover Design: Ryan Bubion
Formatting: Kevin G. Summers

Website: www.GalaxysEdge.us
Facebook: facebook.com/atgalaxysedge
Newsletter (get a free short story): www.InTheLegion.com

KILL TEAM 3 DARK OPS

PVC PATCH

01

"The Angle of Attack is the balance to an Angle of Exposure. For every angle of exposure, there is a corresponding angle of attack for which a minimum of one weapon, ideally more, provides a countering force. The CQB principle of Force Superiority dictates the more guns in the fight, the better. This can apply to every violent encounter and is valid tactically as well as psychologically."
—Legion Manual of Close Quarters Battle

The milk of bright morning sunlight bathed Kel as he stepped into its glare. It'd been dark like the bottom of a mine shaft when he crowded with the rest of his team into the TOC, many, many hours ago. Now liberated from the oppressive throng of Republic officers crowded together to hear the op order, like animals sharing a burrow in winter, he took a moment to breathe in the glorious brightness.

Kel stole small moments like this for himself. Sun on his face, he closed his eyes and thought of a sky of cotton ball clouds. A glade of yellow-leafed trees swaying in the breeze. Of small animals and birds, playing in ignorance of the machinations of the toiling sentients around them. He hadn't seen such fauna here, but he imagined it. Otherwise, there would be nothing to contemplate but the sterile, snow-covered mountain crags around them.

Hardball's steps halted beside him. Kel knew it was him. He announced his presence with a juicy spit of stim-leaf, aimed at some innocuous target in the snow. His own personal bombing campaign. It was a gooey, light green liquid sortie that issued forth every few minutes, never ceasing as long as Sergeant Harding was out of armor, as they all were. And Kel didn't need to open his eyes to identify the next sound, that of a palm slapping a forehead.

"I could choke-slam every one of 'em," Hardball muttered, definitively breaking the silence. "The frellin' idiots."

So much for his meditation.

The interruption didn't bother him. What bothered Kel was that he agreed. They *were* idiots. The leaders of the Scarlet Division were acting the fool. But at the moment what bothered Kel most was that he couldn't join in on dogpiling curses on the Repubs.

It wouldn't be officer-like.

Meadows materialized on his other shoulder. His team sergeant's catlike appearance contradicted his mass. Out of armor, he was the size of a combat war bot. In armor, he could intimidate a capital ship. "They're being baited. They're not even going to make a probe. They're just going to jump right into the middle of an ambush."

"Can say that again, team daddy," Hardball said before spitting out a solid mass of pale greenleaf, only to replace it with a wad of dark, fresh chew from the pouch in his pocket. He spat again. Emerald green. "Plus, they just refuse to consider that the Nems might be able to shut down all their toys. Re-fuse. They wanna rush head on into that valley and get kilt doin' the only thing they know how to do." He spat again. "It's just like you always say. They don't know what they don't know."

What his NCOs said was true. The division leadership was ignoring all the implications of what their recon revealed. That, plus the many odd tech failures that plagued the Republic Peacekeeper force. And the fact that it was the Nemanjic they were talking about here.

The operation order had been a spectacle of bizarre proportions. The colonel nodded approvingly when the staff officer reached the critical moment. A line so rehearsed, so hackneyed, Kel thought the man concealed secret relief when the room erupted in barks and cheers rather than yawns. Luckily, his audience was at least as delusional as he was.

"And then the enemy will tremble at the most terrifying vision in the known galaxy. The skies filled with the arrival of repulsor gliders, bringing silent death from above."

The brigade officers responded to the delivery of his trope with deafening roars, one conditioned by regimental tradition as much as genuine fighting spirit. A reflexive action, like that of a lab rat pushing a lever to get a reward. At hearing the phrase, "death from above," hoot like a madman and receive a food pellet. There was no other way to explain it. Because no one not so habituated could believe the man's hype.

The cap to the operation order was the pep talk from the brigade commander. The colonel took the podium again after the recitation of the order by his staff officers. His wavy silver hair, unnaturally held in place by some cosmetic product, contrasted with his ridiculously tan face. The effect made him look not younger but instead reminded Kel of a weathered bronze statue wearing a novelty wig.

Kel's father kept his own head trimmed neatly all his life. As a teenager, his dad once looked disdainfully at his son's collar-length hair to render judgment. "Hair is a woman's glory and a legionnaire's shame." Unless mission dictated, Kel kept his hair short, always remembering that moment.

"Men," the Scarlets' colonel said, pausing for effect. "I call you men because it is important to emphasize that we are men. And we must do what men do."

A holo flashed open behind the colonel, showing a younger version of himself sitting atop the turret of a heavy grav tank.

"I've led men into combat. And it's times like this when lies won't do. The gym never lies when we see results from hard work, nor does the mirror."

Another series of images floated behind him, all montages featuring the colonel. Kel recognized the planet. It was Praxis Two. A relatively minor skirmish occurred there twenty years ago. Now Kel understood the combat star the colonel wore had come from that campaign, famous for not a single shot having been fired by anyone but the Legion.

"This will be a fight for the history books. And it will be my honor to lead you all into the first major combat our brigade has participated in. I wouldn't ask any of you to do anything I haven't done myself many times."

At that, Kel led the rest of the team out during the colonel's droning remarks, hoping the rapt attention of the colonel's audience had concealed their departure.

Kill Team Twelve's last two pairs of boots made their way to Kel's sunning spot.

"It should really be the Legion taking the lead on this," Wiggy said, his perpetually flat affect sounding even more world weary than usual. "A single company of leejes could prep that battlefield for them. What are we going to do about it, sir?"

Before Kel could answer, Pabon added his protest. "Sir, you gotta try to talk some reason into these basics. This is a terrible plan. There's a lot of kids getting ready to die because their leadership is too unimaginative to conduct anything but an air assault." JP jammed hands in pockets as he assumed his perpetual slumped posture when out of armor. It only made his wide back appear even wider, as though he were concealing wings.

"The captain's already done what he could," Meadows intervened. "These basics always act like a fire and forget missile. Once they have a plan, there's no turning them away because nothing will change their minds. We did our job. The rest is up to them. I'm sorry someday we'll be sitting back talking about how stupid they were to get so many troops killed, but the captain's done what he could."

Kel was actually still a lieutenant. He'd been frocked to captain by the new DO commander to have a little more status among the Repubs. The month Kill Team Twelve had spent supporting the Repubs hadn't convinced Kel his new rank brought with it any extra influence among the closed-minded division staff.

"I'm heading back in," Kel said. "I can't sell them on a better plan. That ship's already jumped FTL. But maybe I can put us where we can do them some good."

"Want me to go with, sir?" Meadows asked. His towering presence would more likely intimidate the basics and make his pitch for a mission more difficult.

"No. Best I go alone."

The colonel had invited Kel to a pull-up contest with him and his officers on their first meeting. "I've heard about you legionnaires. It would be good for morale to have some healthy competition." Kel had begged off, instead training with the team the next morning in their usual combatives. When the colonel prodded him again the next day, he'd seen many of the officers pale and shrink at the suggestion. Clearly they'd been spying on the team's routine training. Blood was a normal byproduct, but that morning there had been a little more than usual.

No, by his mere presence alone, Meadows would probably make the sell harder. Kel would match the giant's intellect and military planning ability against any of the group inside the tent, still gathered in the dark, absorbing the final details of the OPORD. But it wouldn't do to explain his reasoning for leaving his team sergeant behind. It would seem too much like yet more criticism of the Scarlet Division's officers. However well deserved.

"I'm going to get us a job."

Kel was twenty-eight years old. Soon, twenty-nine.

Now more than ever, he missed being a sergeant.

He missed Team Three.

He missed Dark Ops being Dark Ops.

And he blamed himself for its demise.

02

The climb was almost straight up. Kel had a route planned and thought they could make the summit by dark. He would lead, despite his team sergeant's protest.

"The boss is still the best climber, Curt," Hardball answered, defending Kel's plan to the team sergeant. "At least, he's the fastest. Don't git too far ahead of us, sir."

"Not to worry, Gabe," Kel said using Sergeant Harding's first name. Kel preferred familiarity and had always appreciated being addressed so on Team Three. Yet another thing he missed. When he'd stood up the new Kill Team Twelve a year before, Meadows was quick to lay down the law on how it was going to be.

"I was never a fan of the lack of basic military courtesy on Team Three, sir," Meadows had told him their first day together. They'd been close friends. Equals. Kel didn't protest his new team sergeant's molding of the team to one with more Legion discipline than he was accustomed to in Dark Ops. But it didn't sit well with him. Maybe he'd made a mistake not taking Poul with him from Three to act as his team sergeant. Now Poul was the senior NCO on their old team.

A lot had changed.

"We won't sacrifice stealth for speed," Kel assured his team. He knew his own reputation for climbing. Fast. "The Nems may have moved off the floor and up into the peaks since we last came off this range. I've got a different route in mind to keep us out of sight and still put us over where we can spot the bunkers."

"No one I'd rather follow, sir." Hardball spat out his last chew before buttoning up. It would be days before buckets came off again.

Unlike the Republic's grand mission on Haemus, their own mission was simple. It was suspected the Nemanjic had a battalion of troops, maybe more, wintering in the Rila Valley. The overt fighting had slowed down between the human factions in this civil war—the Nemanjic and the neighboring Istrians—but hadn't ceased with the onset of another hard winter.

If it were only humans involved, the conflict would be fairly easy to understand. The addition of the aliens made the situation a murky water, hiding the true depths of the cause of the war. But on the surface was the one glaring beacon that brought them to this mudball. Genocide.

Sometime in the last generation, Planet Haemus had gone from one where humans lived in peace with the alien co-residents, the Bassinus, to one at war with itself. Even Kel had been affected by the SNN holos of the slaughter.

The Bassinus were so human-like in appearance, save for the tiny cleft of the upper lip, the ridged cranium, the pink skin. It would be difficult for a third alien species to differentiate the two side-by-side.

The Istrians stood by the Bassinus and invaded the Nemanjic continent to defend their nonhuman brethren. The civil war had been raging for a year before the Republic intervened. What Kel countenanced was one half-hearted attempt after another by Republic diplomats, Galactic Republic peacekeeping forces, and economic sanctions by the House of Reason, until public opinion forced a response more significant than stern lectures on the daily news.

And so far, what had been accomplished by committing the Republic Army to the planet had been nothing short of underwhelming. Operation Swift Guardian was supposed to change all that. Kel and Team Twelve had done the hardest work, trying to locate the elusive Nems in large number.

The Nemanjic Guard were as close to a peer as Kel had yet experienced. The Nems were master slicers who assaulted commerce and banking data streams around the core and mid-core. There was never proof that the criminals were state-level actors, but there was always suspicion that when a den of Nem slicers were arrested, they'd operated with some level of support above that of a simple crime gang. So, when things started going wonky with the Peacekeeper's tech, Kel saw trouble brewing.

Early in the Haemus emergency, a squad of peacekeepers crashed to their deaths responding to a report of genocide in a Bassinus village. It was thought an unfortunate accident. A result of excessive velocity and poor control by the driver on the winding canyon road. Simply one tragedy compounded by another. There'd been many speeches and grave newscasts mourning the lives of the Aristrean troops lost in the attempt to save another group of beleaguered Bassinus. Then it happened again. Soon the peacekeepers were grounded.

"Until we can prove otherwise, the cause is glitchy isolinear chips in the off-core tech," the Republic army intel officer told them in a brief. Aristrea was a backwater that copied tech rather than purchased it. Knockoffs were never as good as the real thing. "While we suspect the Nems are attempting to slice into military tech, entering a

Republic data stream is virtually impossible. Nem slicers are not considered a viable threat at this time."

At this time. The major was hedging his bets. If the Nems had developed the ability to drop any repulsor at will, the Repub Army efforts on Haemus would be as impotent as the peacekeepers' had been. And this first major engagement would be as legendarily bad as the first New Vega.

Kill Team Twelve was going to prevent that.

He'd purposefully chosen the steepest route, following a series of crevasses up to where they could crest a saddle and make their way over and down into the valley. Kel climbed this last run to the top without anchoring. It was a short chimney. Arms and legs scissored to push against the walls, he locked himself with his upper body, relaxed his legs and brought them up to splay out, and alternated in the short vertical hops until he reached the top. The crevasse widened as he ascended, and he had a momentary pang of doubt before he committed and sprang to one side. With a sure grip from both hands, he eased over the ledge.

That would've been classic, Kel mused, glad he hadn't fallen. He'd lost concentration for a brief moment, picturing himself falling down the chimney, like a woban-ki he'd once seen in micro-G, four limbs thrust straight out in panic. The armor would prevent any serious injury as he collided against the walls, but it would've been embarrassing. It was a difficult balance with the mind.

Considering consequences without letting an image of failure cloud performance.

Never picture failure, he berated himself. *Always see it done right in your mind. Concentrate on the task, not the outcome.*

"I'm going to anchor and drop one to you," Kel said from the ledge.

The sun was setting. Returning to this range would've been easier had they used the ice climbers again. The bikes could've carried them and their gear and put them above the tree line and into the valley in less than a day. This time, it had to be on foot and with mimetic camo deployed. He planned a steep route to maximize concealment from any watchful Nems, adding to the difficulty. There would be some technical climbing needed to get into the valley on the other side. It had to be done this way.

Only a crazy person would come at the Nems from this direction.

"I'd say you achieved your goal, boss," Meadows said, a little strain in his voice as he received the snaking ball from above, the thin line trailing out of it as it descended. "I'd never expect anyone to take this route."

"I'd never take this route," JP said. Everyone knew JP was not a fan of climbing.

Meadows anchored the autoascender. "Set, sir."

Kel triggered the package and felt the carbon line swell and expand, then go taut down its angular course as holds deployed from it like well-ordered quills from a spiny dragon.

Meadows was first to reach the ledge.

"I'll push up and get eyes out," the team sergeant said without waiting for reply. JP came next, taking Kel's offered hand and moving wordlessly onto the first flat expanse they'd had for hours. It was the silence of relief. Disdain for heights or not, JP was as solid an operator as Kel had ever known.

JP had come to Dark Ops when Kel was still a sergeant. They hadn't had the opportunity to associate, but Kel heard the word spreading quickly about the new operator. He was a fanatic. A fanatic about personal combat. Kel could relate. But it was soon apparent that JP was on an entirely different level.

Any unoccupied moment, JP tested his body against immovable objects. A duracrete column would be met by his bare fists, knuckles bouncing off their unyielding surface. In his quarters, he relaxed by watching a holo while rolling a steel rod up and down his shins, every so often treating his legs like a percussive instrument and tapping them with the heavy cylinder. Kel adopted the habit. It hurt like hell, but soon his own shins became dulled to the impacts, and when he kicked the training bot's forgiving surface, it left a dent.

The first of JP's tics that Kel personally witnessed left an impression. Near the CQB complex on Victrix were a stand of pines. One day Kel and Team Three watched from the shoothouse catwalk as the solitary JP strolled over to a particularly straight one.

"Hey, Kel," Poul called to gain his attention. "That's the new guy on Two. Whatcha wanna bet he's going to do something crazy? I hear he's part Paladonian." Paladonians were from a high gravity world and were renowned for their strength. Kel had been there. The new operator didn't have the typical short squat appearance, but Poul had said "part."

The man removed his jacket and wrapped it around the slender trunk as a thin cushion for what he did next.

He struck the tree with his forearm, swinging his arm one way to deliver a blow, then reversing to strike it the other way. Lightly at first, slowly, testing, until the man seemed confident. Then he unleashed.

Kel had never seen that kind of power from a human before. JP assumed a rhythm, driving from his hips as he alternated using the ridges of his forearms in a mesmerizing cadence of blows. Soon Kel understood as the top of the tall pine began to oscillate as though bending to a shifting breeze. JP timed his strikes to match the sine wave of the now swaying tree, each blow increasing the amplitude of its swing, until it rocked. He stopped before the tree broke from the strain.

Almost as soon as Kel had been given the task of standing up Team Twelve, JP approached Meadows, asking to be considered for the new team. Kel was glad he had, his fear of heights notwithstanding.

Hardball followed Wiggy and stood with Kel another moment to watch the ball of the ascender reverse course back to them, swallowing the line as it returned. Gabe stretched to look down over the ledge. "That was fun. Let's do it again soon, boss. Just not real soon."

It had been a grueling climb to get to this point. Kel doubted any other team could have made it as quickly as they had.

Meadows took the lead on the narrow goat trail, the pitch such that they had to balance with a hand against the face of the crags as they walked. Reaching a spot large enough for them to leave their marching file, Wiggy halted and bent forward, hands on knees. Kel knew the strain he was trying to relieve. Wiggy'd volunteered to hump the Stone on this climb. The heavy blaster had the weight to match its power. There wasn't a free lunch when it came to weapons. More power meant more weight. It would normally be toted by one of their DOGR robots, but not even the versatile autonomous combat multipliers could navigate a climb like this. Only a beast born to the task. Or a legionnaire.

Hardball moved to take the weapon off Wiggy's back. "Switch out, man. I got her." Wiggy grunted thanks and gingerly rose to full height again, testing his back as he did.

"Just about there," Meadows encouraged.

Kel agreed. Checking the nav, it looked as close to ideal as he could imagine. The sun set fully, marking their transition to the walking part of their journey by abruptly matching it with the rapid curtain of night. To their HUDs, night was merely a concept, never a constraint. Problem was, against the Nems, the darkness might not be the ally it normally was. The Nems had good tech.

Kel recognized the frozen runnels from their recent visit to this altitude. They bled down the slopes like streams of cold lava. It had been a week of careful, painful work. The five of them had split up and ringed the valley to tunnel hides out of the snow and ice, one scoop at a time.

It was a week well spent.

They were in the valley that first time as proof of one of the earliest lessons Kel had learned about the difference between perception and reality. Of how technology blurred the latter and fed the former. How planners in a dry, warm office chose to see things in their own way. And always, how the person on the ground could be ignored when *his* reality didn't match *their* perception.

The Scarlets sent drones into the valleys and poured over Navy orbital scans, searching high and low for sign of the remaining Nem forces. There was at least a division unaccounted for in their order of battle, and the hunt had been on to find, fix, and finish them. The Scarlets were spoiling to get into a fight, so it hadn't been hard to sell them on his offer to do the legwork to perform a ground reconnaissance of potential redoubts. They agreed, but not for the best reasons.

"Frankly, Captain," the division intelligence officer said, "it doesn't seem like a good use of your talents." The major wasn't as intimidated as some of the other staff seemed of him, but neither was he friendly. "That valley's a dry hole. Three different technical recons have come up with the same answer. It's empty."

Kel didn't want to come down on the man too hard. "Understood, Major. But we need boots on the ground. Drones and Navy flyovers can only get so much. They're not infallible. I can defeat most of that detection without tech. Just good old-fashioned use of the terrain."

That brought a scoff from several around the table.

"Captain, we all know the Legion's reputation," the brigade commander said, his uncomfortably white teeth revealed by the condescending grin. "And I don't doubt your abilities. But disguising a battalion or more of mechs and troops..." He trailed off, leaving his incredulity unfinished. "But, I'm not sure how to use you better." He paused as he considered his own analysis. "You have my permission to perform your reconnaissance. We'll keep up security operations in the hamlets as we continue to locate the last of the Nem Guard."

Kel could tell it was a relief to the room when the colonel dismissed him, the whispers already starting before he departed. Most of the recommendations Kel had presented to the Scarlets had so far gone ignored or unimplemented. They'd gone out on patrol to observe the security sweeps. The Bassinus in this sector lived in a segregated borough of the city and on adjacent farms. The aliens had been relocated out of the city and placed in refugee camps in an effort to protect them. The attempt at stopping the massacre of the aliens had been partially successful. There were still small raids, and a family of Bassinus had been killed last week. But there was little Kel and the team could do. It was a task too massive for five men. The team hadn't really had a function for the past month and getting out of the Scarlets' sphere and on the ground was not only necessary to fulfill his mission to provide assistance to the army, it was necessary for the team's sanity.

By the end of a week spent on their bellies mapping the valley bowl and the foothills that rimmed it, they'd confirmed Kel's theory. The sensors had missed the Nems.

He was impressed. It'd been like finding an object hiding in your blind spot at night. You had to look away quickly to see a shadowy outline of what actually stood right before you, hidden in plain sight. Hidden below were dozens and dozens of concealed warrens, large and small. The Nems not only utilized excellent physical camouflage, they were running a combination of passive and active measures to hide any electromagnetic emissions. Dark Ops armor had the deceptive ability to bend light and change color and texture to suit the environment. Kel kept a mimetic net in his sniper daypack as well. The Nems had something different. It was a field, projected like a holo and not physical, but it hid any emission behind it and gave off a spectral emission almost undistinguishable from the terrain around it.

"Okay. There's something there," the intel major conceded. "I agree the time differential weighted scans show enough background difference that it's not natural. Why weren't you able to get closer?"

The colonel interrupted. "Major Gilbert, I know you'd feel better had the captain returned with a holo of a Nem servicing a tank in one of those dens." He shifted his attention to Kel. "What you've found, Captain, is the first significant indication of the Guards."

This was a first. The colonel's insecurity and overcompensations dropped at the prospect of closing with an enemy. Maybe he wasn't completely self-absorbed.

"Colonel." A lieutenant stepped into the TOC. "We've got activity in the valley. Drone just picked up vehicular movement across the valley floor." A holo over the table showed a combat sled appearing from behind a small rise to float across the valley for several minutes before disappearing behind a rocky outcrop on the opposite rise.

"Someone broke discipline," the operations officer said. "That sled came right out of one of Captain Turner's anomalies."

The colonel squinted. "Gentlemen. We're not going to waste further time debating the significance of this. We're moving the brigade to stage for a sweep of that valley. Start your planning and let's be ready to move."

"We're about there," Meadows said as he halted.

Kel moved up with him and took a long scan. He compared what he saw to the map and the markers they'd overlaid. From here they'd have direct eyes on a dozen of the anomalies ringing the valley. Undoubtably, they concealed the unaccounted-for Guards units. Some were quite large. Definitely large enough to hold mechs. The entrance to the valley floor was just out of sight around the peaks to their right, a narrow mouth between the fangs of the rapidly rising peaks. It was a choke point for sure, and the first target for suppressive bombardment.

They descended to a spot a few hundred meters off the valley floor. Kel thought they should have a good view of what was going to play out from here.

"This is the last spot with decent cover," Kel said as he took a knee and pointed. The lip they now sat on had a variety of boulders, driven by rains and gravity to call this spot a temporary home in the geologic time scale until eventually finding their final resting place somewhere below. The team was high enough to have a good vantage yet low enough to be close to the fight.

"Find your spot," Meadows said as they spread out.

"Feels funny not being in a hide," Wiggy said, not alone in his apprehension.

"Nah," Hardball grunted. "I'm glad to not be in a grave again. Sure, we're burning juice to keep the camo running, but we ain't gonna be up here for a week this time. We can save power soon enough. Once the bombing runs start and the Scarlets drop in, the whole planet's gonna know where we are."

03

"I'm not underestimating our enemy," Brissell explained to his executive officer as he passed his hand over his smooth-shaven head. The enormous mustache acted like a bushy curtain to conceal his mouth. There was never any doubt as to whose voice came from beneath it; Brissell's voice was as hard as his physique. "That I hold them in contempt hasn't clouded my judgment. Not with your constant remonstrations as a reminder. I know why our ancestors abandoned polygamy so long ago. You're like a second wife. Can I say nothing without fear of your criticism?"

Daegor accepted the dig but wasn't so sure his point had found its target with the commander. His loyalty to Brissell was absolute. But being a blind follower was no way to serve. He proudly held the man's laurels, but always tempered such moments with the knowledge that hubris killed. It was his duty not just by position, but by friendship. He made his point about overconfidence as sharp as he dared without severing their relationship.

"We've never faced them in open combat, Brissell. Not in a brigade-sized attack."

Patriotism and pride were fine things. But only Daegor had seen firsthand how the warriors from the core fought. Especially those armored Legion demons. Now, deep in the cave that had been their operations center these past months, he had grown even more uneasy about their commander's outlook.

They'd been together for decades, starting as equals, with Daegor soon becoming the junior as Brissell rose to command. He accepted it without resentment. Family name meant a lot on Haemus. Not that Brissell didn't deserve his command. There was no one he respected more. And despite their friendship, sometimes his role as devil's advocate roused the famous storm and thunder Brissell was known for. Bearing those cataclysms was part of his job, too.

"As you continue to point out, Daegor. But they've not once bested us. Not once. And I agree, in the attack they're going to be a different animal than the one we've stung so many times. The Greens aren't clowns," he said, referring to the Republic Army. "But they are clownish. And conceited. It's their conceit that makes them so unwilling to consider that we've got the technologic edge on them, a poor mid-core world such as Haemus. And they refuse to change their tactics. That's the hallmark of arrogance. And if you can't back it up, arrogance is a sin. They can't. We can. So, they own a sin we'll make them pay for."

Daegor admitted that their slicers had defanged the Greens, shutting down their repulsors at will, turning them into foot-borne infantry cut off from immediate support. But slicing would not win a war for them. They'd used their secret tech sparingly but effectively, judiciously targeting their combat sleds. At first it had been an exercise in probing the closed data stream of Republic tech. The supposedly impenetrable network of their devices. The success in causing small malfunctions had let their slicers map many of the Greens' systems. They'd bloodied the Republic troops in platoon- and company-sized operations, forcing their withdrawal by killing critical systems at just the right time and location. A sled dropping like a slaughterhouse rindar hit by the butcher's bolt had great effect when it was the lead vehicle in convoy on the narrow roads along the cliffs. Intelligence confirmed the Repubs blamed the failures on glitches, never suspecting it was not their maintenance at issue but rather a silent attack by the tech-savvy Nemanjic Guard.

It was an awesome accomplishment, penetrating the Republic's data stream. One he took cautious satisfaction in. Daegor had another source of pride as he considered the upcoming battle against the Repubs: their network of loyal spies.

Brissell's assessment that the Repubs were clownish was correct. Had they sequestered their troops from the populace, gaining an accurate assessment of them would have been much more difficult. Low- to high-level Greens fraternized with the populace to show their good intent. Frequenting shops and places of entertainment in the safe zones was meant to lull the populace into accepting their presence. While the current of Republic credits was appreciated by the local entrepreneurs, it hadn't diminished their loyalty. The flow of information from the naïve Repubs was like a pipeline carrying clear water.

He was not alone in thinking the pleasure girls were patriots. It was hard to be too critical of his enemy for their lustfulness. Nemanjic women were among the most beautiful in the galaxy.

He thought of his own daughter and involuntarily shuddered as he shook the image from his mind. She would never have to sacrifice herself that way. What they did now, they did for her survival. For their entire culture.

The Bassinus would be wiped out and their Republic protectors repelled like the pack of opportunistic predators they were. Hurt them badly enough, the rest would limp away, realizing that it would be too costly to fight a war they didn't need to win. Haemus was unaligned and meant little to the Republic. And they were not alone among independent worlds to resent their meddling. Daegor agreed with Brissell and the others that it was misplaced sympathy that brought them to Haemus. They couldn't see the danger the Bassinus represented, not just to the Nemanjic but to all humans. Once bloodied, their House of Reason would take the expedient route to save face and depart. Then cooler heads would prevail among the politicians at the center of the galaxy.

But first they had to provide the resounding defeat that would send the message that the Nemanjic people were to be left alone. It could be done. He had faith in Brissell's plan. But he feared that not every engagement with the Greens would be as one-sided as their bait and ambush tactics had been to date. Trying to get Brissell to admit that had been a failing proposition, now more than ever since the achievement of the slicers and the false confidence he was trying to prevent his friend from adopting.

"Stop your worrying, old friend," Brissell said to dismiss the topic once and for all. "We've come a long way since our first encounter with the Greens."

The Peacekeepers had been little more than an annoyance then. Especially after the successes at killing their combat vehicles in such a sublime manner. They had the Istrian interference all but silenced, the Bassinus fleeing in droves. Then the Republic entered the picture.

The Greens tried to interfere with the Bassinus relocation. Skirmishes with their small patrols had resulted in heady victories with Brissell's plan at total resistance. They'd bloodied the Greens, and well.

The Greens' next move was unexpected. Bombing campaigns. He had to give the Republic forces credit. Their early efficiency targeting bases and destroying the Guards' ability to fight in the air left them nearly powerless. The loss of fighters and transport craft had been felt. It was like losing an arm, or a leg. The vital tool was missed, but they had more limbs and the will to use them. When the Greens destroyed the last of their air defenses, they transitioned to the ground campaign. The Republic's mistake had been not seizing the day and conducting an all-out assault on the Guard. Instead, they became occupiers. Their next mistake.

The code that pierced the ether to render the Greens impotent was a hidden strength. And not their only one. No, like a seamball player with more than one pitch in his repertoire, their real strength was not found in the airpower or in the few battalions of heavy tanks destroyed so early in the Republic's campaign against them. It was in their combat mechs. Their other hidden weapon. Small, mobile, deadly. Brissell's own grandfather had helped pioneer the technology, and the tactics of the walkers. Verlopov had been a Repub. An academy graduate. When he returned home after a career among them, fighting Savages and quelling civil wars across the galaxy, he returned dedicated to making his own people impervious to what waited in the depths of the black sea of space.

Verlopov taught them that depending on the Republic was no different from calling the cops after the crime had happened. Always they came with too little, too late. Daegor grew up revering Brissell's grandfather. The general who made the Guard what it was. The stories of his combat against the Savages more intense than any fantasy tale he'd ever read. And because of him, they never had to leave Haemus to learn the warrior's craft.

They learned their trade against the Istrians, their neighbors to the west, and against the Malgar to their north. Territorial disputes and wars lasting weeks filled their common history. Nothing to rival Verlopov's record, but enough to allow Brissell to distinguish himself. And Daegor no less than his friend. But family name was family name. It was preordained that someday Brissell would lead. Now Daegor stood with his friend who commanded the forces that would mark the end of Nemanjic subservience to the neighboring nations. And to the sickness of the Bassinus.

The Bassinus.

Like all on Haemus, they'd lived among them their entire lives. So human in appearance that it was easy to overlook the mouth, the ridged cranium, the pink skin. They'd coexisted for centuries, human and Bassinus, if not in cooperation, at least in amicable tolerance of each other.

Daegor was closest to Brissell, but not even he would bring up the subject of Brissell's son and his betrayal. The Millennium Call had brainwashed a generation. If they didn't stop the subversion, the Nemanjic would be lost. So would the Istrians and the Malgar. And the rest of Haemus. All but the Nemanjic were just too blind to see it.

Now they waited. Hidden, not in hiding. Soon the Greens would come. And soon the lifelong friends would know if Brissell's bluster or Daegor's caution was the superior strategy. Because if Daegor's fears were correct and they'd underestimated the Greens, their culture was at an end.

But there was a small hope. One Daegor kept to himself, not wanting to further embolden his friend. Perhaps he was deceiving himself, the worst deception of all for a warrior. Still, it was hard to not feel that small glimmer of hope. If he was right, the Republic underestimated them so much so, that they'd seen not a single Legion company among the invading meddlers.

Therein lay his hope. And their salvation.

It was as a young lieutenant that Daegor had seen the Legion. They were more myth than reality. The tales of General Rex. Of waves of Savage marines falling to Legion fury, unleashed like bolts of lightning from the gods above. That's how Verlopov had made it all sound. Daegor grew up almost a member of the family. Almost a brother to Brissell. Almost equal.

It was at Verlopov's urging he took the year to learn from the Repubs. Brissell was already too proud, even as a newly minted officer, to believe there was something of value to be learned from the decadent core. He detected the general's displeasure at his grandson's intransigence on the matter. Daegor had no such disdain for the Republic Army. Verlopov himself had been one. Even if Brissell cared little, Daegor would not spurn his hero. He would take Verlopov's guidance, even if his own blood would not.

Daegor shadowed the battalion commander closely for months, learning all he could as the junior visitor. He'd been treated respectfully, but he knew underneath their smiles, they thought of Haemus as a backward world and their Guard a toy army. But at the end of his time with them, those who looked down on him had themselves been humbled. Because it was the Greens who'd felt like rubes on that incredible day.

The ratio of attackers to defenders necessary to overcome a static defense was classically accepted as requiring four times as many attackers to succeed. And as the defenders, they had the numbers. Daegor had been taken into the Green officers' confidence. Like the Greens, he relished the battle to come. Because their defense could not be broken. When the enemy finally advanced across the desert, it would be like the beginning of a sweet dance that would end in a passionate coupling and a satisfaction brought only by victory.

Except that's not what happened.

How had their defense failed? And so quickly? The answer came to them by pieces.

It wasn't by clash of impervisteel that they fell.

It was their failure of imagination.

Perhaps the same hubris that plagued Brissell now.

The armored division rolled onto the plain before them. But the coupling was not sweet. Instead it was perverse. Humiliating.

Artillery support was of course notionalized for the exercise, and the graders agreed that every grid square of the enemy's advance would face a rain of plasma and shrapnel. So how did the calls for artillery result in empty air? At the same time, reports trickled into headquarters that a strongpoint on the line had fallen. Silently. Daegor was stunned as the chief referee, a colonel, told the battalion commander that his unit was combat ineffective, his headquarters destroyed. The commander's query as to how this had come to pass was answered with the simplest explanation.

"Legion reapers."

Daegor saw these reapers. Briefly. He left the TOC to assess the battlefront for himself. Iron gorillas moved in packs like running wolves. Visible for flashes as they bounded, then invisible as they disappeared into defilade too small to conceal a man, much less the armored hulks they were. Never pausing as they wreaked their havoc. They continued through the lines and beyond. With their line breached, the division of heavy armor bore toward them like a stormfront, their own defenses shut down by the evaluators. Dead.

The Legion first attacked deep behind their lines, a single platoon neutralizing their artillery support, having infiltrated by parachute from orbit undetected. Another had attacked their air support. And yet another the Corps headquarters and supply trains. Their lines had been breached by another platoon of the armored devils in advance of the tank attack.

A single Legion company had neutered the might of three Republic divisions in the defense.

Had it not been an exercise, the field would have been red with the blood of the entire corps. Back home, few accepted his tale as true, until Verlopov requested a briefing, curious as to what Daegor's time with the Republic had taught him.

"Regardless of what we may think of the Republic," the general said after hearing his report. "The Legion is why the Republic stands. We could hate them for that, but then without the Legion, no human life would remain to bear the jealous spite of them. We can hate the Republic, but we must respect the Legion."

Now he wondered why the House of Reason had not landed the Legion on Haemus. Unspoken to Brissell, he hoped they would not.

04

"Lightning-One transmitting in the blind. We have no guidance or target lock. I say again, we have no guidance or target lock. Unable to deliver payload."

"You hearing this?" Hardball said. "I'm dropping onto the Scarlet command net."

Kel looked skyward and let his HUD do the work for him. The tiny dots grew into recognizable shapes. Two trios of Shark tactical fighter-bombers soared above in trailing arrowhead formation. They would soon be out of the bombing corridor. On a sub-channel, he heard Hardball trying to enter the Scarlet's comm stream.

"Meteor, this is Ghost, entering net. I cannot raise Battle-Six, over."

He repeated the request several times. Kel dropped in and listened. It was a chorus of the deaf singing different refrains, dozens of lone voices without a conductor, each crammed into a single auditorium to perform their solo, lost in the cacophony. It had happened. The Nems had done the unthinkable.

"The Nems have everything jammed," Kel said. He ran a quick diagnostic and tried again.

"JP, launch a drone and get us eyes." If the Nems had comms jammed, only L-comm devices would function. But that only meant they could talk to themselves.

Meadows's voice was full of urgency. "Wiggy, hit those birds with a tight beam and tell them we can direct them onto target by laser."

Kel continued to listen to the chaos of the Scarlets as they tried to communicate with each other. He linked into the orbital to check the location of the Scarlets' forward elements. They should be at the mouth of the valley by now.

Nothing. He tried the link again.

Wiggy grunted. "No dice contacting the bombers. I've got the Sharks lazed and they can't hear me, or won't respond. I don't know how the Nems are doing it, but it's not just low frequency wave propagation they're interfering with. Sharks are out of line of sight now."

"You sure you had them painted?" Hardball asked.

With no hint of irritation, Wiggy replied, "I had a great splash on them. My comm shot should've practically deafened them."

Kel ran through options. "If they can't hear us, maybe we just start lazing targets and hope they comprehend we're down here marking for them. Featherheads aren't dumb. Someone'll figure it out."

If the pilots picked up on it, they could repurpose the ordnance for direct guidance. The payloads would follow the lasers to the undulating splashes painted on the targets by the non-coherent terminus of the beams. It was purely optical guidance. There would be no signal transmission to interfere with. That the Nems had jammed not only communications but also the active positioning guidance from orbit was too impossible to believe. Whatever the Nems had done, it was halting the attack as if duracrete had been poured on the Republic task force.

"Good plan, boss," Meadows said. "We'll be ready when they make another run. Hardball, keep on the net.

You get a hint the Sharks are coming around again, we'll all designate as many targets as we can."

Had it been one of their Talon crews in a similar circumstance, the aggressive pilots would've already dropped to make a low-level pass and hammer targets by sight if they couldn't guarantee a lock for the bombs. The safety of altitude wouldn't stop them from getting in the fight.

"Drone on station," JP said.

Kel opened a window and let it dominate his visor as he oriented to the map view. Marshaled a few klicks below the mouth of the valley were the Scarlets. A squadron of cavalry in light-armored Hardback fighting vehicles was pushing into the valley bowl as they watched. Kilometers behind them, the heavy grav tanks sat motionless. He wondered if the colonel had a holo cam trained on himself perched in one of the turrets to capture the mountains in the background.

"Those cavs aren't holding up," Kel narrated. "They've gotta know the air support failed. They're just rolling in blind, buttoned up in those Turtles like it's gonna make a difference to a particle beam or a chain gun. It won't for long."

Cut off from communication, they were taking the initiative to get forward and get eyes on the battle space.

That's what scouts do, Kel thought. *At least they're taking some initiative. But the armor is frozen. Why?*

"Any sign of air?" Meadows asked.

Hardball grunted. "Negative. They're holding on station quite a ways east. Still transmitting blind and asking for guidance."

"They aren't already clued in they aren't going to be getting any?" JP said. "They gotta get some hate in their hearts and get down here and go to work."

A flare erupted below.

One of the lead Hardbacks exploded in a white and yellow flash. The secondary ignition of plasma boiled the air around the burning hulk with purple haze. As with all violence, it happened in the space of a heartbeat, faster than light, quicker than thought. The first punch had been thrown. Its source was a dark spot within a craggy rise off the valley floor a few thousand meters away. Kel lit the spot in his HUD and applied the full spectrum overlay. Yes, it was fuzzed as he expected, but the interference the Nems ran couldn't completely disguise the hidden position. Not with the HUD plotting a regressive to the source of the attack.

"Wiggy, get the Stone on it," Meadows calmly directed. Wiggy was already moving by the time Meadows had spoken.

"Do it, Wig," Kel said. "We aren't staying here. We've got to get into this fight before..."

"Oh, man! Do you see this?" Hardball said. "They're dropping."

It was impossible to miss. The Flying Freshers were on the move. Dozens of the C-110 repulsor gliders flew into the edge of their overhead view. Each carried a platoon of troops. Didn't the air controllers know the battlefield hadn't been prepped? That the bombardment never happened? The repulsor gliders would be picked out of the air like low-hanging fruit. The Scarlets were flying into certain death.

The Stone fired. Kel closed the window with a click of his teeth and watched. The heavy blaster set on pure particle beam drilled into the dark. Kel didn't have to zoom in to judge the effect. Burning plasma from some type of re-pulsor-powered war machine mixed with the explosions of igniting ordnance, the telltale of a clean shot.

"Nice, Wiggy!" Hardball said. "I'm painting another for you." A cursor appeared in all their HUDs. Another one of the concealed positions to the left of the previous one, farther back and slightly elevated, was now covered with a red triangle. The Stone fired again followed by anoth-er blossom of the familiar colors, unnatural for anything found in nature. Too bright, too powerful, too god-like in its fury.

I've got to stop this drop, Kel told himself. "Ghost-Six transmitting in the blind. Abort the drop. Abort the drop. Aircrew, abort the drop. Veer off. Air support failed to clear the drop zone. The DZ is still hot." Kel left L-comm and pushed out on all bands in the clear, increasing his transmission power to maximum, hoping to overcome any competing signal blocking reception by the Scarlets. They were no longer concerned about revealing their presence with such a comm burst. The team was already on their feet and strapping on carryalls.

"It's going down, boss," Meadows said.

Kel didn't bother to bring up the drone window. South over the narrow entrance to the valley, the gliders came into view. They were nicknamed Flying Freshers for a rea-son. The long, wide craft moved like a toilet with wings, aerodynamic as a duracrete brick. Low and slow and at the same altitude as the team, the C-110s glided in front of them above the valley floor. Kel could have shot them from the sky with his K-17.

The nose of the lead craft attracted ground fire like a black hole sucking up starlight, the Nem ground gunnery drawn almost magically to the perfect spot on the Double-F. The ungainly bird fell in slow motion as it continued its path sharply downward, the ground fire now shifting to the trailing birds as they continued their suicidal glide. The C-110s weren't maneuverable. They were built for stealth and to carry a large load for their weight. They couldn't halt all forward motion like a true repulsor craft. Some of the rearmost birds dropped altitude and made controlled crash landings to avoid entering the maelstrom of blaster fire. Others careened past to be met by the spray of energy beams coming at them from both sides of the valley, only to be shot down like game in a hunting ritual.

"Some of the trailing Freshers made it down," JP said, standing fully erect, disregarding the intense fire below them. "There are troops dispersing into defilade out of some of them. I bet most of them are too beat up from the landing to be combat capable." JP was a medic as Kel had been. He was right. There were likely deaths and injuries from the controlled crashes that rendered surviving Scarlet troopers out of the fight like dropped dishware, shattered and unfixable. The human body was a frail thing when gravity was the mechanism of its assault.

"They're all down," Wiggy said. "Some of the Freshers that made it down should be below line of sight from the rest of the bunkers. The one out front that got clipped first made it down more or less in one piece, but it's a sitting duck." A cursor appeared over the hulk Wiggy was talking about. About two thousand meters in front of them, a glider sat at an odd angle, half on its side but otherwise intact.

"If I thought we were going to have to fight this one for them, we'd have all brought Stones," Meadows said.

Directly below them streams of fire shifted from the sky to the ground targets.

"We're starting with this one." Kel pointed down slope. "If we can give the Scarlets breathing room until the armor rolls up, we can save some of them."

It was too late to save them all.

Kel ignored the fight out on the plain as they hurtled down the slope. He'd almost fallen a dozen times, hastening to locate a landing for his next footfall as they descended at a breakneck pace. Knees and ankles ached as they loped in a controlled crash down the slope, the rock harder than any duracrete road.

They slowed as they neared the rise above the bunker.

"They've got no exterior security," JP said.

At least, not that we see yet, Kel thought.

Held up at a spot just over the lip of the cave, he took another careful scan. Any Nems guarding the reverse slope against should stand out in their HUDs, even with mimetic camo.

"Nothing," Kel said. "They're pretty confident no one's coming up their back side. Their mistake."

Whatever tech the Nems were using to kill the data stream and camouflage themselves, he doubted it was man-portable. It had to be powered by something with some mass to it. If they could find it, they could get this fight turned around. Kel and JP broke right as the other three operators went left, both positioning to get a view into the bunker. Or cave. Or whatever it was. Manmade, natural, or improved, it concealed a source of fire. The pulse of blaster and chain gun fire from within had slowed considerably. No doubt they had exhausted all the targets available from their narrow field of view.

"Be ready. I expect a mech to pop out from there any-time," Kel said. "They have to come out if they want to fin-ish the job they started on the repulsor troops."

As he and JP worked their way down and laterally, he hoped the Repubs were unfreezing their asses and roll-ing their heavies forward to support the bare troops that had escaped from the gliders and gotten pinned down on the plain.

"Mech!" Wiggy said on L-comm just as Kel saw it, too.

Stepping out of the crevice from behind a wall of rock was a steel anthropoid. A mechanized walker sporting a chain gun beneath the driver compartment and a blaster atop. It paused as it crouched to clear the low arched ceil-ing before rising to full height. The monstrosity stayed in place as it swept both guns in collapsing arcs.

Kel expected the blast from Wiggy's Stone momen-tarily, and stepped back behind the boulder as he nudged JP back with him. "Stone coming. Cover."

From his position about twenty meters opposite them, Wiggy hammered the walker. From so close, the harsh buzz of the burst frying the air was audible for a mi-crosecond before the explosion drowned it out. Kel didn't wait and was already moving as he heard Wiggy say, "Target destroyed."

"TBs," Kel said as he brought his K-17 up and launched a grenade into the depths beyond. From his side, JP did the same. Kel faded back behind cover as their grenades arced away. "One, one-thousand. Two, one-thousand."

Opposite him, Meadows and Hardball launched as well, vapor trails hanging in the air for a brief second before the explosions ripped. The first detonation hit, followed by the push. He felt the ground lift and the crush of overpressure squeeze his organs as the thermobarics ate the atmosphere away. He dropped an AP round down the pipe of his launcher and stroked the receiver to make sure the carbine was set on full particle beam before stepping out again.

Through the smoke, his HUD gave clear outlines to the objects concealed within and colored them in with white and red patches like a child's drawing, indicating both human and machine. As he'd anticipated, whatever mimetic shielding had been in place to conceal the hidden position was out of play now.

Kel started hammering.

Two more mechs in the cave, one crouched, the other standing. Both temporarily frozen. Identifying the driver compartment of the one on the left, JP joined him, sending blasts at the cramped bubble. Armored or not, the blasts tore into the shielding and hot, white sparks cascaded on his HUD. The mech on the right fell to a barrage, its hatch open, a cauldron of flames boiling out of it. The driver must've been stepping into the cab as their grenades hit. Scattered on the ground were another dozen troops. As they moved on line through the cave, the team joined Kel in making sure they were all dead, using lower powered beams to put shots into chests and heads.

Meadows was first to flood the space with his infrared torch. The rest joined to pan around the excavated space. He sighed. "You know how you eat a rindar all by yourself? One bite at a time. Next."

05

They followed a path around the next spur, the slope affording little more than a flat contour wide enough to place one foot at a time toward the next of the inset bunkers. Meadows and JP dropped and crawled to where the spur crested.

"Sentries out ahead. They're learning," Meadows said. "Hit 'em."

Both unleashed their blasters, staccato and even. The Nems were wearing a light spectral camouflage, nothing near strong enough to hide from their HUDS. JP sent one more blast at a twitching body just as Kel slid next to him.

"Three down," Meadows reported. "Just like the last troops, they're very lightly armored. We can burn 'em down on low power."

"These guys had eyes out," JP added. "Our surprise advantage is over."

"Wiggy, bring the heat to 'em," Kel said.

"Moving," was the trotting man's sole response. Hardball followed close behind Wiggy as they skirted along the spur and descended. The rest of them stayed prone to crawl down the slope to a spot level with the top of the bunker overhang. Kel could just see the dark wavy curtain of energy that hid what lay behind. Wiggy paused at the edge of the last cover and stepped out as he lowered the Stone to point into the mirage.

Kel slaved the view from Wiggy's HUD. The Stone aimed into the mist covering the entrance and fired. The concealment of the cloak dropped with the first explosion revealing a two-legged mech. Hardball stepped around him and sent an AP into the cave. With the concealment field down, it was clear this bunker was smaller than the last and contained only the single mech and a few troops on the ground near it, bodies at angles too acute to be compatible with life and burning in a horrific yet satisfying way. Such visions were always accompanied by the silent motto of the infantryman, unchanged since the Stone Age of humanity.

Better you than me.

"Works both ways, losers," Hardball said as charge packs and explosive ordnance cooked off within. Their own mimetic armor and EM shielding defeated detection by the Nems just as theirs had confused the Repubs. "Nice work nailing those sentries. We got the drop on them. They never got a shot off."

"Don't get used to it," Wiggy said. "They're going to leave concealment soon. S'bound to happen any time."

"Moving," Kel said as the rest of the team slid down the embankment behind him. "Behind you," Kel said as he passed behind Hardball to inspect the bunker.

The fires within burned less brightly now. Wiggy and Hardball moved in to make sure there was nothing left alive. He paused a moment to make sure they needed no help. When he heard no blaster fire, he moved. "With me," he said, pushing past the scorched bunker and started climbing.

The next anomaly was five hundred meters closer to the valley mouth. Meadows and JP pushed higher up the slope, trying to spot ahead as they moved.

"Hold up, boss," Meadows told him. "The next one is small like this one. Seems to be the last one on this side of the valley."

"Yup," Kel agreed. "Wiggy, Hardball," he called out, multitasking as his team sergeant talked. "Need help in there?"

"Good to go," Hardball said. "Coming out. On your six, sir."

The pair moved to Kel where he knelt behind a large pile of rocks as Meadows and JP talked in the background. From where they were, the crashed repulsor glider was in view. Kel was anticipating the coming suggestion just as Wiggy dropped to both knees and laid the Stone in front of him. "I've got one more charge pack for the Stone. Start passing me extras, boys."

Hardball dropped his daypack next to him. "I'll hump it if you want a break."

Wiggy's negative head shake made clear his feelings about the pain versus reward calculation. "Just give me your spare pack for the Stone so I have it handy."

Hardball complied and pulled the cylinder out of his pack to place it in the empty spot on Wiggy's armor. It stuck and he released it.

"Ball hog."

Kel took a sip of water from his bucket nipple. "So, what are you thinking, Top?"

"That downed C-110 across from us."

Kel took a step back from behind cover to scan across the plain. Directly across from them was the forward most of the Double-Fs. It had landed in an ideal spot, below the line of sight of the opposite side of the valley, but directly in front of the two positions the team had just taken out. It had obviously been on the receiving end of the barrage

from the now destroyed mechs. The top half of the fuselage was gone; scorched fuselage and ragged chain gun
holes peppered the top of the bird. The wings and weapons pods were fractured and lay on the ground. At least it
was not burning.

"What do you see from up there?" Kel asked.

"There's troopies about two hundred meters on
the other side of the wreck, hunkered down in a gulley,"
Meadows said. "And another group behind them spread
out around the rocks. Best cover they had. They got lucky
where they crashed."

"I know where you're going with this, Top. You're
right. We have to get them into the fight. We can't do this
by ourselves."

"Where the hell is their heavy armor?" Hardball asked
rhetorically. The drone showed them the answer. The
tanks were marshaled and not moving, still kilometers
away. The light reconnaissance vehicles were moving
though, inching past the burning wreck of a Hardback,
taking a course up the west side of the valley.

"Okay. We have to do this the old-fashioned way," Kel
said. "We have to go get them."

They moved at a combat run, keeping the wrecked
Double-F between them and the troops. Without comms,
there was a risk the Scarlets would fire at them as they
approached. They'd gotten no response to their laser
challenge, looping and flashing the invisible beams at the
Fresher, hoping to get a response. The Scarlets must have
an observation post on this side of the crash site, though
they hadn't yet spotted them. Kel saw nothing, but knew

it was the ones you never saw that killed you. And friendly fire was no exception.

No one shot at them as they neared. "Legion at your front!" Kel yelled over the external speaker as the wreck came into full view. Yelling was inelegant, but there wasn't going to be another way to make contact.

"Legion at your front," Kel again yelled around the tail into the night.

Between them and the wreck, a visor appeared to reflect back at him. A man stood with it, revealing himself fully from out of a low spot.

"Nova!" a voice yelled.

"Promethium," Kel replied to the running password. A second head appeared out of the fighting position. On their backs, a void in his HUD was caused by the balled-up ghillie suits attached to their carryalls. That and the long rifles they carried identified the men as snipers.

"Advance to us, Legion."

They trotted the last fifty meters and the team spread out into a perimeter while Kel talked to the basic who'd brought them into the Scarlet lines.

"Captain Turner, Legion," he said.

"Sergeant Rogers, sir. Recon company."

"Who's in command here? We're here to get you into the fight."

"I'll take you, sir. About a hundred meters that way is the platoon CP. Such as it is. Lieutenant Leslie is in command, well, would be, but he's out of the fight. Bad head injury. Sergeant Major is running the show."

"Take me to the sergeant major then."

"No, sir. That's his name, sir. Major. He's the senior squad leader. Platoon sergeant didn't make it."

Meadows pointed at Wiggy. "Why don't you post up with his partner here while we go sort the situation?"

"Easy day," Wiggy said as he moved over to the other sniper.

"Davis and I watched you guys hit that bunker," the sergeant said as they moved toward the main body of Scarlets. "Hey, coming in," he said as he flashed an infrared beacon. The running password was again exchanged as they neared the depression. "We knew there was Legion somewhere with us. We seen you guys hanging around the TOC. Didn't get the word you were part of the spearhead into the valley, though, sir."

"Just worked out that way, Sergeant."

"Sergeant Major," Rogers said to introduce Kel to the acting unit commander as a thin NCO moved to them. "This is Captain Turner. He's running the team we watched hit that bunker. It was you guys who hit that other one first, right? The really big one back in the cut? We couldn't get eyes on you from where we were, but it looked pretty big, judging by the ordnance we saw being exchanged on both sides. Thanks. They were grinding us down."

"Glad to help. Three mechs were holed up there with a couple of squads' worth of grunts. They were the ones who did the most damage to your glider. Did you see us signal you with our lasers that we were coming in?" Kel asked.

"Yes, sir," Major answered. "We did. I thought it best not to light you up in return. Anyone with eyes on the valley knows where we are. Seemed like we'd be exposing you to a lot of attention if we responded in kind."

"Thanks, Sergeant," Kel said. "We appreciate the tactical wisdom."

Kel meant it. This was an unusual situation. Probably no unit in the Repubs practiced large unit tactics under a total comms blackout. It was simply a contingency they'd never had to consider. When Kel thought about it, L-comm was a tech that the Legion was completely dependent on, as well. If someone could disable encrypted Republic comms so completely, was it beyond imagination that it could be done to L-comm, too? How would they function in such a situation?

"Sir," Major said. "Our comms are out. Can't raise anyone in the company or higher. The net's scrambled."

"It's the Nems, Sergeant. The whole division and everything overhead in orbit are jammed. Don't know how they're doing it, but it's the only explanation."

The sergeant spat. "So, it's not just us."

"No, Sergeant. Not by a long shot."

"I thought as much. That answers a lot of questions. What a disaster. We're the most forward that made it, far as I can tell. I sent a fire team back with orders to make contact with any other platoons that made it down. They were to pass the word to move to objective Bravo, then I told them to keep going until they make it back to the line of departure to let brigade know our situation. Doubt they've made it too far. Any idea why the armor isn't here yet, sir?"

"Good news," Meadows chimed in. "I see some movement on the drone. The heavies are rolling."

Kel didn't bother to look for himself. "Sergeant, we need to get your platoon into the fight. There are more of those bunkers. Any more that we can take down will let the heavies get deeper into the valley in numbers. Then we can let them take the lead."

Kel knelt to get below the rim of the depression, inviting the sergeant to do the same. He punched up a holo from the link on his forearm. They were a kilometer from the mouth of the valley, a narrow isthmus before the valley widened into the expanse where they now hunkered. This end of the valley was a choke point for their relief. Where air cover was supposed to demolish the surrounding cliffs but hadn't.

"The next bunkers are here, and here." Kel pointed on the projection to a pair of side by side draws on the opposite side of the valley. "Then this one," he said, pointing to the smaller one on their side of the valley that they'd ignored to instead retrieve the landed glider troops. He punched up the overlay of the suspected anomalies hiding bunkers. "Open your link." He bounced his data to the man.

"Hmm." The sergeant looked at his own link. "Would've been nice to have had this earlier."

Kel winced. How could the ground troops, especially the recon element, not have all the target information? Was Team Twelve's work locating the anomalies all wasted effort?

If the suspected fighting positions never got shared below the brigade level, it certainly was, Kel thought.

"Our next target should be these bunkers," Kel said. "We need to knock them out so the tanks can get a foothold into the valley. Where's your platoon leader?"

"Dying. Medic's got him tranqed. Busted femur. Head trauma." Two life-threatening injuries.

"Gonna see if I can help, sir," JP said without asking permission and then left them.

"Sergeant," Kel said. "Anyone who can move out is coming with us. Wounded stay put. We're going to knock out these bunkers and get some armor in here."

The sergeant nodded vigorously. "Yes, sir. Can do."

"How many combat capable do you have?"

"Almost three squads. Twenty-eight, including me."

"Meadows," Kel said. "Let's get them organized. You're taking a squad with Major and hitting the last bunker on this side of the valley by yourself. I'm taking the team and we're splitting up to take the rest to hit the two on the other side."

"You'll need Wig and the Stone for sure, sir," Meadows said. "Both of those bunkers make that first one we hit look like a little fish. You're after whales over there."

Meadows was right again.

They should've all brought Stones.

06

"Got what you need?" Kel asked Meadows before they parted company. Meadows took a moment and surveyed his new rifle squad. Though they didn't have a Stone, the platoon's anti-tank penetrators now sat across the shoulders of a couple of stout troopers.

"That we do, boss. I'll keep you updated and we'll plan on link-up behind what should be the new forward line. That is, if the tanks get here."

Kel thumped the larger man on the chest. "We may have to double-time down there and drive them up ourselves."

Meadows laughed. "Ha! Maybe we shoulda just done the whole attack on our own. You and I each in a tank. JP I'm sure could figure out how to fly a Shark. How hard could it be? Wiggy and Hardball could run the artillery. I think it's a new model for the Legion."

"See you soon, Curt."

"Roger, boss."

Kel's two squads were ready to move out. Major took direction from the team to get everyone stripped down to essential equipment. If it wasn't charge packs or water, they didn't need it. They had to cover a lot of klicks in too short a period of time, and arrive ready to fight.

"Ready to move, sir," Hardball said as he took the last item out of his carryall and attached it to his armor. He closed it up and placed it next to the rest of the team's gear in the middle of the perimeter of wounded Scarlets remaining behind. Those that could had their weapons out in front of them. Those too injured lay on the ground. JP ministered to a man sitting with his back against the depression, placing a patch over the man's bare chest. Kel thought the man must have suffered a collapsed lung from broken ribs sustained during the crash; maybe fragments from the fuselage had penetrated the trooper's light armor. The chestdoc would continually monitor the pressure in the trooper's chest and relieve it with a needle puncture if needed.

"I've done what I can before we move out, sir," JP told him. "They need evac. Their medic's done a good job, but there's nothing more he can do. I crossloaded him with what I could spare to treat the squads going with us. I'd say they're as ready as we can make them for the next fight."

Hardball spoke. "We're heavy on charge packs and grenades, light on everything else. Doubt we'll miss those cutting charges. Sure won't be needing those rats." Rations were the last thing on anyone's mind.

"Hope not, Gabe," Kel replied, thinking about the few demolitions they'd hauled up the backside of the mountain with them and would now leave behind after all the effort. "Got our route?"

"Check." Wiggy narrated as the map projection appeared in their HUDs. "We've got a lot of low ground we can utilize and natural cover between us and the other side of the valley and any mechs waiting. If Meadow gets to work on that last bunker soon, we shouldn't have anything at our backs by the time we reach here—" A way point appeared on the map, the first leg of their route taking them southeast. "Then we start to scoot north again to the other side. From the ground elevation reconstructions, it looks like we should stay below any potential eyes on us unless they're at least five hundred meters up in the hills. If so, we should be out of observation and fire until we reach here to jump off to the targets." A red triangle glowed at the objective rally point, a spot along the eastern valley from where a few foothills and a ridge would conceal their movement to the next two bunkers.

"We've given the troops as good an op order as we had time for," Hardball said, gesturing to Sergeant Major. "They have the route and know the movement order."

"Nothing to do but to do it," Kel said. "Let's get on it."

They were sacrificing security for speed, but Kel saw they had little choice. They trotted in a loose double column, following Wiggy down a winding, snow filled creek bed for most of the first leg. Where it petered out, they navigated across the plain between a series of low rises toward one of the rocky islands jutting out of the rolling valley floor.

He'd assigned Sergeant Major to bring up the rear and take the role of assistant patrol leader, responsible for sending up a head count after every significant halt. Kel stayed with Wiggy up front, monitoring the drone feed for any change in the battlespace and leaving Wiggy to concentrate on their route.

"Eyes on the bunker, sir," Meadows voice came over L-comm from behind them. "Starting our attack."

"Roger." Kel bumped Meadows to a side channel, dimming his voice to a minor presence in his bucket. Now a thousand meters from them, the sounds of blasters and plasma grenades made their way through the valley from the direction of the assault.

"What do you say, Bart?" Kel said as he surveyed the horizon and readied himself to burn down anything that appeared.

"I'll take the first squad with me," Wiggy said. He stooped to the corporal whose name Kel thought sounded like "platoon," but wasn't. He'd already forgotten it. The corporal and his squad were crouched, some of the men peeking out of the shallow ditch in anticipation. Wiggy switched to his external speaker and spoke at little more than a whisper.

"Bring your squad with me, Huntoon. We're going to haul ass for the next cover."

"Yes, Sergeant," the young trooper said, a familiar trepidation in his voice. Kel had been there. He understood. It was times like this that made any sane person anxious, not knowing if they were about to expose themselves to a hail of deadly particle beams to which there was no protection. If a mech did have a line on them, it would be over before they knew what hit them.

"No rushes," Wiggy said to the men hunkered down around him. "All the way. Don't stop until we get there. Ready? With me." Wiggy broke into a run, the ten men with him matching his pace. Kel and the rest of the team stepped out with them then dropped prone, ready to return any fire that came out of the dark. Wiggy's voice bounced rhythmically with his running.

"All-most there. No one. Shooting. At us. Yet."

Kel stole a glance. They were covering the distance rapidly. It was a few hundred meters. The lightly armored Scarlets had no trouble keeping up and in another minute were splayed out behind the rocky features for cover.

"All quiet, boss," Wiggy said with an exhale. "Tell you what, these kids are sprinters. A few of 'em burned past me. We're set. Come to us."

JP was already getting the next squad on their feet. Hardball carried the Stone and would be the heaviest and slowest of the team. He strode to the edge of their cover and patted JP. "Moving," he said and broke into a run.

"With me," JP said to the squad and trotted forward.

Kel waited for the rest to pass until Major reached him. "I'm last, sir. Good count."

"Beat feet," Kel said and ran. He half listened to Meadows's voice in the background as he shouted directions to his squad. They were fighting into the bunker, and Meadows was telling the gunner on the penetrator to pour it on.

Ahead of him was a lone trooper carrying one of the tank-penetrators across his shoulders, his rifle bouncing on his chest as he kept both hands balancing the long tube draped behind his neck as he trotted. Kel didn't envy him. He'd humped a similar weapon years ago as a seventeen-year-old legionnaire. It was pure dead weight. Until they needed it, its only purpose was to bring pain to the one who had to carry it.

"WALKER!" Wiggy yelled.

A bolt hit the ground ahead of Kel. He kept running through the cloud of debris, conscious of the bodies that were once men, now only portions of men. He vaulted over the carnage and slid behind Wiggy and his troops, crowded behind the rocky cover until he spotted a place to crawl to and return fire.

"Light it up!" Wiggy yelled.

JP's voice was somewhere in the chorus encouraging his squad to do the same as bolts from their K-17s joined the N-16 blasts from the Scarlet troops. Kel rolled to look at what remained of two bodies caught in the Nem blast. The sizzle of another bolt splashed off the face of the rocky cover they hid behind.

"What've we got?" Kel said as he rolled back to his stomach.

"A single walker," Wiggy answered. "Five hundred meters. My twelve. Moving to our left. He's trying to flank us."

Kel raised onto a knee above a pile of rubble to his front as another blast hit the rocks to his right. Sparks from a chain gun showered from the mech and yellow trails poured at them like golden arrows. Kel swiped the side of his grenade launcher. The HUD automatically brought up the reticle and showed green as he settled it on the mass. He launched and dropped. Seconds passed as he waited for the report of the grenade explosion, blasts and projectiles soaring overhead back and forth without pause. The electric hum of the grenade cooked and sizzled. Kel rose to kneel again to see the purple plasma send a blossom of sparks off the mech just as a thunderous boom followed a second behind a telltale trail. Burned in his retina was the momentary line of white that came from somewhere to his right from the other side of the rock mass he hunkered behind. The Stone.

Hardball had sent a blast at the same instant Kel's grenade ignited, the purple arcs illuminating the two-legged mech briefly before the blast from the Stone hit it square on. The grenade's discharge illuminated the Stone's impact so that even the Scarlets' poorly enhanced visors let them witness an arm hurtling away along with the top blaster cannon and the hatch of the crew cab just before the light faded. His HUD readjusted and he could again see the mech, now face down on the dark plain, the power plant discharging to bring another artificial sun to life for hundreds of meters around it.

Kel retasked the drone deeper into the valley. It was as he feared. Mechs were leaving their dens and moving out to take covered positions on the valley floor. He panned back to the valley mouth. No armor in sight. A kilometer behind them along the west valley wall, the Hardbacks of the cav unit were slowed to a snail's pace, hardly farther than when he'd last checked. Meadows's attack and their recently finished fight with the mech had deterred the cavs from advancing, rather than spur them ahead.

"Mechs out ahead. The nearest is three klicks up the valley. Nothing closer. We can keep moving. No time to wait for those Hardbacks to roll up," Kel said. "We need to hit those bunkers. Let's keep pushing. But it's time to bound in case another walker sprints out of nowhere. I'll take the first squad. Sergeant, get us ready to move."

"You heard the man," Major said as he moved along the splayed-out line of prone troops. "Second squad, get ready to travel. Wedge out. Six meters between you. Legion'll get us to an overwatch point, and we'll cover the next squad's bound. Carver, I want you and that penetrator ready to bring the hate if another mech shows up. Get ready."

JP rose with Kel.

"Move out." Kel trotted, slow enough to let the squad rise and get moving to keep up. He had a spot picked out a hundred meters ahead, choosing his spot to dropped prone as he ran. As he dropped and got his K-17 in front of him, he sensed bodies do the same to his left and right. The two-meter-long barrel of the penetrator, their only anti-armor weapon besides the Stone, wavered in the air as the gunner fought to stabilize the ungainly weapon without the repulsor pod underneath it yet activated.

"JP, call the ball," he said over L-comm. "I'm checking the drone."

"Rog," JP said. "Wig, Hardball, we're set. Bound past us."

"Moving," Kel heard two voices say. JP was talking to Major and the troops as Kel let his attention shift to the drone. About a dozen walkers had crouched into what must be prepared fighting positions around the valley. Mechs were best utilized as mobile firing platforms. Their advantage lay in their speed and maneuverability in terrain not conducive to larger armored platforms. Using them as static weapons was to their disadvantage. There were enough of the concealed fighting positions that Kel knew there must be many, many more still in reserve.

At least none of the mechs are headed at the downed Fresher, he thought. One mech they might be able to deter. Two working together would turn the perimeter of wounded Scarlets into a last stand. He felt bad leaving them, but the bunkers were the priority. Where was the air support? Why weren't they hitting targets of opportunity by now under visual guidance?

To his right, two armored bodies trotted ahead of a half dozen green-uniformed Scarlets, continued past and beneath his line of sight for a moment as they went down a dip, then up again to plop onto the next rise.

"Set," Wiggy's voice assured them.

They repeated this alternating pattern several more times before Kel halted them up, both squads on line with each other. They'd made it, and done it near as quickly as a Legion platoon could've. Better yet, they'd made the advance without getting fired upon as they reached the last ridgeline separating them from the next bunkers.

"Boss," Hardball said. "On the net. Sounds like the Sharks are coming in for a run."

Kel had ignored the chaos of the Repub comm net. *About bloody time*, he thought. He tuned back in.

"Lightning-One, transmitting in the blind. We are assuming an attack run. Any Republic troops, we are assuming an attack run."

"Light IFFs, everyone," Kel said. The pulsing beacons on their buckets would provide a visual indicator to the pilots that they were friendly troops below them. It would also reveal their position to anyone else scanning. "Oba only knows where they're going to lay ordnance." With both theirs and the Scarlets' transponder signals rendered useless by the Nem scrambling, the infrared beacons were their only hope of avoiding being identified as "troops in the open" by a hyped-up pilot looking for an easy target.

"Of all the times for them to find their courage," JP said with disgust.

"If they lay into those mechs in the open, we'll be alright," Wiggy consoled. "And if not, see you on the other side. It's not worth staying here and fretting over."

Kel agreed wholeheartedly with Wig's existential summary. They were doing what they could to control the situation. Like putting on a crash harness. If the bird was going down, there wasn't anything else to do. Worry profited them nothing.

"Time to push to the ORP and get—"

"Captain, situation report," Meadows interrupted.

"Send it," Kel said.

"Bunker destroyed. No casualties."

Kel's patrol hadn't been so fortunate.

"I see you're near your ORP," Meadows continued. "I'm going to head for the cavalry unit on your side and light a fire under 'em. I'll roll support up to you ASAP, even if I've gotta hijack a Hardback and drive it myself."

"You won't get here in time. We're moving ahead with our attack. Watch out. Sharks are transmitting blind they're getting ready for a gun run, and there're mechs out in the open deeper up the valley."

"Saw that, heard that," Meadows replied. "Still, we're closer to the cav platoon than anyone else. If we can link up, I'll encourage them to push up." The cav officer leading the platoon would see it Meadows's way, or Meadows would be the new owner of a Hardback. Maybe all of them. "There're at least two crash sites between us and where those Hardbacks seemed to be stalled out. I'm going to rally any troops we can along the way."

"I'd stay away from any crash sites until the Sharks have finished their runs. They might mistake a crashed Fresher for a mech. Consider lighting your IFF and do what you think best, Curt. We're on the move."

"Roger, sir. Meadows out."

Kel took a breath.

"JP, Hardball, Wiggy. Time to move. Major," Kel said aloud switching to external. "Get your two snipers. Once we're in our ORP, I want those two up and out, getting us some eyes ahead."

"Here, sir," they said in unison, the two snipers now in their full camo, cradling rifles.

"Good. You heard, then. I'll push you two out once we get into the ORP and I leave to do my recon."

"Yes, sir!"

"Lead off." Kel pointed at both JP and Wiggy, then touched Major's shoulder to hold him back for a moment.

"After I get eyes on the first bunker and get the rest of my team and a squad hitting that, you and I are taking a squad with the penetrator and moving on to the second. Understand?"

"Yes, sir. If it's alright with you, sir, I'll pull two off the other squad to go with us. The first squad has your Stone and the rest of your team. We'll be a little lighter on firepower than them, and can use the extra two to make up for our losses, plus losing Davis and Rogers on our objective so they can overwatch."

"Do it," Kel ordered.

"Sharks inbound," Hardball said.

Before he heard them, he saw a trio of the aircraft appear overhead a few thousand meters off the deck, followed by the hum of their engines a second behind. They slowed further before dropping to bank away behind the rising terrain and head up the valley. A quick look at the drone window showed the craft firing guns and releasing plasma bombs onto the valley floor.

"No time to admire the fireworks," Kel said. "We've got our own work cut out for us."

07

"Coming in," Kel said over L-comm just before he and Hardball came back around the short draw and into sight of the rally point.

"Come in," Wiggy answered.

Kel picked up the pace as they hit a wider part of the slope and moved to where JP and Wiggy waited, Wig now again in possession of his precious Stone. Wiggy made it clear he'd had enough of a rest and was feeling separation anxiety from his most favored child.

"You've had a shot," he told Gabe. "Appreciate the spell, but now it lives with me. Unless I buy it. Then you can have it back."

"Sure 'nuff, big man," Hardball said, relinquishing the heavy blaster once they reached the ORP. "Wouldn't want to keep you from achieving a seamball kind of score with the number of kills you're going to claim after this. One with the Stone was good enough for me."

"Hardball, you run the play," Kel told them. "You and the team take the first squad. I'm taking Major, the penetrator, and the second squad, and we're pushing over to the next draw to hit bunker number two. If we get bogged down, well, I hope you'll be in a position by then to bring us some help with the Stone. I've doubts about how well that penetrator will do on a mech."

The mechs had duranium armor, an energy ablative field, and sharp glacis-like surfaces that defeated anything but a straight-on heavy particle beam. It was one of the reasons they were so effective. Against anything short of the kind of heavy armament a Shark or Talon could bring to bear on them, focused energy weapons like the penetrator weren't as effective.

"We've got another eight full-power blasts left on the Stone," Wiggy said. Each charge pack gave the Stone, the most powerful man-portable blaster made, two blasts. They had four packs left for the beast. The K-17s on full power were capable of defeating most armor, but they'd eat up the last of their charge packs for the K-17s quickly if that's all they had to take on more of the mechs.

"Then let's hope we don't run into the planet's repository of the krelling things in these two bunkers," Hardball said. They heard no more ordnance from the valley. "Sounds like those Sharks made a single run and beat it for parts unknown. I'd like to say we've been in worse spots, but right now I can't think of any. Good luck, sir."

"Luck, sir," JP said.

Wiggy saluted.

Kel felt a lump in his throat. "Luck to all of us. See you soon. Sergeant Major, let's move."

Kel watched his teammates and their squad veer away until they disappeared from sight behind the ridgeline. He wished they weren't splitting their force and was trying not to second-guess himself about his tactical decision to hit both bunkers as simultaneously as possible.

Too late for that now, he thought.

Like most things in life that required a tough choice, it was only in retrospect that you knew if you were right or not. He hoped he wasn't going to look back on this as a regret.

"Over this ridgeline, a wide draw, then another rise where we can come up over the plateau and set up for our assault," he summarized for his squad. "We're going slow in case they have an OP/LP out. I'm pretty sure they don't have the ability to use remote electromagnetic detection systems. Their scrambler has to knock out their reception as well as ours. My bet is they have old-fashioned hard lines of comm between outposts. Once Hardball and the guys hit their bunker, ours will likely start spilling mechs going to their aid. We've got to keep them off their backs."

"Yes, sir," Major said. "You heard the captain." He pointed at each member of the squad. "Low and slow. Captain's got the best chance of spotting any sentries, so don't get in his way. Ready to move, sir."

Kel led. At the last rise, he dropped onto his belly, and the squad copied his movement as they crawled up to peer down onto the last concealing terrain. Looking down, the draw and the hidden bunker lay deep at its head. The grade was steep but leveled out around the rim surrounding the deep head of the draw. More of the piled scree and loose boulders rested along their path, sharp craggy outcrops forming detours to their path.

"Sitrep, sir. Starting our attack," Hardball informed him.

"Good hunting."

He switched to his external and whispered to those nearest, "They're starting their assault."

Blasts came from behind their left flank, confirming his warning.

"Time to ease down and get closer," he said to the men on his left and right.

He rose to a crouch and started a creep down the embankment. The slope was loose material for footing, not frozen in place like it had been at the higher elevations. Kel had to steady himself, dragging one hand against the ground to keep from losing balance and taking a sudden slide down the grade. The men with him did the same, loose rocks and soil freeing themselves, sending small avalanches racing down with them.

If anyone's looking this way, we're about as subtle as a herd of bullitar coming down the mountain, he thought, his grimace stretching his skin tight.

The whine of Shark repulsors came from over the valley again and particle cannons made a rhythmic dull pulse from beyond. Lights flashed from blaster fire rising from the valley floor, trying in vain to intersect with the fighter bombers, yellow blasts following a straight path until they faded into the dark. He didn't hear secondary explosions from successful contact with any mechs, but was glad for the distraction. Glad the pilots were forging on to get into the fight. Glad they weren't alone.

"Mech ahead!" Major said, a little too loudly. It was a different experience working without L-comm. Kel snapped his eyes up. A mech faced away from them as it took a few strides out of the depth of the draw, seemingly oblivious to their presence as it tested itself with a few cautious steps. The ground in the bottom of the draw was the same rocky, loose soil they found themselves on. It had probably been frozen when they entered the bunkers. Days of sun had warmed the valley floor considerably.

"Carver, get your ass down here and hit it!" Major yelled as they all took a controlled slide to reach the bottom of the slope, larger parts of the slope sliding down with them. "Hurry."

Kel reached the end of their ride first and fell forward onto his chest, far enough over the lip of the narrow ridge to see down into the draw. With a swipe of the receiver, he settled the reticle on the back of the mech just below the exhaust ports and fired twice. "Ninety-eight meters," his HUD told him, and he registered the information unconsciously. Without waiting to see the effect, he launched a high energy grenade at the same spot.

"Carver, hit it!" Major yelled.

"Clear," the trooper yelled, warning others not to be too close to the ports on either side of the heat sinks that flared off the two-meter length of the tube. A long red pulse flared, intensifying as the gunner held the beam on his target, painting the back of the beast. Kel imagined a hole drilling deeper and deeper through the armor, anticipating an explosion that didn't materialize despite his fervent wishes. He kept up his own fire, blasts from N-16s on either side of him flying at the metal monstrosity, most missing their mark to send earth and rocks into the air around it like mini rock-spewing geysers.

"Fire discipline!" Major shouted. "No spray and pray. A sight picture for every shot!"

Kel was about to give the same command, beat to the punch by his young sergeant.

The penetrator beam ceased. The mech sank slowly to its knees like a slowly deflating balloon. No explosion issued. Kel watched another heartbeat's interval. Smoke came from the mech. Its wicked arms and gun turrets still, but not yet limp.

"Carver, give it another," Major yelled.

"Changing coolant cell and charge packs," the trooper yelled.

"Hold fire!" Kel yelled.

The mech seemed out of commission. Best to save what few blasts they had from the penetrator until they needed them.

Then Kel's world became a chaotic mix of blur and noise as he felt and heard the crush of an explosion with him the center of its fury. The man to his left screamed. The loudest moan was his own, rolling around his bucket like a deafening jet blast until he realized he alone could stop its source. Grunts and groans returned to his bucket as external sounds reentered his world closed.

"Captain, Captain, are you alright?"

It was Major, kneeling at his side and rolling him to his back.

"Captain, can you hear me?"

Kel shook his head and gasped. "AP mines. Who got hit?" Kel checked himself. He felt no pain. The world tilted back and forth in his HUD as he tried to sit up. He squeezed his eyes shut and groaned, forcing his brain to clear and his ears to stop ringing. "Grrrrrr." He shook his head again. "Who got hit?" The teeter-totter motion of the world eased back to normal.

Of course. The Nems had mined the slope above the bunker. It's what he would've done.

"Satterwhaite's dead." The man to Kel's left. To his right, another man lay face down, unmoving.

"Check him," Kel said, pointing to the downed man at his other side.

Where's my carbine?

Kel rolled back and searched the ground in front of him. His K-17 was there, the optic smashed, ragged holes spilling isolinear fibers from within. He checked the charge. Fifty percent. It seemed otherwise functional.

"Sergeant, we've got to assault. Get that penetrator up and ready. Take it and anyone able and get down there. Hit anything deep in the draw. Keep them inside. I'm going right. Move."

"Sir, you alright?" Major again asked.

"I'm fine. Let's move!"

"Are there more mines ahead?" Major asked.

Kel swayed. He was still dizzy. "Probably. Lay down fire down as you move. Wide dispersion. Try to detonate any still waiting. Get moving." He moved, stepping over the body of the wounded man.

Two stunned troopers waited for his direction.

"With me. Let's go," Kel said as he swiped the side of his K-17 back toward himself, then downward. He sent a blast at the ground a dozen meters in front of him, then again at the slope, trotted ahead, and repeated the effort. He tried to pick obvious spots where a mine could be but was rewarded with nothing for his effort. Maybe the Nems had been satisfied with the one line of charges they'd stumbled into?

"Captain, sitrep," Hardball's voice came over his bucket. "We're pushing into the bunker. Small one. Two mechs destroyed and troops neutralized. How copy?"

Kel stumbled to speak. "Copy. Good copy."

That means I understand. Seems right, he told himself. He contemplated the path that would get him to the first decent spot where he could put fire back into the draw. *Got to get down there. Got to get a spot to fight from.*

"Captain, what's your situation?" Hardball's voice came again.

Kel stumbled and caught himself. His leg felt weak. There was no pain.

"Captain, do you hear me?"

Kel fell, picked himself up again, and trotted down the slope.

"Gotta get to where... I can... get some fire into that bunker."

"Hang tight, sir. On the way." Kel heard some chatter on the team channel, but it meant nothing to him. He found a narrow channel between jagged rocks and paused to look back. The two troopers were moving slowly behind him. He pointed. "Move down and find a spot to get guns into that bunker. Keep them pinned in there. Don't let up. We've got to do this. Go."

"Moving," the lead trooper replied. He was wounded, but ignored it. The larger man in trail moved around to grab the injured man by the waist.

"C'mon, Lupe, lean on me. I'll get us there," the larger trooper said. Blood leaked from under Lupe's armored chest to stain his uniformed shoulder. "Just a little farther and we'll rest. We're gonna have a great spot to shoot from. You'll see."

"Right you are, Sobieski," the wounded man said as he let the larger man help him.

Kel headed into the narrow. He crawled over a small boulder between the two sharp walls forming the passage to step onto a thin ledge. He knew he was in a good position, because of the excellent view he had of the crouched and damaged walker. He knew doubly so because coming out of the depths of the draw, looking right up at him, was another. Kel snapped his carbine up and fired. To his right, red dragon breath appeared, holding on the chest of the mech as metal welded and vaporized in sizzling smoke. The mech's chain gun opened up and sprayed steel and flames, the muzzle pivoting left and right wildly.

He pressed the trigger of the grenade launcher. Nothing happened. A warning icon in his HUD flashed. *Malfunction.* Kel grabbed a grenade off his chest, stroked it, pulled back, and threw. The red beam stopped, the end of its trail following the point to the mech to terminate like the fletching of an arrow sinking into a soft target before disappearing.

The chain gun fire stopped. The mech paused in place. Kel's squad rained blasts from N-16s into the draw from both sides, at the mech and past it into the hidden bunker. From behind the halted mech, a sharp yellow blast whizzed past, coming from what could only be another mech. This one raked the walls around Kel. Debris rained into the air, some of it pelting Kel's armor as he tried to backpedal. There was nowhere to retreat to, on the ledge as he was. The new mech stepped into view. Twin turrets, high and low working in opposition, sprayed metal projectiles and blasts, lighting the canyon and the mechs in a demonic red glow.

Kel had a single vision.

Dark hair brushed back to reveal smiling green eyes and white teeth, arms outstretched and beckoning. He heard Tara's sweet words. Sweeter than anything he could've imagined. Because they were real. He'd heard them before.

"Oh, sweetheart. We're going to be so happy."

A blinding blast erupted and his HUD flashed out from the intensity.

"Don't shoot. Coming in!" Hardball yelled over L-comm. "It's us. Coming in!"

Heavy fire filled the little canyon from the direction of the mouth, filling it like the rush of a tsunami and bringing death with it. Blasts and steel and white flares passed him, turning the channel into a rising river, flooding it with the energy of a thousand suns. The mechs burned and exploded. Kel winced, instinctively expecting spall to pelt him, waiting for the hot steel to cut through his armor and into his flesh. He opened his eyes. The last mech to emerge from the bunker fell on its face as more blasts pelted it on the way down, a boxer punching his opponent all the way to the canvas.

"Captain Turner. We're here. Don't shoot. It's us. Where are you, sir?"

"I'm here, Gabe. I'm okay."

From the mouth of the draw stepped a mech. Kel startled and was bringing his useless carbine to bear when he realized it had been the source of his salvation. Trotting beside it on the ground was Wiggy, the Stone on his shoulder.

"Hardball, is that you? Are you in a mech?"

"Got dat right, boss. And I ain't ever giving it up. Wiggy can have his Stone. This is the only way to kill."

08

"I'm heading out to make pick up on the wounded," Kel said after he caught his breath, surprised to be alive.

"Keep your head down, boss. Still hot down here," JP warned. "This one's pretty deep. We'll clean it out and I'll be there as soon as I can. You okay?"

Kel ignored the last. "Roger. Turner out."

He stumbled back along the crevice passage and down to where the two troops, Lupe and Sobieski, had posted up. *I remember their names*, he realized and felt relief. His brain had been frelled for a while. *I must not be too far gone. Maybe it jogged something loose.* Kel had a difficult time remembering names under the best of circumstances.

"Lupe. Sobieski. Where you at?" Kel yelled ahead as he descended, following the faint trail of thermal imprints left by their steps on the rocks. His mind was clearing. His vision sharp again. There was muffled blaster fire from below. Definitely one-sided instead of the two-way variety.

"Here, sir." Sobieski, the larger man, appeared around the rocks. "Lupe's going to sit this one out. He's lost some blood. I've got him patched up and lying down behind cover. I'm ready to go with you and finish this."

"Stay with him," Kel ordered. *Maybe their commander is an ass, but by Oba these men make me proud.* JP had just told him they'd cleared the rest of the bunker and he was leading help to them. "The bunker's knocked out. Help's coming to make pick up on our wounded."

"Yes, sir. Say, sir... does the Legion have mechs now?"

Kel laughed. "Today we do."

He climbed, leaning into the grade as he did. "JP, I'm heading to the top of the rise. We have some seriously wounded up there. We walked into a spread of AP mines."

Kel told him where Lupe and Sobieski were and dropped a cursor on their location, then another on his destination.

"Roger. I'm already heading up the other side. I'll pick up Major and whoever's with him."

"I'm coming up behind you with help, Captain," Wiggy's voice entered the conversation. "You weren't sounding too good there for a while, boss. You okay? Stay put until I get to you."

Kel grunted. "Negative. I'm heading up top. Meet me there."

He kept pushing, anxious to get back to the site of the mechanical ambush that had rocked them. He knew there were at least two severely wounded men there. The man that had been on his left, Satterwhaite, was dead. Kel saw that right away. He crested the rise and traversed the last rocky outcrop and there they were. He broke into a trot and almost fell, his left leg buckling again. A throbbing dull ache in his thigh was apparent. He limped to the first body. The man's chest rose and fell with a gurgling sound. His HUD added a blue filter and Kel scanned for bleeding. Small amounts of blood glowed brightly from the wounds that peppered his unarmored extremities, but nothing rushed out in torrents. Kel knelt and rolled the man onto his side, bending his legs and tucking his arm underneath his head like a pillow to keep the man on his side and his airway clear until he could return.

He scanned around for the other man he knew to have been gravely wounded. There! The other body lay just past the pile of scree that had separated him from Kel during their brief time together before the mines did their work. As he moved closer, his question was answered. The back of the man's chest was torn open, large fragments of his body armor fractured and splayed outward, the wound beneath too large for anyone to have survived.

"Captain!" JP said as he came into view. He led a squad with him, one of them Kel recognized as the medic.

"There's a man twenty meters behind me. He's alive. This man's gone."

"Dunham," JP said to the medic. "Go check it out. I need to check the captain."

"On your six," Wiggy's voice came out loud from behind them some distance.

"Sir, you're bleeding," JP said. "Sit down and let me check you."

"I'm good, JP, just a little dazed. Must've been a spread of APs hit us from behind." Kel pointed to the rocky elevation behind them. "We laid down right in their path." He zoomed in on a scorched patch where a mine had obviously been planted, aiming right for the ledge where they'd laid.

"You took a good shot all over the back of your armor to prove it, boss. It looks like a street sweeper peppered you. Peeled off a chunk of the armor on your left thigh. I'm going to leave it and put some extra hemopatch into the wound. Hold still."

Kel twisted to try to look around JP to inspect his own wound. Impossible. His view was completely blocked by

JP's mass. His thigh ached more now, dull, not yet sharp. Kel knew it would come later.

"You breathing okay? Your vitals all look good."

"Yeah, JP. I'm good."

"Miracle you didn't get it worse. We get you off the hill and down to some cover in the bunker. I'm going to strip you and make sure we didn't miss anything." Kel didn't feel like arguing the point right now, but wasn't about to let that happen. The fight was still on and there was an entire battlefield active in front of them.

"How's the boss?" Wiggy said walking over to them.

"I'm fine," Kel answered.

JP lifted his shoulders and threw up his hands. "Yeah, yeah. Whadda I know? I'm just the team doc. You say you're fine, you're fine."

"What about Lupe and Sobieski, Wig?" Kel asked.

"I found 'em. They're heading down to the bunker with some help."

"We're ready to litter Birdsong, Sergeant Pabon," the medic Dunham said from behind Kel. "I've got him stabilized. He's unconscious. I gave him some nociblock. We need to move him down and get a better look at him."

"Okay, Corporal Dunham. Get him littered and we'll move him. We'll come back and make pick up on your dead after we get Birdsong and the captain down."

"It's Satterwhaite, Sergeant Pabon," another man with Corporal Dunham said, gently and without anger, letting JP know that their dead friend had a name.

"Satterwhaite," JP corrected himself. "We won't leave him up here for long. Wounded out first, though."

"I can walk fine," Kel said, annoyed. "Let's get all our people accounted for and off this hillside. We need to reconsolidate and get back into the fight."

Hardball's voice came over L-comm. "Things are about to get a little easier, I think." Before Kel could ask what he meant, the Repub command net erupted in Kel's ears.

Hardball broke in again in his left ear. "The scramble is down. I think we may have found their interference generator. Or something. Whatever it is, it's all slag now."

Wiggy stood and looked out over the plain below. "I'd say it's too much of a coincidence. Look."

Ground fire rose into the night sky. Explosions from the valley floor reflected heavenward in twos and threes, indicating the bombers were hitting targets. Kel searched the skies. His bucket identified two trios of Sharks at altitude, the lead birds veering away as the trail group dropped ordnance over the valley. His HUD enhanced the aircraft and a faint white aura danced an outline of the falling bombs, tracing them to where they dropped below his line of sight. More flashes and delayed booms followed, spreading up and out into the dark.

"I'd say that's proof the stream is working again," Wiggy said flatly. "Sharks have target locks."

Kel clicked over to the drone view. It was still on station a few kilometers up the valley. Mechs ran at full tilt, singly and in pairs. They were making for the cover of the bunkers farther up the valley, firing into the sky as they lurched away. Flames sparked around the valley floor like campfires.

"Meadows, give me a sitrep," Kel asked over L-comm.

"Just about to bounce you, sir," Meadows voice hit him. "I'm on my way with the cavalry, so to speak. About a klick out from where I have your locator. Are you in need of fire support? How copy?"

"Negative. Come in cold," Kel answered. "See you in a few." He sighed. He watched JP and Wiggy pull out an insta-litter and wrap it round the body of Private Satterwhaite. Had he waited longer, Meadows could have brought up the Hardbacks for the assault. Meadows must have set a new land speed record to have traversed the battlefield after his own assault to reach the stalled out cavalry and get them moving. A lot happened while they were concentrating on hitting the two bunkers, independent gears driving the momentum of the combat machine from different spokes of the battle space. Too much to keep track of while he tried to run a small unit on the ground in active combat.

Kel looked back up the rise at where the AP mines had been waiting for them. Something lit in his HUD. Something linear and sharp. He took a step to one side to expand the view between two staggered rock faces and hit it with his infrared torch. "Wig, check me on this. See that?"

Wiggy moved to him. After a moment he hummed. "Signal emitter. Has to be. It's in a bit of a bowl, but from this high up, it would broadcast over quite a distance. Wish we'd picked it up earlier. We could've knocked that out and probably gotten the same result to kill the Nems' scrambling."

Kel shrugged. "Maybe. We'll pass it on for someone else to check out. The techies are going to flood this site as soon as I can make it happen. It's time we clip the Nems' wings and their ability to mess with Republic comms permanently."

"Check it out," Hardball said. "The armor's moving."

Kel zoomed out on the drone view. Hardball must've already tasked it to pan back to the valley mouth. A column of grav tanks was spread out across the widening valley as more swept through the choke point of the lower pass to follow, and soon divided into three clear echelons moving left, center, and right up the valley.

"Meadows," Kel called. "Mark us as the forward most line and get their commander aware we're up here. I have doubts about their trackers being updated to our current positions."

"Ahead of you, sir," Meadows responded. "I've got you marked on their battle tracker and the cav has verbal comms with the armor. The rest of the task force knows where you are. Where we are, I should say. Coming on line with you now."

"Sure 'nuff," JP said, just as a pair of Hardbacks floated into view a few hundred meters away.

"Let's get off this rock," Kel said as he stood. He placed all his weight on his left leg and tested it. It held. The tension of the hardened dressing pulled on the skin of his thigh as he stepped off.

Kel looked at his ruined K-17 and its shredded optic. The mine at Kel's back had sent a rod just over his prone head to strike the top of his carbine. He knew the type. The mine he lay in front of had likely been angled too high, and most of the projectile spread passed over him, the balls that rimmed the periphery of the charge peppering his back and legs. Had it been aimed a degree lower, and the rods found their mark instead of just the pellets, it would've turned him into a sieve.

Like Satterwhaite and Birdsong.

"I turned the cav loose to get back on mission, sir," Meadows said as the Hardbacks floated away. "Coming in."

Meadows led the third squad into the draw. Kel and the rest of the platoon gawked, mesmerized by the three downed mechs smoldering at its head, smoke billowing and drifting off the sides of the canyon and over the lip of the bunker entrance.

"Sergeant Major," Meadows said as he put a hand on the man's shoulder. "Check your men. Anyone injured, get them to the casualty collection point with JP." He pointed at a niche providing some cover where JP worked on Private Dunham. "Then get everyone else into pairs and form a security perimeter starting here, here, and here." Meadows again pointed to locations around the mouth of the draw.

"Yes, Top," Major said, adopting the address the team used for their senior NCO.

"These are good troops," Meadows said to Kel after Major left to get security established as the team sergeant directed.

"I couldn't have asked for more from these kids," Kel said in agreement. "They never quit."

The sky was showing the first hint of the new morning.

"When you got to the cav, what were they doing?" Kel asked him.

Meadows grunted. "Not a whole helluva lot. You might say they were paralyzed by indecision. The captain running the show saw the light pretty quickly. At first, he was adamant that he needed further guidance before proceeding. He'd sent one of the Hardbacks back to the line of departure to make contact with the armor and was still waiting for it to return with instructions." He sighed. "It didn't take much convincing that he had to take some initiative. Once I had a mission for him, he found his purpose in life. Now that he's back in the fold, I'm sure they're racing to get out front and scout targets for the armor."

Had the comms scramble really been such a halt to the entire operation? Kel pondered.

"I guess I lost attention during the op order. Maybe I'd already walked out. Did they brief a contingency plan for comms loss?" Kel was still finding it hard to believe the lack of combat initiative that was shown by the Scarlets after losing the comm net.

Meadows nodded. "Beats me. Maybe we need to pay more attention if we work with the Repubs like this again. Why didn't the armor roll through?"

Kel thought he knew why as he pictured the chiseled features of the Scarlets' commander, frozen in pose atop his tank like the holo still.

"We're going to have a very significant contribution to the after-action of Operation Swift Guardian." If he were to compose the report on the spot, it would end by calling for the silver-haired commander's head on a platter. "Let's get in there and see what Hardball found."

Meadows joined him as they walked deeper into the draw, inspecting the wrecked hulks of the mechs as they passed. The crew compartments were popped open, the charred remains of their pilots roasted in place like so much burned meat.

"How in the name of Rex did Hardball get a mech?" Meadows said as they walked into the bunker. It was a massive excavation. Across the fifty-meter front chamber, support columns held up a smooth roof over a level floor. It was more finished by far than the other bunkers they'd encountered. In the middle sat Hardball's heisted mech, crouched and with its canopy open.

"Figured I better leave her in here," Hardball said as he spat, his bucket hanging from his side. "Enemy configuration vehicle and all. Wouldn't want any pumped-up Repubs to forget this is behind friendly lines now."

Kel removed his own bucket. "Alright, Gabe. Spill it."

Wiggy came from somewhere deeper in the bunker to join their conversation. "It was just sitting in its own little revetment at the back of the first bunker, prepped and ready to go. Gabe beat me to it."

"You wanted the Stone so badly—no way I was going to let you have this, too," Hardball said after spitting again.

JP walked in behind them and took up the rest of the story. "We jumped as soon as we heard what you'd stumbled into, sir."

Hardball nodded. "I slaved into your HUD. You needed some help. This mech was just sitting there, ready for me. I've trained on similar before. These ain't the only planetary armies who use 'em. This one's purty nice compared to some of the others I've used. It ain't Sinasian but it'll do. Legion's still got a company of ones bigger than these in the Wolfhounds."

The Wolfhound Legion Regiment was in another arm of the galaxy, far away from the 131st and 187th. Kel had been in the 131st, as had the rest of the team before coming to Dark Ops.

"Wiggy hopped onto the dismount spot on my back and we took off," Hardball said. "If she hadn't been prepped, we'd have been screwed. As it was, the keys were in her and she was practically running."

"I thought I was going to have to jump ship a couple of times there," Wiggy said. "You were pretty close to tipping us over getting around that rockslide."

"Close only counts in nukes and ener-grenades," Hardball retorted and then spat. "And don't think your helpful encouragement along the way wasn't appreciated, brother. Never heard your voice go that high before. Anyway, sir, Wiggy hopped off with the Stone and took the short side of the draw while I drew fire from their mechs as I moved across, no differn't than CQB. Worked like a charm. This baby pasted them Nems faster than light speed."

Wiggy nodded. "The Nems were probably even relieved to see another mech coming into the draw. For a split second anyway. Until we ruined their day. And by the way, Gabe, *I* nailed the last mech with the Stone. You didn't get it by yourself. The captain and his squad had already hit two of them. I checked the replay in my HUD. Every one you hit had already been tagged by someone else. Don't oversell it, okay? But thanks for the backup."

Hardball frowned.

"Alright, ladies," Meadows interrupted their spat. "What happened next?"

Hardball spat. "Seemed best to stick with what worked. I plowed ahead into the bunker and dusted everything in sight. That caught my eye pretty quickly, though." He pointed to the rear of the bunker complex. A pair of hardened fighting positions with medium blasters lay in front of a wide passage, melted and wrecked with bodies splayed around them. "That seemed pretty obvious as something important to them. I just laid it on 'em until it was too tight to get the mech in any farther, then I dismounted and the rest of the boys and me, we went in and cleaned it up. Lemme show you what we found."

Hardball led the way over blasted chunks of duracrete and impervisteel down a wide passage that ended in another set of fighting positions, as equally destroyed as those at the entrance to the passage.

"We sent TBs down their alley and then Wig hit it with the Stone." Hardball spat again.

"It was the last shot we had," Wiggy said. "Almost like it was meant to be."

"We all sent as many ener-grenades down there as we could."

Hardball led the way again as they stepped through the ruined blast door. Kel moved Hardball aside and raised his bucket to shine its spotlight into the depths. Meadows joined him.

"What do you think, Curt?" Kel asked him.

Rows of consoles and conduit filled the space.

"A lot of tech in here," Meadows said. "Seems like it was critical. Too coincidental to the Nems' scramble dropping to be anything else, I'm thinking."

"Okay," Kel said as he moved back into the main chamber. "I'm buttoning up and getting a sitrep off to the TOC. They need to get S-2 and the techies up here. I think we found some treasure for them."

Meadows returned from checking on Major and the rest of the men posted outside. Kel spoke with two officers from the intelligence section as a team of technicians with handheld lights navigated over the rubble and into the ruined control center. A platoon of fresh Scarlets stood around the chamber gawking at the crouched mech while Hardball leaned against his pet, a wad of stimleaf in his mouth as big as a seamball, enthralling the fresh Scarlet troops with tales of driving the beast into battle.

The intelligence officers departed to follow their technicians, and Kel walked over to where the rest of the team stood.

"There's no off switch for him," Wiggy said, thumbing at Hardball and his captivated crowd. Hardball's relaxed country drawl seemed even deeper than usual.

"Yup. I reckon we oughta go back to these babies. Been awhile since the Republic used 'em. I gotta hand it to them Nems. They knew a good thing when they seen it. Stole the design for themselves, I reckon. Made 'em pretty good, too, for a bunch of unaligned hicks."

Gabe spat before continuing, the mesmerized troops fresh, clean, and as yet unmarred by combat, hanging on Hardball's every word, the font of combat wisdom.

"Nope. That weren't their mistake. Their mistake was frelling with the Legion and your fellow badass drop troopers."

"Sergeant Major," Meadows yelled. "Front and center."

Major trotted to the team sergeant. "Yes, Top?"

"Get the rest of the platoon in here."

"Yes, Top," he said and took off.

Kel squinted in puzzlement.

"Make a hole." The Scarlet troops parted the way like polar magnets as Meadows strode through their congregation. It was that, or get crushed by the human tank. "Alright, Gabe. Just this one time. You there, Private." He pointed at one of the kneeling troops that had been captured by Hardball's presentation. The trooper popped to parade rest.

"Yes, sir?"

"Here." Meadows produced his link and handed it to the young man. "Get a few of us. Don't screw up. I'm counting on you."

The young man accepted the device and nodded vigorously, performance anxiety plastered all over his young face.

"Sergeant Major, get your troops around that mech. Gabe, you hop in the cab. Sir," Meadows gestured. "After you."

Kel laughed. "Okay, Top. I guess it won't be the death of all things sacred to capture the moment."

The team crowded to either side of Gabe. Major and the Scarlet troops kneeled in front of them. Gabe grinned so wide that green drool ran out of his mouth and onto his armored chest.

"Say Tyrus Rex," Meadows commanded.

"*Tyrus Rex*," they all chanted as the private tapped Meadows's link furiously.

"Got it, sir."

Kel laughed as Meadows inspected his link and nodded approval. Kel looked around at his team and the Scarlet troops still in place around the mech. This was the best of times.

"That's goin' on the team room wall," Hardball said as he wiped his face before breaking into another grin.

"Sure thing, Gabe," Kel said, his own smile fatiguing the muscles of his face.

It had been a day of days.

09

It was a total rout. A catastrophe. Daegor knew the end was near. Bombs continued to fall, joined by artillery barrages smacking the peaks around them.

Brissell's plan had brought them to this inglorious ending.

What had given Brissell a feeling of invulnerability, a high ground advantage delusion, an adolescent omnipotence fantasy, was built on nothing more than parlor tricks and street magic.

The slicer's sorcery had not conjured them a victory.

Against small groups of peacekeepers and light patrols, the magic had been stunning. The beam projector dropped repulsors out of the air. They'd proven it. The slicers proved they could intrude into the impenetrable data streams of the Repub's communication nets. It was an incredible achievement. Much more so than the banking systems slicing the State Security Bureau did to make the Nemanjic wealthier and stronger than their neighbors.

"Daegor," Brissell wheezed. "It's time for you to go." Red spittle sprayed onto Daegor's face with each word as his wounded friend struggled to speak. "It's up to you now."

Daegor shielded Brissell with his body as the roof above them rained dust from the widening cracks. Outside, the cliffs above the bunker thundered with the deafening impacts of another artillery barrage, showering shards and splinters of rock into the entrance like a deadly hail.

Daegor was shocked when Brissell's mech limped back to the TOC, showering sparks and in flames, returning alone to spill out the burned man he barely recognized as his oldest friend. He'd cautioned Brissell against joining the fight, but had there been another mech for him to pilot, he would've joined his friend. A final attempt to hurt the invaders with the erratic and high speed gun runs that only their mechs could execute. In any other battle, against any other foe, they would've won. Instead, Daegor stayed behind, awaiting the inevitable.

Why hadn't the Repubs taken the bait and poured tanks across the valley? Why hadn't they advanced when it was obvious it was their only option? Had the Repubs figured out their plan somehow?

Part of Brissell's prediction was right. With the tech of the core rendered impotent—guidance for their munitions blocked, communications made medieval—the Guards themselves lay unmolested in their undetectable spider holes and bunkers. The only choice for their commander would be to drive his tanks ahead and into their trap. Pairs of hunter/killer teams waited to ambush the Republic's floating behemoths, ready to knock out their repulsor drives with the code-crushing beam projectors, leaving them frozen and vulnerable as their mechs danced and pulverized them. Faster. More agile. Unpredictable to even an AI-assisted gunner.

Why hadn't the tanks spearheaded the drive into the valley once it was obvious they had no other option? The answer came to him again and again, as clearly as the crumbling walls of the bunker around him.

The Repubs were better. Their commander wiser, more cautious than Brissell.

"Daegor," Brissell coughed again. His voice was alien. Dry and raspy behind the burned lips. "You must go. It's up to you now. Lead our people. You must continue the fight."

"Water. Bring me water," Daegor said over the thunder and tremors of another barrage.

"No," Brissell ordered. "You must go. The millennium call. You cannot leave our people undefended against the fanatics. Fight. Save us from the Bassinus." The dying man winced. "Oh, Matthias. Why weren't you stronger?"

"Your son loved you, Brissell," Daegor said as the man passed.

"Sir, we have to go," the lieutenant said to Daegor, thrusting a rifle at him. "The colonel's dead. The phased array generator is failing. This location won't be hidden much longer. A direct hit and the passage will certainly close. It's our last chance, Colonel."

Daegor knew he was right. He accepted the weapon. "Lead the way." As they crawled through the rubble to squeeze one at a time through the narrow crevice, Daegor mourned his friend. Brissell had many faults. He'd always been headstrong. He'd always been conceited. But he'd always been loyal. Not only to the Nemanjic, but to Daegor. He swore his oath.

We will resist. We will fight to the last. If we can't convince the rest of the galaxy of the evil that threatens us, then we'll kill every Bassinus before we're extinguished.

Kel still cradled his damaged K-17 as he rode on the Hardback's deck. The rest of the team was around him. They floated across the valley in style, afforded the chance to witness the battlefield from relative comfort. His bucket was silent. He checked. It seemed everyone but him was flaked out and asleep, lulled by the rocking of the Hardback as they inched along. Every so often they passed a smoldering mech, sometimes in pairs, like the burned skeletons of an old couple dead in a house fire. Their smallness struck Kel as they glided by from atop the armored reconnaissance platform. Not with a thousand walkers could the Nems have held off the assault. The sun was overhead and glinted off the snowy peaks. It was going to be a beautiful day.

The major fighting was over. They hitched a ride with the reserve force, moving up to take the lead in the next phase of the operation and sweep the passes and mountains for remaining resistance. A new command post at the base of the mountains was formed, and Kel was anxious to get there and find a new task. There could be more holdouts in bunkers, maybe even high-value leadership targets waiting to be captured. There would be no one better suited to the task than Team Twelve.

His first attempt at securing another mission failed. He'd been unable to task any air assets to lift the team and his Scarlet platoon to act as a blocking force on the other side of the mountain range. He had no doubt there would be Nems who made it out of the valley. He wanted to be there to bag any trying to escape. Once at the command post, he would try again to sell this next mission for Twelve. They needed to go on the hunt. And that required light, mobile troops to go into those passes. Not being truly independent and with his own support was a new experience, and one he wasn't enjoying. He'd had to give up his Scarlet platoon, too.

"How you doing, sir?" JP asked.

Kel had been lost in thought as he stared at the landscape. He'd been composing his valor recommendations for Major and the Scarlets who'd fought with them. He would make sure their bravery was recognized. They'd been every bit the warriors that the Legion were.

"Not sleeping, JP? Take a break. At this rate, we're not going to arrive for a couple of hours."

The mounted patrol was moving cautiously—not a bad posture to take, in Kel's opinion—even if he preferred to get the ball rolling faster. Sometimes it was just like this. Stuck and with nothing you could do about it. The large-scale fighting was over, but the battlespace was nowhere near uncontested. The gunners in the Hardbacks swept sensor pods and turrets in continuous search patterns, looking for targets. There could definitely be more mechs, hidden and waiting to attack.

"How's the head, sir?" Kel noticed JP had bounced him on a private link and anticipated what was coming next.

"Fine," Kel said, annoyed. "Stop asking. I'll be the first to let you know if I'm not, okay?"

JP harrumphed. "You know, irritability is a major sign of head trauma."

Kel's annoyance grew at the suggestion, then he broke out laughing at the irony. JP was right. "True enough, man. But I'm fine."

"Boss, I really think you should let me evac you to orbit to get into a Navy medcomp."

Kel scoffed at the idea. "It's more important I stay here. We have work to do. This isn't anywhere near over and we're needed."

JP tsk-tsked. "I could tell Curt. He'll carry you off and put you on a transpo to orbit if I tell him what's at stake."

"You wouldn't!"

"You know as well as I do that if you had a bad brain slam and any axonal shear doesn't get repaired as early as possible, there could be long-term consequences. You don't want to be one of those guys who looks back—if you can even remember today—and wonder if you'd been proactive *now* that you wouldn't be the mess you are *then*. There's going to be a future for you past this mission, past Dark Ops, past the Legion. One where you'll appreciate your brain working."

Kel felt a lump in his throat. He thought about his vision of Tara when he was sure he was about to die. He didn't mean to say it out loud, but it came out—from his heart straight to his mouth—so quietly that for a moment he thought it had remained inside him and unshared.

"Once upon a time, I thought that was true."

JP remained silent. When Kel said nothing, JP broke the moment. "Do you want to talk about it?"

Kel took a deep breath. No. He didn't. He changed the subject.

"JP, you're a hell of an operator. And a great medic. A better medic than I ever was." For being a stone brute on the outside, JP was a man of spiritual depth and compassion. He supposed it was no different with any of the other men in DO. Except for Meadows. He was purely a killing machine.

"I know for a fact that's not true, boss. But thanks. If you won't let me ship you out, at least get some shut-eye. I'll take the watch. First let me give you another nano boost and check that patch on your leg. I'm gonna put a stim pack on it too while you rest, okay?"

"Okay. Fair 'nuff."

Kel knew JP was right. About everything. But he was right, too. There was something important yet to be done. And he knew he was the one to do it. Whatever it was. He lay back and let the rocking of the Hardback fill his senses. He thought about the last time he was on a boat with his dad before he drifted off.

"Wounded! Very careless of you, Captain. Lack of aware-ness in the combat environment and failure to maintain mission command in favor of a little glory in personal combat is not commendable. Not at all."

The colonel had barely looked up from the hovering battle board. Grav tanks formed a perimeter and at its center a canopy shaded the command post. Field desks and floating holos rimmed the gathering of the colonel and his staff.

"Still, I'm pleased with your results."

Kel knew he didn't have to stand here and take the criticism from the Republic officer, just as he knew he *did* have to stand here and take it if he wanted to secure another mission. He wouldn't let the colonel's berating criticism of him taint his own military bearing. Kel was a Legion officer. He wouldn't protest to defend himself and his actions.

"Sir, I'd like to get my team out there and back into the fight."

The colonel continued to stare at the battle board, gazing between it and the datapad in his hand. "What's that? No. Major Shields briefed me on your proposal. It's unnecessary. I won't have your team get bogged down by being too exposed and wasting combat resources to come rescue you. Request denied." He returned to his staff. They were expecting a visit from the division commander. The staff was briefing the progress of individual units and their locations around the battlespace.

Kel remained in place.

The colonel cast a sideways glance, seeing Kel had not moved. "Major Charles, would you...?" He tilted his head in Kel's direction. A fit major with hair cropped as close as Kel's broke from the circle and walked over.

"Captain, come with me please."

Kel fell in step with the man as they passed from the shade and into the sun before the Scarlet officer found his chosen spot and paused to lean on the back of one of the grav tanks. He reached into a pocket and produced a stimstick. He offered one to Kel, who declined with a shake of his head. His anger burned too hot for him to risk words right now.

"Captain, the commander is sending you and your team back to the rear area as soon as possible. You did an outstanding job. You and your team deserve a break from the fighting. You don't have to do more to prove to us the Legion's reputation is well deserved."

What the major said was a sharp contrast to the dressing down he'd just received from the colonel in front of his entire staff.

The major took a drag from the stick before continuing.

"The colonel knows what you and your team did. There's no question what an important contribution it was to this fight. It was an outstanding example of combat leadership and initiative."

Kel didn't know what to say.

"Captain, please don't think I'm being disloyal when I tell you this." The man was leveling with him. "I've been with the old man a long time. I know how he comes off. He's unable to share his admiration for your actions. He can't say it, but he recognizes it. And he rewards his subordinates in ways that really matter. With promotions and commendations. He always prefaces praise with criticism. It's just his way. He's not the egotist you probably think he is."

Kel doubted that, but as he thought about it, he understood some of the strain the colonel was under, and how that might manifest as he tried to lead his brigade to victory. It just wasn't how *he* would do it.

"Also, with the division commander about to arrive..."

Now Kel understood. If Kel were around to add witness to the initial failure of the colonel to embrace maneuver warfare instead of being paralyzed into inaction at the loss of comms, it would be embarrassing for the colonel, to say the least. Possibly career ending. Now the colonel could emphasize the successful result rather than have the initial chaos be the focus of the visit from their commander.

"I'm tracking, sir." Kel was sure he truly was, but didn't elaborate on his suspicion.

The major flicked his dead stimstick away.

"It was a helluva job, Captain." He extended his hand and Kel took it in return. "A bird's coming in to pull your team out."

That raised Kel's eyebrows. The colonel really did want him out of the area before the general arrived.

"You've got a bright future ahead of you with the Legion. You have the thanks of the Scarlets. It won't be forgotten."

Kel watched him go, staying just long enough to see the colonel sneak a glance at Kel, checking to see if he'd left yet.

"Top, coming your way," Kel said as he stepped away from the tank perimeter. "Get us packed. We're heading out of the AO. We've been fired."

"I'm going to check in with Three," Kel told Meadows as they sat, backs leaning against the grounded Hardback, waiting for their ride. "I need to update Braley and Radd."

"Pfft," Meadows scoffed. "They're probably sitting poolside in the capital."

Poul Radd did have a special ability to ensure Three always had good accommodations whenever possible.

"You know, Curt, I wouldn't bet against you on that."

Kel sent out a bounce to them both, and after a delay, it was Poul who answered.

"Hey Kel, how's Twelve? We're hearing big things about Swift Guardian. The task force ops center has been boiling over. Losing the command net had everyone shook up. What's the word?"

"We're good. We made a difference. I'll tell you all about it when we get in."

"You're heading back? Good. Braley's in with the task force intel cell now. The order will be given soon, but Braley was getting ready to pull you back with us, anyway. He's got us a new job."

That was good news.

"What's the gig?"

"We've been green-lit to go on the hunt. The gloves are off. Kill or capture everyone in the Nem leadership."

10

Excerpt from the private letters of Harlan Squibb-Davies, Exaltus Academy of Sciences, two hundred years prior.

To say the Bassinus represent one of the grandest symbioses of exotic and familiar among the known alien races is a reflection on the inadequacy of human language to communicate the sublime. After three months on Haemus (the human-imposed name for the world—I use it because I must, Reginald; I know you are frowning right now) I accept I am ankle-deep in an ocean of knowledge, its true depths unknowable from the shore.

I have enough material to steer the research from Liberinthine. After fifteen years, it's time Shelia proves she can swim among the dethfins. Her work has been uninspired. If she can't make her bones with the Bassinus, she won't ever be able to stand on her own feet academically.

I feel conflicted about giving her this opportunity but am reminded of your kind demeanor and strive to emulate some of your better characteristics. I will allow her a minor coauthorship on the work, which should be worth some gratitude on her part.

Either way, she should have everything she needs to finish her post-doctoral, and will be out of my department once and for all. The experience has been tedious. She's not a bad exoethnographer but maddeningly unable after all these years to shed her xenocentric viewpoint. She's rather like Quillion in that regard, and we all know how her work continues to filter through and taint the field still.

I wish you were here to share in the excitement. Yes, no need to remind me that there is little of interest for you in sentient life that so closely resembles the human form. Bipeds and carbon-based metabolisms are anathema to your curiosity. Thank you for remaining a friend all these years despite my plebian tendencies toward the mundane.

Oh, only if you were here could I change your mind! The Bassinus are a marvel. Will humanity ever rise to the heights of their social achievement? They live in blissful harmony with each other and even with the interlopers of our pathetic race. I know, Reginald, the Bassinus aren't native. Let us not go down that road again, you and I. They themselves settled the world only two millennia ago. In the grand scheme of this ancient part of the galaxy, a mere blip in time before our own kind appeared like beggars in their garden. Haven't we polluted enough of the galaxy with our presence, that we had to contaminate the Bassinus as well?

It was no human impulse of benevolence that transformed the colonists from pioneers with conquistador tendencies to cohabitants upon discovering the planet was already occupied. Since the original colonists found the Bassinus as exalted as do I, perhaps I shouldn't hold the ape of those ancient times the object of my malice— though he be of a vile race, childlike and stunted in growth. Despite the close relationship, those of our kind have been most incurious about the history of their alien neighbors. Fortunate for me, I'll grant. What little they have produced demonstrates all the biases of our history. Hardly any of it is scholarly. I have the first crack at recording the culture of the Bassinus with conscientiousness.

We know so little of the galactic origin of the Bassinus. Shelia and the team will hopefully gather the clues with some diligent effort. Interestingly enough, the Bassinus have little interest in their own ancient history. They have a sense of the eternal but live in the present. When they speak to you, it is with their full attention. I sense the depth of their connection to the environment and the universe at every level. Perhaps that is one of the things I find attractive about them. They are so unlike myself, who only finds peace in the past tense.

Still, the humans and the Bassinus live integrated lives here. That is due solely to the nature of the Bassinus, I assure you. Their ethos is one of all-encompassing compassion and acceptance. Otherwise, how could they have allowed the human squatters to join their polity? It's an arrangement unique in the galaxy I have traveled.

It's a wonder I cannot explain that the humans have not caused alienation over the years of their shared history in the planet. Normally, acculturation would be the path to coexistence. Human culture here has all the recognizable elements with none of the refinement one would hope should have been adopted from so close an association with the Bassinus. Nonetheless, the Bassinus more than tolerate the Haemians (there, I've used the accepted name for the humans here). Though the apes are inferior, the Bassinus accept them as equals.

Reginald, I think I have at last found the race that will prove genetic pro-galactic homology. Humanity is the inferior offshoot of another superior galactic race. Ancient, hidden, or extinct, unknown to us still. The Bassinus are cousins to us at least, maybe even closer to the progenitor race. *The geneticists will do their mapping. We will do our part and observe. They express qualities our kind has only fantasized about evolving toward embodying. I'm more hopeful than ever we can find the last piece of the puzzle to prove my theory once and for all.*

We have but the glimmer of our genetic forebearers. This mongoloid may yet reconcile his racially imposed limitations to bring that realization to all humanity.

I look forward to sharing more on my return.

HSD.

11

"Don't crowd him," Poul said. "We aren't going to lose him, so don't spook him by getting too close. We want him to carry on about his usual business and lead us up the chain."

"Yeah, yeah, dad," Woobie replied. "How about you don't spook them with the drone, how about that? I'm farther back than it looks from your overhead view. There're five vehicles between us. No way his crew has me made. I've done this before, Top."

"I highly doubt that, Woob, but I appreciate your enthusiasm. Now, do what you're told."

"Yes, Top," Woobie said, properly chastised.

The target vehicle slowed, made a turn, and picked up speed again. "I've got him on the drone," Sims said. "He's on Kray-so-jik Street, or however you pronounce it. You're out, Woobie." Sims was in another civilian speeder and in street clothes like Woobie. They knew the general location where the under-minister of internal affairs was likely headed. Sims had been making random patterns around this part of the city, monitoring and anticipating his opening to leapfrog into place and tail behind the target. "I'll have eyes on him in a minute."

"Your replacement is a bit of a smartass," Poul said to Kel over a private side-channel.

"The king of all smartasses should know one when he sees one, I guess," Kel teased. Poul's ability to say the wrong thing at the wrong time was legendary.

"He didn't start out that way, of course," Poul continued. "He came to us prim and proper as a schoolboy. That lasted about a month."

Kel had only briefly met Woobie back on Victrix. He'd been too busy getting Team Twelve running to worry about how Braley and Poul were making out with their new teammate.

"But he's fun. And he's as good as you'd expect. He did his time in an assault company and had a stint as an instructor at Legion urban warfare and sniper school. Kinda reminds me of Tem."

Tem had been the last man on Three to die, Sims his replacement. Now, Woobie had taken Kel's place on Three, though for a different reason. It sometimes felt like a kind of death to Kel, becoming an officer. It wasn't the same life he'd had before.

The capital was cloaked under a layer of thick clouds and a light misting rain that promised to chill them for the next several days. Which was good. The weather was to their advantage and served to reduce awareness of their movements by the supposed professionals guarding the Nem leadership. The entire population was clothed in wet winter fashion, umbrellas and wide brimmed hats the norm.

Kalspyra was like most capital cities, a mix of old and new. Kel only read about it in the area study, while Three had been on the ground here since their arrival. It was very much a separate region, the center of Nemanjic government and culture, with no Bassinus influence in the architecture and planning of the rest of the subcontinent.

Like many immigrant worlds, the settlers had brought much of their own culture and transplanted it to the other side of the galaxy to make it more like the home they'd fled. It always morphed into something much different from what they'd left behind, alien in its own peculiar way despite the traditional touches.

"He's slowing," Sims narrated. "Definitely stopping. Stopped. I think this is it." Everyone in buckets was watching the drone feed in a HUD window from the back of the lorry. Kel and his team were crowded together, Wiggy at the helm of the tinted cab. The blue sedan Sims piloted stayed in its lane as it floated on. "I'm past them now. Gonna circle the block and find a place to post up."

"I'm doing the same from a block over, Sims," Woobie said. "If Braley thinks this is the spot and our man's going to be there for a while, then we're set up about as good as we can be. You and I'll hit his PSD from different directions. I only see two. Easy."

"Okay," Braley's voice entered the conversation for the first time in many minutes. "But stay put until I tell you to go for them." Braley and Poul were in another chase vehicle, Poul monitoring the drone and Braley driving and acting as mission commander. Three still being short an operator meant Kel's full-strength team was best suited to act as assault, much to Kel's preference.

"This is what I have on the building they entered," Poul said as a new link popped open in everyone's HUD. Kel sent it to his wrist link instead and pushed out two windows, one showing a ground view, the other a ghost schematic of the elevations.

Poul recited the major characteristics. "Five story. Sub-basement. Central lift and stairwell. Enclosed fire escape. Office and residential mix. Service entrance from the alley."

It was big. Too big for them to lock down by themselves.

"What do you think, Kel?" Braley asked him.

"It's big. That's what I think."

"What we lack is information. I'm launching the Inquisitors," Poul said, anticipating their need before Kel asked. The larger drone sat directly above the building as three smaller drones dropped from it onto the building. Poul would partly direct them, partly let the AI program guide them to spy through exterior windows and, if there was enough time, allow them to enter and send interior views as well.

From the top down, the ghost schematic filled in a floor at a time with new details. Translucent holos of people in residence on the top floors appeared, going about the business of living, seen easily through the unobstructed windows and overlaid on the framework of the 3D map.

Lower floors filled in with details indicating offices, most unoccupied, some spaces active with workers behind desks, working at holoscreens. Nothing so far showed groups of more than two or three.

It was the second story that remained blank.

"Braley, I think it's level two that merits attention," Kel said.

"Agreed. Poul and I will hit the service entrance and work up from the fire stairwell. You hit the front entrance and plow up that grand staircase. Let's get set. Sims, Woobie, you ready to start your foot approach?"

"Moving now," Sims said.

"Same, same," Woobie replied. "Dropping to side band," meaning he and Sims would be communicating with each other on another channel, allowing the team to still hear them, but off the main. The two would likewise hear the rest of the team's chatter as a secondary comm stream in the background.

"How long do you need before you're on top of the protective detail?" Kel asked.

Sims's voice came back. "Wait one. Woobie, I see one by the sedan, another posted up at the foyer entrance. You take the chauffeur; I'll get the muscle at the door."

Woobie broke in. "If assault is ready, I'm ready to start my approach. It'll take us two minutes to reach the building at a walk and take them out."

Braley said, "Do it."

Kel spoke to Wiggy. "Call the ball, Wig."

"Moving," Wiggy replied as the lorry eased forward.

Meadows had his hand on the side panel door as they continued their glide down Crasoyjic Street. There was light pedestrian traffic on the walks and a vehicle behind them blared a request for them to speed up as faster traffic passed on their left.

"Thirty seconds," Wiggy said. "Hang on."

They lurched forward for a spurt and Meadows pulled the panel open, waiting for the lorry to flare to a halt. Meadows was first out, Kel on his back as they ran to the main entrance. Sims and Woobie were dragging two stunned bodies off the walk and out of the way. Sims had pinned the old-fashioned entrance panels open just like a doorman preparing the way for guests to dash in out of the rain. The team poured through. Wisps of purple light faded, and Kel saw only a single body, a woman, stunned on the floor ahead. Sims was a one-man welcoming committee. He'd cleared the way for them with a stunner. It was heavy handed and wouldn't win them any friends among the Nems, but it was the best of bad options.

Kel and Meadows hit the grand staircase running.

"Moving to two," Kel said.

Braley came back to him. He and Poul had used the service stairs from the alley. "We're on the second-floor landing. Eyes out on the main corridor. No one's the wiser."

Just then Kel turned the corner at the top of the landing to see Braley and Poul paused in a threshold at the end of the hallway, several doors in between them both.

"Meadows, fight left. I'm going right with Three."

"Roger, sir."

Kel cranked the penetration of his HUD up to max. Human forms appeared behind the thin walls. He prioritized as he moved. Behind the middle door a sitting room led to a much a larger room where four figures stood around a seated one. The seated figure glowed in blue and yellow thermal relief, pointing at the person he was addressing. This was a boss.

"Middle door it is," Kel said as he paused in front of it just as Braley and Poul met him from the other direction.

"Meadows, work your side. We'll holler if we need help," Kel said.

"Roger, sir. We're good here," Meadows answered.

"Breacher," Braley said, and stepped back slightly to let Poul pass in front of him. Kel kept his gun up. The antechamber on the other side was still empty.

"Electronic. Not mechanical," Poul said. "Wait one." Poul manipulated the link on his wrist. "Set." He stepped back and Braley resumed his place on the door with Kel.

"Breach," Braley commanded.

The door slid open and they glided inside.

"Compromise," Kel said, seeing figures on the other side of the next door startle and face the entrance as the three entered. They'd done so silently. An intrusion warning must've been sent as they'd overridden the exterior lock.

Poul took a slight lead, a strip charge already in hand and placed it on one side of the door. He faded back as Kel and Braley stepped up, prepared to rain hell if the door suddenly opened.

"Ready," Poul said.

Wordlessly Kel took a step left and back from the door; Braley mirrored him.

"Breach," Braley again commanded.

Across the door the man closest to Braley and on his side was producing a weapon. A cold, black object in his hand, a red glow coming from the grip, hotter than the yellow of the hand that held it. Kel had the best shot at him. The plasma charge burned and Kel shoved the portal with the muzzle of his K-17. As he stepped through, he saw the man extend the object in his hand. There was no doubt in Kel's mind it was a weapon. He raised his carbine the last few degrees, and as the reticle in his HUD floated up to the base of the man's neck, the soft depression just above the sternum clear in Kel's mind, he pressed the trigger. He continued to step to his right and checked the corner out of habit. Just because his thermal didn't register a body, didn't mean there wasn't one there. The corner clear, he swung back across the room.

Braley had been a molecule's width of space behind him and was on the left side of the room, Poul next to him. A thug on the left side of the room held a pistol at his side, frozen for the moment.

"Don't move!" Poul yelled. "Drop the weapon."

The thick man hesitated. Poul sent a stun blast from his K-17, a bluish pulse hit the man in the chest and reflected back an even lighter blue. It was a less-lethal alternative, but not foolproof. Kel had his gun on the thug as he knew Braley did, ready to finish the job if the stun had a less than instantaneous effect. The thug dropped like a rag doll.

Kel turned his head to check the man he'd shot. Still down. A nice-size hole open in the front of his chest and neck. He wasn't going to resurrect.

"Hands up. Higher," Poul again commanded. "Don't move."

Two men remained standing, the one in the chair making no effort to leave his throne. All complied. Kel made a clicking noise with his tongue and his HUD returned to an unenhanced view.

The mouth of the plump man in the hung open.

"Vice Minister Pidoshkin, you are under arrest," Poul said in syncopated syllables. "Stay seated. Keep your hands up."

"Meadows, jackpot," Kel said over L-comm. "We need some hands if you don't have anything better to do."

"Moving, sir," Meadows said as two armored leejes came into the room. "We're just holding the hall. Other rooms are clear."

Poul commanded them one at a time. The crew alternated acting as cover and control to ener-chain each of the men, including the stunned and the dead man. Braley and Kel moved to either side of the target and chained him where he sat, one snaking around his chest and upper arms, another around his wrists and forearms in front of him.

"Let's get the hell out of here," Braley said. "Let the MPs know they can roll in and police up the rest of the day's catch." The military police were holding for the call to pick up any additional captures.

"Captain," JP said from behind him. "What do you think this is? Looks like blood."

JP was kneeling to look at the man Kel had shot. JP held up the hand that had been holding the blaster to show him the knuckles and back of the huge mitt. It was smeared with something. The same something was also on the man's shirt, as though it had been wiped there. Kel knelt to inspect. Blood. He let his HUD run a spectrum of wavelengths over it. Blue didn't enhance the stain like human blood would. The green band made the blood glow brightly.

"Check it out," JP pointed. Drops of it led deeper in the room and stopped at a wall.

"We've got something here," Kel said. "A blood trail leading behind this wall."

"Stash room," Poul said. "This wall is blocking out my HUD, but I've got the seam of a door here." Poul reached over his back and pulled off his monomolecular blade and ran it down the seam as Kel watched it grow wider.

"Meadows," Braley said. "Tell the cops to get here with enough help to seal this place and have them roll in an ambulance." Braley was thinking the same thing Kel was.

Suddenly the panel gave way and pushed in. Wiggy reached past and dragged the wall section to the side. Kel was tall enough to see over JP's head as he followed him into the room.

It was a small windowless space. A slab sat at its center and on it, a naked body. A drain in the floor completed Kel's picture of what the room's purpose was. It was the first Bassinus Kel had seen this close. Unclothed, the Bassinus male looked less human. Perhaps it was partly because this one was worse the wear for having been tortured. Purplish blood pooled underneath it and green bruises were raised all over its body. Before Kel could say anything, JP was digging out his aid kit and had a vitals card on the man's forehead a second later.

"Braley," Kel said. "You better take the rest of the team and our critical leadership entity. I'll stay with JP and await the cops."

"I'll stay back, too, Braley," Poul said. "I'll bring them out in our ride and see you back at the wash point."

"Okay," Braley said. "Agreed. We want to be out of here in case this place gets too much attention." Spiral News Network reporters were on the ground in Kalspyra. More so, this was a site housing hardcore Nem resistance. Support from their underground could be rolling on them right this moment. "You should only have about five minutes without help. But we won't leave if it's not calm outside."

The plan had been for them to all to have been gone by now, racing to the protected black site where the Nem critical leadership entities were going to be held. Finding the abused Bassinus had been wholly unexpected and changed their exfiltration plan.

"Thanks, Braley," Kel said. "I'm not really worried about it."

"I'll be posted up where I can see the main entrance," Poul said as he followed the team and the prisoner out. "I'll guide the cops in. Be ready to come running if I holler, Kel."

"You know it," he answered.

"Sir, he's trying to speak," JP said.

The Bassinus was semi-conscious. JP had wrapped him in a thermal blanket and spoke soothing assurances. "We're here to help. We're getting you to a hospital." Synthdressings dried over the gashes on the bald cranium. The man mumbled, not in Standard, before his eyes came fully open and his incoherence disappeared.

"Peace and blessings on you for joining the fold, my children. Elandru awaits."

A split lip smile came over him and his eyes closed again. A shiver went down Kel's spine.

"If I didn't know better," JP said, "I'd swear he thinks we've bought his brand of cosmology. Sorry, buddy, I'm just here to keep you from joining your own afterlife. I won't be seeing you there."

12

Uniformed Nem police had a perimeter of pedestrians pushed back from the building. Kel and JP trotted from the service entrance to the smaller lorry waiting in the alley. Poul eased the sled past the uniformed Nems and armored Republic Army MPs securing the scene. Teams of investigators searched inside, the medics removed the Bassinus victim, and yet more cops interviewed the other occupants of the building. Poul pulled a J-turn and sped off.

"Braley," Kel got on L-comm. "We're starting our counter-detection route before we switch vehicles. We'll see you at the site as soon as we can."

"Negative, Kel," Braley answered. "We're heading back to the house. You might as well do the same after you're satisfied you're not being followed."

Kel was curious. "Why's that?" He fully expected to be heading out almost immediately to another target.

"Republic Intelligence and the Army investigators have the package now," Braley explained. "It's going to be some time. They don't have a feel for how we do things yet. There's no reason to have everyone hanging loose waiting. I say we keep working our own leads from the house until we hear differently."

"Makes sense," Kel said. "Alright then. See you at home."

Poul slowed as they neared a checkpoint before entering the high speed lane. Another pair of uniforms, Nem police and Repub MP, waved them through as Poul bounced his clearance ahead without waiting for their permission to speed off.

The leadership of the Nem police had all been arrested or dismissed. The majority of the local police force, the actual cops on the beat, had been retained to help keep civil order under the supervision of the Republic army military police. Dismissing the entirety of a local police in a situation like the Nemanjic Crisis was a recipe for disaster, one Kel was relieved to see was not being repeated here. The Republic had done so in regret many times in the past, with unemployed police turning into violent insurgents, incensed at losing jobs as much as having to deal with an occupier, doubly motivated to exact revenge on an invading force.

This way, the cops kept being cops. There was still petty crime, domestic violence, civil disputes, and the like. Someone had to deal with it to keep the society safe and functional. Their own people were the ones best suited to do the work. With vetting, some of the leadership might be brought back onto the police force. Others would likely have to be hunted down again because they would become auxiliaries for a building Nem guerilla resistance, or actual guerillas themselves. But all that would come later.

"Where'd you get this baby?" Kel asked Poul after they switched vehicles in a dim garage where a half dozen wheeled and repulsor sleds of different sizes and makes sat. The sport sedan was just big enough to fit their three armored bodies, built for luxury and speed rather than utility. Kel insisted on driving.

"We made friends very early on with some of the criminal element." Poul was laughing as he spoke. Kel merged into another high speed lane and revved it. "The embassy security office has connections. One of their secretaries, Martina, has a brother. Nice girl, by the way. Anyhow, the Nems have an interesting culture. Business ventures that might not be exactly aboveboard are acceptable so long as the victims aren't other Nems. So, her brother Crawdjic had a ready source of vehicles for us, already scrubbed of transponders and ID codes. I guarantee they're all stolen from Istria. The civil war has hurt the heisted vehicle business, so we got everything for a steal, so to speak. He even helped us find the garage space."

"Is he trustworthy?" Kel asked.

"Of course not," Poul spat with incredulity. "But he won't go against his older sister. That's what the RSO says, anyway. You know how it is, though—profit is the motive, not nationalism. He'll work with us until he gets a better thing going."

"Or the Republic does enough damage here to alienate all the Nems against us, even the moderates."

"Or until then," Poul agreed.

In back, JP grunted. "Have him find us something a little roomier next time."

They turned off into a residential area and past a checkpoint manned by another of the mixed Nem/Repub security teams. High rises and walled estate-size homes typified the borough. It was a safe zone where most of the off-world diplomatic missions, extra-planetary corporations, and bankers housed their employees and families. An underground garage beneath a moderate-sized building was guarded by plainclothes security. Kel pulled down the ramp and settled the speeder to rest.

"Home sweet home."

Kel returned the wave of the man at the head of the ramp before the door sealed closed. The guards were Istrian contract security. They carried blasters concealed and stood a roving patrol around the team safe house. Kel couldn't tell any difference in ethnicity between the Istrians and the Nemanjic, but knew they would undoubtedly be insulted if Kel were to make such a remark to one of them. There was a fractiousness in much of the galaxy that permeated some societies. Speculative sociologists believed it had to do with how the galaxy was settled from old Earth—if you bought into all that. Old grudges, old biases, old hatreds lingered. The only surefire thing that had united the galaxy was the war against the Savages. Would the Nemanjic civil war even be a thing if the donks were here?

Kel shuddered at his train of thought. Maybe humanity always needed an enemy. It was a tragic possibility.

On the main floor the rest of the team waited, already stripped out of armor and performing weapons checks and maintenance. A ritual more important than bathing or eating to a legionnaire.

"How's the vic?" Sims asked, referring to the Bassinus victim they'd rescued.

JP pulled his bucket off and shrugged. "He was speaking when we turned him over to the medics. I think he's going to make it."

"What do you suppose they were trying to get out of him?" Hardball asked. He was spitting into a cup, his cheek packed full. "That obviously wasn't some random Bassinus."

Braley sighed. "Agreed. The fusion cell will have more for us later, and maybe we'll get an answer."

Kel hoped Braley had established their team's hierarchy within the intelligence machine that put them high in its circle of importance. He was content to let Braley fight that battle for them all. He'd had enough of wheedling concessions out of the intelligence types, who seemed to always forget that their purpose for existing was to get information to the operators, not massing critical information like a dragon hoarding treasure, never spending it, only piling it higher and higher in satisfaction.

Meadows spoke up. "Take another thirty segs to finish getting equipment refit, take a meal break, then we after action this hit."

"Yes, team daddy," Wiggy sang.

Sims and Woobie looked to Poul for agreement, who nodded in reply. Two teams working together left some ambiguity as to how things would be run. Meadows always dominated any interaction. Poul was more of a collaborator, one of the qualities Kel missed on his own team. After a quick fresher break and a meal, the two teams gathered on the main floor and the round-robin started.

As the ground assault commander, Kel led the after-action. There were no significant criticisms or recommendations for changes, and after everyone had their say, the talk turned to the list of critical leadership entities they hunted for.

In the center of their gathering, the faces of the Nem CLEs they hunted were arranged in a floating mass, more of a ball than a tree. Pathways that looked like neural connections led between and around faces, connecting individuals to each other, some with numerous lines between them, some with none, the lines themselves in different colors and all with specific meanings.

Kel was working overtime to try to learn the symbology of the target matrix for himself. Team Three had been establishing it while Twelve had been working with the Scarlets. Two faces stood out to him. The polished head and bushy mustache of Marshal Brissell was dimmed and a fine red X had been placed over it. Kel had barely returned from the battlefield when the update had been made that the Nem Guard ground commander had been recovered. Dead.

Kel thought only another moment about his deceased adversary before concentrating on the face below Brissell's, still very much bright and without an X. The face of another Guards officer. There was nothing that stood out about the man. Dark, neatly trimmed hair sat above a narrow face devoid of facial hair. He was the prototypical gray man: indistinguishable and lost in the crowd. He was a number two man if Kel ever saw one. Missing from the battlefield. Colonel Daegor.

The man Kel would bet was about to turn Haemus into a blazing wreck.

His attention had drifted.

"...so we'll keep at it independently as well," Poul was saying. "The interrogator drones are still on site at the last hit. They're inside and pulling feeds for us. The AI will have everyone mapped and any connection to the target matrix soon, and we'll compare it to what we get from the fusion cell tomorrow."

It was a plan Kel very much liked. Their mandate was open: kill or capture CLEs. They would work with the Repub task force to do just that, but would not be hampered by them if they failed to be adaptable and flexible enough to keep the op tempo high.

"What do you suppose we're going to find out about that building we just hit?" Sims asked. "A torture room hidden in an upscale office, and swanky private residences in the same building? Not exactly the kind of secure location for extracting confessions out of people without attracting attention."

"It's a headquarters for organized crime," Woobie said matter-of-factly. "Reminds me of it anyway. Just like home." Wolodarski was from some mid-core world Kel never heard of. That he had a gritty background didn't surprise him. There were all kinds in the Legion. A man's background wasn't held against him. Only what he did was important.

"Those upper apartments, those are brothels," Woobie continued. "The office—that belonged to a boss." He pointed at the face of the target they'd just captured, floating above them in the matrix, a green halo around it indicating he was in custody. "Pidoshkin may be a vice minister in the treasury, but he's tied to organized crime. He's no economist. I'm betting he's a part of their intelligence and security apparatus. This was a good capture."

"I think your instinct on this is spot on," Poul said.

"I like your analysis, Woobie," Meadows chimed in. He had no small amount of experience himself analyzing similar networks. "By tomorrow we'll have more trails leading from this. We're close." Meadows was always sparing with praise. That he doled it out now struck Kel as a mark of high regard from the grizzled operator.

"Thanks," Woobie replied earnestly. "It just takes one to know one, is all."

There's a story in there somewhere, Kel knew. He'd dig it out of Poul later.

"I'm going to suggest we call it for tonight, then," Braley said. "I say let's hit the ground running early tomorrow. I'll hit the fusion cell and anyone who wants to join me is welcome. The rest can stay here and keep working what the AI pulls out from the latest haul, and I'm anticipating we'll be planning for another hit tomorrow night."

The group broke up. Kel headed up to the room he and Braley shared. The space wasn't big enough for them to each have their own bedroom, so everyone paired up. Except Meadows. JP, Gabe, and Wiggy tripled up in one of the larger rooms. Curt's snoring was legendary.

He was going to work out, but suddenly lost the drive. He plopped back onto his mattress and stared at the ceiling. He'd had a recurring image that he kept pushing away, only to have it return at moments of quiet when nothing else occupied his mind.

"*Oh, sweetheart. We're going to be so happy.*" Tara's face hovered, her words echoing in his mind over and over.

"Hey, Kel," Poul said as he opened the bedroom door without knocking. "Braley and I are going to work out. Want to go some rounds with us?" Braley pushed in and started digging through his gym bag for gloves.

Kel didn't respond. He stared at the ceiling.

"Kel?" Braley queried.

Kel rose to his elbows. "Come in and close the door."

Poul shrugged and complied, then joined Braley to sit on the edge of the other bed.

"What's up?" Poul asked, concern on his face. Kel realized as he sat up that his eyes were moist. He wiped his face.

"I made a big mistake."

13

"Not this again, man," Poul sighed. The war against the Scarecrow had been a nightmarish episode for them all. "None of that was your fault. None of it."

Braley pushed one of the local beers into Kel's hand. Whereas he normally would pass on the beverage, he didn't hesitate to accept it.

"I know. It's the other stuff, the stuff I could've changed but didn't that I regret." He took a swig. Bitter. Just the way he felt.

"You mean, Tara?" Braley asked.

Kel sighed. "Tara."

"Her family's in the clear. We ended that problem for them. Permanently," Braley summarized. "So, what's to keep you from trying again?"

Kel didn't have an answer. "I dunno. I figure she's moved on by now. Let's not talk about her anymore, okay? There's other stuff I'm ate up about."

"More than just letting the love of your life get away for all eternity?" Poul said.

Braley sucked wet air through clenched teeth.

"Oba's beard, Poul." Braley elbowed him. "Take it easy on Kel."

Kel chuckled. "S'okay. I kinda need to hear some of Poul's crass commentary right now. Makes it feel like old times, being together."

"Alright then, spill it," Poul said. "I'll shoot you straight. What else has got Kel Turner down in the dumps?"

"For one, I hate being an officer. I should never have taken promotion."

Poul accepted another bottle from Braley. "Okay. Too bad. That horse is outta the barn, *sir*," Poul teased. "What else you feeling guilty about?"

"Dark Ops. I'm not happy about how Dark Ops is changing. It's not the same unit." Kel's suspicion was that the combination of the Primus Pilus and their own ad hoc team had sparked a chain of events that resulted in the changes occurring in Dark Ops. Not even Poul knew the full extent of the war against the Scarecrow, especially Kel and Braley's part in ensuring the conspiracy was crushed once and for all.

"No, it's not," Braley echoed. "And I don't think it's any kind of a coincidence that Hartenstein and Nail retired almost immediately after our little independent op to bring down that cabal of twarg eaters."

"I bet we rattled some cages," Poul added. "Even if no one knew who did it, there are only so many folks in the galaxy with the capability to do what we did. Anyone with some brains probably put two and two together."

"So, Steiner was the one to do the figuring," Kel said, referring to the Legion Commander. "He sussed out we worked outside of official channels to solve the problem ourselves. Maybe even the politicians and RI caught a whiff of it. The general forced Hartenstein and Nail into retirement so as not to raise a big hubbub with any kind of investigation, and gave us Colonel Chatsworth."

The new DO commander had never been an operator. He was an unusual choice for leading the covert action unit, unless of course, General Steiner's purpose was to bring a new kind of Dark Ops into existence. One with less autonomy. Reigned in.

"Battle Matrix Preparation is not exactly a DO exclusive mission," Braley said. "Though we do it well, any Legion company could do it."

"We've been doing more and more conventional missions and less special operations work, wouldn't you agree?" Poul asked.

Kel did. "So. I killed Dark Ops."

"Not this again," Poul blurted. "Get it through that thick skull, buddy. None of that was your fault. Those people extorted you to try to get control of Dark Ops. You didn't ask for that. If you hadn't stepped up, who knows where their conspiracy might've led? What they'd have tried to do to us all? So, we had to kill a politician in the end? Kill 'em all, I say." Poul knew how the episode ended—with the death of the senator. He and Meadows had been in the next room, so to speak. What he didn't know was that their mission had a special level of help from a source more secretive than Dark Ops.

Braley winced, again. "No more for you, Radd." He took the bottle from his hand. "Oba, but I wish I'd have run a dampening field before we started. We're not supposed to ever talk about this. Remember what the colonel and Nail made us promise?"

"My fault," Kel said. "For real, this time. I'm the one who brought it all up."

"So, what are you gonna do, Kelkavan?" Poul said mockingly, in the same way their teammate Tem once did. "Complain, or fight? It's not like you're going to quit."

Kel sighed. "First I'll complain. Then I'll fight."

Braley laughed. "You did it right. Complain to your brothers, then go back to work. We're here for you, man."

"Got that right," Poul said. "It's us three, then Dark Ops, then the Legion. That's where my loyalties lie. It doesn't matter what the team room door says. The three of us are a team unto ourselves. And gimme back my beer, Braley. Two isn't nearly enough tonight."

Kel woke with a bad taste in his mouth, but otherwise felt good. The sun was just rising. Braley was out cold. He tip-toed around the bottles on the floor and out of the room. Kaff was his first priority, then he'd work out. *Someone's up already*, he thought as the smell of morning juice hit him from the second floor landing. Meadows stood in the main room with a cup in hand, alone, studying the float-ing cloud of their intelligence tree. It had grown during the night, and more golden lines had been added between some of the faces.

"Morning," Meadows greeted. "Didn't expect to see you so early."

"Big day ahead, Top. Early bird gets the critical leader-ship entity, and all that."

"You get everything worked out, sir? Feeling better?"

Kel thought he'd concealed his funk better. "Was it that obvious?"

"No. But I've known you a long time, boss. And we've seen a few things together, you and I."

Kel wondered if Meadows was reminding him that he was a part of the inner circle of Kel's closest friends, too, though he'd been left out of last night's therapy session. He quickly dismissed the idea. Meadows didn't really have human emotions like loneliness or jealousy.

"That we have, Curt."

"Don't forget it." Meadows pointed at the cloud, abruptly changing the mood. "I'll get you a cup while you study this. Tell me what you see when I get back."

That's as close as Curt and I are ever going to get to a hair-braiding moment, he mused, sensing Meadows's discomfort at having made reference to their many shared ordeals. It was Kel and Three who'd been there for Meadows when his entire team was murdered by I-squared troops. And it was Meadows who'd been there for Kel when he was at his lowest. He felt a little guilty about wishing earlier that Poul had been his team sergeant instead of the fearless giant.

The cloud had in fact expanded. As he inspected it, the other obvious change struck him. He reached up to the new face and pulled it out.

"First Bassinus we've seen in the matrix," Meadows said offering a cup to Kel. "The fusion cell got us something on the guy we rescued yesterday."

"Doesn't look like much, though," Kel said with disdain. Thin gray dotted lines connected the Bassinus victim to the Nems they'd captured. No other strings of any color or type linked the split-lip face to well-known others in the cloud, much less a golden cord to indicate the strongest of associations.

"Sir, what's your take on the genocide thing? I know we've been out in the boonies for most of this time, but I have to admit, I don't have a handle on why the Nems have gone high order on the aliens. They've lived together peacefully for centuries. I understand working the problem to stop the symptom, but I don't understand the cause of the disease."

Kel took a sip. Unlike most missions where immersion in the local culture was a necessity, Twelve had been linked to the Scarlets almost from the start. Though Kel complained that battle matrix preparation was a conventional mission, a part of him had grown weary of the intricacies of working with alien cultures. Now it was time to put that aside. Which meant if they were going to understand the situation better, he would need to tap the diplomats and Republic Intelligence.

"I'm in the same boat, Top. I'm playing catch-up. But I've got a feeling we're not the only ones."

The night's target was another high-ranking member of the Nem government. This time, a member of the internal security service. Sims picked up a tip from one of his local sources and scrambled the teams to reproduce the same model for success they'd used the day before.

Kel and Twelve were crowded in the back of the sled as Wolodarski and Sims took turns in pursuit of the target vehicle, Braley and Poul coordinating efforts and running the drone surveillance. Sims got the address in the thick of the city from his agent, and followed the target as he left. Once they captured him, they'd let the cops raid the location for additional intel.

"This guy's taking the long way around," Woobie complained after an extended stretch of silence. "He missed the turnoff to his city home, but he's headed the wrong direction for his country cottage. He's going somewhere we don't have a lock on from the intel."

"Then we're on our way to more treasure," Sims added with anticipation. "Unless he's just going to his girlfriend's or the market."

"Doesn't strike me as the type to do his own grocery shopping," Poul said. "He may be well educated, but he's a thug."

Their target was a suspected member of the ISS, the Nem secret police. His profile listed military service, an advanced degree, and time as a cop. It was his thick neck that made Kel think he'd pulled out more than a few fingernails in his time.

Meadows spoke from behind the controls of their darked out sled. "Boss, check me on something. I've seen the same guy behind us three times."

Kel pulled up the external rear view.

"You'll see him. Gray sedan. Driver and passenger. Males." Meadows pulled into the left lane and sped up to pass several speeders before drifting back over rapidly to take an off ramp. The gray sedan followed.

"We've been made," Kel confirmed. "Braley, we've got a tail. Our target's leading us on a joy ride to try to draw us out. Let him go."

"You sure?" Braley asked.

"If our tail is part of their detection attempt, then they've already alerted the target. Your call."

Braley huffed. "Screw it. Sims, Woobie, take him out. Maybe we don't get his whole crew, but we'll get him. We're going to catch up to assist you. Kel, you guys do your thing."

Kel was ready for some action. "Meadows, don't to try to lose them but get us some breathing room so we can get set to take them."

"Hang on." Meadows gunned the sled down the ramp and made a quick turn. Another tight turn down a warehouse row and he flared to slow just long enough for JP and Wiggy to leap out. He gunned ahead, then reversed into a side alley.

"Here they come," Wiggy said. He and JP were set, hidden.

Kel had a foot on the running board of the open side door. Meadows sped out and turned to the approaching gray sedan, angled to block the narrow street. Kel and Hardball popped around from the side, weapons up. Meadows stepped out and no sooner brought his K-17 down into the open space between his door and the front corner pillar than the gray sedan flared to stop.

Three blasters pointed at the driver had the right effect as the vehicle bounced in place after the sudden stop like a boat riding waves. Before it could regain stability, the driver attempted to reverse course. Without prompting, Wiggy and JP stood up from behind a parked vehicle and fired together from broadside, knocking out the repulsor sponsons front and rear. The sled dropped.

The two Nems were face down on the ground and chained before they knew what hit them.

"Get 'em loaded and let's go before we draw any more attention," Kel said. A few curious heads popped out of thresholds to see what the commotion was about. "Braley, we're taking two to the wash point. Gimme a sitrep from your end."

"Good to go. We'll meet you there. We're bringing in the target. Woob and Sims did a smash and grab. Guy's a little dinged up from the collision, but nothing we can't handle until we get him to the medics. Had to take out a trailer vehicle with two goons. Got some biometrics on them before we split. DRT."

Dead right there.

"Sounds like Radd and Captain Yost got into a little gunfight with the target's chase vehicle," Wiggy said. "We're going to have to look at Sims's source. This was a setup to try to draw us out."

"Does seem a little bit too organized," Hardball agreed. "I'm thinking these Nems have got our moves figured already."

"Hey, dummies," JP said as he finished putting gags and hoods onto their two prisoners. "You don't know us yet, but we put the capital 'T' in thug. You kelhorns messed with the wrong guys."

Kel was gulping down water, a little dizzy after his workout, when his link buzzed. It was Braley for the second time today. "Kel, get the place picked up. I'm coming back with company." Braley left early for the fusion cell and by midday bounced Kel to let him know there wasn't anything in the works. It seemed something had changed.

"Company?"

"You won't believe me if I told you. Get everyone to stand to. Out."

Twenty segs later, Kel had everyone gathered in the main room when Braley pulled into the basement garage.

"Who's he bringing, General Steiner?" Sims asked.

"He'd have told us if it was anyone we had to impress," Poul replied.

Meadows looked annoyed. "I hate theatrics. Captain Yost could've told us who he was bringing into our team house."

The door opened and Braley stepped aside for the two visitors behind him. Kel's jaw dropped.

"Papa Bear! Zero!"

"Holy sket," Poul said as he leaped to his feet to join Kel in trading hammer blows with the two. Meadows threw a lazy salute from where he sat.

"Turner, Radd, Meadows," the bearded man said to them one at a time in recognition. "Good to see you're all above ground."

"Who're these guys?" Hardball whispered to Sims.

"Who are you, junior?" Zero said. Zero's manner hadn't changed since Kel knew him. His voice was so flat that it made Wiggy's speech seem musical in comparison. "We're the guys sent to unfrell your mess."

Meadows stood. "As blunt as ever, Zero. And what mess do you think you're here to help us untangle?"

Papa Bear stepped between them. "Now, now. Let's let bygones be bygones. Truth is we've been sent to... to... well, no there's no mincing of words, here. We've been sent to help you boys give a better showing of yourselves. Using the same vehicles twice in a row for a surveillance and snatch? Tsk-tsk. You can't tell me you don't think you frelled up a bit there, eh, Meadows? I taught you better."

Both Braley and Poul looked at their feet in embarrassment. Meadows's mouth opened, then closed. The tiny voice that finally came out was unlike anything Kel had ever heard from Curt. "Sorry, Papa Bear."

"Who are these guys?" JP said aloud, louder than Hardball's discrete query.

Braley stepped in. "Papa Bear and Zero are former unit members. They were senior operators when we first got to DO."

"They brought me in," Kel said, pride exuding.

"Yes, we did," Papa Bear said. "And up till now I've always been proud to admit it." The wide grin on his face confirmed the rebuke was in jest.

"What are a couple of retired leejes doing here?" Wiggy asked.

"We're contractors," Zero replied. "Lanthanum Concepts."

"LC!" Meadows spurted, caught off guard. "We ran into a couple of leejes working for them when we were..." He stopped himself. It had been during their pursuit of the Scarecrow.

"Fine lads," Papa Bear confirmed. "They told the tale well. Spoke of you all in the highest regard. I'd have expected no less. We can talk about it some other time."

Kel's head was swimming. Was their secret operation not so secret after all? How many people knew about the Scarecrow mission?

Poul harrumphed. "Private contractors. Okay. What's your job?"

Papa Bear grinned. "We've been on Haemus for the last six months, working the problem from the Istrian side of the border for our clients. They get a little short-handed at times and need ready professionals to fill in the manpower gaps, so to speak."

"Your clients?" JP interrogated further.

"RI," Kel answered. "They're private contractors working for Republic Intelligence. You've been sorting out the civil war for the Istrian intelligence service, yes?

Papa Bear grinned even wider. "Nice folks. Easy to work with."

Poul accepted the tag from Kel to take over. "So, who sent you here then?"

"Your fairy godmother," Zero replied.

Papa Bear winked. "Your new sergeant major thought you could use a little assistance navigating the dark waters of Haemus. Since we've been on the ground for so long, he thought we could improve your acclimatization, so to speak."

"Bigg sent you?" Meadows said with disbelief.

"You're never far from his watchful eye, children," Papa Bear laughed. "Since he couldn't be here himself, he sent some adult supervision."

14

"Let's see if this doesn't go a little smoother, shall we?" Papa Bear said from the back of the lorry. He moved pieces of a holo around him as he spoke. "There's a time to go it alone, then there's a time to play well with others. Bring out all the toys in the bin, don't you know?"

There wasn't a lot of chatter from Kel or the team as Papa Bear and Zero helped plan this hit. It had been a while since he'd felt schooled. Humbled was more like it. There was a lot they'd been failing to consider in their operations. The two retired operators were at least kind by not rubbing it in as they more or less took over their operation.

Papa Bear and Zero moved into the team house and spent the next few days working around the clock on the target cloud. The cloud had grown considerably, and links extended to form webs in new directions and with more connections. Now when Kel tapped on a face, more information than he could process spilled out of the holo. Work addresses, home addresses, vehicle registries, medical records, family members, social media acquaintances, paycheck sources, banking, and tax records. More information than the human brain could sort.

The Nems were no different from any other modern society. Everything was available on the data stream. It only took a skilled analyst to put the available information to correct use. While the AI program sped the process up,

126

it was producing better connections because Papa Bear and Zero constantly tailored and tweaked parameters as a result of what they learned studying the targets. The intuition of a skilled operator ruled supreme.

"Capturing them on the move is a beautiful thing, especially as these gentlemen like to keep moving around." Papa Bear kept a running commentary going from the back of the sled as they rolled. "They still feel very safe moving about their own city. We're going to change that. Keeping them holed up will slow down their activities. Then we can hit them in what they think are their secret hidey holes."

"We got a frequent flyer coming up along the route," Zero said. "Third time I've picked him up. Registration tracks to the cousin of a member of the economic ministry. The owner just linked into his office workstation. So, he's not flying it. His family tree only pulls up the one potential player—the credit counter. And of course, we know the Nems like to use the economic ministry as cover for their secret police." A mug shot from an ID badge holo appeared. Zero swiped and a second holo appeared beside it. A live drone image enlarged to show the same face behind the controls of the speeder. "It's the cousin all right. We need to take that vehicle out." Zero spoke into his link then swiped a bounce into midair. "The MPs are on the move. He'll be out of play in a minute."

"I've got another one, Zero," Papa Bear said. "Vehicle registration and transponder don't match. Listed as belonging to a little old lady who only takes it out for evensong twice a week, I bet. But not from the grave, she doesn't. Everything about that one is as shady as what's beneath my own dear granny's skirt. Send the cops after that one, too."

The target was a captain in the Guards. It was unknown if he'd been in the Rila Valley with Marshal Brissell. He'd been off any security feed for months, only to pop up in Kalspyra two weeks ago. The timing was too coincidental. He was either in hiding—a deserter—or was part of the resistance.

"This guy's not a deserter," Zero said. "And I don't believe in coincidences. He's got secret police security running interference against us. That confirms it for me."

Papa Bear smiled. "I love my work."

"Okay, Major Yost," Zero said. "I think we have our target isolated from any support. Let your boys try now."

Braley took the cue. "Okay, Sims, Woobie. Poul sent the drone high. It's all on you for close eyes. Don't lose him, don't spook him, and keep us in the loop."

"I'm on him," Sims said. Pulling the drone out was a precaution. The drones were stealthy, but not completely unobservable to Nem tech. The Nems couldn't bust into the L-comm encryption, but the presence of a drone would be enough to let the target know he was compromised and send him to ground. One of his spotters was currently held up in a traffic stop, trying to explain to an MP and a Nem cop why he wasn't following traffic laws. The other was stuck behind a stalled sled blocking three lanes of speeders leaving the city for the suburbs. The captain right now would be getting the word from his support crew that they were out of play, but nothing was amiss. Just bad luck.

"When I go fishing, I don't just want to catch a big one." Papa Bear kept up his monologue. "I like to limit out. Big. Small. I like to catch them all. Let's see if this fishy takes us to where the rest are schooling."

"Woobie, I'm out," Sims said. "He turned into the residential section. I'll circle back."

"Rog," Woobie answered, barely concealing his glee. "He's not getting away. I'm with Papa Bear. I like a stringer full of fish."

"Yeah, yeah," Poul said. "Less fish talk, more eyes on the target."

Kel switched to the slaved view from Woobie's specs. The green speeder slowed and pulled between two homes. Woobie slowed and crawled past, craning to show them the view down the shared drive between the homes. The man was already out, the door from the drive held open for him by a man with a military-style haircut. A detached garage beyond held three more vehicles.

"Jackpot," Woobie said. "Sims, I'm going to ditch the ride and make my way back on foot."

"Already on foot," Sims said. "I'm coming from the next street over."

Braley spoke on the main. "It's on you, Kel."

"Two minutes," Meadows said from behind the controls. They'd kept a kilometer off of the trailer vehicles. Now that the target house was known, he'd already been closing the distance in anticipation. Now on the residential street, Meadows floated them along at a casual pace.

"Same here, Kel," Poul replied. "They've got no way out by vehicle except the drive. Braley and I will be right behind you."

If everything went smoothly, the leadership of Team Three would only be needed to help Kel's team control suspects. If they needed the extra two guns, it would be a bad night for them all. Especially the Nems.

"One minute," Meadows said.

"No one outside," Sims said. Though he and Woobie were in civvies, Kel knew the two were covering the house with their K-17s. The image intensifiers wouldn't let anyone hide from their sight. "Roll through, Twelve," Sims finished.

Kel was in the air and running as Meadows floated over the tiny front lawn and halted on the drive. He shot the front door on wide dispersion and launched a stunner right after it as the light door shattered. Hardball followed him as he plowed through the front room. Another stunner sailed to the back of the house from Gabe's weapon as warm purple flashes backlit three men caught in the paralysis of the plasma and fell.

"Going high," Meadows said behind him as he sprinted up the stairs, Braley and Poul with him.

"Basement locked down," Wiggy said. He and JP had taken the side entrance and plowed down the stairs, anticipating the typical layout of residential homes in Kalspyra. "Three stunned and in chains here. Starting secondaries."

Kel and Hardball finished the main floor. Two bedrooms and a sitting room contained two more suspects, stunned, but not unconscious, only catching the periphery of the stunner sent long into the house.

"No suspects upstairs," Meadows reported. "But secondaries are going to bring out a haul. There's a comm network up here and more datapads than I can count."

"The garage is clear," Sims said. "Woobie and I will stay out here and keep things secure until help arrives."

"Coming in, boys," Papa Bear's voiced boomed from the front door. Hardball had just finished chaining the last of the suspects as the bearded giant appeared, Zero slinking in just behind him, a small grav container in hand. "The locals and our Repub MPs will be on scene in a moment. Do one of you gentlemen want to greet them? Zero and I have some work to attend to."

Kel marveled as Papa Bear rolled a suspect onto his back, then snatched him into the air like a rag doll, holding the man by the back of his shirt and using the other hand to lift the man's chin as Zero flashed a holo of his face. Papa Bear released the hold and grabbed a limp hand to offer to Zero, who captured a bio-scan. "That's one." The flaccid body was returned to its resting place like a rejected shirt off a clothing rack, the wrong size or color unsuitable, and another heaved upright and presented for Zero's inspection.

"They're like an old married couple picking vegetables from the garden," Braley said, paused in the foyer to watch the process with Kel. "I'll be out front."

"This old married couple's going to get us another target," Zero retorted. "Don't take your buckets off."

True to his word, as the MPs were hauling away the last chained suspect, Zero motioned them close. The target cloud sprang out of his pad. Though smaller than the projection in the team house, the spaces in between were filled with more gold threads, now making the holo seem fuller, solid, less ethereal.

"This guy next," Zero said, pointing to a chubby red face.

Papa Bear smiled wryly. "I couldn't agree more. Nicely done, Zero."

"Who is it?" Kel said, not alone.

"He's an old lech, is who," Zero replied.

"That's a 'what,' not a 'who' answer, Zero," Papa Bear chastised.

"I know! That's the double-eleven," Hardball drawled, referring to the target's simulated place in the stack of playing tiles they'd used to organize the highest value targets. "He's numero deuce in the secret police."

"Greoshj Slokov," Papa Bear continued.

"He goes by 'Uncle Happy' on the romance site he's hooked on," Zero scoffed. "Funny how a thug trained in counterespionage can't come up with a way to hide his tracks better when it comes to making a love connection."

"I'm lost," JP said.

Papa Bear held his palms up. "Love is sometimes the ultimate disarming flaw. That smooth-faced young man there has a sister." He pointed through the blasted front door at the last suspect the MPs loaded into the sled. Kel squinted to see why Papa Bear referred to him as smooth-faced, since a Nem policeman had put a hood was placed on him. "Our 'double-eleven' is at her apartment right now."

"How do we know that?" Wiggy said, more lilt in his voice than usual. Kel was curious how this was going to come together, too.

Zero explained. "Baby Face chats with his sister constantly on the local net. She likes to post a lot of holos. A partial of an older, fat man came up. A shoulder and part of a double chin. A partial reflected in the lenses of another girl in the holo still. Not much, but enough. Even then, it was on her closed group page. Not safe from us, though."

"So, you got him there?" Hardball asked.

"She looks good in a swimsuit, by the way," Papa Bear threw in.

Zero continued as though no one had interrupted. "Not in one step. His workstation, though encrypted, logs a site he accessed on a personal link. Very private stuff.

No faces in the clear. But one little honey he comms with frequently, though she wears a wig and mirrored specs, still shows enough of her face that when we ran it against her public profile, bingo. Then working backward, the partial of the fat man gave a high probability match for mister double-eleven."

"Okay. They know each other. Well, it seems," JP said.

Papa Bear took up the trail. "And since we know who each of them is in the real world, knowing he just received the 'come on over' signal, we know where he's at. Her place. Right now."

"Think her brother knows his little sister is keeping company with his boss?" Poul said.

Zero shrugged. "He's not the only one. He's probably just the best paying. She's an escort."

They rolled in all their vehicles to the apartment complex. "Let us handle this, fellas," Papa Bear said. "No need to rile up the neighbors."

Kel objected. "He's got a PSD."

"Nope," Zero said. "Not here. And if he does, I think we can take care of them, kids. But thanks."

Kel waited for Braley to offer resistance, but he just shrugged. "Suits me. Call if you need us."

Hardball slid the door open. Papa Bear and Zero hopped out and soon disappeared through the stone arch and into the apartment courtyard.

"This is nuts," Wiggy said.

Kel considered the assessment. "Nah. I've seen those two do *waaay* crazier things than this."

Hardball mumbled. "I'll consider the source. No one's done crazier stuff than you."

Kel ignored him. After a few minutes, Papa Bear and Zero came out of the entrance, a portly man, hooded and chained, between them. They marched him to the smaller sled where Poul and Braley waited and sat him in the back. "Drop him off, if you'd be so kind, gentlemen. I think that's what we're going to get tonight. Let's give the fusion cell a chance to do some work, eh? We don't have to carry the whole load."

"No trouble?" Meadows asked as he pulled away, Papa Bear and Zero again sorting holos in the back of the sled as they rolled.

"Not once we explained the situation," Zero said.

"He could come with us, or the Republic would bomb his family's ranch into atoms," Papa Bear added. "You know the saying."

Meadows sighed. "Which one is that, Papa Bear?"

"A smile and a gun will get you further than a smile alone."

Meadows groaned.

Papa Bear yawned. "I love my work."

As they floated on their way back to the team house, Kel stared out the one-way screen at the city. The freeway was deserted this time of night, the police checkpoints halting all but official traffic after midnight. The city was clean and orderly. If not for the military presence, it would be unremarkable except for its normalcy.

"Papa Bear," Kel asked to first be sure he had the senior man's attention away from the holos he sorted.

"What's up, Captain Turner?"

Kel shook his head. "I'm frocked for this mission. I'm still a lieutenant. But I wish you'd just call me Kel, or Turner, like you used to."

Papa Bear chuckled. "Another thing we can discuss later. What's on your mind?"

"You've been on the scene a lot longer than us. I've been trying to get caught up on a few things. The Nem civil war on the Bassinus. What flipped the switch that made the Nems start killing their neighbors? I've been digging into the xenoanthropology and the history..."

"You've been reading Squibb-Davies's brand of rot?" Papa Bear said with no small amount of criticism in his voice.

"Not many other sources to turn to. It's in the area study as a primary reference."

"Oy. So, after digging through ole HSD, you can't figure out how the most exalted race in the galaxy became the subject of genocide by a seemingly civilized society like the Nems, yes?"

"Got me in one. I haven't been out with the Bassinus, so I don't really have my bearings..."

Papa Bear sighed. "I'll save you the trouble, Turner. As twisted as this may seem, the Nems may be in the right after all."

15

Kel's hand reached for his blaster. He'd just gotten a full grip when he realized it was Poul in the doorway. "Hey, we got trouble. One of the hamlets is under attack."

Braley's feet were on the floor. He was already donning armor. "What do we know?"

"The net traffic is pretty chaotic. The MP company sent out a 'troops in contact'. Mechs and ground troops are hitting them pretty hard. Must be Nem Guard. Multiple casualties. The basics are sending a Hardback battalion to the scene. Listen." Poul swiped his link and an audio feed exploded in a frenzied exchange of voices.

"I can't reach anyone at the main gate, or any of the patrols." The voice was adolescent. High-pitched, but not panicked. "Mechs plowed through and hit everything. I'm holed up in the command post. The lieutenant took out a patrol. I can't raise her or anyone else."

"What's the enemy strength and composition?" another voice said.

The youthful voice came back. "I don't know, sir. Walkers and dismounts. I was under fire all the way to the CP. I still can't raise the lieutenant. The civilians are getting hammered. I'm going to move out to try to rescue any I can."

"Negative. Stay put and stay on the link. Help is on the way."

Poul muted the feed. "That MP kid is talking about fighting mechs to save civvies. Good troop, but they were right to tell them to stay put."

Kel rushed to catch up to Braley's state of readiness. "I thought we slew the last of the mechs in the Rila Valley?" He rubbed the last of the sleep from his eyes as his K-17 snapped to his chest. "Guess not. I also thought the full-on attacks on the Bassinus were a thing of the past."

There hadn't been an overt attack on a village since before the teams arrived on the scene. The peacekeeper forces, the strategic hamlet program, and the airstrikes had halted the genocidal assaults quickly.

The rest of the team was downstairs, the last armor applied, carryalls and weapons at their feet. Their two guests appeared, kitted out as well. JP whistled.

"Is that how Lanthanum struts around?"

Their armor and buckets were a mottled gray that shifted through variations in tone in the light. Active camouflage. Not mimetic like Dark Ops tin cans, but very effective. Their carbines were shorter, sleeker than K-17s.

"How you like them Thuringian masterpieces?" Hardball said as he spit his wad of stimleaf into the trash before taking a final rinse of kaff. "Tidy li'l package. Only played with one once. Liked it."

Thuringii arms were sexy, at times temperamental, expensive, and a choice for those who wanted the luxury arms to say something about the user. Like dating a holo model.

"I'm getting nowhere with air ops," Meadows said. "We can hit the airfield and try to 'jack something, but I can't get a priority. They're too disorganized." The hamlet was a hundred klicks from the city center. Sleds would put them there in time to dig graves, not in time to fight.

"I'm talking to the fusion cell right now," Braley said aloud to those without buckets on. "We'll get SLICs and gunships overhead soon. They stopped keeping aircrews on a hot standby two weeks ago. Great timing, that."

"We need air," Papa Bear said. "I've got the Lanthanum skid inbound. It's thin-skinned and unarmed, but it'll get us there fast. Our pilots are raring to deliver if you're wanting, Major."

Braley gave a thumbs-up. He was comming with the fusion cell again.

"I'll bring them down close," Zero said. He flashed a holo of an intersection barely a block away. "Here's where she's going to set down. Let's grab everything and hoof it."

Their roving guard startled as the garage door slid open, almost a dozen armored figures loaded for war coming up the ramp.

"Don't wait up, girls," Hardball said. "We'll be back late."

It was crowded on the skid. Kel sat in the door with legs dangling, everyone shoulder to shoulder on both sides of the aircraft. Braley and Poul took the two crew seats in the center of the deck. The two commed with the Scarlet light-armored group floating toward Lubanya at best speed.

The city thinned out below him, tilled fields and orchards becoming more frequent.

"Two minutes," the co-pilot said overhead.

Poul spoke. "A low pass east of the hamlet, then circle 'round. We'll drop drones and go on the hunt from there. First sign of fire, ground us."

"No worries there, leej," the pilot said. "Stay strapped down. May be some crazy banks coming up."

Kel slaved into the nose camera. It was a better view than he had from the door but still limited. Fires burned in the hamlet. They dropped to treetop level and began a slow clockwise bank. Kel had a straight down view from the starboard side of the skid, centrifugal force keeping him glued to the deck. Back to a direct view, he amped up his HUD to scan for activity. The fight here was over. The Nems had hit and run. On a side channel, he heard the call.

"Troops in contact. Requesting close air support."

The bird banked hard left so all Kel saw now was his feet in the air.

"There's an MP QRF getting hammered. Between the hamlet and the garrison." Braley said. "Twelve klicks west."

With nothing to see as the pilot fishtailed and rolled, Kel pulled up Poul's drone feed. Pushed high and hauling for the site of contact, Poul ran the drone as fast as it could fly. Kel listened in to a side channel between the fusion cell and the hamlet, recognizing the voice of the MP troop who'd made the TIC report only twenty minutes before. He broke in using his net override.

"This is Quasar Two-Six. We're overhead. What's the situation on the ground? I see no combat activity in the hamlet. Can you confirm?"

The MP answered his hail. "In the air above us, Quasar? Are you leading the QRF?"

"We're moving to assist your QRF from the garrison as we speak. You're still on your own for now. Can you confirm fighting in the hamlet currently?"

Pause. "Negative, Quasar. The mechs are gone."

"Keep this channel open with us. We'll be there ASAP. Quasar out."

"Got 'em," Poul said. Scattered on both sides of the road, a convoy of up-armored sleds was in a disorganized halt. Two intact sleds continued to fire into the distance from raised blaster mounts above the cabs. The rest were burning, destroyed, others empty of troops, abandoned. "Sket! The Nems are still able to drop repulsors."

"Unit in contact, this is Quasar, airborne above your location," Braley repeated several times without reply. "Scarlet Control, Quasar One-Six. QRF observed. Heavy damage. We are continuing pursuit. Nem mechs spotted, heading for MP garrison Lubanya, how copy?"

While Braley managed information, Kel was ready to act. "Get us ahead of the mechs. They're making a straight line for the garrison. Low and fast. Meadows, find us an LZ and get us where we can block."

"Rog," Meadows said as he crab-walked out of the door then stayed on knees to wedge forward between the pilots. He switched to audio and began directing their flight path.

"Ready to get that Stone workin' again?" Hardball said, naturally to Wiggy. Blaster fire rose from the tree line to their port side as the pilot jogged violently away.

Kel pulled his feet in as the skid brushed across the treetops.

"Got leaves in my teeth on that one," Wiggy said next to him.

Poul broke in. "They're on an azimuth through the woods, straight for the garrison. I've got four of them lit. A few troop sleds with them."

"Thirty seconds," the pilot said as they slowed, and made a slow swing to fit between the tall, skinny conifers that lined the two-lane roadway.

"Thanks for the lift, Terry, Dan," Papa Bear said. "Get back to Kalspyra. We'll call if we need help. Good job as always."

"Okay, boss," one of them replied, obviously not in agreement but obedient to Papa Bear's judgment. "If you insist. We'll wait for your call."

"Off with you, now," he said as he dropped off the deck onto the road.

"They'll cross the road," Meadows said. "If they're smart, they'll bump across. If not and they just plow through like an undisciplined mob, we can make them pay."

Kel checked the drone overhead. "They're moving straight as a laser. Let's move!"

Poul tagged the projected intercept point with a red star where the Nems would come out on the road. Without a bend in sight, most anywhere the Nems crossed would put them at a disadvantage.

"Ambush is murder and murder is fun," Hardball said on a side channel.

It was an axiom Kel lived by. "Braley, Twelve will take East. You and Three take west."

"Two-hundred-meter separation should give us a wide base. Do it, Kel," Braley said.

"Hustle it, Twelve. Everyone, start dropping hasties," Poul said.

Kel took a knee as he dropped his carryall and pulled out a sphere. He rolled it off the road into the ditch, then took off. The rest of Twelve joined him, the impacts of their armored feet on the hardball road making thunder as they ran full-out.

Sims spoke from behind them. "All showing command lock. They won't do much against the mechs, but they should slow down the sleds."

Kel's had sprouted its six legs by the time he took off running. By now it was on its own path into the woods, its AI searching for the repulsor signature of a combat sled. The hasty mines were a pursuit deterrent but would work equally well for an ambush.

At the front, Kel was past the intercept point. Another hundred meters and they'd dive into the woods and roadside ditch, ready to hit the Nems as they neared the linear danger area that was the road. *Terrible choice on their part*, Kel thought. *Lucky for us they're in a hurry.* Two hours till sunrise. Wherever the Nems were planning to escape to, they were running out of time.

Kel peeled off the road, down into the drainage ditch, and up again into the wood line. "This is the place," he said, dropping prone. "Wiggy, with me." The Stone hovered, the repulsor pod activated, and Wiggy assumed a cross-legged position underneath it.

Kel dialed up the thermal on his K-17 and aimed across the road into the woods. Like a shooter simulation, the drone feed burned through the tree cover, red and yellow glowing mechs in black outline lurching toward them, weaving between large trunks, plowing through small ones. The crack of snapping timbers pierced the air. Kel's pulse quickened.

The sleds trailed behind the plowing path of the mechs. Still deep in the woods, the first mech came into sight. "Wait for it," Meadows said. "Let them get clear of cover." Three of the mechs stepped cautiously forward.

One remained at a distant trail behind the sleds, hot bodies packed onto their decks.

Sims spoke. "Hasties are almost there."

Hell erupted. Staggered explosions blossomed in the dark. The overhead reminded Kel of an aerial bombardment, like a cluster of bombs falling at steady interval in a random pattern. This death came from beneath the unsuspecting Nems, not rained from above. The hasties trotted purposefully through the underbrush, attracted to the sleds like bees to a flower, pollinating the undercarriages with neutronium pellets at the speed of thought.

One of the lead mechs pivoted and fired in a wide dispersion to the flanks, suppressing an ambush from a direction void of ambushers. Without prompt, Wiggy fired. Hot white flares filled their HUDs.

"Good hit!" Hardball said. "Loading." Gabe swapped a new charge pack into the Stone.

Kel sent full particle beam fire at the nearest mech, Meadows and JP doing the same from his right at the next exposed walker. He paused to launch a grenade, then dropped the charge pack as he fed in a new one. The pure accelerated atomic setting drained a pack in a just a few bursts. From the opposite side, beams raked into the mechs as well.

"Loaded," Gabe said, Wiggy responding affirmatively by firing again. Some of the beam was dispersed through the trees, felling them and setting a blaze to the kindling of the splintered giants.

"You got more juice, hit him again!" Gabe coached.

"Yeah, yeah," Wiggy droned back. "Quit nagging." The path clear, Wiggy fired again at the same mech.

Another flash fed Kel's hunger for destruction. *Splash two.*

"Down!" Kel yelled reflexively as he forced himself flat. White meteors showered overhead, chain gun fire from a mech sizzling the air above them. From the other side, Three hammered at the single mech firing wildly, Kel raising his head just in time to see the walker fall.

"Twelve, shift fire," Braley said. "We're assaulting through. Nail that trailing walker. It's coming your way."

"On line," Kel said as he strained to see the fourth remaining walker. Switching to the drone feed, deep in the woods and obscured from direct view at ground level, the fourth mech trotted away. "It's moving past us. Let's move."

Kel hit the road at a full run, trusting that Three had the kill zone contained. The mech was picking up speed. It entered a clearing and catapulted ahead at a run until it made a sudden turn toward the road.

"Wiggy, it's coming across. Hit it!" Kel dropped prone. One last check of the drone window to project where the mech would appear, and he lowered his face behind his optic. *678*, the HUD read. Almost seven hundred meters. Kel sent blasts into the projected path, joined by the rest of the team, impacts from their blasts causing trees to explode, foliage to burn. It happened faster than he could blink. The mech appeared. Wiggy fired. The flash of the Stone faded, leaving the line of the afterimage in Kel's retina, the birdlike knees of the mech bending and bouncing to spring the machine forward. It disappeared across the road and into the woods.

"Missed it clean," Wiggy said, disappointment heavy in his voice. "Sorry, sir."

"Scarlet Command, all stations on the net, there's a mechanized walker headed to the Lubanya garrison." He repeated the message.

A reply came from the fusion cell, many klicks away in the capital.

"Quasar, how far away from the garrison is it?" Poul had the drone locked on it and was bouncing the link over the entire net.

"At its current rate of travel, it'll be on the garrison in fifteen minutes," Poul advised.

Kel rolled to his side to check on the rest of the team.

"Sorry, sir," Wiggy said next to him. "No excuse for missing."

"No way, Wig," Meadows said. "Too damn far, moving too damn fast. That mech driver's on a suicide run."

"Yeah, well, I gave him the opportunity," Wiggy insisted. "He's a dead-ender, alright. And he's going to make it, too, if they don't get a Shark to intercept."

"Enough, Wig," JP said. "No one could've done a better job."

"We've done what we could. The basics are going to have to step up. Let's get back to work," Kel said before breaking back to the common channel. "Braley, what's your sitrep?"

"We're mopping up. Block from your side and work toward us. There may be some hoppers who made it out of the kill zone. Stay sharp."

"Moving," Kel said. "You heard Three. Let's get to work."

On line and moving cautiously, they crossed the road and moved into the woods, patrolling back to the ambush. Fires blazed, trees and brush in yellow flames, the non-organic materials of the destroyed war machines burning red and purple as leaking plasma continued to burn, black smoke feeding a layer of cloud cover in the treetops.

"We've dead-checked everyone," Braley said. Poul and Sims squatted in a quiet spot, working invisible holos in their HUDs as they worked with the Repubs to give chase to the escaped mech. Papa Bear and Zero examined corpses, taking biometrics and holos, ever mindful of the need for more information on their assigned adversary. "If they hadn't bunched up, we'd have been in for a tougher time."

"If we hadn't grabbed hasties," Kel added.

"True," Braley said, leaving the point settled.

Above, the rumble of aircraft rolled over them. The treetops obscured them, but Kel knew the sound of the Shark fighter-bombers when he heard them.

Sims wandered over. "Top's bouncing the feed over to the pilots. They should have..." Booms echoed from nearby. "I'd say they're on him."

Kel pulled up the feed again. Flashes and eruptions of earth rained around the mech, the song of the storm reaching them a few seconds later.

"Gentlemen, feel like a follow-on mission?" Papa Bear asked as he joined their group.

"What do you have in mind?" Kel asked.

"I'll call our taxi. We need to survey the Lubanya hamlet. This may have tipped the Nems' hand enough that we can shut them down for good."

16

The ride over the hamlet was less harrowing this time. Kel's feet dangled over the edge and he wished his legs were bare to feel the refreshing wind against his skin. The orange morning sun cast a single long shadow from the lone remaining spire of a Bassinus dwelling as they circled above. Repub troops swarmed around the hamlet.

The Hardbacks arrived on scene while the operators had fought alone to punish the murderers. And it had been murder of which the Nems were guilty. Kel prepared himself for what they would find from the moment Papa Bear recommended they return to the scene of the massacre. He didn't want to see the barbaric result of the Nems' war on the innocent civilians, but steeled himself, knowing that he would regret it if he lost the opportunity to bear living witness to their crimes.

Medical SLICs were on the ground near the main gate and forms carried stretchers to them like ants bringing crumbs back to the nest. From between the pilots, Papa Bear pointed. "Set us down in the center of the village." The skid slowed and descended in a tight orbit to rest in what he pictured had been the center of a ring of pyramidal towers.

"We can take a lot of stretchers on this deck," Kel said.

"Sorry, Turner," Papa Bear said. "Not just yet. You gentlemen pitch in where you can. Zero and I have work to do. We'll be back for you."

JP grabbed the med kit from the engine well of the skid before hopping off, not asking permission of the air crew. The skid lifted and was gone.

"I'll find who's running the recovery and join in," Meadows said. He broke off onto the Republic net.

None of the surrounding buildings had search symbols painted on them. "Might as well start here," Kel said. "JP, take Wig. Hardball, with me. Braley, you guys take that side. We'll let you know what we find."

"Roger," Braley said as Three broke into two groups and headed out.

Remnants of mirror-smooth walls broke through the rubble to show what it had once looked like. "This one's flattened. I get no life signs," Hardball said as he lowered his link. "I'm running all bands. It's cold. Let's keep moving, sir." He took out his torch and burned an X into one partially intact face of the glass-like edifice.

"Over here," JP said. "Got something hot. We need a hand."

Kel trotted to where JP and Wiggy bent to lift a slab. "About a meter down," Wiggy said. Meadows joined them, the slab seeming to levitate as he added to the effort. The wall careened over and crashed. A bare arm protruded from a crevice. "Got one," Wiggy said, the first to attack the next large piece of debris pinning the frail flesh.

JP's speaker came to life. "Help's here. We've found you. We're not leaving." JP's words spurred them all to keep digging, to lift the tomb away, one piece at a time. Kel pulled a vitals card out and ticked it in a chest pouch. He crawled under the ledge of a truss, his bucket light shining ahead into the tight cavern. The back of a hairless cranium lay whole. "I've got you."

Meadows spoke to the medic station and called for a sled. "We've got a live one, our location."

"More to come, medical," Woobie entered the comm. "We've got at least two in the same group, adjacent structure."

"Roger, Legion," the voice replied. "We're short anyone to send at this time. We've got your tag. Good work. Keep us informed."

More hands appeared around Kel and soon light pierced through the jagged canopy of the rubble. He extinguished his lamp. "JP, grab two auto-tourniquets. The legs are pinned below the knees." JP appeared over his shoulder. The bands wrapped around the thighs and JP pulled his vibro-blade.

"I'm amputating," JP said as he worked. "We'll never get him out otherwise."

Kel observed as JP cut with a sawing motion across the first knee, then the other. "We're free," JP said, sheathing his blade. Kel protected the head while JP rolled his patient over. It was a woman.

Meadows knelt and lifted the small body like a giant scooping up an infant, and walked back to where Gabe had a litter prepared, laying her down as gently as he would a sleeping baby in its crib. Kel applied the vitals card to her forehead.

"I'll get her," JP said. "Find us another."

The sun was burning overhead by the time the last body had been recovered. Kel popped his bucket and took a swig from a hydration pouch as the last body was hoisted onto a sled and floated away. Not all of the bodies had life signs. Not all of them had been adults. Not all had been Bassinus. Two bodies, though badly mangled, were unmistakably human, dressed in Bassinus robes.

"They flat-out shot some of 'em before they dropped the buildings on top of them," Hardball said with fury. "They cleared some of these places, room by room, then hit them with the mechs."

Kel offered his pouch to Wiggy who took a long pull. "The Nems worked fast. They knew they'd miss some on their first sweep through. Figured dropping the buildings would finish anybody left. Bastards."

Kel thought about what Papa Bear had told him just the night before.

"As twisted as this may seem, the Nems may be in the right after all."

"What's that mean?" Kel asked, shocked. "How in the name of Oba could they be in the right?"

Papa Bear and Zero kept working on their pads, small holos of the target cloud floating over each of them as they took the ride back to the team house after the success of nabbing double-eleven.

Papa Bear shook his head. "No. Terrible choice of words. They're not in the right. But they have a reason. And the Republic had a hand in it."

Hardball was listening in. "Why am I not surprised? This I gotta hear."

Papa Bear had everyone's attention as they floated on. He swiped away the holo and Zero copied him, leaving the rear compartment dark as Meadows piloted them home.

"What do you know about the Bassinus, Turner? And their settlement on Haemus?"

Kel knew he was being led on a journey to his answer. It would not be a simple revealing of all Papa Bear knew. It annoyed and intrigued him at the same time. He sighed heavily.

"The Bassinus settled here. They're not native. Their origin world isn't clear."

"Correct," Papa Bear encouraged.

Kel continued his recital. "The area study cited roughly two thousand years of Bassinus presence on Haemus. The Nemanjic and the other human ethnicities arrived here less than a millennium ago to find the planet occupied."

"All true," Papa Bear again rewarded. "What's missing from the studies is essential information about the nature of the Bassinus."

"They're peaceful," JP offered. "Pacifists, even. They haven't raised a hand to defend themselves against the Nems."

Papa Bear nodded in the dark. Kel waited, knowing there was something important to come once Papa Bear felt ready. After an interminable silence, he continued.

"More is known about the Bassinus than what's been revealed publicly. One of the most important being, they're highly telepathic. The other being, their genetics are very adaptable. So much so, there's good evidence they're mixed with not one, but perhaps several non-Bassinus genetic lines. There's human DNA in their genome already."

That was true of several species that were practically near human. Not the telepathy, but the human DNA. Kel was ready for the big answer. The bombshell. When it wasn't forthcoming, he took a stab.

"Papa Bear, what's this 'millennium call' thing?"

"Go to the head of the class, Turner. I know you want this wrapped up neatly, but it's a lot to take in all at once. The long and short is that the Bassinus are disarming predators. When their race hits a certain communal stress every thousand years—maybe it's some kind of internal clock—the Bassinus find it necessary to assimilate a new genetic line into their own."

"How's that work?" Hardball burst. "They ain't got the gumption to kidnap nobody."

Kel thought he had it. "Telepathy."

Papa Bear grunted. "They're very strong telepaths. They project placidity in their dealings with others. The psychs think it's a survival adaptation. But every millennium or so, they exercise the racial need to go beyond coexistence with other races, and move to incorporate another gene pool into their own."

JP scoffed. "How can that be? Speciation by selective breeding? I'm not sure how to characterize it. Do they have some kind of genetic manipulation tech?"

"It's not tech," Papa Bear said. "When stressed, they produce gametes compatible with mates of any humanoid species."

Hardball packed his lip and found an empty hydration pouch to spit in. "Is *that* why they look almost human? They done this with humans sometime in the past?"

"How do you know all this?" JP asked.

Kel knew. "Lanthanum."

Papa Bear's voice betrayed a kind of superiority. "We hire the same xenobiologists and other specialists the Republic does. We get the material from the same sources, just unfiltered. The Bassinus genome has elements of many races, some the brains can't identify. They think the Bassinus may have absorbed several races completely. The House of Reason, RI, the diplomats from Ex-Planetary, they already know all this."

Kel connected the dots. "The Millennium Call. It was time for the Bassinus to assimilate new neighbors. Only, the Nems being a particularly stubborn variety of human with aggressive, even tribal traits, they didn't sit back when some of their people responded to the call."

"Things kicked off here a few years ago," the older operator continued. "From out of nowhere, a movement to convert to the Bassinus religion started. The youth were particularly susceptible. Soon teenagers were shaving heads, donning Bassinus robes, and moving to the cloistered communes of the aliens. Some adults went as well. The Nems responded as a society first by appeals to cultural resilience and anti-Bassinus propaganda."

"But there's no reasoning against mind-control," JP said.

"So, where's the Republic come in?" Wiggy asked.

Papa Bear took on a weary tone. "The Nemanjic government reached out to the Republic for help. The diplomatic mission brought in teams of xenoanthropologists and the like. They studied the situation. They reported. And what they advised was..."

"They're a unique and vital race in the galaxy," Kel interrupted. "You've no right to interfere, you have to co-exist, it's your fault for being so close-minded, blah, blah, blah." Kel had heard it before from those who thought the zhee were a faultless race. Unique and beautiful among the creatures of the galaxy. Being simple and true to their nature. It was humanity's duty to accommodate. Resistance was sinful. Acceptance was mandatory.

Zero spoke for the first time. "The Nems realized they were on their own. They're a culture that fled their home world as a result of persecution. You might say they're historically primed to see an existential threat and react with... genocide. The Nems see themselves in a fight for their very survival. Against a bunch of hairless scrawny wimps."

"That part of the story's never made the Spiral News Network," Hardball said after a huge spit, as though it had been building with the story.

"History's full of the stuff not in the books," Papa Bear said, sadly. "It's probably not the first time the Bassinus have faced such resistance. The specialists think their millennium call has been successful in the past, and they've completely absorbed some races. Other times, they've had to flee for their own existence. They may be galactic pilgrims, assimilating others or wearing out their welcome, one race at a time."

"Kinda like less successful Savages." Hardball spat again, this time missing the target of the pouch as he shook his head, vexed.

JP was as exasperated as Kel felt. "So, this is the best the House of Reason could come up with, sending in the military?"

Kel's head sunk into his hands. "Welcome to our Republic."

"Excuse me, sir?" A basic trooper approached. She came just close enough so her voice would get attention, but put into practice the caution someone had likely told her to use when dealing with legionnaires. They were unpredictable at times.

Kel was closest, and still had his bucket off. "Yes, Corporal? How can I help you?"

She stepped closer, but remained wary and out of their reach, less timid but not yet trusting. A puppy unsure whether it would receive scratches or a smack on the snout.

"Are you the legionnaires who spoke to me this morning? Quasar?" The trooper had "MP" stamped on her sleeves.

"Know any other leejes on the planet, Corporal?" Wiggy said with annoyance, the only other of the team to have his bucket off. Kel frowned at him. "Sorry, Corporal," Wig apologized. "It's been a rough day and a night and a day."

"Corporal, are you the soldier that called in the TIC last night?" Kel recognized the voice.

"Yes, sir." She stood at a loose parade rest.

Kel gestured her forward. "Stand easy, Corporal. You were very cool on the net. Very professional. I've seen soldiers with more combat time than you not keep so calm."

The young soldier blushed. "I didn't feel that way, sir."

"Tell us what happened," Kel gestured her to join their circle. The team had settled in a loose perimeter at the base of a building only partially demolished, enough of a wall remaining to cast good shade. It had been warming up and after their exertions, seeking relief was comforting as they tried to deal with the carnage they'd sorted through. The sole Bassinus spire rose above them, the only thing untouched in sight. Some of the armored group were napping and stirred at the noise. Kel made a double-thumb gesture and the rest of the team popped lids. JP hopped up from the boulder he sat on and pushed a pouch into her hand.

"Come sit with us, Corporal," JP insisted, practically forcing her to take his place.

"Thank you, sir." She was still uneasy, and sat erect and stiff.

"What's your name, Corporal?" Braley asked, hoping to put her at ease.

"Corporal Kristie Hudson, sir."

Kel smiled and spoke extra softly. "Corporal Hudson, tell us what happened last night."

"I was on roving patrol when they hit. We heard the commotion and the net erupted. My Nem counterpart Luka and I sped to the front gate. The control point was already under heavy fire. Our sled got hit and Luka was killed. I tried to help him, but he was already dead. The sled was burning, and I had to leave him."

Kel and the team stayed silent and let her speak. Every soldier needed someone to listen and understand.

"The walkers just plowed through. I've never seen anything move so fast. I always thought when I got into combat that I'd know what to do. That I'd have time to react. I didn't have time to do anything. Not even think. Everything around me was exploding and burning."

"It's like that," JP said. "For everyone. When the violence starts, it happens at light speed."

The corporal nodded. "I stayed low until the Nems were past me. I raised the lieutenant. She told me to make my way to the CP, that she was taking the next shift out to engage the Nems. I know she made it out of the command post with the two patrol teams waiting to come on shift. Two MPs and two Nems. Our augments are good cops. I've learned a lot from them." She stopped. "When I got to the bunker, it was deserted. No one answered my comm. I figured it was up to me to skip to higher and give a sitrep."

"You did right," Wiggy said. "Knowing when the chain of command fell to you, then taking action, that was the right decision."

She gulped. "I wanted to get out there. The CP bunker was safe. Everyone else went out to do their job. The civilians were being slaughtered. But when I was ordered to stay put, part of me—part of me was relieved at first. Then as the noises died down, all I felt was... " Her guilt at surviving when her comrades had not was pouring out. She slumped.

"Stop it right there." Meadows rose from where he'd been lying just outside of the circle. Kel thought the taciturn giant had been sleeping, or uninterested in the interaction all together. He thumbed at Woobie who took the cue and surrendered his seat on the boulder next to hers. Even seated, Meadows towered above her. The young corporal looked fearful, her eyes wide, posture turned rigid again as though expecting the worst.

Kel was unsure what was about to happen. Meadows's idea of gentle interaction was a chokehold instead of a vibro-blade to the kidney. The corporal was near tears. Kel was about to raise his palms to beg an easy hand from the ogre, when Curt spoke. There was a softness Kel hadn't heard before.

"Hudson, that won't help. You need to hear this. And there's no one better to tell you."

Kel held his breath.

"We all fail. Every one of us. We all fail."

A tear ran down the corporal's cheek.

"You don't get to save them all. Sometimes, you can't save any of them. Sometimes all you get to save is yourself. You don't get to choose."

More tears ran down her face.

"A warrior knows when they've done what they could. They accept it and move on, ready for the next fight. Because if you're ready, eventually another fight comes, and you can pay back the ones you couldn't save."

The corporal wiped her eyes. "I'm not sure why I had to find you. You recovered more survivors than anyone else in the relief. Everyone's talking about the legionnaires. I figured this was the only chance I'd ever get."

"The chance for what?" Kel asked.

"When I heard your voice on the net last night, telling me you were on the way, my first thought was, 'I hope they know I'm not hiding. I'm not a coward. I want to be out there fighting, like my mates.' But I had orders. I stayed on the net. And I sat there and listened to the fight. Alone."

"You're no coward," Meadows said sternly. "No one thought that." The rest of the team grunted agreement. "You did your duty. You were as cool as any legionnaire who'd called in a TIC a hundred times. Was that your first combat?"

The young woman took a deep breath. Her tears were gone. "Yes, sir."

"How old are you, Corporal?" Woobie asked.

"I'm eighteen, sir."

"And already a corporal? That tells me something." Meadows held up a finger, indicating he'd be right back. Meadows dug in his carryall, and returned to kneel in front of her. "May I?" he asked as he waited her permission. He moved to pin something on her uniform. Kel exchanged confused shrugs with Poul. Both leaned to see around Curt, curiosity bubbling. It was a Legion combat star.

"This was my grandfather's. I carry it for luck sometimes. The Legion doesn't wear them anymore. I'd like you to have it. I hope it brings you luck, too. When the next time comes and you get your chance to KTF, you'll be carrying the honor of your comrades with you."

The corporal fought tears, and when she looked up from the tiny five-pointed spiral galaxy on her chest, the battle for her emotions was won by a confident grin.

Meadows leaned in and whispered. "I wouldn't let your sergeant major see you with that on your uniform, though."

"Headed your way," Papa Bear said over their common net.

Lanthanum Concepts might have a lot of toys, Kel thought, *but L-comm isn't one of them.* "On the ground in ten. Ready to move out?"

"We're ready," Braley answered for them. "What's next?"

"We're dropping you off at the team house. Zero and I are headed in to the fusion cell. Get yourselves refit and ready. We may break this thing wide open tonight."

"What've you got?" Kel asked.

Zero answered. "The Nems moved the mechs into place by rail. We found their trail from the tracks. We checked the orbital surveillance record. Sure enough, they loaded up at a railhead from the southern province. We've got the fusion cell pouring investigators and signal intercept crews all over. We're close to finding their base of operations."

"This was too big and not very well concealed," Papa Bear said. "This took a lot of support to pull off. We've got enough new faces that, coupled with the physical trails, we're close to double-twelve."

A bounce opened on Kel's link and a face appeared. Colonel Daegor.

"He's directing this last gasp," Zero said. "Let's end him."

17

"Be careful, gents." Papa Bear and Zero were disappoint-ed, but understanding. While Lanthanum had provided the two the best of everything in the galaxy, even the best was not on par with Dark Ops armor and L-comm.

"These boys are dead-enders if there ever were," Zero said with as much emotion as he was capable, slightly above the temperature of an ice cube. "Remember that. Pull out if you're compromised and we'll recover you. Don't push your luck. To sket with what the basics want."

"Thanks, Zero," Kel said as rolled his body net and stuffed it away. "We've gotten a good feel for how these kelhorns think. In and out. We'll be back with the goods in a week, tops."

"See that you do," Papa Bear said. "These Repubs ar-en't patient. Not with the politicians hounding them for results. They're likely to come barreling in any time. I'll keep the pressure on for them to remember that all good things come to him that waits."

There was only one potential bucket propped over a door that could drop on them: a certain silver-haired colo-nel. But after Kel's meeting to coordinate with the Scarlets' fire support officers, his confidence in the Repubs was at a new high. With all eyes on the Scarlet commander, per-haps this operation would be different from their last ex-perience together.

"We're doing this op to suit," Poul reminded, removing some of the items duplicated in his and Kel's individual layouts. The order of the day was travel light. Poul and Kel would be a team. Meadows and Hardball. Sims and Woobie. Wiggy and JP. Braley would stay solo to stage centrally to receive and evaluate all the information from the reconnaissance teams.

"But it's amazing how they throw the Legion to the wolves when it suits *them*," Braley said. It was unlike him to criticize the other services. While sharing a room in the team house, Kel told Braley about Twelve's experience working with the Army. He could speak plainly with another officer about his frustrations. "Appreciate you keeping the Scarlets calm while we do our thing."

"A pleasure, Major Yost," Papa Bear assured. "Another advantage of being a Lanthanum contractor. Our employer grants me a rank equivalent to the basics' top boys. We'll be the voice of reason. Still, we wish we were going with you."

Hardball had a double cheek full of stim. "Tell you what, Papa Bear, when I'm retired, last thing I'm gonna miss is crawling around the woods like some kinda critter. At your age, why would you want to? Don't your body talk to you after all these years?"

Hardball had taken to the older leej, and Papa Bear to the less polished Gabe. Kel saw them in deep conversation on many occasions. Both knew each other's personas were ostensibly incompatible with what some might think was the mold for a Dark Ops leej. Papa Bear was a master of diction and careful speech and at times used his superior language skills to intimidate. Gabe took pride in his simplified language and used it to disarm those who might judge him by that alone. Outwardly, both were physical brutes.

"Love of king and country keeps me youthful, Gabriel."

Hardball's usual accent dropped out, sounding almost urbane. "And if the cause be just and honorable?"

Now it was Papa Bear's turn to laugh. "Look out for this one, Captain Turner. He's a sandbagger. Behind the window dressing of a simpleton lies a refined man of letters. Don't play tiles with him."

The operators were going in alone to comb the forests and hills of the southern range for the remaining Nemanjic Guard. The techies were close to a solution for nullifying the Nem disruptor black magic. Going in on foot and using only L-comm while on the search was decidedly the best option for locating the last of the Nem resistance undetectably. Kel's first suggestion had been dismissed.

"Bomb the whole range from orbit. Flatten it." Kel spoke at the first pause in the intel briefing without waiting for the gathered group to solicit advice. At Braley's insistence, he'd broken down and accompanied them to the fusion cell. The pair of Lanthanum operators presented all their findings to the combined civilian and military chiefs. Kel couldn't help but stare, casting death rays at the silver-haired colonel from the Scarlet brigade. Kel assumed the man had already been sent home. Apparently in the aftermath, the Repub division commander had not judged the conduct of the Battle of the Rila Valley in the same way Kel had.

The embassy man scrunched his face in disdain, repelling Kel's suggestion like he'd tasted curdled milk. "The House of Reason is quite clear on this point. A tribunal will be held. The accused must be tried publicly. Evidence of their crimes will be presented for all civilized beings in the galaxy to witness. Simply bombing them will not serve that greater good."

So here they were. Ready to crawl on their knees and bellies. To silently scour the region. Turning every stone and staring into every dark hole. To find a monster big enough to satisfy the pols. All so that the guilty could be hung in front of the galaxy and prove the House of Reason represented justice.

As much as Kel hated to admit it, it was a task appropriate for a kill team.

It took two drivers to pilot the massive dump truck. Papa Bear and Zero were dirty, dusty, greasy. They would pass for miners. Well-armed, but without their hard armor, they were deadly but not dressed for a big fight. Quarries ringed the southern range, producing the constituent materials for duracrete and the large substrates needed for construction. The Nemanjic were talented engineers. The hidden bunkers and caves they discovered in the Rila Valley taught them that. Kel suspected they would find similar subterranean redoubts hiding the remnants of the Guard somewhere in the depths beneath these bluffs and peaks.

"First drop point coming up," Zero warned by link as the ridged wheels of the gargantuan truck pummeled the rocky road beneath them in a constant grind. The path wound around the hills, climbing slowly as the bed of the dump truck vibrated and shook like the fault line between tectonic plates.

"My teeth are coming loose. Glad we're first off," Sims said. He and Woobie hung from the top of the tailgate. When the truck slowed to a crawl, they activated their camo. The mirages of their two forms slid through the slit beneath the cover and disappeared. The vibration started up again and they rolled on. Another thirty minutes passed without conversation, the operators locked in their own private torture chambers. It did no good to constantly comment on it. There was a time for chatter, then there was a time to suffer in silence.

"We're next," Poul said. Kel was ready. He had a mild headache from the constant jostling. At Zero's warning, they climbed and copied the same deft performance of Sims and Woobie, their envy ending as they hit the hard ground.

"Last step's a doozy," Poul said, helping Kel stand. "PLFs come in handy still." A parachute landing fall was used to cushion the body when contacting the ground at the end of a successful parachute descent. Balls of the feet, the calf, thigh, buttocks, and side of the back were laid down in that order to absorb the energy of contacting the earth. For the most part, it was a technique they left behind, living in the world of freefall parachutes. A graceful glide and stand up landing at the end of a long ride was a fine way to arrive back on firm ground. But some things were never forgotten by a practiced body.

"Feet, knees, and face. Landed like a bag of sket, just like always," Kel said as he joined Poul to trot off. He was secretly satisfied he'd pulled Poul as his partner for the recon. Meadows picked the teams, with Braley the only one dissatisfied at having to hole up by himself and take the role of data manager.

"With rank, responsibility," Meadows answered when Braley groaned.

"I'll pay you back some other time, Sergeant Meadows," Braley joked. Partially.

A trail led around the empty quarry and soon they were over the first ridge and concealed in the woods. They paused and let the sounds of the forest return. "You've got the most time in the boonies here, Kel. Anything stand out from your last jaunt over hill and dale?"

The Rila Valley had been desolate. The southern range was forested and reminded Kel of hunting grounds he'd tromped.

"This terrain is quite a bit different. But I've got some sense of how they like to lay things out." Kel and the team briefed Three on their experiences searching for the Nem hideouts. The techs agreed the Nems would have to use the same external transmitter stations to broadcast the disruptor. If they could spot one, it would be the same as finding an open for business sign.

"We're going to give a wide berth to any bunkers we find," Kel said. "They'll have learned their lesson after Rila. I bet every one of them will be ringed with mines."

"Gun shy?" Poul teased.

"Smarter," Kel replied.

Poul guided them to the first grid. They split up and made the flower-shaped paths of a search, scanning on a wide spectrum and looking for visual clues that would betray evidence of a human presence. Deep draws and other terrain too steep or narrow for a mech or for anything less versatile than a pair of boots were scanned, searched, cataloged, and quickly ignored.

"Let's take a breather and move on," Poul said. In a small depression they dropped their carryalls. Kel kept watch while Poul updated their map, confirming and marking where they'd been. When he was done, they switched. Kel took a quick break to eat a concentrated energy bar and swish some dental rinse before putting his bucket on again.

"Let's do it. It'll be dark soon. Lead the way, brother."

"I'm glad we got partnered, Kel," Poul said as he negotiated up the rise. "I wish we were still on Three together. I half thought I might be called to go with you when they stood up Twelve. We'd have made a great combo, running a kill team together."

"You were my first choice," Kel said. "But it was Meadows's time, you know?"

"I didn't take it personally. But that's good to know, man. Thanks."

The sun set. Night was still day in their HUDs. They made another search across a grid square with less steep terrain, hopeful they might find the first signs of a Nem bunker. The more agreeable area was no more conducive to a discovery.

"Time to move on," Kel said. "You need a break?"

"Nah. I'm good. I'm getting to be more like you, buddy. Anymore I find I only need to eat once a day."

"Spoken like a true recon leej. Off we go."

It was well after midnight that they found it. Poul froze ahead of him. He crouched and Kel took the silent cue to do the same. "Come look at this," Poul said. Kel eased forward. Poul parted the ground in front of him with careful hands. A cable the diameter of his bare finger, smooth and unnaturally straight stood out just below the loamy surface. "Darn near tripped over it." Rain had exposed a narrow span of the cable, just enough to stand out from the features around it.

"It's an isolinear conduit," Kel said as he brought his link out. "It's shielded, but not enough to completely block emissions from this close."

"What say we trace it. Up or down?"

"I'll take up," Kel said. "Drop rucks and meet back here?"

"Be talking at you," Poul said as he descended, link in one hand like the old-fashioned magnetic compasses they trained on back in Legion basic land nav. A man, his mind, and a compass. It was a tried and tested way to find out who could keep their wits all by themselves, in the middle of nowhere.

Two hours later, Kel trudged down the slope where Poul waited in the depression, his camo net over both him and their rucks. "I followed it for a good three klicks," Poul said. "It split, then went too deep and I lost the trail. With the techs in tow, we could probably pick it up again."

"No need. When you're rested, let me show you what we've got."

"I'm good, unless you need a break. Say when."

"Now. This is too good to wait."

The canopy was a woven mat that blocked the tops of the trees and the stars. Under the ferns that carpeted the forest floor were the cold telltales of mech tracks in the ground. "Braley," Kel called. "We've got a positive on mech sign." He bounced the location and some stills. L-comm was not limited to line of sight, but did not have unlimited range, and a good-sized mountain between operators did tend to block signal. Braley was headed to a spot high enough for all the teams to maintain comms with him as the central switchboard.

"That makes you and Poul the grand prize winners," Braley said.

"Not so fast—it's not who called in first, it's who located first," Woobie said. "Sims and I found our Nems an hour ago. We just had to crawl out of this valley to reach big daddy."

With Braley acting as the relay, Kel heard them as if he were in the same grid, though they were on the other side of the range. His map updated with a flashing icon marked the spot Sims and Woobie had found.

"Yeah, but do you have a disruptor field tower located, children?" Poul fired back. "'Cause we're on our way to laying a command det charge on one now. How about a little more effort and a little less whining?"

"Age before beauty, Top," Sims said.

"We're the same age, Sims," Poul said. "Radd out. Oba, become a team sergeant and everyone assumes you're as old as Bigg."

They followed the cable emissions, mapping where the hard line branched, one trail leading to the floor where the tracks lay, the other continuing higher to where Kel had located the signal emitter. Nestled on a precipice and barely visible was the top of an emitter. With some careful climbing, Kel could reach it. He was planning the route when Braley's voice interrupted.

"Meadows and Hardball are compromised."

Poul sighed. "So much for sneaking and peeking."

Kel grunted. "Let's find out if it's time for seeing and fleeing."

18

"Braley, what's happening with Meadows and Hardball?" Kel asked.

Braley delayed answering. Kel knew Braley was a one-legged man in an ass-kicking contest at the moment. "They stumbled into a sentry."

"Are they being pursued?"

"Not at this time," Braley said. "He and Hardball were separated when a spider hole opened and a Nem popped out. It was just bad luck. Meadows doesn't think it was a response to being detected. He's carrying the body out with him."

Kel aborted his climb to mine the emitter. Poul was already attaching a splicer onto the isolinear cable he'd exposed. They would tap into the line like the others they'd already spliced and see what information it pulled. It could be voice communications, which would be very useful assessing the strength and locations of their enemy. It might just be power and command data. They'd find out once they got out of the area and could analyze the take.

The units could also sever the line on command, or set it for a delay to do the same. That alone might not be enough to bring down the disruptor field. But an artillery round would certainly do it. They had the emitter locked onto the map. The cannon cockers could drop a round on a dime—with enough targeting support. But that relied heavily on all the technology remaining functional.

Just then Meadows came on the comm. "We're on the move." There was no strain in his voice. "Take us about an hour to make it to the other side of this ridge and put some terrain between us and the bunker site." Kel imagined Meadows carrying a dead Nem over his massive shoulders as he climbed, like a hunter carrying a kill. Meadows was as skilled as Kel with a vibro-blade.

"Rog, Meadows," Braley replied. "Keep me advised."

"What's the plan, boss?" Kel was glad he didn't have to make the call as to what their next action was. They all knew the compromise plan—pull out. But if their presence remained undiscovered for some time yet, they had options.

"Sket. Our IPB has barely begun," Braley complained. The initial intelligence prep of the battlespace had been interrupted like a thief caught breaking in at the front door. "I'm bouncing FS our target locations right now. The Nems could figure out any second we're here. They punch up the disruptor and turn our guardian angels in fire support deaf and blind, we'll have no choice but to hightail it and let them bomb this place into a piece of flat land."

"Agreed," Kel said. "I recommend we set the splicer to cook off for one hour. It'll give all of us time to get some distance from the targets without tipping our hand to the Nems. A missing sentry—they might not get too riled up about just yet. But that *and* a hard line disruption—it'll be the same as advertising we've moved into the neighborhood."

"What's everyone else's score?" Poul asked.

"You two have the best find," Braley answered. "Sims and Woobie have a definite with signs of mechs like you have. Meadows and Hardball—we just don't know how extensive a target they located. Wiggy and JP are empty-handed. I've got everyone moving out. Like I hope you two are. Set that splicer and beat feet. Now. Clock's running. I've got to work this problem with Scarlet fire support. Out."

Braley was hard at work, burning brain power at a rate much higher than Kel and Poul were burning in muscle juice humping up the peak and out of the valley. They'd formulated an event template with the Scarlets' fire support element. The artillery brains were a model of enthusiasm about the most efficient way to kill from a distance. It made Kel glad he'd never come under the guns of competent cannon cockers.

Pre-mission, Poul and Kel took the task of coordinating with the Scarlet fire support team. Legion companies were highly variable in their configurations. All had mortar support. Some had actual artillery, light and even heavy armor. Braley pushed Kel to take the task. Kel's time in the regular Legion had been in an assault platoon, then Legion Reconnaissance, before becoming an operator. Coordinating fire support was not a strength he possessed. Poul was a very competent heavy weapons specialist. Both had been cramming in anticipation of meeting with the Scarlet gun bunnies; pragmatism coupled with curiosity as to how these things were done.

They sat with three Scarlets at their base, a table in a quiet hab quickly deserted at the sight of the operators. Two legionnaires drew a lot of attention, making Kel wistful to return to a world where he wasn't on public display. With lids popped and introductions made, Kel tried to set the tone for what he hoped would build their relationship for the upcoming fight.

"I don't have any experience working with Republic Army assets at the brigade or division level," Kel admitted. "And our fire support looks a little different from how the army organizes things."

The solid-looking lieutenant colonel spoke first. "And to be honest, we've never worked with the Legion before, much less folks from... Silver." The officer used the Dark Ops cover name. The boulder blocking the path between them had been nudged a few centimeters.

The major put his shoulder into it. "So, if we can count on you not to skin us and eat us..." The boulder was rolled aside.

Poul was first to squelch his belly laugh. "Not on the first date, gentlemen."

"We have PTB that should work to keep them in place if they're penned in their holes," the Scarlet artillery major offered. Plasma thermobarics. "They'll tunnel well, not quite a bunker buster, but they'll get us at least ten meters of penetration before payload detonation." He continued with more deadly options, listing them off like a master chef describing his specialties, pride and glee bubbling through the surface of his nonchalant recitation.

"We can offer EMP if you want it. Local field about five hundred meters. Cyax. Shouldn't be a problem for you leejes buttoned up, so long as you don't mind a full scrub later." Cyax was a lethal agent inhaled or with enough skin contact for absorption. Things would have to get very, very bad to pull out the chemical warfare tools.

"We've got loiter rounds we can send if you have troops to pursue. We release ground control to you for terminal guidance." The artillery could launch anti-personnel rounds that had the ability to hover on station for fifteen minutes, and had a travel range of five kilometers

GALAXY'S EDGE

from their hold point before either deploying or going inert. The rounds would stay airborne, await a target command, and could pepper a grid square with deadly frag.

"And of course, plenty of dual-purpose conventional plasma-fragmentary," the colonel said with a wry grin. "M779 will take care of most any problem. The battle calculus is pretty straightforward. Five M779 per mech kill, and we can deliver tons of it."

"No nukes though, sadly," Master Sergeant Jacob Kelly shrugged. "No great loss. The Nems don't have anything left that's big enough to be worthy of our specialty munitions." He reminded Kel of someone just dressed for a date, only to get the bounce their partner was canceling at the last minute.

"Why didn't you guys get used earlier at Rila?" Kel asked.

Major Kelly looked as though he were swallowing sour bile until the colonel spoke up. "Well, you might say we didn't get invited to dance until the band was playing the last song. But we like to think by the time we were done, we brought some class to the whole affair. Likewise, your special reconnaissance will have a lot in common with the exploitation and pursuit we did that ended the Rila Valley campaign. But this time, we get to be there for the band's warmup number."

An event matrix and contingency for a dozen courses of action planned, by the end of their eight hours together, time had compressed into mere minutes for Kel. It had been an education.

"We can't thank you enough," Kel said, exchanging firm grips with his new comrades. He felt he'd grown to know the hearts of the warriors the many kilometers behind him on the battlefield.

174

"When you call, we'll be there," Colonel Halloran assured them.

"In my next life, I want to come back as an artillery officer," Poul confided to Kel when they were back in buckets. "Those guys are giddy about killing. I like that."

"You just love to unalive people in spectacular ways," Kel said.

"I'm no liar. I won't even try to deny it."

"Smoke on the way," Braley said. "TOT, one minute." Braley made the decision. To cover their escape, the artillery could cover the range in obscuring refractive smoke. Airbursts would rain clouds of the dense dust dropping curtains of fog too thick for even sensors to penetrate. It would paralyze any pursuing Nems. It wouldn't hamper the leejes' ability to navigate in the slightest.

"What changed?" Poul asked as they picked up the pace, leaning into the uphill slope as they trotted, the narrow animal trail a virtual highway.

"Someone's getting pursued," Kel replied knowingly.

"Kel," Braley said. "Cook off all the splicers. Wig and JP are in contact."

Kel brought up the menu and executed the command. "Done." He listened to Braley on the side channel communicate with the fire support until they no longer replied.

"Kel, do the splicers read back fired?"

"Rog, Braley. Did the Nems kill the data stream again?"

"Yeah. We are full-on cut off from FS. Watch yourselves. I'm going quiet. Gotta try something."

"So much for being the invisible eyes of the Legion," Poul said. "We ain't going to live this down." Kel wasn't worried about their reputation at the moment. Wiggy and JP might be in a fight for their lives.

Braley returned. "Got 'em back! Kel, you guys knocked out the scramble in a corridor over your target. I've got a drone over it and I'm bouncing a tight-beam link through it to fire support. We're back in business."

"What's the plan? How can we help, Wig and JP?" Braley dropped to a side channel to speak to the two.

"Smoke was a good call," JP said. "We're getting some distance now." The bounce in JP's voice told them he and Wiggy were running. "Braley, we've got mechs on the move. Bring the rain while they're blind. Don't wait. Do it now."

"Roger," Braley replied, not nitpicking for more detail. If they wanted fire support, they needed fire support.

"Braley," Kel interrupted. "Before you call for fire, listen to me."

"Go."

"You can request DPICM for the mechs in the open. Hit the other targets and areas of interest with PTB and EMP till they're tired of sending it. But our target, go light on PTB then call only EMP. Got me? The big boys want someone to hang? Then let's go find them someone to hang."

Even kilometers away from the nearest impacts, the ground shook like riding in the back of the earth hauler. From the rocky tree-lined bowl they'd adopted as home, the world beyond the ridgeline was as violent as creation itself. The drone Braley had hanging overhead read out the score as the game progressed. Impacts hammered the map like blossoming meteors, striking deep in the valleys surrounding the mountain range. Nearest them, Braley walked two penetrator rounds onto the spot Kel registered, then—the show of shows. Less impressive airbursts and ground strikes preceded bands of expanding radiation, visible in the microwave spectrum to their sensors. The EMP. The waves rippled out, collided, rebounded, amplified, and covered the valley. A new assault followed. Then another.

"End fire mission," Braley said. Larger drones appeared. The artillery was sending in their own forward observers. No longer affected by the Nem blockade, the large birds covered the territory. Any escaping Nems would be met with more raining death.

"Coming in," Sims said. Kel spotted them now through gaps in the thick trees, ambling down the military crest of the ridge.

"By the time they get rested, we should be ready to go," Poul said. Their armor and weapons were well shielded from EMP. But walking into a zone so filled with high-energy pulses was asking for trouble. The two operators dropped rucks and leaned chests against the rim of the natural foxhole.

Kel rapped each on a shoulder. "Take a break and then we'll make our way down. We're not waiting for anyone else on the team. We're it. Let's find a CLE to take home."

"Well, I'm not popping my lid," Woobie said. "Those guys mix up shells and send a chem round our way, I'm not ending up doing the funky chicken while you guys laugh."

"It wouldn't be anything like that, Woob," Sims said. "You'd just turn cherry red and die. But, I'm with you. I want to hit these guys while they're on their heels. Let's head out now."

"Poul?" Kel asked.

"Another twenty minutes isn't going to make a difference, more or less. It'll take us an hour to make the valley. Good by me. Let's nab us a critical leadership entity to make up for our inadvertent misadventure of a recon." Poul mumbled as he bent to retrieve his ruck, "Not that I'd let anyone say that to our faces."

"Kel, is this really a good idea?" Braley asked. He was still moving off his mountain perch, the rest of the team also well on their way to the valley where Kel made the fourth for a short-handed three-man kill team. "The smart play would be we keep anyone alive barricaded, send drones in, and wait them out. The Scarlets can get troops SLIC'd in and up here within a few hours. Let them do the heavy lifting. Or at least wait for Meadows and Hardball to join you. They only need another hour at the rate they're moving."

"I know, Braley," Kel said. "But that might be enough time for our boy to escape and start this all over again. This is our best chance to do what Papa Bear and Zero talked about. End it. Now."

The silence telegraphed Braley's feelings about his plan. "This isn't like you, brother. Don't be headstrong. Be smart." He sighed loudly. "But I'm not down there. Just promise me you'll pull back if it's too hot."

"I promise, dad."

They took the last rise cautiously under full mimetic camo. The PTBs hit with precision, deep cuts into the earth revealing the bunker housed beneath. Duracrete and graphite rebar mixed with thick tree roots and brown earth mocking a natural disaster like an earthquake. The only difference being the charred and scattered human remnants betraying the synthetic source of the cataclysm.

Wordlessly the operators spread out and moved on line as one, HUDS, audio sensors, and infrared lights probing into the darkness of the visceral opening. "Tossing," Poul said as three tiny Inquisitor drones flew off into the chasm. A window opened and a map came to life, growing like a time-lapse holo showing the growth of a branching plant. "I'm sending two long, and I'll keep one just ahead of our route for a live view."

The hulk of a mech lay scorched, crushed, and dead as a spent charge pack. A tunnel wide enough for the walking tanks sloped downward. "At a fast move," Kel said as they let the drone be their forward eyes.

"This is a massive network," Poul said from just behind. Sims and Woobie were on his shoulders, guns raised to send the invisible lights from their K-17s deep ahead. "The whole complex rings the valley but doesn't run deep. Wherever this fortress has been breached, the EMPs will have flooded in. I'm betting... contact!"

The tunnel continued a curving path. Fifty meters ahead, it opened up and an unmapped area waited. The mapping Inquisitors were well ahead of them, following the tunnel route. The third drone hovered from ceiling height to show the open blast doors, the Nem troops gathered just beyond, and a still mech poised in front guarding it all. No light of any spectrum issued forth. The Nems were blind.

"That mech's dead," Sims said. "They don't have any tech better than a candle working, and it doesn't look like they have that." A few dim glows indicating handheld chemical lights, barely strong enough by which to read large print, were apparent.

"Hit 'em hard," Kel said. Even if their electro-optics and blasters were fried after the fierce EMP assault, the Nems had projectile armaments. They could kill just as well as any blaster. "ROE stays the same. They raise a weapon, don't hold back."

Kel slowed. He stepped around the corner. He launched a stunner past the frozen mech and shot the two troops at its side as three guns joined his. Another stunner launched through the open blast door from beside him, and Kel followed the trail of the herald angel past the bodies and the stalled mech, through the wide opening, inviting him to probe its secrets. The dance of purple arcs faded as he stepped into the room. Stunned Nems sprawled around. One struggled to rise and Kel shot him.

"Three o'clock," Sims said.

A trio of bodies disappeared behind another blast door, this one swinging shut. Kel joined in the instant response and fired. A pained voice came from behind the door, no longer in motion. Poul was with him as they flooded to the door, and shouldered it open again as he slid with it, making room for two guns. Kel activated his white light and flooded the space beyond. The Nem reflexively threw an arm across his face.

"Hands up, don't move."

The man stuttered in place, the disruption causing hesitancy, his movements bewildered. The stunners had shocked him, but not neutralized him.

"Hands up!" Kel said again.

The arm came down from across his face.

"Colonel Daegor, don't make me kill you."

The hair was slightly longer. The face was even thinner, but it was him.

Poul fired through the threshold at something Kel couldn't see. "All clear but the corners," he said over L-comm.

"Colonel, it's over," Kel said aloud. "I don't have to kill you. Raise your hands."

The colonel's arms remained at his side. "You're not one of the green devils of the Republic, are you? You're Legion."

"Hands up, Colonel," Kel repeated.

"I think you'll have to kill me, Legionnaire. I'm not going to be judged by some farcical tribunal. Some bug race, a ridiculous dog-man, a donkey, sitting in judgment of me and what I've done to assure the survival of my people? Never. I'm afraid you'll have to kill me."

"Right hand, Kel," Poul said. The colonel had kept his body angled, concealing a weapon. "Frell this." Poul's grenade launcher made the familiar hollow plop. The colonel collapsed. Poul sprang into the room, racing directly for the falling figure.

Kel followed on Poul, cleared his corner, turning back to see another armored figure had poured in with him to clear the other side. He stepped over the body at his feet. To his side was the other body he expected to see, the one Poul shot from the threshold.

"Were you certain that round didn't have enough distance to arm?" Kel said as he moved to where Poul was chaining Daegor. A handfrag lay at the colonel's side, dropped when Poul's grenade bounced off his chest.

"Or that the colonel didn't have an activated grenade in his hand?"

"I've seen this holo before, remember?" Kel did. Poul had once saved them and a hostage from a grenade-wielding fanatic. "It was either a blaster or a grenade in his right hand. He never had two hands where I couldn't see them at the same time, and it takes two hands to arm their frags. Either way, after all the trouble we went to, I thought it was worth the risk."

"Well, let's hope you didn't stop his heart when you punched him in the chest with that forty-seven-millimeter fist."

Daegor was silent as they carried him out into the sunlight. Soon, the first of the Scarlets appeared, then more. Now the valley floor was teaming with green uniforms and visored helmets. Kel searched the faces for those of his repulsor glider troops. JP ministered to the leader of the Nem resistance, an oxygen hood now on the older man, and a pain stimulator on the base of his neck. The rest of the team stood with Kel in a protective perimeter as JP worked.

"Make way for Six," a voice yelled as Scarlet troops parted.

Glimpses of a tan face appeared through the forest of troops, silver hair poking from underneath the helmet coming into view as he strode closer.

"Report, Captain."

Braley stepped between them. "I'm Major Yost, the mission commander." Braley detoured the colonel as Kel turned away.

"Figures," Hardball said. "Here to grab some glory."

In a few minutes, L-comm broadcast Braley's warning. "Headed to the CLE with the Scarlet commander.
We're transferring our prisoner. Let's make the handoff
and get out of here."

JP talked with a pair of medics. The captured Daegor
sat chin slumped to chest.

What's he thinking? Kel wondered. *Does he wish he'd
had that grenade prepped*?

Poul bounced his ener-chain code to a captain, then
joined Kel where he waited with the rest of the team.

"Hey, what gives?" Woobie said. "What are they doing?"

Daegor was being stood. The oxygen hood removed.
From either side, a pair of Scarlets carried the man up the
embankment and into the wrecked entrance of the bunker, followed by another dozen green-uniformed troops.

"This isn't right," Hardball said. "Captain, you
seeing this?"

"It's okay," Kel said. "Just watch."

The silver-haired colonel moved to a position of
prominence amid the rubble. Three links were held aloft
around him to capture the moment. On cue, Scarlets
walked from the darkness of the bunker and into the
light, the ener-chained Daegor in their midst. The colonel removed his helmet as the prisoner was brought to
stand before the taller man, who looked down, stone face
squinting in judgment.

His voice was loud enough for the whole valley to hear.
"The House of Reason has come to deliver its justice."

"Can you believe this?" Wiggy said, another episode
of uncharacteristic display of emotion in his voice. That
was twice. Kel would store the events for future reference.

"That's some kinda nerve," Hardball coughed.

"He's been practicing that line," Meadows said.

"What a disgrace," JP said.

Kel disagreed. "Let's put this place in our vapor trail. I'd say everything's as it should be."

19

Papa Bear's grinning face filled Kel's link. "Catch you at a bad time, Turner?"

Kel had been working out by himself. He caught his breath.

"Nope. What's up?"

"I want you to take a little jaunt with me. There's someone I'd like you to meet. Or more correctly, someone who wants to meet you."

"Should I get Braley?"

"Major Yost isn't invited this time. You won't need to armor up. Let's be low-key, shall we? I'll be by in ten." He broke the connection. Kel cursed. He'd just started his workout, and it irritated him that Papa Bear was being cryptic.

Exactly ten minutes later, Kel was standing outside the team house exchanging pleasantries with one of their security staff when a blacked out speeder pulled up. The gull wing door on the passenger side opened. Papa Bear sat behind the controls of the luxury racer.

"Thought you'd appreciate a little gourmet dining. It's almost lunch and there's a nice spot just up the road. Shall we?"

Kel hopped in. This part of the city was returning to normalcy. Umbrella covered café tables had sprung up with the improvement in the weather. It was still chilly, but the rain and sleet hadn't come down in a week. The mild rise in temperature sparked as much street activity as had the Republic's announcement that the civil war was over. It was like the Nemanjic were awakening from a long winter's sleep.

The Bassinus issue had yet to be resolved. With combat operations winding down to the odd police action, the Republic flooded cultural specialists and social scientists by the repulsor load into the country. The two kill teams were packed, their lift into orbit scheduled for the morning. They'd be on Victrix in a week's time. As he signed his report, Kel vowed to cease his ponderings about the Haemus civil war. He couldn't resolve the conflict, and doubted the Republic experts could either.

My new outlook is to be disciplined enough to know when I can't help anymore. I will leave it all in the past. Meadows is right. A warrior knows when they've done what they could. They accept it and move on, ready for the next fight.

"Who wants to meet me?" Kel asked.

"My boss."

Papa Bear had told the truth. The restaurant was only a few blocks from the team residence. It had a stone-walled courtyard for parking, security guards out front. The influx of more Istrians with the Republic mission had heightened tensions in the city in a different way than when the Scarlet MPs had patrolled. The Nemanjic civilians were friendly to the Repubs, or at least neutral. The Istrians they outwardly disliked; some spat on the heels of passing Istrian police patrolling jointly with Nem counterparts. Kel still couldn't spot any difference between the ethnic twins. Smart business owners wanting to capitalize on the return to commerce had hired security to deter violence between locals and the occupying visitors.

"Captain Kel Turner, please meet Grant Odom." A fit man in a tailored suit rose from the booth.

"How do you do, Captain Turner? Please, join me. I've come a long way to meet you."

Papa Bear held a hand up to a waiter, halting the man from approaching. "Lanthanum Concepts is based on Andalore, but we have branch offices across the core," explained the man Papa Bear referred to as his boss.

"It's a long haul from Andalore, just to meet me," Kel said.

"I was headed here to check on Brian," Mister Odom said. Brian was Papa Bear's first name. He'd never been curious. "It was also an opportunity to make your acquaintance. There are a lot of people who speak very highly of you, Captain Turner."

"Just Kel, please."

"And I'm Grant. This has been a very successful contract. No different than any other that Brian's managed for Lanthanum. The bonuses that come from a win like this add up not only for Lanthanum, but for our specialists as well.

"I'll come to the point, Kel. Lanthanum would like to offer you a position."

"Good morning, Captain Turner," the bearded operator said as he passed Kel in the hall. The man was sweaty and dressed in cut-off shorts and a T-shirt riddled full of holes. Kel didn't recognize the man but returned the greeting. A raised body mod on his forearm caught Kel's eye. Before Kel could identify the mark, the man was past them, down the hall at Six's team room door.

"Fresh meat," Meadows said dismissively as he led them around the corner. "Knows who you are, though." Meadows grunted. They pulled their grav containers along. They'd unseal the team room and start sorting gear, then get the large pallets downstairs unloaded and start the process of topping off all expended items used on the Haemus mission.

"Look what the wobanki dragged in," Bigg said, leaning against their team room door.

"Hey, smaj," Kel said gleefully, excited to see his old team sergeant and surrogate father. He traded chest thumps with his hero.

"Glad you're back, Twelve. Good job."

"What in the nine hells is that?" Hardball spurted.

Kel saw it now. The nondescript "12" was missing from above the team room door. Emblazoned on the door itself was a large skull. The Legion sword pierced it. It sat on a background of the five-pointed spiral armed galaxy that was the old Legion combat star. On the skull in red was their team number.

Meadows pointed. "Who did this?"

"Colonel's directive," Bigg said. "One of the first things he did. The Legion approved our unofficial insignia as unit heraldry."

"Official heraldry," Kel said in disbelief. "Dark Ops. A covert unit. Has. Official. Heraldry." Then it hit him. The body mod the operator had tattooed on his forearm was the same insignia.

"I didn't want you to be surprised," Bigg said.

"I couldn't be any more surprised if I woke up with my head fused to the carpet," Hardball said.

"Probably not a new experience for you, Hardball," Bigg said. "Let's go in. There's more to talk about as you unpack."

Meadows placed his palm on the biometric pad and the door slid open.

Kel coasted his grav container to a halt and plopped onto the float behind his small corner desk. "What is it, Bigg? We're expected at a dress parade for the change of command for the new Legion Commander?"

They'd gotten the word on the flight back. General Steiner was out. General Barrow was in. None of them knew much about the new Legion Commander. He'd been sector commander over the 187th before his bump up.

"Nothing like that," Bigg said. "But there are more changes coming. The colonel's expecting you, Captain Turner. Make your way down. I'll bounce that you're on your way."

"Okay, Bigg," Kel said, getting to his feet. "I'm not about to get blindsided by something, am I?"

Bigg shrugged uncommitted. "Time for NCO talk. Beat it, sir."

Kel found Braley waiting with the commander. The office was essentially the same, but Colonel Chatsworth's "I love me" wall replaced the collage of Colonel Hartenstein's mementos from a career in the Legion and Dark Ops. Kel had only briefly met the new Dark Ops commander before shipping out for Haemus. His initial impression had been rushed. The new commander came from a career in the 187th and had never served in Dark Ops. Kel's fears seemed to have cemented into reality. Insignias. Tattoos. Dark Ops was a changed unit under the new leader.

"I have good news for both of you gentlemen," the colonel said from behind his desk. He was thin and wiry.

He kept a shaved head. His forearms were corded and vascular. "You're both no longer frocked to your ranks. They're both permanent. Congratulations, Major Yost, Captain Turner."

Kel was shocked, not for the first time today. His intuition tingled and told him there was more to come. Braley reached over to shake Kel's hand. He returned the grip absentmindedly. What boom was about to fall?

"And like everything that accompanies your new ranks, there are new challenges."

Kel felt dread coming with the next words.

"Major Yost, your time in Dark Ops is coming to a close. The Legion needs you back."

Braley nodded. "Yes, sir. It was bound to happen."

"Captain Turner." Kel swallowed hard. "The new directive from Legion command is that officers may spend only a single four-year tour in Dark Ops before returning to the Legion. You're closing in on near a decade in DO, almost two of those as an officer. Your status is not yet settled. For right now, it doesn't matter, though. Neither of you are leaving DO just yet."

The enormity of what the colonel just said was like a bad dream for Kel.

"Psydon is in rebellion. They think they're leaving the Republic. A full-scale invasion is in the advanced stages of preparation. Top off and repack your teams. This unit is going to war."

"Dark Ops is being gutted," Kel said as they walked across the quadrangle. "Practically every team leader has been here more than four years already."

"At least they're leaving the NCOs alone. They're the strength of DO."

"It's a purge," Kel said. "I told you. It's a response to the Scarecrow Op. Just like the rumor we heard from that Navy guy on the cruiser. There are points in the regular Legion now. Meadows checked it out. Turns out it's true."

The appointed officer program allowed for the direct commissioning and promotion of officers in the Republic armed services. Favors given to ensure loyalty to the political elites by the officers they raised to prominence. The Legion had never permitted points in their ranks. Until now.

"It's a move to subvert the power of Article Nineteen," Braley said. "It's transparent."

"It's a move against the constitution, is what it is," Kel said. "Somehow the snakes in the House of Reason got Steiner to sign off, and still they cashiered him. What could they be holding over his head?"

"Maybe nothing. We don't really know the sequence of events. Bigg will tell us what he knows when we get him alone."

Kel whispered. "What's the Primus Pilus Society's take on these things, I wonder?"

Braley held the door for him. "We're going to have to wait to find out. We've got a brand-new war to win."

20

"Psydon is the third planet in the system. It has an orbital axis perpendicular to the ecliptic, a nearly coplanar rotation around its sun, and experiences a clockwise rotation with a period of twenty-six hours. As a result, the weather on Psydon is remarkably constant. It is largely an environment of dense vegetation classified as jungle with warm seas and small uninhabited polar ice regions."

Kel was only half paying attention. He'd been through the material. He was certain even the most lackadaisical of legionnaires had done the same. As for the five thousand basics crowded into the bay with them, who knew? What Kel had discovered about the Repubs was that the individual troops were frequently high caliber and motivated. As an organization, they were mired by inefficiency and an orthodoxy reminiscent of some ancient religion with traditions and methods consecrated by time.

But that assessment rang hollow for Kel because as he thought about it, the Legion had a few inexplicable quirks of its own. He tried to identify the different Legion and Republic units gathered for the briefing. The troop transport *Tenacious* had been brought out of hermetic stasis from its rest around Tarrago moon. It hadn't been used since the Savage Wars. Not even the invasion of Antione— the largest of large-scale combat operations Kel had ever been involved in—had needed its holding capacity.

The 187th Legion was waiting on Okella, the staging planet for the invasion. Psydon resided in the 187th sector, so they had been deployed almost immediately. A single star system away from Psydon, Okella was a habitable world with a biome that resisted every attempt at modification. The native species was a burrowing creature that reminded Kel of a rodent that dug holes in his mother's garden. The gophers lived in large communities for safety from larger predators, of which there were several. They made fundamental tools and used fire, so qualified as sentient, though the xenobiologists estimated it would be a million years or more before truly so. Such a long period of time that the Republic didn't bother to isolate the planet. The Savages had no consideration for the sanctity of a developing race, so neither could the human and other civilized races during their war for survival.

The 131st Legion was already on the ship when they shuttled from Victrix up to the waiting *Tenacious*. From his stadium view of the massed troops below, an island of leejes in gray combat uniform stood out from the green sea of swaying bodies around them. Somewhere in that drab grouping would be the current generation of recon leejes of the 131st, Kel's old unit. Would it really be so bad, going back to the regular Legion to stand with the massed troops below? What if he ended up commanding the Legion Reconnaissance company? Somehow, he knew the Legion would make sure to find a place for him a thousand light-years away from wherever the 131st was.

"Hey, Kel," a voice whispered behind him. The kill teams were crowded together on the observation deck, separate from the other troops on the ship. A hand came forward. "Didn't get a chance on Victrix to say congrats on the bump. You deserve it, man."

"Thanks, Beeks. Appreciate it." Mike Beeker was commander of Kill Team Two. He hadn't seen his friend in over a year, and the same span before the brief exchange that had been their last chance meeting in the halls connecting the team rooms. Kill teams were gone more than they were home. Theirs was a friendship of commonality rather than familiarity.

"Hey, Beeks. Any word where you're headed to back in the Legion? You came from Wolfhound Regiment, right?" The Wolfhounds were a named Legion within the regimental system. It was a good example that caused Kel to reexamine the criticism he'd leveled at the Repubs. The Legion had numbered regiments, which it referred to as Legions—though they were regiments—and named regiments that were understood to be Legions. If ever there were an organization defined by tradition, it was the Legion. The difference between them and the basics being, the Legion discarded what was inefficient. Dogma, gear, tactics, and even basic organization evolved constantly based on its need above all to be deadly.

"No word." Beeker leaned closer. "But if it's back to the Wolfhounds, it won't be so bad. You?"

Kel joggled his head. "The CO made it sound like my status hadn't been decided yet, since I don't quite meet the letter of the law of having four years as an officer in DO."

"Lucky man. If I don't see you for another year, have a good one."

Kel turned his attention to the holo broadcast above the tiny dais where the briefer stood. He was still prattling on about the system background.

"The doro are not native to Psydon. They are descended from pack predators, and their social and military organization follows a psychosocial model that emphasizes

many of the same characteristics as their primogenitors."
He faded out again. There was going to be nothing new to
learn here, but Colonel Chatsworth had insisted all operators, though quartering separately from the other forces,
would participate in every joint service brief. Chatsworth
was already on Okella with General Umstead, the sector
Legion commander, and Legion Commander Barrow,
planning the Legion role in the invasion. If they didn't attend, he would never know. But it wasn't how things were
done. Orders were orders.

"The doro have a canine similarity. Utilizing a quad-
ruped's ability to run at high rates of speed, they have
evolved to apex predator with the ability to stand on two
legs for superior situational awareness."

JP mumbled. "If we all chip in, we can hire a company
of wobanki mercs and drop them on Psydon, just for the
entertainment value of it."

"Cats and dogs only fight in cartoons, JP," someone
said behind him.

"Nip it," Meadows said.

Kel knew the doro were canine-like. The briefer was
telling him nothing. Now, the Wolfhound Regiment. Kel
knew less about them. They were stationed at the darkest
edge of the Cygnus arm, a sector having few human-set-
tled worlds and many bizarre non-humanoid alien races.
They had a battle record in the Savage Wars as dense as
any regiment in the Legion. Being so isolated, it was a regiment that by reputation had the best organic support of
any of the regiments. The Wolfhounds had assault companies like all the legions, but also companies of heavy
tanks, light mobility armor, artillery—they had as much
diversity and capability as a full Republic army division.
It was one of the only regiments with its own aviation.

Legion crews flew Legion ships in support of the Legion, making it independent of the Navy's ability or desire to do the same.

If Kel were posted to the Wolfhounds, he would be almost starting over in his education as a Legion officer. Placed in any role except that of an assault company officer, he would have to be trained from the ground up for any other position of responsibility. It was simultaneously frightening and exciting. He still had a lot of curiosity about other combat specialties. His experience with the artillery team from the Scarlets had ignited that desire to challenge himself. He hadn't been forced to study a new discipline in a very long time.

"Top, how long you figure this goes on?" Wiggy said next to him covertly. Holos showing the dense jungles and rushing rivers of Psydon played over the massed troops.

"For too long," Meadows said at an attempted whisper. "But we aren't going to disobey the colonel's directive, so button it."

"You got it partly right, Meadows," another voice said from somewhere behind. "It is going on for too long."

"We've got real work to do," came another. Joe Crane. Kel had caught up with Joe before they lifted, proud that his friend had recently been given the top spot on his own kill team. He was another choice he'd considered for Twelve's team sergeant before Nail pushed him to take Meadows. There were only seven kill teams—less than thirty-five operators—on Victrix and available for the Psydon invasion. Some teams were cannibalized ad hoc from partial teams to form a full one, like Joe's Team Ten. Others like Twelve had only just returned from another mission with barely time to drop uniforms in sonic scrub and grab new charge packs before being spun up.

Individual missions, partial team missions, schools, combat injuries, and needs around the galaxy meant there was never a full complement of operators on a kill team, and never a full house of kill teams on Victrix at any time. Three was still short a man, Poul and Braley satisfied to continue as they had on Haemus with just four instead of the usual complement of the five or six that made up a kill team. Their plea that breaking in another operator would hamper them had a sympathetic ear in the unit's sergeant major. Three was still the most storied and re-spected in DO. If there were a mission of missions in this invasion, Kel felt sure Three would get it. He wondered what would happen to Three when Braley was forced out.

"Pipe down, girls." Bigg's voice came from the rear, just loud enough to be heard at the front railing where Kel and Twelve stood as the vanguard of DO's representation for the brief. "I'll turn you loose after the Republic division commander has his say."

Even at this distance, the small figure in green uni-form that rose to the dais was imposing. The holo cen-tered on the new speaker's face. Older, but not shrunken. Gray at the temples. He stood tall. Two stars on the collar. The Black Horse on his shoulder.

"This is a time when all soldiers wonder of themselves if they have adequately prepared their hearts and minds for the task that lies ahead." For the first time in an hour, Kel's attention was focused. The general spoke with dig-nity and without bravado. Like a father.

"You are the sons and daughters of privilege, here to-day because you stand among the few who stepped for-ward to answer the call of duty in a Republic full of men and women who choose personal safety and comfort over the honor of service. The few who know that freedom comes at a price and that we are never more than a generation away from losing it.

"From the Savage Wars to the tyranny of a thousand aggressive races, the only thing that has guaranteed the survival of humanity and the Republic has been the sacrifice of your fellow warriors.

"Today you have been asked to make a leap of faith. Asked by your leadership and your government to plunge into that gravest of endeavors—war—and to trust that our cause is one vital enough to warrant the risk of your precious life.

"I ask of you only that you remember it is for the person to the left and right of you for whom you fight. And that in a time many years from now, you will look back on your service in Psydon with pride, knowing your honor is intact. For though you will carry the soldier's heart forever, know it was burdened so for the cause of your fellow warrior."

The soldier's heart. Kel knew what the general meant. He carried the soldier's heart. The weight of it. He felt it daily. And he wouldn't have it any other way.

"Men, let's make a quiet departure," Bigg said as the division commander left the screen to be replaced by one of his staff to continue a mundane but necessary part of the briefing, significant only to the soldiers of the Black Horse. The operators were silent as they filed out. The general's words had touched more than just him.

"Glad we stayed, Wiggy?" Hardball asked as they waited their turn to move through the hatchway.

"I am," Wiggy said in a breaking voice. Was Kel mistaken? It sounded as though he was choked up. Were Wiggy's eyes moist? Kel filed it away. Three times now he'd detected emotion in the taciturn Wiggy. And in two words, Wiggy had proven to Kel he was as human as the rest of them.

Two days on Orion Station meant a brief break from the cramped spaces of the *Tenacious*. There were no separate modules for DO as was common on large Navy ships, but they had a deck section to themselves and their own mess. Kel could not remember when so many operators had been together in one place at the same time. He admitted that there were names and faces he did not know. Operators came and went. Some of them without Kel ever having known they'd been there. But even his mild melancholy at the thought didn't reduce his desire to get out of this ship and spend some time alone, or at least with just his own team.

Orion Station was flooded with troops. Youthful greens and jaded grays filled the concourses, restaurants, and shops. Though the stop's purpose was to pick up yet another division of army troops for the invasion, it was a well-planned interlude. For many, this might be the last opportunity for the comforts of the civilian world. There would be few on Okella and definitely none on Psydon. Sometimes, it was the memory of something as simple as a hot meal, a cold beverage, or the smile of a beautiful stranger that reminded a soldier of what awaited at the end of the journey.

"I know a spot," Kel said. He and the rest of the team wore the same loose gym garb they'd worked out in. "It's deep in the station, closer to the commercial port terminal. We can beat the crowds of basics and leejes and get a booth." Kel led them to the pub where he'd first met the Yomiuris, so very long ago. He didn't feel nostalgic or sad at the thought, just hungry after the intense workout. He was past sadness. Now there was only the mission that awaited them, whatever it would be.

The place hadn't changed. Holos buzzed over every table. Sports, news, entertainment of varieties Kel couldn't catalog. What he had in mind was a thick steak. Maybe two. It was the same spot where he'd learned from the Spiral News Network he'd been unknowingly helping to overthrow a government. Kel chased it from his mind as he ordered off the screen.

Kel tore the flatbread and dipped into the common bowl, loading it with the paste. The other men watched with curiosity. JP copied Kel as the two steaks on his plate waited. "Hey, this is pretty good."

"It is. Been a while," Kel said. "Got used to the stuff on a place called Meridian. Kind of surprised to see it's made its way here." Kel chewed his own steak, lost in thought as the others kept up their usual banter between bites.

"Don't know what we'll be doin', but I doubt we'll eat this well fer a while," Hardball said as he chewed.

"You don't know that," Wiggy said. "It's a planet of carnivores. I bet they have steak. Of something."

JP paused his chewing. "Their domesticated agriculture consists of raising a small rodent and a large lizard. I bet they're not for pets."

"You would remember that out of everything in the area study, medic," Wiggy said.

"You don't know either wouldn't make a good meal," Meadows said. "Ask the man who's been everywhere and tried it all. Isn't that so, sir?"

"Huh, what?" Kel had been scrolling on his link. He swiped it at the holo and received a ping back. "I'll catch you guys later. Meal's on me." He slid away without explaining.

"What's up with the boss?" Hardball asked.

Meadows shrugged. "He's a man of many talents. Probably meeting Bigg for drinks, trying to wrangle us a good mission. Like a good officer should."

The terminal was busy as ever. He dodged bots and carts to make his way to the gangway lock. The *Callie Supreme* answered on the first hail. "Can I help you? You asked to speak to the captain. I'm Captain Sullivan." The captain reminded him of the Sullivans he knew, red hair and pink skin under the radiation-induced tan of a lifelong spacer.

Kel impulsively decided to visit the *Supreme* when he saw it on the list of ships in port. He'd scrolled the port authority schedule out of boredom. Or had he? There was a part of him hoping the *Callie*'s name would appear, part praying it wouldn't. To see the *Supreme* here was a shock, like turning over a log to find the snake you half expected to find was actually there.

"Captain Sullivan, I'm a friend of the Yomiuris. I've shipped on the *Dream* with Eric and Caroline. I wonder if I could have some of your time to get caught up on things?"

The captain's eyes widened in recognition. "You're Mister Turner."

"Kel."

The captain silently considered his request, then acquiesced. "Come up to the wardroom. Someone will meet you, but I'm sure you could find your way."

The captain invited him to sit after pouring them both kaff. "I don't suppose I should ask, but are you working? Something to do with all the soldiers running around Orion?"

"Yes," was all Kel said.

"I see. What's on your mind, Mister Turner?"

Kel understood he wasn't being received as an old family friend. "I was hoping to find out how the family was doing, how the business is going, anything you'd care to share, really. I've been out of touch."

"Hypercomm not working?" The captain's sarcasm bit Kel fiercely.

"If you know who I am, then the Yomiuris have also told you something about what I do."

The captain seemed to accept Kel's explanation. "Merchant shipping on the edge is an up and down industry. Business was very good for a long time. I was under the impression you had something to do with that."

"Indirectly, but yes."

"Just like it's my understanding that you were responsible for our downturn in fortunes."

Kel frowned. "Not exactly true." He sighed. "But not exactly false, either. It wasn't me that harmed the family business." That was as much as he was going to explain himself. "So, I take it business hasn't been good?"

The captain checked his chrono impatiently. Kel sensed the polite veneer was about to come off. "What is it you really want to know, Mister Turner? You didn't come here to inquire about shipping contracts."

Kel found himself mute.

"I'll answer the question you won't ask. My niece hasn't left home in a year. She's... hurt. And you and I know who's responsible."

Kel wandered the main concourse. A walkside table opened up and he ordered a kaff. His link out, he typed using his specs, deleting and restarting again and again, dissatisfied with each effort. The kaff sat untouched and cold by the time he read this last effort a final time, then pressed send to bounce it to his hypercomm mail account. If there were a reply, it would come long after he was already in isolation on Okella, preparing for his next mission.

His link buzzed. It was Bigg.

"Hey Bigg, what's up?" Kel's stomach knotted.

"Meet me at the Navy yard. Now, please. There'll be an escort at the gate to bring you in."

"Sure, on my way. Anything you can tell me?"

Bigg smiled. "You're the favorite son. You can thank me later."

21

"Twelve is leaving the *Tenacious*. We've got something better to do than continue to cruise with the steerage class," Kel told the team once he had them alone. He was still high on the surge of adrenaline. "You can thank me later," he said, using Bigg's same words. Kel had in fact thanked Bigg.

Meadows's eyebrows raised. "Sounds like a buckets-on time to me." Once everyone had their lids secured and were on the private team channel, Kel spilled it.

"We've been assigned to take out the doro command authority. We're going in first to locate and neutralize the doro Pack Leader Supreme. Him and all his tribal deputies."

"Yes!" JP shouted.

"Legendary," Wiggy said.

Hardball traded chest thumps with the rest. "I hope Three has fun on Okella. This is Twelve's time."

"Nice work, sir." Meadows offered his hand. "I knew you were off to politic for Twelve to get the best mission. Job well done."

Kel took the giant mitt. "You bet," he said, grateful for the timing of it all. "We're headed to the other side of the station. Bigg's got us a locker in the passenger port with a freefall and a mission support package already waiting for us. Get our grav containers together. We have an intelligence liaison meeting us there, too."

"Space dive?" JP asked.

"You know as much as I do right now," Kel said, knowing JP wasn't fond. "Better safe than sorry. Best be ready for anything. Bigg's seen to that. Let's be ready to leave ASAP."

Kel made a last sweep of his rack and closed his personal carrier and placed it on top of his larger kit container. *Armor. Weapons. Charge packs. A freefall and MSP waiting. What more could I want for?*

"Captain Turner, there's a station lorry waiting your team at the aft cargo gangway," a voice came over his bucket.

"Let's move." Kel found himself humming as he walked.

"Where're you guys headed?" Sims asked from the companionway where he perched, making room for Twelve and their gear as they wove through the corridor.

"Ta-ta for now, you buncha bridesmaids," Meadows said from the rear of their procession. Heads were peeking out of staterooms as they passed. "Next time you see us, the war will be won. On behalf of Twelve, you're welcome."

The code opened the locker hatch and as promised, inside the small warehouse space were two plain shipping containers—their MSP and FSP—and a third coffin-like package. A table and chairs sat at the other end, several bunks, and a fresher. The lockers were for shipping container preparation and packing. Sometimes they were used for temporary crew quarters or for quarantine of goods and personnel.

"Make useful, boys," Meadows said. "The captain and I will check the FSP, you guys check the MSP and make sure we're good to go. There's still time to get any defi-ciencies filled."

"What's this, a saff-suck?" Wiggy asked. A slaved, freefall support container was a bot that could follow them in freefall, and keep up in most any terrain while carrying their equipment. "A little bigger than most."

"Looks that way," Meadows said.

Kel checked the biometric ID pad. "It's an old friend. I'll introduce you all later. Let's get to work."

"What about it, sir?" Meadows asked as the FSM doors split open to reveal racks of parachute containers and equipment delivery pods. "Hard to anticipate what we might be missing without knowing more. I assume RI will be facilitating procurement of any other special needs to support the mission."

The access door chimed and opened. A broad man in civilian clothes walked in. He took a moment to assess the men and the space.

"So, this is my kill team." The door sealed and he walked past them to set a small case on the table. "I'll make it quick. We've got a few hours until we move out." The case opened and the man swiped a screen. "Field's up. Pop lids and let's talk."

Seated around the table, the man continued. He had the bearing of a soldier, not at all like the intelligence of-ficers he'd worked with. *That's a plus*, Kel thought. The man's bushy black eyebrows didn't conceal the bony ridge underneath, and the crooked jaw told Kel he'd been in his share of fights.

"We're going out on the *Xaylan Three*. She's a passen-ger cruiser for hire that shuttles small loads throughout the sector. She's on par with your *Shinshu Maru*. Crew is all civilian contract, but not cleared for mission information."

The man had yet to identify himself. Telling them he knew about the covert DO delivery platform, the *Shinshu*, was meant to put him in a position of power.

Kel wasn't playing.

"I'm Turner. You haven't introduced yourself yet."

"I'm Barnett. As I was saying, the *Xaylan* will get us in-system. By the time we arrive, I expect to have information that'll determine how we're going to proceed onto Psydon."

"Barnett," Kel said with his hand up. "Let's back things up a bit. Who do you represent? What information are you waiting on, and from what sources? We're going to need to be read-in a little better than what you've done so far."

The man discounted Kel and looked back at his link, dismissing him. "That's all on a need to know basis. As I was—"

Kel shot out. He had Barnett in the air, feet somersaulting overhead, landing him on his back with a crash that should have collapsed the table. Kel had the shocked man pinned to the table, his fist still full of the opposite shirt collar across the neck in a strangle, his vibro-blade against the pulsing carotid artery. Meadows' and Hardball's blasters menaced him from either side. Wiggy and JP were already at the door covering the entrance.

"Whatever your name is, listen carefully." Kel spoke softly, almost tenderly at the upended turtle on the table below him. "There's no one in the galaxy more on a 'need to know basis' than me and my team. If that doesn't work for you, then I'll stuff you out the nearest airlock. We don't need you. You are an intermediary placed here by people we don't trust. If we don't trust you, then there's no reason to keep you alive. I'll only ask once more. Who are you with?" Kel relaxed his grip slightly but kept his blade on the man's throat.

"Oba's beard, Kel," Barnett strained to say, little air available to push out his words. "I'm with Nether, okay? You're charged up hotter than a cheap plasma coil."

"You know this gutter, sir?" Meadows asked.

Kel didn't. "Never seen him before."

Barnett sucked a deep breath. "It's Shuck. Lev Shuck. From recon."

"Shuck?" Kel released his grip. His vibro-blade went away. With two blasters on him, Kel wasn't worried about letting him up.

Barnett took a deep breath and rolled to sit, coughed again, and rubbed his neck. "Sorry. I didn't manage that part well. I promise it'll be smooth from here on. I forget sometimes, though I shouldn't. My own mother wouldn't recognize me."

"Shuck?" Kel asked again, incredulous. "I haven't seen you since Antione. What happened?"

"You do know this guy, sir?" Meadows confirmed before lowering his pistol farther.

"I've been biomodded so many times, I don't even remember what my own face used to look like."

Kel motioned his men to put their sidearms away. "We were in recon together. He's a leej. Was," Kel corrected.

"Nether Ops, huh?" Meadows said, reluctant to holster his sidearm. "We don't give a sket how secret your little gang is. Why'd a leej come off so high and mighty with us like a kelhorn, huh?"

Shuck/Barnett shrugged. "Sorry. Institutional inertia. Force of habit."

Kel burst out laughing. "How'd that work out for you?" He laughed harder. *Lev Shuck?* he marveled. *The galaxy is a small place, sometimes.* "When were you planning on telling me, Lev?"

"I hadn't figured that out yet, Kel." He rubbed his throat some more. "You've got issues, you know that?"

Meadows mumbled as he holstered. "You have no idea."

The men helped the crew load grav containers and the support packages onto a bot lift. Meadows nudged closer to Kel though they were on L-comm. "Hey boss, next time you think you need to commit murder, how about a little heads-up?"

"I thought you were always ready to commit murder, Curt."

"Fair 'nuff. Who's this Shuck, then?" Their Nether Ops guide was on the ship waiting.

"He was my squad leader in 131st Recon. He was a good leej, back then."

"And now?"

"I like how he came clean but, we're just going to have to wait and see." Kel shook his head while he laughed. "If I'd known that was the way to get the spies to open up, I'd have tried that approach a long time ago."

"You and me both," Meadows agreed.

Underway and in the bay that would be their mission prep area, Shuck sat at the head of the table and opened up a holo of Psydon. "Let's try this again. By the way, I'll take it personally if you do that again, Kel. Try using your words next time if I'm not living up to your expectations for forthrightness, okay?"

"Sorry, man." The team followed Kel's lead to join in his self-deprecating laugh. "It's been a rough few years dealing with RI and the like." Kel was a little embarrassed at having reacted so violently, so close to being out of control.

"So, what do you wanna be called?" Hardball asked. "Shuck or Barnett?"

"Stick with Barnett. It's what the flight crew know me as."

"Who are they?" JP questioned.

"Some are former Navy. The rest are just aviation pros. They're contract from one of the private companies we use for support."

"Lanthanum?" Meadows inquired.

Barnett nodded affirmatively. "We use them for a lot of odds and ends."

"Seems like you're not the only one," Hardball added. "We've run into their folks more than once. They use a lot of former leejes."

"They deliver what they advertise," Barnett said. "And they're quiet professionals. But they don't do it all. You're the kinetics. They're enablers."

"Got it," Hardball replied. With his bucket off, Gabe usually had a mouthful of stimleaf. Kel noticed it had been days since he'd seen Hardball with a stuffed cheek. His normally thick accent had tapered off somewhat as well. "So, can we assume you have a target package put together to get us started?"

Barnett swiped. "I've been on Psydon for months." The holo split into a stack of rotating images of the capital and the Pack Leader Supreme Council building, power plants, military installations, and the spaceport. "I've done the target assessment of most every site myself. I have a good idea of where the target moves, but when he does so is somewhat random."

Decapitating a government always had the same difficulties. Guaranteeing the location of a CLE for a precision bombardment was a guessing game. A gamble as likely to fail as it was to succeed to sever the command authority from its minions. Predicting the exact location of a leader and getting the timing right for an orbital strike was as difficult as catching a comet in a seamball glove while wearing a blindfold. Trying to coordinate it with the start of an invasion to achieve maximum surprise—and cause total chaos within the enemy chain of command— was even harder.

"There are limited opportunities for a human to move about and observe on Psydon. The capital is one of the few places off-worlders are common, and even then, there aren't many. My cover as an arms dealer allowed me some flexibility, but it still took months for me to build enough trust to get access to any of their military installations."

"Arms?" Wiggy asked. "What kind of arms did you supply the dog-men?"

"Tauran blaster rifles."

"HA!" Hardball spat. "Taurans! How'd you pull that off? Are they broke, or just stupid?"

"They're not stupid, believe me," Barnett said. "But they do have a budget. In some areas, they went first class. They have a quantum orbital air defense system they bought from the Ootari. As good as any core world. Small arms, they scrimped a bit."

"We can forgive you for selling them that junk," Meadows said. "Half of them won't work out of the grav container, the other half will overheat and shut down after a dozen full-powered blasts."

"Tore-rans. Torched-hands more like it," JP mocked. "Seen more than one of those burst when the charging chain seizes and the stripping chamber overheats. I'd hate to be holding on to one when that happens."

"Sorry to say not all of them are going to be garbage," Barnett apologized. "And like I said, they're not stupid. They have competent armorers. They've upgraded internals with aftermarket modules. They know how to get the most bang for their buck."

"So, why didn't Nether Ops in all its brilliance slice the software so you could shut them down on demand?" Meadows asked irritably.

"You know why. I've been working for months to get on the inside. If the code was discovered, I'd be dog food and we'd have nothing."

Hardball scoffed. "And what do you think you'll be when the friends of all the troops that are going to get killed by those blasters find out who gave those weapons to the enemy?"

Kel intervened before things escalated. "All right, all right. We all know how the galaxy works. Barnett's not responsible for that. Let's focus on the job. We'll solve the ethical problems of the universe some other time."

Barnett clucked. "Once we have the CLEs out of play, this invasion is going to go like clockwork. The Republic offloading shoddy blasters on the doros for my cover will be a minor concern."

Meadows grunted. "We're going to hold you to that, leej."

"We have less than a week to make it happen," Barnett reminded. "With or without a successful decapitation, D-day is at 2500 Zulu, seven days from now."

A mass system jump by the assault force would accompany the Navy's bombardment of all critical infrastructure and military targets. A pair of Shadow 8s hung over the table. Flat and pointed like the tip of the Legion sword, stubby swept wings, no visible protrusion for a cockpit, only on close examination were the fine sawtooth edges and sharp rippled surfaces apparent that assisted the tactical bombers in their invisibility.

Barnett looked grim. "We'll have these two assigned and on call. Ours and ours alone. Their only purpose is to flatten what we tell them."

"When do we meet the crew?" Meadows asked.

"We don't. Our next stop is Psydon orbit for insertion." Barnett said it a little too matter-of-factly, a little too dismissively. Meadows wasn't having it.

"Back up. What do you mean 'we don't'? Let's review. I ask a reasonable question regarding how we plan for mission success, and you answer it. Dictating to us how things are going to be done is going to make us repeat our introductory lesson." He had Barnett's attention, the Nether agent reflexively rubbing his neck. "I don't know what you remember from your recon days, but air coordination takes work. It's not fair to the pilots to expect them to nail this blind, and it sure isn't fair to us. Say we do locate the target, we call in the strike and they blow the bomb run, it goes down as *our* failure."

Barnett pointed to Kel, who was ready. "Let's talk about it with our tactical air controller. We'll leave it to him." Kel placed his palm on the biometric pad of the coffin. It opened and out stepped Bertie.

"Greetings, Captain Tuner, and congratulations I might add. Overdue, if you ask me." The eight-legged bot stepped out of its container, made the usual tests when it was awoken from dormancy, flexing and performing small jumps in place. "First round at the pub's on me. Mister Barnett I've been keyed to already, but how 'bout the rest of you fine gentlemen give me your biometric lock and then we'll all be properly acquainted. Sergeant Meadows, you first then please, Top."

JP was the first. "No. Way. That's no saff-suck. That's an AI DOGR! I heard about them but didn't believe it." Medic bots were common in Repub line units. Deployed operational ground bots were only slightly smarter than SFSCs. Combat bots in any variety of AI were a thing of the past.

"Autonomous combat multiplier, or ACM if you must, Sergeant Pabon," Bertie replied, snaking around to look at the speaker. "But I'm just Bertie to you team boys; no need to be so formal."

It was a bit off-putting until one got used to it, the square bot head moving at unnatural angles and independently of the rectangular body. Kel remembered his first meeting with the ACMs, how their personalities and comedic accents at first made them entertaining and later, somehow commonplace. Just another quirk among the multitude of unique traits of the family of operators. Phillip and Bertie ended up being perfect teammates—selfless, resourceful, and deadly.

"Where's Phillip these days, Bert?" Kel asked.

"Slumming with Eight, don't you know, sir. We're sorry to be split up, but I'm not the slightest bit ashamed to say being with Twelve makes it a bit like old home week, plus the opportunity to make some new mates. Bloody proud to be along for the ride, sir."

"This is our JTAC?" Hardball's skepticism was loud and clear.

"That I am, Sergeant Harding. And so much more. I've already been working with our air assets. Few know as much as yours truly about working with a kill team, and those lads are quite enthusiastic to make a good showing for you. They're ready to pull a suicide run if need to be."

"Suicide run?" Wiggy asked.

"Oh, manner of speaking, Sergeant Wiggins. There's enough data stream running that if they do buy it, they'll be uploaded and shoved into a new core."

"Huh?" Meadows said. "Are you telling me the Shadow pilots are AI, too?"

Bertie bobbed his head in approximation of agreement, reminding Kel of a trick horse answering a yes or no question for the audience. "Those are Shadow 8Es, Sergeant Meadows. They're not mental giants like me or Phillip—the Republic still has its thing about weapons of mass destruction being autonomous and all—but they're smart enough to jockey those Shadows and drop the hate where it's needed."

"Feel better now?" Barnett said coarsely. "Give me a little credit, guys. And also, give me more than a single sentence to give you the answer you're looking for." He frowned at Meadows. "I've put my neck out to get us this far. And whether you know it or not, being out there alone without another leej to back you up isn't all it's cracked up to be. Cut me some slack, huh?"

"I do know," Meadows said with some sympathy. "But if you're really working with the team, you have to be *with* the team. Got me?"

Barnett nodded. "Got it. It's just been a while. But by the time we get to Psydon, I promise I'll be meshed with you. Especially if we jump in. Looking forward to diving again."

"Jump with us?" Hardball said. He stuffed his mouth full of stimleaf. "Guess I ain't quittin' just yet."

22

"Pack Leader Supreme Rask moves with his alphas between a few locations. Rask travels with his war council, a pack of a dozen war chiefs. They move between the main council hall and a handful of hunting lodges around the planet, all in dense jungle, so that gives us a certain advantage if we need to move overland."

"Hunting lodges?" Wiggy questioned.

"The hunt is a cultural necessity, but whether Rask has to do so to maintain status or he just likes it, he's in the jungle tracking dreex at least every couple of weeks."

"Dreex?" JP asked.

"Kind of like a doober," Wiggy clarified. "Seen holos."

Barnett assisted by pushing a new image up. "Not as big, but twice as fast. Mouth full of double-rowed teeth. Not hard to kill with a blaster of course, but the doro hunt them with spears. Finish the kill with their teeth."

The six-legged predator had a tan spotted coat that helped it blend into the lower foliage of the jungle floor. The muscled hunter stalked through the jungle then rose on its hindmost legs to sniff at the base of a tree, coiled, and leaped gracefully straight up at least five meters. When it landed, a small primate was in its jaws.

"Nice," Meadows said. "We just figure out where the best dreex hunting is, set an ambush on a good trail, and wait till the whole party's in our kill zone. Ought to take us about a year to pull that off. If ever."

Barnett pushed another holo forward. "Caza-Han is the capital. Major spaceport. Industry. The doro live spread out so there's a sprawling suburb, but a small population. Less than fifty thousand. The jungle separates farms and domiciles by pack-family." A terraced compound rose out of the jungle, five successively smaller levels topped by a crystal roof and colonnades, ramps leading to adjoining buildings between the tall, swaying trees.

"Rask and the pack council supreme spend most of their time here. There's good hunting, and it's where most pack business gets done. If we know he's here, a port landing is a good option. I have ground support and we can get the team anywhere around Caza-Han by transport. With tensions rising, everything will be well searched, but I've planned for that."

"If he's not in the capital?" Wiggy asked the obvious.

"There're only a few spaceports around the planet for commercial and passenger travel between major population centers. The doros don't travel much. Mostly they stay in pack-family territory. In the best of times there are only a few lanes of air travel used. With an invasion imminent, any aircraft headed over one of the lodges would be tough to stealth well enough to avoid their detection grid."

Kel already knew where Barnett was leading. "But you travel frequently to deliver arms and provide tech support. If we know Rask and his band of hunting buddies are at one of the lodges, we make an airborne insertion from one of the commercial lanes and hit him in his hobby hideout."

"So, the sooner we get into orbit and you can check with your eyes on the ground, the sooner we'll know whether to prep 'chutes or not," Meadows said.

"Let's look at the lodges," Kel said.

They were versions of the main council temple in Caza-Han. All surrounded by dense jungle and many kilometers away from what little civilization interrupted the rich forests. He was already running plots on his link.

"This one on the Gred-Ahn Peninsula is less than a hundred klicks off the nearest sky lane. That's one of the closer ones," Kel recited as he let his program do the calculations. "We'd only need to exit at ten thousand meters to make that flight under canopy."

"This one near the Cuchin is closer to double that from the nearest lane," Meadows pointed out. "That's a transatmospheric lane, though. Good thing. We'd need to duplicate a trajectory like that to have enough altitude for that kind of glide."

"Even then, that's a real stretch," Hardball added.

"When's the last time you were under a canopy?" Kel asked their Nether-leej.

Barnett showed gritted teeth as he thought. "Last year. I had a period where I was jumping regularly, but then got busy."

"It happens," Kel commiserated. "But a year is a long time, and sport jumping isn't quite the same, is it?"

"No," Barnett admitted. "But I can do it. If we're going to HAHO, it's a short hop and pop, then follow the leader."

"We'll spend some time together for a refresher, starting tonight," Meadows said. They could do sims that would recreate most aspects of the experience and test Barnett's ability to respond to malfunctions and unexpected conditions while under canopy for the long, silent ride to the ground. "What about weapons quals?"

"I'm the cell combat instructor. Nether's populated with a lot of guys like me. We don't let combat skills slip."

Kel smiled. "Good. Wig and Hardball, let's divide up the sites and get contingent drop plans made for each of them. I want sub-orbital and high altitude options from every air route plugged into the drop program. Top, you and JP figure gear loadouts for freefall and ground insertion options, including what we can crossload on Bertie."

"Give me everything you got, gents," Bertie sounded off. "And don't be shy. If there's a square centimeter of space left unused in or on me, then we didn't bring enough stuff."

There'd been little to do but PT and wait. JP led them in combatives, proving he couldn't be driven back by even Meadows. JP launched bone breaking attacks, driving forward and through an opponent like a grav tank in a never-ending assault of ridged surfaces, knuckles and open hands, punishing any target offered. His stout form repelled grasp like the surface of an unyielding boulder, rough and heavy, unable to be deterred in its slow and merciless roll to crush anything in its path. Blows bounced off him like rain off durasteel.

"If you had to catch me on the run, you'd be plumb out of luck," Hardball teased as he rubbed a bruised thigh. JP always finished last in team runs.

"Running promotes cowardice. Taking pride in how fast you can run's never seemed warrior-like to me."

"Yeah, yeah," Hardball brushed him off. "Don't know how you got through Legion basic being so slow."

JP grinned. "I was a lot smaller then. My people don't get their biggest or strongest until they hit thirty Standard. I'm nowhere near my prime."

Four days and a few hours later, they were kitted up and waiting in the bay. Barnett excused himself. "Thirty-minute warning from the pilots. Once we're in orbit, I'll have about an hour to make contact with my agents, all while we hold Caza-Han ground control at bay. If the doros are spooked, they may insist we land at the capital for inspection before we can proceed elsewhere."

"When we drop out of jump, I'll ping the Shadows," Bertie assured. "So long as I get a ping back, we know the delivery went as scheduled and we're in business."

The Shadows piggybacked past Psydon on a Jaberwotha merchant vessel and were hiding on the second moon. Once the stealth bombers received confirmation, the two invisible ships would make their approach to the planet, and join the party.

"I'm going under," Barnett said as he opened a pad and started working, the faint hum of the security field around him to silence and conceal the surroundings as he worked.

"Time to get this game in action," Hardball said. "I've had about all of this bay I can stand."

"Out of stimleaf?" Wiggy asked. "Been noticing you slacking on your favorite pastime."

"No. Just time for a change."

Everyone also noticed how much Hardball had been reading, as well.

"Whatcha reading these days, Hardball?" JP asked. Hardball had something running on his link or specs at almost all hours, his link reading to him even while he worked out alone.

"Papa Bear had some good recommendations," he said. "He's a pretty well-rounded individual. He gave me some stuff he thought I might enjoy. Some of it I knew of but always thought was out of my wheelhouse. It'd take me a lifetime to read it all."

"Like what?" Kel asked, curious.

"A lot of ancient lit. Some of those guys knew the real deal. Right now, I'm reading one called *Meditations*. Guy who wrote it was an emperor. It ain't like today. In those days, royalty and politicians were trained to think as warriors. Just to survive the family squabbles and assassination attempts by those who feared you as a rival was somethin'."

Kel loved history but hadn't heard of that one. "What else?"

"Some stuff from another period. There was a group who spent a lot of time cultivating their minds as well as their warrior skills. All warfare happened up close and personal—bad-breath range. Swords, spears, and arrows. These guys studied poetry and art to deal with it, and only thought about death and how to die beautifully and with honor. They might stop in the middle of a battle to compose a poem, that sort of thing."

The team remained silent.

"You see, a monk studies the warrior to learn courage. The warrior studies the monk to learn compassion."

"Oba, Hardball," Wiggy groaned. "Papa Bear might've frelled you up giving you all that nonsense."

"It ain't nonsense," Hardball said offhandedly. "It speaks to me."

Meadows's eyebrows raised. "Well, no poetry while we're busy trying to KTF, agreed?"

The pilot's voice interrupted them. "Dropping out of jump now."

All eyes went to Barnett. He was speaking, swiping holos with both hands, and typing on a floating keyboard, all in the silence of the field around him. He gave nothing away as he worked, no indication of good or bad in his expression.

"Hard to read," Meadows said.

"He'd be hell to play tiles with," JP said.

Bertie had been curled up dormant. Kel knew the AI was always active, even when still. He might have been talking to the food processors or waste management AIs on board to pass the time. His neck extended. "I've got a ping returned from the Shadows. We're in business."

"That's good news," Kel said. "Let's hear what else has happened in the neighborhood while we've been in jump."

Barnett stood and the field ceased its translucent glow around him.

"Well?" Meadows said. "Don't keep us waiting."

Barnett's expression turned from blank to dour.

"It's as I feared. The doros are getting spooked. We have no choice but to land at Caza-Han. I can get us through the inspection. I'm not worried about that."

"What is it, then?" Kel asked.

"Rask and his council left the capital yesterday for parts unknown."

"So, we don't know where he is?" Wiggy inquired.

"I didn't say that," Barnett replied evasively. "It's just going to be more difficult to locate him with precision. I've got trackers on all the hoppers and his yacht."

Kel anticipated the problem. "They're passive, right? To avoid detection. And they have a relatively weak output. How close do we have to get to get a bounce back from one?"

"Five hundred klicks, give or take. The jungle is so dense it can eat up a lot of the e-band."

"What about orbital eyes?" Meadows asked.

Barnett shook his head. "The doro don't allow orbitals for the most part. They have them, but other than weather, comms, and positioning, they don't want them. It contaminates the sky for the hunt. But that's just a convenient cultural excuse, if you ask me. The real reason is they're paranoids if I've ever seen any. The idea of a platform circling overhead makes them feel like they're being observed, like they're prey and not predator."

"Great," Hardball said. "We've got less than three days to do this. What does your agent net say? Is there a best guess? Otherwise we're splitting up to fly the friendly skies all over this ball trying to get a ping. That or we don't hit him until D-day-plus until after we own the skies. I don't like that option."

Heads nodded all around.

"I don't have all my agents on comms. Once we're on the ground, I've got to make contact directly."

"Mister Barnett," the pilot said. "We're ready for final approach unless we have to wave off."

"Objections?" Barnett asked. "No dissent, Captain. Caza-Han it is."

"Let's get ready, team," Meadows said.

Barnett hesitated. "Kel, Meadows, give me a moment, will you?"

Meadows was putting on his bucket and paused mid-motion, surprised at the inviting tone. The time Barnett spent with Meadows had sparked a more fraternal attitude in the Nether Ops officer. He was acting more like a leej again.

"I've had a partner on these runs before. The doros wouldn't think it out of place if one of you joined me. If things are tense on the ground, it would help me to have someone watching my back."

"You take it, sir," Meadows said. "I hear these dog-men like to pick fights. I'm just big enough that it might draw too much attention. I'll stay buttoned up with the team, ready to bring the KTF if needed."

"Suits me," Kel said. "Let me get stripped and into my scruffies."

"Wear a knife," Barnett said. "It's a status thing. Anyone without one is a slave or at least an inferior."

"Good hunting," Meadows said as he moved off to join the team to move equipment and themselves into hiding. Barnett was correct. The *Xaylan* was fitted out much like the *Shinshu Maru* with shielded and concealed spaces disguised within a maze of compartments for smuggling humans and cargo.

"Where're we headed?"

"Once we clear inspection, we need to mark a drop for a meeting with one of my assets, another we can contact in the open at his business in the foreign sector. By the end of the day, either we have clearance to deliver this latest shipment of blasters to Ar-Song, or we take our chances and bust out of here without permission. Either way, we follow up our best leads and start pinging transponders, or we have a target locked."

"Agreed," Kel said. "What we won't do is sit tight. We have to make it happen, or we're going to be watching the show go on without us."

23

Kel took a dislike to the doros almost immediately. The dog-men were not men and they weren't dogs, but the worst of each archetype blended to make Kel's skin crawl. The customs inspectors sniffed at everything and left drool on every surface. The chief authority supervising the small pack sleuthing the *Xaylan* spoke Standard that was understandable enough between growls and gurgles.

"Barnett. You cleared," he said on two legs, swiping his pad in Barnett's direction. "Go Ar-Song, deliver hardware. Pilot instruction. No flight plan deviate. Air defense shoot down."

Barnett made a grunting sound in reply and some more guttural growls in the syllables of the doro language. The head dog-man made a panting sound and left.

"What was that about?" Kel asked.

"Just polite banter. I wished him a good scent for the hunt and for his mate's heat. We sealed up?" he asked overhead.

The pilot replied. "Sealed again. They're giving us four hours before our turn in the flight corridor to Ar-Song. If we need to miss it, I'm going to have to fake a breakdown. Give me as much heads-up as you can, if that's the case."

"Got it. We're leaving the ship. Out."

They pulled out of the spaceport onto a two-lane road shaded by jungle canopy creeping over it from both sides like an awning. Kel had worked in dense jungle many times. If the jungle growth was this heavy in the capital's spaceport, out in the wilds it would be near impenetrable. Bots crawled along the shoulders of the road, beam cutters mowing back the intrusive green tangle.

"Where to first?"

"Load the message drop for a meeting. My agent is in a rival pack-family of Rask's. When a new pack leader supreme takes power, the loser's pack gets absorbed. Not quite slaves, not quite equals until the packs are well bred together. Rask hasn't been in power for more than a litter season. My guy's a holdout, hoping to restore his pack to prominence if I can keep my promise to get Rask out. He might be who we prop up when it's all over. If he lives."

"No idea we're planning to invade?"

"I haven't tipped our hand. He thinks we're maybe planning a subversive campaign to overthrow Rask and reestablish Republic ties. I've supplied his crew with arms and promises of more when the time's right. That, and Republic credits. Guy's no patriot. He wants to avenge his pack brothers who lost the fight for leader and get into power himself. Same old story."

"Was it Rask who pushed the doro into leaving the Republic?"

"Yes. But we think there's outside influence. More mid-core unrest. It's not all coincidental, either. There's a movement. We don't have the players identified yet. When we do, it'll be game on."

They took an off ramp heading into a built up area.

"The ex-planetary twarg-eaters here really dropped the ball. We got zero warning Psydon was pulling out. There's been too much of that lately. We almost lost Sonestra last year, you know? Blind luck it didn't go under."

Kel remained silent. His memories of Sonestra came up too frequently still.

"I got sent in to play catch-up. I inherited this first doro we're going to visit from my RI predecessor. He's an interesting character. Sometimes he's moody and doesn't volunteer much, but he hasn't flat-out lied to me about anything. Has a weapons shop in the free trade zone. You'll understand when you see him."

After a brief stop where Barnett drew a squiggle on a corner block of one of the ziggurat-shaped buildings, they took off again. "He should see that. He's supposed to check it twice a day. If he monitored the landings like I've instructed, he should be checking it more frequently. He's hungry for guns and credits. At least he's dependable that way."

The free trade zone was where most of the off-world presence clustered. There was a single hotel lodging visitors, a stylized version of the local architecture, durasteel and glass rather than the stone or facsimile used locally.

"What are the Ootari doing here?" Kel asked as they passed one.

"They still have a diplomatic mission running independent of the Republic. Plus, they sold the doros the air defense system. That bug is either a consultant or a member of the mission. Or both. Every Ootari act is done in concert with their hive government. They do everything together in lock step. In that respect we're probably lucky they chose to join the Republic, because I don't think there's a way to factionalize them if they decided to work against us."

The moktaar he saw reminded Kel of the doro in some ways. Neither were fond of the wobanki, who were decidedly not represented. "There's our source's shop." The square building sat in the sun; the rough barked trees present everywhere else absent. The building had undecipherable doro script over the arched entrance over which a stuffed dreex was mounted. The sign hanging out front pictured a multi-barbed spear crossed with a rifle. Translation was unnecessary to understand what wares were offered for sale inside.

The shop was empty save for the lone doro at the counter. Racks of blasters, slug-throwers, spears, halberds, and short swords lined the walls. The display cases were full of knives and hand weapons including pistols. Kel stopped and picked up a slug thrower from one of the wood racks. The doro hand was similar enough to human that the grip was unmodified, but the trigger guard and trigger larger to accommodate the wider, shorter digits. He examined the Stonewell and checked the bore. It was a solid piece. The action was smooth.

"Your associate likes the traditional, Barnett?" the doro behind the counter said through a voder. "I prefer the slug thrower myself. It makes for more of a challenge."

"Hello, Prawg. I brought a friend along who appreciates good weapons. How's business?"

The doro was missing an eye. Kel noticed he sat on an elevated stool, one metallic hind leg dangling in a flexed posture. A prosthetic. In a culture like the doros', a disfigured or impaired member of the pack would be cast aside. Prawg had a much-needed skill unhampered by his war damaged body; he built fine weapons.

Prawg whined. "Could be better."

"Can we speak?"

The doro panted. He swiped a paw and the front entrance sealed with security shutters. "Let's go in the back." He eased off the stool until his prosthetic touched, a cane

Kel hadn't seen acting as a third leg, balancing his stride as he led them behind the counter.

The shop was filled with machines. Filings and shavings from metal and exotic woods collected underneath the benches. Kel paused to look at a side plate of a hand blaster lying on one of the benches next to a magnifier visor. In relief, a hunt scene was recreated. He shifted position for a better view of the relief, surprised by the perception that the carved dreex ran a step farther with each angle viewed, the hunters cocking and releasing spears as it charged.

"You have an appreciation for artistry," Prawg said. It didn't translate as a question but a statement. "Lately my wait list is shorter. If there's a project you have in mind, I might be able to deliver it within a few months, depending on how detailed a piece you have in mind. Frequently my wait times are over two years."

Barnett placed a stack of credits on a benchtop. "We're always interested in the artistry of a master craftsman like yourself. Perhaps you'd hold this to reserve your time while we decide on the specifics of the project."

Prawg settled onto another stool. The sharp breath he took through his snout told Kel he was in pain. "You're respectful, Barnett. I half believe you appreciate my skill. But I know what you want. I don't know where the pack supreme is. Some of the chieftains purchase new weapons before a hunt, especially lances, since even the finest break hunting the dreex. Even mine. But I've heard no boasts or taken orders from Rask or his pack for a month."

"Do you hear anything? Not just the supreme pack appreciate your wares. You have admirers among the warriors of all the pack-families."

The old doro panted. "There's talk that a once-in-a-generation dreex been spotted. If the Pack Leader Supreme brought in such, it would be fortuitous timing, given the war some think may be on the horizon. It would leave little doubt as to Rask's ability to lead and fight."

"Where's this dreex been spotted?"

"Raranda."

Prawg pulled out a link and swiped. Kel blinked to open the window in his specs. The territory was in the other hemisphere. He enlarged the view to see the relief of mountains, huge rivers flowing into the central sea, and only a single population center.

"The largest dreex recorded have come from Raranda. This one's prints measure seventy centimeters. It would be the largest in many generations if it proves as big as its spoor would tell."

"Where on Raranda?" Barnett pushed.

"Hunters are secretive. A pack rarely gives up such information."

"Master Prawg," Kel said, speaking for the first time. "May I ask you about one of the pieces I saw in your shop?"

His ears perked up. "Go and retrieve it." Kel returned carrying a hand weapon. He laid it before its creator. The receiver was unusual in that it was duranium, colored in a swirling pattern of deep blues, cobalt, and green. The grip was of a wood unlike any Kel had come across, sure that it must be from a species native to Psydon. Curled and wavy patterns of grain changed in the light.

"Slug throwers are weapons of beauty that require skill to wield," Prawg lectured. "It is a 10.8 millimeter capstan. It holds but eight rounds. Why does this anachronism interest you?"

"It has a soul," Kel said. "The craftsmen put much of himself into its creation. Is it line-bored?"

Prawg's ears stood straight up. "It is."

"May I test the action?"

Its builder panted again, and barked. "You must."

The actuator turned the capstan into battery with a solid click, with an assuredness that traveled through his fingers to his heart, speaking wordlessly that this weapon was ready to translate his will. He pressed the trigger, then repeated the process several times. A glass rod snapping in two was less defined in its break than was the certainty with which the actuator dropped, producing a rich metallic ring each time.

"This is not a weapon for war," Prawg said. "Though it would serve for such. This is a soul-forger. A really good weapon is not for use without. It is for use within. A tool of self-discipline. A weapon such as this can only be used to its full potential by one who masters himself. A blaster is the tool of efficiency. This is the anvil used to forge the character of the one who would learn what secrets it could teach its student."

Barnett interrupted. "Prawg, we're short on time. Is there anything else you can tell us?"

Kel frowned at his friend, telling him to back off.

"Master Prawg, is it for sale?"

Prawg's ears lay flat. "Few have ever inquired. It has been here for many turns around the sun because it is not for sale." Kel waited. "But I would send it with you." Prawg turned to Barnett. "The last war took my eye, but not my sight. The Republic will not let Rask's brazen threats go unanswered." He gestured around the workshop. "This may not survive, nor may I. The war Rask seeks has no purpose. He is not hunting dreex to keep the heart pure.

He wishes to prove himself great in the eyes of others. Off-worlders, even. Folly! As though they cared for the pack!"

Prawg barked, then met Kel's eyes. "All the prime packs have left for Raranda. I do not know where Rask has gone, but Harancha was here yesterday, boasting to me of the territory he would hunt in Raranda." The craftsman sent another bounce. The map in Kel's specs enlarged, a glowing tint shading the Kanna Valley.

"That is what I know. Come, warrior. I have things to send with you along with the soul-forger."

"Master Prawg," Kel began. He wanted to tell him to run, to flee into the deepest, darkest jungle to save himself from what was coming.

"It's alright," Prawg halted him knowingly. "Duty is harder than durasteel."

In the speeder again, the weight of the soul-forger warmed his lap in the dreex-leather pouch Prawg placed it in. He was still humbled by the bonding he'd made with the gunsmith. A pack of young doros eyed their speeder and showed teeth as they passed.

"On to meet your other agent?" Kel said, snapping back to the present at the sight.

"No. Prawg's smart. There's a reason he told us about Harancha. He's my other source. He's gone, trying to kill this monster dreex for himself. Let's get back to the ship. We know where we need to go next. It's time to get on the hunt ourselves."

"The lodge on Raranda is close to the Kanna Valley. It makes sense as a target." Kel was climbing back into armor as the team listened to Barnett.

The aircrew joined them. "We can fudge a little on the trajectory to Ar-Song. I can shave a few hundred kilometers off the horizontal distance. It shouldn't draw any attention or at least, not get us anything more than a warning from the air controllers." That was fortunate. One of the contingencies if the target had been too far off the beaten path was to simulate a crash, and drop below sensor level to take a nap of the earth flight to the destination. All of the Postremadon in their medbags couldn't keep them from coating their armor in breakfast for such a rough ride around the globe.

"Repulsor lift in ten," Barnett ordered. "We've burned four hours to the minute and we're lucky that's all. D-day's almost here."

Chutes were laid out on the deck. JP and Wiggy worked to rig Bertie. Kel eyed his grav container and the N-22 that lay inside. There would be limited opportunity for long-range work in this jungle. He placed the soul-forger in its pouch next to his sniper rifle and sealed it. His personal container wouldn't find him again for some time.

"You jump with this heavy blaster before, Bertie?" JP asked. "Might play havoc with your stability."

"I've jumped more and from much higher, Sergeant Pabon," Bertie sang in response. He was in high spirits. "I've got a bit of advantage over you meat sacks," he said, testing the flight surfaces of his shell, panels opening and closing like the feathers of some parading bird plumed in display. "No offense, mate."

Wiggy saw his opening. "Bet you wish you could do that, JP. Keep you out of those spins you're so apt to induce."

"Once," JP corrected. "Once. The FCA froze. And as I recall, I recovered and hit the drop zone right next to you." The freefall compatible armor overlays had control surfaces that aided a jumper's stabilization in thin air freefall. Like any device, it could fail, and always at the worst time. "I'd say that gives me a better track record than you. What was your excuse for landing in that canyon again? Something about vortex winds?"

"Yeah, yeah." Wiggy shrugged him off.

Bertie tsked. "Glass houses, Sergeant Wiggins, glass houses."

Meadows and Kel checked the drop computer plot together, Barnett following along as they reviewed. "At twenty-five kilometers AGL, there'll be a point where we can slow for a safe exit," Meadows said as the simulation of the *Xaylan* reached the apex of its trajectory. The pilots worked mathematical sorcery to calculate the repulsor engagement sequence to battle gravity long enough to allow the jumpers to exit. Even in thin atmosphere, the heat envelope around the ship would be so intense as to fry them at hypervelocity. To time the stutter in the *Xaylan*'s velocity at the top of its arc, then regain speed without burning out her plasma coils, was black magic.

Seven dots dropped from the tail, fell for a moment, then arrested into a glide. The planet rotated, the pulsing course projection traced a line down, passing over the Crystal Sea, the Howling Moon Range, the Kanna Valley, and the rolling tops of hundred-meter-tall trees that covered the landscape in all directions.

"The sensor penetration is fair, enough that we can feel reasonably certain the floor of the DZ is solid."

The ziggurat lodge was visible in outline through the forest. A circle glowed ten kilometers before it, indicating their drop zone.

"Any clearing is going to be too much of a risk. Tree landings will be the order of the day. No avoiding it."

Kel agreed. There'd been the briefest of time to choose a DZ location. There wouldn't be an easy one, no matter how much they agonized over trying to find one on the map. Even so, a clearing present on the most recent holomap might be gone by now. The jungle could swallow hilltops, produce new ones, carve creeks and impassable rivers, all within the span of a single rainy season. And on Psydon, every season was rainy season.

Meadows touched his bucket. "Six minutes," he said over L-comm.

Barnett wore the same armor he'd seen Papa Bear and Zero wear, the FCA adjusted to the thinner profile by Meadows. On Legion armor, the overlays made them look even deadlier, as though they could fly without wings. On the sleek, smooth surface of Barnett's armor, it looked like luggage strapped to the outside of a Wheldon speeder, ruining the sexy lines of the luxury vehicle. Side-band encrypted comms made Barnett a part of their communication network. In the jungle, his range was limited to a few meters. Weak, but as close to undetectable as the non-L-comm tech could be configured.

"It's gonna be tight," Meadows urged. "Get close."

They'd practiced the exit dry, dozens of times. Barnett was surrounded in the core of their formation, Bertie the last behind their layer of durasteel. The hum of the grav

decking below was strong, the whine of the inertial dampeners competing for his nervous system's attention.

"One minute."

The dampeners shut off.

The ramp opened, the molten glow in their trail fading,
the light of the green world below now visible.

"Thirty seconds."

As they edged to the ramp, Hardball spoke. "Forged
in heat and fire, I do not lose myself, but find salvation by
leading the charge."

"Go."

24

Kel activated his deployment sequence then looked up to see the huge square above him. They fell for less than a minute before deploying chutes, just enough time for the FCA to stabilize them for a safe opening. He was next to Meadows, in the lead. The rear view showed four jumpers with Bertie's boxy form trailing slightly above them beneath his double canopy.

He checked the steering link. A quick toggle left and right, and the chute obeyed.

"Good luck from the crew of the *Xaylan*," the pilot's voice said, their contrail dissipating into the high altitude clouds. Once the crew delivered its cargo to Ar-Song, they would lift again and hide, spectators for the arrival of the assault armada due in two days. "We'll be on moon two if there's a service we can perform for you again."

"Good job by the pilots," Kel said on a tight beam aimed at Barnett. "How you doing?"

"All good. I'm reducing my canopy. I don't weigh as much as the rest of you and the program's a little behind in adjusting." Barnett was higher behind the pack, his canopy providing too great a glide ratio to stay in formation with the rest of them.

"Stay on heading 275," Meadows said. "Don't be afraid to spill some air. If you overshoot, we'll never link up."

An hour passed floating in the darkness without even a pinpoint of light to betray a doro presence below. The region was deserted or, as he suspected, the vegetation so thick that light from any source less powerful than a laser couldn't break through to freedom. Halfway down to the jungle, Kel's legs and arms were numb as they usually were on the long ride under canopy. He shifted in his harness and flexed his joints to keep blood moving. Finally, the faint radiation of heat retained by the stone blocks of the lodge registered dimly below.

"The tag I have on Rask's yacht answered," Barnett announced. "It's parked below. He's there for sure. Jackpot."

"Then as long as we don't land right on top of him and his crew out in the woods, we're going to catch them dead to rights." Kel felt the rush of the hunt. This was much better than chasing an animal.

"We're locked onto the drop zone," Meadows said. "Anyone see anything?"

"Negative," Hardball said. They'd all been burning the region on full spectrum. Soon, they'd be too low to change their landing site even if they detected life signs on their DZ. "I've got nothing. You'd think we'd pick up animal life at least."

"This stuff is so thick, nothing's going to punch through," JP said. "We could very well land right in someone's lap. It'd be a surprise for the both of us."

"Be ready to fight as soon as we hit," Kel said. "Double-check blasters are on suppressed mode." His was across his chest, just waiting for him to pop the belly band holding it in place.

"Maybe we'll drop in on that giant dreex and bag him ourselves," Wiggy said. "That'd look good on the team room floor."

"Two minutes," Meadows warned.

Kel took hold of the manual steering toggles. The roof of the primeval forest was a thin mask disguising a killer beneath. Between it and the floor a hundred meters beneath were layers of flora and fauna, many of them deadly. But the jungle was neutral. It helped or hindered them no differently than it did their enemy. Like all terrain, it served the one who knew how best to use it to their advantage.

Meadows broke through the leafy surface and was swallowed. Kel clenched his teeth in anticipation of a violent stop and flared his chute.

He was falling. Branches broke strain and snapped as he dropped. Feet and knees stayed locked together, his fear of landing astride a huge branch motivating him to imitate the form of a writing stylus: thin and smooth. Finally, he came to an elastic stop, recoiling up again at the bottom of his downward travel like a yo-yo at the end of its string. His body swung like a pendulum. He anticipated his chute tearing free and dropping him like a stone any second. When it didn't, he released his carryall and eased it down. It halted on solid ground. Even with his spectral enhancement at maximum, the image in his HUD was dark. Celestial light didn't penetrate this jungle.

With a blink, the descending line released from his parachute container. He found it and passed it over his chest. The descender grasped the line and a green icon flashed in his HUD.

Now or never, he thought. *I'm secure, or about to take one hell of a first step.* He keyed the release and eased out his harness seat. He slid a few meters as the line grew taut, then rappelled slowly to join his carryall. The ground was spongy but firm beneath the top layer.

"I'm down," Meadows was first to speak. An icon showed him only twenty meters away. Nothing but shades of greens and blacks defined the world through his HUD.

"At your six," Kel said as he let his carbine snap to his chest and pulled his ruck on. He hit the destruct key and the carbon fiber webs of his parachute lines, canopy, and container turned to dust.

"I'm stuck," Wiggy said. "Hung upside down. My feet are wrapped in my suspension lines."

"I've got you, Wig," Hardball said. "I'm right below you."

"JP?" Meadows inquired. An icon showed JP fifty meters away.

"Moving to help get Wig out of the tree. Can we risk some active wavelength? This is ridiculous."

"Negative," Kel said. "Feel your way with your HUD guidance."

"Barnett, are you good? Need help?" Meadows asked. No reply. It meant either Barnett had landed so far away his weak comm signal couldn't reach them, or he was injured. "Bertie, retrieve Barnett."

"I've got him," Bertie said. "He's fifty meters from me. But he's... I don't have an adequate explanation just yet. I'm using a weak mapping sonar. This terrain is relatively flat, but he's subterranean. I'm heading to his location now."

Meadows met him, both moving to where Wiggy was trapped. "This is some dense stuff," Meadows said, half tripping over a tangle of roots.

"We can risk using cat eyes," Kel said, and activated the pair of tiny glowing infrared marks on the back of his bucket. The dim eyes gave the person behind a visual reference as they followed the ghostly apparitions. The bobbing motion and angle of the eyes taught the next person how to anticipate the terrain and obstacles ahead.

The first hint of starlight illuminated a small patch through the trees. Upside down and a full fifty meters above them, Wiggy hung trapped in his suspension lines like a bug in a spider's web. Hardball scaled the nearest tree and was tossing a line underhand as JP used Wiggy's lowering line to drag him nearer. Wiggy missed the line; Hardball coiled it again for another attempt.

"Assistance needed," Bertie said. "I've found Barnett."

"Moving," Kel replied. "You guys got Wiggy?"

"We got him, boss. Go," Hardball said as he coiled the line again for yet another toss.

"Hurry," Wiggy said. "My head's swelling, I've been upside down so long."

Kel and Meadows followed Bertie's icon down a gentle slope to where the DOGR waited, his long neck plunged into the puddle of a mostly dry creek bed.

"Bertie, what've you got?" Meadows asked.

The ACM's head appeared from the pool. "There's a sink hole at the bottom of this creek bed. It's huge. Barnett's submerged below."

Now Kel saw it. Barnett's canopy was caught in the brush above, the nearly invisible shroud lines disappearing into the water. The Nether agent was trapped below.

"Pull him out!" Meadows said as he started gathering handfuls of the carbon fiber lines. "Bertie, straddle the mouth. We'll use you as a fulcrum to pull him out."

"Roger," Bertie said as he stretched his fore and aft legs across the pool.

Hand over hand, they pulled the lines across Bertie's back. Barnett's bucket broke the surface.

"Thank Oba!" Barnett's voice exploded. "Help me up. There's a current under there. I couldn't get out." Strain and exhaustion told the tale. He'd been submerged for close to ten minutes.

On dry ground, Barnett collapsed. Kel checked his readouts. Stressed, but otherwise good vitals.

"What happened?" Meadows said as he joined the man on his back.

Barnett gasped. "I thought I was free and clear. I crashed through an open spot in the trees." He took another deep lungful of air. "I thought I was headed for a soft landing. Then before I knew it, splash, I was under."

Peeking out in high spots between puddles, the creek bed was some kind of limestone. If an unarmored person fell into one of those holes, there'd be no escape. Only a dark death in the current, pushed along the subterranean channel no differently than falling through river ice to drown below an unyielding ceiling.

"Reminder to self. Don't travel the creek beds."

Meadows rose and offered Barnett a hand.

"Duly noted."

Bertie managed the best. Eight legs buried into the soil up to his knees, pulling one at a time out of the soft ground, he climbed the slope. Even on hands and knees, Kel couldn't imitate his success. Halfway up the grade, shallow roots gave way along with part of the hillside. He slid back to where he started.

"Now *this* is jungle," JP said as Kel stopped at the end of his ride.

"Line coming down," Bertie said from above. He anchored his rear legs onto a large trunk as he tossed the line to them. The operators slithered up the hill one at a time, clinging to the rope as they crawled.

"How far?" JP gasped at the top.

"We've made a kilometer in the last hour," Hardball said between sucks of hydration from his bucket nipple. "A little better than our last leg. It's getting easier."

"Should've landed right on top of that pyramid thing and fought our way down," Wiggy said. "They'd never have expected it."

To Kel, everyone's silence meant agreement. Or exhaustion. Even he found himself winded.

"We've got a full day to get eyes on the lodge," Barnett said. "We'll make it."

"Sun's rising," Meadows said. "We'd best get hidden and send out sensor bots before we try to go farther. This spot's as good as any."

On his belly and covered by his mimetic net, Kel took his turn at rest and checked the sensor map. They sent out a few dozen of the mini-bugs, small drones that crawled out a few hundred meters in concentric layers to give them warning of approaching threats. The sensors sniffed and registered seismic activity to indicate patterns of movement. A ripe fruit falling onto the jungle floor would be recorded as an event. But a series of such events would alert the program that a footfall pattern was detected, and send a warning to the monitor.

Once they'd settled into the silence of their perimeter, the constant pitter-patter of water droplets was joined by the rustling noises of small animal life returning. The program had already "learned" the differences between the activities of the small ground nesting rodents and the arboreal primates that occasionally dropped out of their leafy apartments to forage. Kel marveled how even with sunlight peeking through the heavy cover above, visibility in a straight line was still limited to a scant few body lengths.

"Bertie, how's that drone progressing?" he asked.

With a net and foliage draped over him, his boxy form was concealed only because he'd dug a grave in the loose soil to lower his profile.

"Almost there, Captain." Bertie supervised navigation of one of the larger bots to find a spot from which to transmit a view of the lodge. "It's making a slow crawl up a tree as we speak. There are some primates that call this one home, but the buggers don't seem to have noticed our snooper just yet."

"See that they don't," Kel said. "Take your time."

The primates lived in groups of ten or twelve including the babies, and for no obvious reason sounded off in choruses of howls every so often, answered by other tribes off in the distance like a kind of link. "We're here, Smith family, and we Joneses are fine—how about you?" they seemed to say.

"We're ready for a visual," Bertie said after another twenty minutes.

Kel checked team vitals. Everyone's pulse and respirations increased, including his own. They were at a fifty percent security status, but neither Kel nor the other half of the team supposed to be resting had slept. It was time to turn their imaginations of what the jungle hid into reality, the thing you'd dreamed of made concrete. Or in this case, stone.

The view was limited. The lodge was large, the right angles of the structure peeking out between leafy projections. The vertical stabilizers of the yacht were partially visible in a small clearing just beyond the ziggurat.

"Bertie, do you have a solid lock on the building and surrounding grounds?"

"Roger, sir, down to the last centimeter. I can guide the strike perfectly with what I have from here."

Kel checked. With this latest update, the computer made the lodge just over two thousand meters from their location. Far enough for a safety margin, close enough from which to do a timely bomb damage assessment. "We call the strike in from here, let it cool down, then make our BDA."

Barnett interrupted. "We don't have any confirmation whether the head cheese is in residence or out on his boondoggle in the jungle somewhere. We've got eighteen hours. I'd like to get a live look. There's only so much the crawlers can do for us."

"Agreed," Kel said. He was on the way to suggesting the same before Barnett cut him off.

"You and I should take a leader's recon. We can sacrifice some of the sensor drones and walk them into positions closer to the lodge to at least give us movement information." The bots were dull and couldn't be trusted to take the most concealed route into a decent proximity around the target.

"Boss, it shouldn't be you," Meadows said. "Let me and one of the guys go."

Kel considered before answering. "I'll take you and Hardball with, but we'll split to get eyes-on from two directions. Twice the risk of compromise, but twice the help available if needed. That's my final offer, Top."

"Then we head out at last light," Meadows finished. "Swap security. Me, Hardball, Wiggy, rest. Captain and JP, you're up. Barnett, if you keep acting like a leej, I'll let you pull security like a member of the team. But if someone hears you snoring, you'll never know when I stick the blade in your skull."

Barnett took the abuse. "Yes, Top."

"That's what I like to hear."

Kel startled awake at Wiggy's voice. Another alternating round of security passed with the bot staring at the lodge transmitting nothing much. He'd swallowed some taste-less paste with another appetite suppressant before doz-ing off. There'd be no popping lids while on the ground. The doro had acutely sensitive noses. The team and all gear had a UV scrub before they left the *Xaylan* to neu-tralize any traces of biologic remnant that might give off scent. Hydration and low-residue protein paste were go-ing to remain their fare until this was over.

"I've got movement. Linear. 150 meters."

Kel came fully awake. He pulled up the map. One sen-sor at a time highlighted movement, a path projected straight for them.

The sun was dipping lower. The movement was com-ing from the direction of travel they used to occupy their present location. Someone had picked up their track. The ACM was closest.

"Bertie? Talk to us," Kel asked.

"Running all spectra. Still too far out to get enough penetration for a scan."

"JP, Wig, shift rear with me," Meadows said. "Slowly. Don't give up our position."

"Hundred meters," Wiggy said.

Kel kept on his front and watched the sensors. Another bug pinged, then disappeared. *Why did a sensor go out?* he wondered. *Did someone step on it?* They were small, but something as unnatural on the jungle floor like the tiny bots would be noticed underfoot. Meadows crawled slowly behind him, brushing his foot as he passed.

"Bertie?" Kel asked. "Anything yet?"

"Negative, Captain."

"Another sensor disappeared," JP said. "Someone's found them."

"Get ready to light them up," Meadows said. "Suppressed."

"Bertie, get ready to call the birds in for the strike. If we're compromised, bring them in immediately."

"Roger, boss."

"What's that?" Wiggy said. "It's not a doro. It's some kind of... I don't know what it is. It's eating the frellin' sensors."

Kel's curiosity raged. He crawled next to Meadows and rose up on elbows.

"It's some kind of tank on legs," JP laughed.

He saw it now. A waddling creature the size of a bathtub, covered in armored plates, pushed the ground with a flat nose extended from its shell as it mowed across the jungle. Kel checked the sensor map again. Nothing else pinged around them.

"I don't remember seeing anything like that on the flora and fauna flash cards," he said. "Rare species?"

"If he eats anymore of our sensors, I'm going to have to blast it," Wiggy said.

Just then the animal paused to root, burying its nose deeply in the wet ground. It dug frantically with clawed toes until it found its prize. The head poked deep into the excavation, then returned, a writhing white slug fighting as it was pulled like a string from its tunnel, then sucked like a noodle into the narrow jaws. The animal took a new azimuth and waddled away into the brush.

"Cancel calling the strike in early, Bertie," Kel said.

"I don't know, boss, that could've been a doro probe," Bertie quipped back. "They might have a whole platoon of those things heading this way to overrun our position."

"Must have a burrow nearby," JP said. "Little guy just popped out for dinner. Now he's heading home after a grueling day at the office."

"Well, he's taking three of our sensors home with him," Wiggy said. "Hope he gets a bellyache."

"When they reappear on the map, we'll know he's done with them," JP said.

Wiggy made a rare chuckle. "I'll let you go get them, JP."

"Two doro around the firepit. No movement from the lodge," Kel said.

He had a better view than what the bot had given them. Down one side of the lodge, a receiving area sat in front of a recessed entrance, a ring of manicured trees and flowering bushes fencing it all like a front lawn. A frame of timbers stood in the open; ropes hung from the cross beam.

"If I had to guess, that's a station for gutting and skinning game."

The two doros had rifles laid beside them as they tended the small fire. From any other angle, its light was consumed by the jungle.

Meadows spoke. "We've got eyes on the landing pad. The yacht and the hopper are cold. Haven't moved in days. There's no sign of doros tending the vehicles."

"Rask is on the hunt," Barnett said. "Those are servants. He's out with his pack. They could be days away from here, following a track."

Kel checked his chrono. "Everyone, drive your bot to a best position and make your way back to the rally point. Maybe we get lucky and Rask returns home victorious with his kill in time for the strike."

"And if not?" Barnett asked.

"Rask doesn't leave this valley alive."

25

The jungle hummed and sang to them from the black. When the fleet arrived, it would be like a meteor shower above, but they'd see nothing of it from here. The tiny patch of starlight Kel had been concentrating on that illuminated a sawtooth bush was now just a ghost image in his mind. The weather front that brought the steady rain had erased the real thing. With two hours until D-day, around Psydon were too many targets and not enough kill teams. Seven teams were too few to prep a planetary invasion by themselves.

Somewhere, 131st Legion Recon Pathfinders were strapped into a dropship, ready to exit a transport carrier as it broke from jump space. The dropship would cast off, ready to hit orbit, and deposit the leejes to take the long, lonely leap to the surface. Same with the 187th Recon, but Kel didn't have the same connection with them. He'd done it with 131st, and it was them he thought of just now. He'd been first on a planetary invasion with the Pathfinders. Few could say that. He still thought about it with pride. First on the ground, first to kill, first to seize and hold. First.

The Pathfinders would drop, direct tactical strikes by Talons to neutralize defenses around whichever airfield they were assigned, then guide the Goshawks to drop the rest of Recon at the lowest of altitude across the airfield. Seized was a powerful word. It would be the trickle to give rise to a turbulent cascade of overwhelming force. Legion assault companies would arrive violently, followed by Repub divisions, each bringing another wave of creeping, rolling annihilation.

But first the surface would burn. The Navy would drop out of jump, so low that to anyone below looking up, the capital ships would blot out the stars. Firing solutions would lock within seconds, particle beams hammering the ground orbital defenses. B-101 Boomers would launch and carpet the planet with plasma bombs. The jungle would burn for the first time since Psydon's volcanoes went dormant.

Kel thought Three would be assigned to hit the equatorial orbital defense site in the western hemisphere. It was the largest and best defended, built into a chain of volcanic peaks. The toughest target needed the toughest team. Being first on the planet was a distinction, and it was Twelve's. But hitting the toughest target was an honor above all others. He was certain the honor would be Three's.

The first strikes would need to be precise and dispatch the ground-based particle cannons swiftly. He imagined his old team delivering a neutronium package, or even a Mark Four nuke to the complex. Kel felt pride knowing he'd done that, too. Were he planning the invasion, he'd have chosen Three for the task.

Could he someday be the one to plan the special missions for such a massive operation? If he went back to the Legion, would he someday be allowed to return to Dark Ops as its commander?

Maybe there's something to be said about going back to the big Legion to get schooled, he considered. *I could run this show. Someday.*

The melancholy he'd felt thinking about Tara was not even a memory. Only the mission remained. All warrior again, he analyzed. If it were up to him, what targets would he assign to each kill team for this invasion?

Psydon was rich in alkane hydrocarbons. Its infrastructure was primitively powered by stuff dug or piped from below the surface. And that was wonderful. Kel had hit such targets in his career, too. Energy plants and grids of physical transmission lines crisscrossed huge areas, targets impossible to defend and simple to cripple. If he were assigning missions, he'd assign no more than one kill team to hit the most massive of the plants: the one Kel witnessed billowing the smoke and water vapor from the combustion that fed Caza-Han. The rest of the plants would get orbital bombardments. More ordnance for maybe the same effect, but no guarantees. Precision weapons were only as good as the quality of the terminal guidance. Knocking out power to the capital was a target worthy of the limited asset that was a kill team. And while the gears of the greatest war machine assembled in a decade meshed together somewhere in the ether, Twelve lay on the jungle floor, waiting to kill just one doro.

"Party returning," Barnett said.

"How many?" Meadows asked.

Bertie answered. "Six."

"Is our head honcho with them?" Kel wanted to know. If so, the mission needed to launch immediately, before Rask got the urge to leave.

"Unknown, Captain," Bertie said. "The sniffers don't have enough DNA, and there's not a visual clear enough for a match based on Rask's gait or physical characteristics."

Barnett spoke hurriedly. "I'm authorizing the strike. Call them in now!"

"I concur," Kel said. "The clock's ticking."

"Working," Bertie said, then went silent. The ACM was speaking in the language of machines, not the crude vocalization he mimicked to communicate with the humans.

"Two minutes," Bertie said.

"That was fast," Meadows said.

"I've been talking to our Shadows all along. Our heavenly angels reached low orbit an hour ago. They just made a stealth reentry into a corridor not well covered by the orbital defense sensors and are at Mach three, nap of the earth, now." Traveling three times the speed of sound at less than fifty meters above treetop level was a feat only an AI could perform. "Go for audio, Shadow Leader."

The voice was unaccented, clear, neutral, and hard to place for region or culture. It was a perfect copy of an SNN female news reader.

"Slowing to attack speed. Confirm ground party safety range for us, Quasar."

"Two thousand, Shadow."

"Stand by."

"Here it comes," Bertie said.

A pause.

Then creation itself.

The first crackle and sharp sizzle was followed a moment later by the thunderous explosion. Purple plumes danced through gaps in the canopy, the energy released shifting to orange.

That would be the aircraft burning, Kel acknowledged.

A second series followed the first. The Shadows screamed overhead, their repulsor whine mixing with the echoes of the explosions.

"Clear for second pass, Quasar?" the perfect voice returned, soft, calm, soothing.

Bertie confirmed. "All clear, Shadow Leader. No change target location, no additional targets. Proceed."

"Roger."

"Hit 'em again, girls," Hardball said on the team channel. "I want to see nothing but a smoking hole when we get there."

The same run repeated. It sounded like each bird dropped two plasma bombs, the *thud, crackle, snap, pop, boom* was interrupted before the *boom*ing sequence began again, with another round from the trailing Shadow. The second sortie was a perfect copy of the first, the light reaching them from a different angle, brighter now. Kel assumed that the first run vaporized so much of the jungle, it was like opening an aperture to let more photons escape.

"On exit track, Quasar. Happy hunting."

"Roger, Shadow. Quasar out." Bertie broke communication. "Very polite for a relatively dull AI," Bertie said. "She was all business on the scramble, but warmed up a bit once we started talking like real folk. Nice girl. A bit dumb, but fast, and packs a wallop. My kind of woman."

"What's the countdown?" Kel asked, ignoring the ACM's banter.

"D minus one hour," Barnett said.

"Make best time to the target for BDA, Twelve," Kel ordered. "Go active emission as needed. Bertie, punch ahead with terrain sonar, find the fastest route. Get us on solid soil and don't avoid traveling the high ground. Movement to contact, weapons free. Move out, Bertie."

For the first time on Psydon, the gain on Kel's HUD had to dim the incoming light around them. The skeleton of the parked aircraft and the hopper burned a metallic white. Ground fires found new fuel as a ring of flames pushed to edge the blast area, underbrush behind the fires consumed and smoldering. Beyond, the wet woods resisted succumbing to the inferno but were losing the battle on a hillside as the overlying forest burned away, treetops bursting into flames and exploding like grenades. As much as he anticipated seeing a huge swath of the jungle disintegrated, the destruction was an area not much bigger than the landing pads and a footprint a hundred meters around the lodge.

"Pushing out GSS," JP said. What ground surveillance sensors they had left were crawling at best speed out into the jungle.

"Here's a search plan," Meadows said. A window opened in Kel's HUD. "By pairs."

"I'm with you, sir," Hardball said as he raised his carbine in a direction pointing around the cracked and toppled stones that had been one of the corners of the lodge, now little more than a mountain of rubble. "Those Shadows did a number on it. Not a living thing out of anything but the deepest bunker could've survived that strike."

Kel agreed. "Look at this tree." He poked the surface with a single gauntleted finger and a meter-long patch of bark fell off, revealing a charred core. "It cooked too fast to burn. The atmosphere for five hundred meters around here boiled. But we have to make sure."

"It's happening," Barnett said.

Above them dark shapes appeared in flashes, one after another. A dark shape filled the sky at the edge of their view above the trees. A particle cannon fired, the yellow ball leading a red trail bright enough to dim his HUD, the after image still burning when his vision returned.

"Get some, boys," Hardball said.

"Love to see what's on the other end of that strike," Wiggy said.

"Never in my life did I think to see a thing like this," JP said. "Not from the surface, anyway. A planetary assault. It must be like the Savage Wars."

"You all act like you've never seen an invasion before," Meadows interrupted. "Enough gawking. The fight here's not over. That's how leejes get killed. Stay sharp and on mission."

Kel and Hardball finished their cloverleaf search pattern. No hidden bunkers. No doro bodies. Just singed and burning jungle, the occasional piece of fractured masonry resting hundreds of meters from where it had been hurled. Hardball found a wooden chair none the worse for wear, out of place with its colorful cushion, sitting ready to be used by a weary hiker.   "How does something like that survive untouched?" Hardball asked rhetorically. "One time when I was a kid, our ranch got hit by a nega-cyclone. When we came out of the shelter, the only thing left was my pee-paw's rocker. Just sittin' there, waitin' for him. It's like Papa Bear says. There are more things in the galaxy than are dreamt of by our science."

"I'm not sure that's an original Papa Bear, Gabe, but I get your meaning. Let's head back."

The rest of the team were gathered around Bertie on a cool patch of duracrete that had survived both sorties.

"The doro planetary data stream is jammed, gentlemen," Bertie said. "The invasion is full-scale underway. Drops are being made on every continent and major city. An all-bands transmission announcement is running on continuous loop."

Bertie projected a holo. Fleet Admiral Thomas Cutler's faced floated in front of them. "To all Psydonians. The armed forces of the Republic have taken control of the planet. All airspace and orbital traffic are grounded until further notice. Do not attempt to lift or you will be destroyed. The Republic does not wish harm to civilians and other noncombatants. The Rebellion of Psydon is over. Civilian leaders are ordered to comply with the directions of advancing Republic forces. Military commanders are ordered to surrender unconditionally to the nearest Republic military authority. Any resistance will be met with overwhelming military force." The message repeated.

"Bertie," Kel swiped his wrist link. "Tight-beam encryption to nearest receiving orbital." His situation report was brief.

Double-twelve's nest destroyed. BDA: One hundred percent effective strike. Commencing detailed search. His identifier sealed the message. It would be transmitted up the chain of command within seconds.

"It's cooled down enough to get sniffers working," Barnett said.

Kel reacted to Barnett's suggestion. "Top, let's get a perimeter pushed out. Bertie, stay with Barnett for security and help him with the search. Rest of us, let's push out where we can do some good, in case we didn't get them all."

Kel and Hardball went back to their search grid, then pushed out even farther to where the jungle was clean and unaffected. From a small hilltop, they scanned the surrounding area and watched the map, only four of the insect bots left between them to deploy as early warning.

"Wonder how the rest of the boys made out," Hardball said as he lay raised on his elbows, his chin resting on the stock of his K-17.

"There'll be a lot of stories when we get back," Kel said. "Let's hope Barnett finds what we need."

An hour later, the Nether-leej's voice came over the team channel. "Good news, bad news, team."

"Send it," Kel said.

"We've got ten dead doros. We counted six in the returned hunting party. Two, we saw on site before the strike. There were two more deeper in the lodge we never laid eyes on. Guards or staff servants. Sniffers were able to access every major area of the ruins. Ten distinct genetic remains."

"But no Rask," Kel interjected.

"No Rask," Barnett confirmed.

"Bertie, did you piece together routes of travel in and out of the area?" Kel inquired.

"Yes, sir." Three trails following map contour lines appeared on the map.

"Team, there's nowhere for him to go but back here." Kel bounced a new message for Bertie to transmit.

Negative confirmation on double-twelve. Continuing search.

"There's not a settlement or travel lane for a thousand kilometers. We assume he was far enough out to avoid the strike, but not so far that he won't make his way here to see what the commotion was about. He's coming to get eyes-on and to find a ride to take him out of here, or his only option is to make the long walk out.

"Hardball and I will take the south trail. Meadows, stick with Wiggy and take the west. JP, you, Barnett, and Bertie get on the last. We dig in and ambush him when he comes back. The mission is to kill Rask and to have evidence for all of Psydon that we killed their big boss.

"Make it happen."

"We're set," Meadows said.

"Set," JP sounded off.

"Set," Kel completed the report.

The sun was up. He and Hardball made best speed on the jungle trail, making for the spot Kel imagined would be their best lie-in for the ambush. Kel took them off the shoulder-width superhighway to skirt through the deepest growth leading to a spot overlooking the path. They took turns leading. Wait-a-minute vines snared their legs, sharp spikes protruding in rings around thin, hard trunks splintered off their armor as they pushed ahead. A naked soul would be torn to shreds, dropping strips of ground meat carved off as they scraped past the needles of the forest.

"We don't know if this trail is even used by the dogmen, boss," Hardball said from beneath his camo net next to him. "The sniffers aren't good enough to check it for old doro scent."

"Doros are no different from us, Gabe. Nothing travels through the middle of the jungle. If they're trying to make best time, they'll use a trail."

The spot was just as Kel pictured from the map. The track followed over a spur on the other side of a shallow draw, rising just high enough to be seen. Behind them a steep cliff of vines and needles protected their backs, a hilltop hidden somewhere deeper behind in the rising jungle. They crawled forward on belly to the edge of the jungle and folded the underbrush gently down, then eased back.

"I've got a good view of about three meters of the trail," Kel said.

"Ditto," Hardball said as he described the terrain and what landmarks he could see. "We've got about ten meters of the route covered between us. If they come from my direction, I'll wait for you to initiate when the lead doro walks into your kill zone."

They waited.

The fatigue was catching up to him, the adrenaline pumped into his body by anticipation fading. His eyelids grew heavy and he bit the inside of his cheek to fight sleep.

"How many could be with him?" Hardball asked. "I figure if his war party is twelve, then we only took out half of them in the strike."

"That's my math," Kel replied. "Rask has figured out something big went down. He's cut off from comms. Maybe he's seen the all-bands surrender message. He's going to make a bee-line for the lodge. It's his only move." He was willing it to happen. He felt some of the adrenaline return with the blood he swallowed.

They waited. His chrono rolled. Eight hours passed.

"One ping. Two pings," Hardball said. "Three. We've got company."

Kel snapped out of his trance.

Hardball whispered, "Lead dog sighted. Wait for it. Wait for it."

Kel brought up the icon he had pushed to the side. It flashed brighter.

"They're halted. The lead dog's sniffing. He's motioning the rest to halt. They're on our scent. He's raising something in our direction."

Kel blinked the command. The mines detonated in series. One. Two. Three. A chain of explosions tore the jungle with thousands of dense needles of their own, making the black thorns of the jungle seem benign.

"Assault," Kel said as he rose, his K-17 firing without a target into the green sea ahead of him. He broke through the curtain of jade mesh and launched a grenade, firing blaster again, then dropping another into the tube to launch another grenade down the trail to explode out of sight. Purple arcs mixed with flying mud and foliage like the tailings from some mad bot-harvester loose in a field. Bodies lay on the trail and he kept firing, aimed now, giving each one a blast before he repeated again. One, two, three, four. Four still dog-men bodies in unnatural repose. Hardball broke onto the trail beside him, running off into the tunnel of branches and thick fronds.

"I got you now, puppies," Hardball said from out of sight. Kel sprinted after him, then dropped when he saw Hardball's feet, his body prone over a slight rise. Kel crawled to his friend's side in time to see the back of a doro fall to a blast, its fur burning beneath the charred hole in the uniform.

ANGLES OF ATTACK

"Move," Kel said, firing ahead as he got his feet. A pair of doro bodies smoldered on the trail ahead.

"We miss any?" Kel asked. Hardball was as at his shoulder.

"No. Any get past you?"

"Negative. I cleared left to right."

"I started at the end and worked left. We better push down the trail and check, sir."

They moved cautiously off the trail and advanced. "Any pings on the bugs?" Kel asked as he checked the map.

"Dead quiet down there. Nothing went farther back than the last doro I dropped. Let's make double sure these ones don't reanimate, boss."

"What's your sitrep?" Meadows's voice pierced their buckets.

Kel took a few deep breaths before answering. His lungs burned and his heart hammered in his chest. He smelled the jungle and the ozone from their blasters in the same breath, but that couldn't be, not sealed in his bucket. His armor couldn't keep his senses bottled up in the shell. Not at a time like this. He was fully alive, a hunter, a demon of death, a life-taker extraordinaire. There was no feeling like it.

"We've got six dog-men down in our kill zone, Top."

"Deader than a black hole, too," Hardball said as he kicked a rifle out of one doro's paws.

On a side channel, Wiggy's dim voice cursed. "I knew I should've gone with the captain. He's the luckiest leej that ever lived. Dammit."

"Hardball," Kel said. "Come look at this." He'd made it up the trail to the body of the first doro caught in the ambush. In his hand was a barbed spear. His chest was open and a mush of red and pink organs sat exposed deep in the well of the narrow rib cage. From under the top of the burned uniform, just beneath the neck, a tuft of gray fur protruded.

"Pull up your scanner, Gabe. Check me. Is that Rask?"

Hardball brought his wrist up and ran it over the body, hovering over the snout a moment before he knelt to pull back the lips. The lower incisor, a slightly yellowed ivory, had a small chip. "If not, it's his double."

"Team, make for our location. Barnett, it looks we have double-twelve. I'll wait for your quantum DNA scan before I send it in, but it looks like we got him."

"Fantastic!" Barnett yelled. "I knew you were the man for the job. We're on our way."

Gabe scanned the trees.

"What is it?" Kel asked, sensing Hardball's discomfort.

"How'd they sniff us? Did we blow the ambush site? Did they see us? Rask must've been quite the hunter because he knew right where we were."

A rumbling, throaty growl came from above them. Kel snapped his carbine up.

"Don't shoot," Hardball raised a hand. "Look at it!"

At the top of the rise above their ambush site was a dreex. It growled again, louder, longer, but made no move to retreat. Its chest expanded as it raised on front legs, the mottled brown spots and tawny coat shimmering in the rays of light that broke through the clouds. The giant head raised and its maw opened. An even longer, deeper howl vibrated though Kel's armor as though the roar came from his own chest. The carnivore dropped. It bared teeth at them, grunted, then turned and was gone, his point made. There was only one hunter in this jungle.

"I've herded rindar steers by myself. I dropped a man-killing cat with a needler once. That's the biggest critter I've ever seen this close," Hardball said, still staring at the spot in the jungle from where it had laughed at them.

Kel was awed. "It was twice as big as the holos. That had to have been the trophy dreex. It was a king."

"Hear that, Rask?" Hardball said to the body at his feet. "So close to greatness, yet so far. Just wasn't your day, doggo. First you missed your trophy, then you got dead. You're a two-time loser. Dumbass."

26

"The decapitation hasn't had the disruptive effect we'd hoped for. The doro military are adept at working independently and without central direction. Despite the death of their Pack Leader Supreme and the chief war council, the individual pack-family battalions continue attacks on Republic forces and display confidence in their movements and operations in most sectors at this time."

"Thank you, Major Grantham," said the four-star army general in charge of all Republic forces, General Revan Harris.

The army intelligence officer took his cue and stepped back from the lectern. Kel hadn't noticed before, but the man had a prosthetic leg, maybe two. Only the faint click of a servo announced their presence. Prosthetics were becoming less common since limb regen had gotten faster.

General Umstead briefed the outcome of Legion operations on behalf of the 187th, the 131st, and, without naming them, Dark Ops. Legion Commander Barrow sat silently, he and Umstead the sole representatives of the Legion. Senior officers from the Republic army filled in the rest of the seats. The general from the Black Horse division who'd spoke on the transport ship was there, his fatigues soaked in jungle perspiration and rain. He'd come directly from the field for this briefing, mud scraped from his tropical boots. Kel pictured the man out with his division, leading from the front, whereas the rest of the assembled leadership were dry and clean.

"General Weyer, can you update us on operations in sector A-one?" General Harris indicated the rugged older man. Kel hadn't known the Black Horse division commander's name, though he'd impressed him by the address to his troops.

"Yes, General. I'd just like to say that the first strikes, though failing to bring about a rapid resolution, were nonetheless impressive and well executed. The guided airstrikes and strategic target destruction by the Legion teams accomplished their goals. The central government decapitation may have had less of an initial disruption of command and control than we'd hoped, but will undoubtedly result in a significant effect once the combat effectiveness of remaining doro units has been further degraded. In addition, the power grid and critical infrastructure in our sector have been completely disrupted. Well done, Legion."

Umstead nodded appreciatively. Colonel Chatsworth pursed tight lips in acknowledgement of his kill teams' work. Bigg sat a row farther back with Braley and Kel, gathered in the joint command center for the briefing and representing the only two kill teams back from their initial mission. The Black Horse leader continued.

"Our armored brigade spearheaded the drive from Caza-Han north."

The Black Horse division raced from the spaceport in Caza-Han up the highway to engage the doro armored unit. Grav tank against grav tank. Not a single Magnus had been nicked. Every doro tank was a smoking hulk. The holos showed one burned out tank after another, the flat and wide single-turreted doro armor nothing more than scrap to be pushed into mass converters for salvageable energy. They dotted the roads and village thoroughfares like grave markers.

"We've flattened the headquarters and surrounding installations of the doro Hunter Maximus Division, and large-scale military opposition is degraded significantly. As G-2 stated, smaller elements as large as battalion size continue to operate in rural areas."

The invasion commander spoke in a way that made Kel think he knew the older division commander well, as though he had once been the junior, now risen above his old mentor. It was with humility that he spoke to the older, yet junior general. "The Black Horse did an amazing job, General. Please convey my respect to your division for your combat accomplishments. Now, what strategy are you implementing with the changing threat composition?"

"We're moving to a firebase centered strategy."

Locating the doros was proving difficult. Army units had been performing search and destroy sweeps on foot through the jungle with limited success. Kill teams had been acting as reconnaissance, seeding huge areas with sensors, then calling in the mobile strike force of a Legion company in response to significant enemy concentrations. So far, the body counts of doro fighters weren't adding up to numbers indicating they'd eliminated any major opposition.

"There are at least three brigades of doro infantry estimated to be in sector A-one," the Black Horse leader continued. "Drawing them out is taking time. We're establishing firebases in the middle of the jungle throughout the sector. We have five partially constructed and ready for the Pachyderms to lift in our Magnus Fours."

It was a sound strategy. Much of the jungle would deny armored vehicles the ability to operate. The repulsors would tear into the loose soil and sink the heavy grav tanks no differently than it would an old-fashioned tracked or wheeled vehicle. In a firebase, the tanks could be used in defense, plus the three main guns on its multi-turreted body had nearly the range of static artillery. Where the tanks were actually able to operate in closer support of infantry operations, the platforms would devastate an enemy faster and surer than any air support.

A rodent-like man with a pencil-thin mustache and wearing colonel's boards spoke in the ear of one of the other division generals seated at the table. A pair of Sevens, mirrored and inverted to form an hourglass, was on their shoulders. The general frowned and said, "Not now," loud enough for Kel to hear. Undeterred, the man rose to full height and stepped into the light. "Why is it so hard to locate such large enemy units in your sector, General?" The man practically sparkled, as though he'd just stepped out of the studio shoot for an officer's uniform catalog. Behind him another officer held a link, capturing the moment. "The Seventh has had no such difficulties rooting out the rebellious doros. Delegate Dewitt is expecting a full report as to why the pacification of Psydon is slowing rather than accelerating." He was about to say more when the seated division commander intervened.

"Sit down, Colonel. Your benefactor in the House of Reason gets no more justification for the progress of this invasion than does any other member of the government. Sit. Down."

The colonel scowled, but slunk back to his seat.

"Apologies, General Weyer, General Harris," the commander of the hourglass division said. The island continent the Seventh occupied had virtually no doro military presence.

Bigg mouthed a word so Kel could see. "Point." So that was an appointed officer? This was another first for Kel. The Legion supposedly had them now, as well? Why wasn't the insubordinate man taken out in chains? Kel knew without asking. Politicians and their allies wielded a power that interfered and corrupted in ways as sickening as the results of a bomb dropped on an orphanage.

General Weyer took the disruption in stride. "Seismic sensors indicate systems of tunnels and caves that conceal we don't know how many doro troops. Short of carpeting huge areas with ordnance to have unknown effects, improving intelligence collection or drawing them out is preferred. Harassing artillery fire has also been difficult to interdict. Their weapons are not only hidden but change locations more rapidly than our kill chain can respond to. We've not found evidence of a single doro artillery piece on damage assessment. In addition to excellent decentralized tactics and use of the environment, the presence of technologic enhancements not yet discovered is a strong possibility. My staff and I suspect that the Nemanjic may have exported some of their tech to the doros. At least, that's one consideration given the intel updates from recent galactic developments."

Nem concealment tech? Here? Kel was caught unprepared for the possibility. The Nems sold anything to anyone, just as they stole anything from anyone. It hadn't occurred to him that their illicit tech could have found its way to Psydon. The idea quickly gained traction in the slippery evolution of his analysis of doro capabilities.

One by one, the army division commanders reviewed their combat successes, failures, and current strategies.

The pattern observed by the Black Horse commander was repeated with little deviation from most of the other sectors. Large-scale combat operations? Settled. The Republic forces led onto Psydon by the Legion rapidly dominated and destroyed the doros' defensive capabilities. Did the Republic hold Psydon? Decidedly. The only offensive capability they had was in small-scale combat which still raged across the planet, in the jungles and around settlements everywhere. The doros fought when they wanted to fight, appeared out of the jungle, then disappeared just as mysteriously. Enough to sting, but not enough to kill the conquerors. The unasked question that hung over the room burned at Kel, too. Because its answer rested with the politicians on Utopion.

Would the Republic continue to hold on to Psydon?

The intervention to crush the Psydon Rebellion had now become a war of attrition.

General Umstead and Legion Commander Barrow approached. Kel joined the others at attention. "Gentlemen, I'm off," General Barrow said. "I'm expected on the floor of the senate. They want to hear from the Legion how brilliantly the invasion was conducted. That part will be the unvarnished truth. With competence and honor. Silver made the Legion and the Republic proud, as did 131st and 187th Legion." He hesitated. "How the war on Psydon will proceed is another matter, one for the next Legion commander to explain, would be my guess. KTF."

So, Barrow thinks this is going to turn into a slow-burning dumpster fire like I do, he thought as he sprung back to attention at the general's departure.

General Umstead indicated they should draw closer. "In discussion with Colonel Chatsworth, Silver is going to take the lead in locating and destroying the remnants of the doro army. By the time General Barrow is on the senate floor, I want reports following close behind him that the Legion is pulling the fangs out of the doros by the ton."

Colonel Chatsworth smiled the legendary smile of the man who'd been given the keys to the kingdom. "I'm organizing us along the lines of a model that's been used successfully in similar conflicts. Major Yost, you are to be my executive officer. Team Three is joining Twelve to become Command and Control North. The other five teams already out are being organized as CCS, CCW, CCE, CCC, and CC Oceania."

Umstead resumed. "We have Talon detachments assigned to each who will work independently and with the support of the respective army divisions and Legion units in the assigned sectors."

An abrupt commotion from the other side of the room made the general stop. The colonel with the black wisp on his upper lip made haughty noises to a group of officers gathered around him.

"The House of Reason will not stand for indecisiveness. When Delegate Dewitt gets my report, I don't doubt there will be immediate changes in how this war is being run."

Similar noises came out of the other toy soldiers gathered with him.

General Umstead frowned. "I haven't yet had the opportunity to speak with you all personally about the appointed officers you may encounter in the 131st and 187th, so I'll tell you what I've already told the commanders of those Legions. I expect you to act with the professionalism of a Legion officer at all times.

"But if an appointed officer in our Legion interferes with the conduct of operations, the successful accomplishment of our mission, or the safety of our legionnaires, just remember..." He lowered his voice. "The jungle swallows the good and the bad alike."

Braley waited until Chatsworth left. "Well, Kel, you finally got Three away from me. Congrats."

Kel felt a lump in his throat.

"I'm just kidding, brother." Braley hammered him on the chest. "I know you had nothing to do with this. The colonel sprung it on me this morning. The colonel, Bigg, and I'll be based out of the Black Horse headquarters compound with you. I'll be seeing you daily when you're not out in the field or when I'm not running around Psydon to run interference for the other teams. If you're messing up, I'll know it."

"First me, now Braley," Bigg said. "Three's torch has officially been passed."

"Radd's still carrying it," Kel said. "And I won't let it go out either, Bigg."

"See that you don't, CCN Commander," Braley said. "Oh, and for the duration of our time here on Psydon, Dark Ops has a new cover."

"We're not Silver, here?"

"Nope. SIG. Strategic Investigative Group."

27

The pattern locked into the mimetic camouflage made their armor as invisible as the adaptive sensors normally would no matter the surrounding, but the fixed camo pattern burned no power. The greens, scant browns, and purples matched the Psydon jungle so well Kel had to admit it was a smart move. Bigg's suggestion, of course.

Chatsworth was proving an anomaly to Kel. The DO commander's actions made Kel rethink his assumptions about the kind of leader he would be. Special operations was a canix of a different stripe, an animal requiring a different set of skills to capture and tame. Maybe Chatsworth hadn't come from Dark Ops, but his response to the changing mission on Psydon was impressive. Kel had to admit, had he been in command, his leadership might not measure up to that of the adaptive Legion officer.

He resisted pulling his legs back into the SLIC for fear of whacking the treetops as they skimmed over the night jungle. Slower, unarmored, but quieter, the lightly armed birds were better suited. The Talons were just too loud at low altitudes. They found that out when a full doro company was on them not five minutes after hitting the LZ. Never again.

"One minute," the pilot said, voice tremulous from the vibrations of the SLIC.

"Check rigging," Poul said.

Kel had done so several times, but checked anyway. It wouldn't do to push off the deck only to tumble through the treetops to break his neck somewhere below in the darkness. If he lived, it would be a permanent embarrassment. Better to die on impact than hear the tale told over and over in the Century Club.

The SLIC hovered and dropped slightly, its belly resting on the bed of branches, as low as it could go without clogging intakes. The repulsors blew leaves back into the cabin in a vortex, making it like the collector chamber of a vacuum.

"Go."

He pushed off and made it past the top layer, relieved the growth opened up under the top canopy, and took a smooth ride down, releasing the line as he came to rest. All around him armored boots sank silently into the soft ground. Kel was moving by the time he heard Poul send the free and clear to the SLIC.

He flooded the way ahead with both his bucket and weapon light. There had been many things they hadn't known about the doro and the Psydon jungle. They'd figured out the doro could see in the infrared. Finding the right wavelength for their illuminators took some experimenting. Broadcasting electromagnetic radiation in any wavelength, even invisible light, was an abomination in the eyes of Oba, but they hadn't found a single indication that the doro scanned for emissions in the jungle. And nothing of the doros' was hidden behind cloaks of disruptor waves. The Nem tech they feared had made its way to Psydon, hadn't. The deep ache that lingered in Kel's thigh made him grateful for that with every step.

The doro preferred their natural abilities as hunters to protect them. Their mistake. The operators had no scent.

And movement, well, everything moved in the jungle. Warm-blooded, cold-blooded, plant, insect, and, given time, even the ground. Operators were stealthier than most animals, looked like the foliage, and could stay out for weeks if need be without breaking discipline.

He looked forward to his next encounter with the doros. Hubris was a gradual poison, taken regularly enough. Eventually, the toxin killed. Confidence, on the other hand, was a tonic. The doro weren't the masters of the jungle they thought themselves to be. And the prospect of proving it as many times as they could filled them all with the light of pure joy, as strong and as real as the beam from Kel's carbine.

The shortwave UV lights illuminated the jungle such that they could finally see like daylight. It had been a missing piece in their puzzle to own the jungle. They patrolled ahead, some of the flowering plants responding by spreading petals, saw-tooth ferns popping open to slice at the grazers come to dig up the soft roots below it. It took him most of their first patrol using the new spectrum to ignore the motion the stimulus produced in so many of the plants, but now he counted on it.

"Security halt. First rally point," Kel said. They'd stopped performing anachronisms like taking a knee or going prone unless there was a reason. Low on the jungle floor they were concealed, but blind. They stayed in a perimeter, silent, letting the natural sounds return. Waiting. Watching. Rucks stayed on. If they made contact and had to move, there'd be no time to leave the fight to pick up a carryall. Shoot, move, communicate. Shoot, move, communicate. That's all there was.

A ruck was a leech. It sucked energy, slowed movement, pressing ever downward to drive you into the ground while compressing the shock absorbers of spine and knees. Not even armor fully resisted the constant crush produced by living with the extra mass. Force, really. The mass times the acceleration of gravity was a force. A force trying to grind you down. But for all it took from you, it also gave back. The charge packs, grenades, mines, and other implements of destruction were more necessary to life than anything else they could carry. Food, they carried none. Water, yes. Food, no. Some tasteless protein paste, sure. Just enough for a mouthful once a day. Changing containers there was always the chance that scent might escape. No good.

The nanite packs ate their waste, and what little they made wouldn't necessitate a swap for a week. Kel got over the idea he was drinking his own recycled urine many years ago. There was no taste. It was just water, and it reduced how much extra they had to carry. If you couldn't cope, you could never be a recon leej. Because there was no filling a pouch or canteen from a stream or vine. Irradiated, sterilized, filtered, there were still bugs or toxins their nanoimmunos couldn't recognize, rendering you combat ineffective from a tiny swig.

"Thirty minutes," Kel broke the silence. "If we were spotted, we'd know it by now." When the doros detected a team on infil, they massed quickly and attacked rabidly, almost like they couldn't help themselves. A switch flipped. Madness took hold. They fired wildly, rarely with discipline. When they ran dry, some of them dropped onto all fours and charged, red tongues curled, teeth barred. They'd come to enjoy those types of attacks. It was like a holo simulation. A game. How many could you cut down and how fast? The dog-men weren't the fastest learners, but they were learning. Adapting. Getting smarter. Experience was their teacher, too. And they'd given the doros enough bad ones that it was showing up in their tactics. Restraining, focusing, making them more disciplined.

Kel feared the salad days were coming to an end. Finding the doros, baiting them to reveal their lair, then destroying them so easily, might soon come to an end.

But likely not today.

"Time to split up." Meadows let him know when they reached the branch of the river. "First one in contact gets to choose."

"Sure thing, Top. It just won't be you," Kel kidded. It was a little thing, but choosing the main course for the post-exfil barbecue had become a point of contention between them. After days without, Kel thought any meal was a good meal, but to some of the team, it was a big deal.

"No more of the giant rats," Woobie said. "I don't care who gets to choose. Just no more. Please."

"You can fight it out with Meadows," Poul said. "He's the only one who really likes it."

"You guys are crazy," Meadows grunted. "Cappies are better eating than rindar." The local herbivore was more of a rodent than ruminant. Kel thought it was too chewy. Maybe they just weren't preparing it correctly.

"The Black Horse guys got a stasis freezer full of rindar steaks, and that's what we're having 'cause we're finding 'em first," Hardball said. "No worries, Woob."

"See you boys later," Sims said with a wave as he brought up the rear behind Meadows, Woobie, and JP. They blended in with the foliage in a few steps, and were gone.

"I'll take the plunge," Poul said, dropping his ruck, not waiting for a volunteer as he eased down the bank.

Kel diffused his light to cover more area downstream and searched for the reflection of glowing eyes. It was as good a place to ford as any, the curve better than most, but it was still a linear danger area. If they were caught while crossing, it would be a bad day.

Poul mumbled curses as he crawled out of the muck and onto the other bank. "Gotta be one damn river with a gravel bed somewhere in this Oba-forsaken swamp."

Kel chuckled. He agreed. The rivers were muck-bottomed and deep. More than once he'd gone under trying to cross without a line to anchor to.

"Set," Poul said.

Kel came last. He snapped his ruck onto the line and dragged it and Poul's ruck behind as he pulled his train across, half floating, half suspended from the single line bridge over the pulsing river. Hands grabbed him on the other side and pulled him from the rippling current. Poul retrieved the line with a command. Releasing its anchor, it dropped slack and returned to the spool, the tail end flipping a stream of water across Kel's bucket. "Sorry, Kel."

He shook his head and the spray bled off his visor. "Cleanest it's been today."

They kept a steady pace. Slow, cautious, careful. Ready to assault through the kill zone of a doro ambush, grenades and blasters punching through the jungle with the destructive force of an angry god. There was no other way. The Talons weren't circling overhead to provide a steel rain to save them. The name of the game was simple: be ready to respond with overwhelming violence and fire superiority at all times. They had pouches and rucks filled to make it just so. When they ran low, it was time to get out of the pool, dry off, and go home.

Wiggy spoke from ahead. "If it's anything like the others, the main encampment is dug into this next series of ridges." He keyed the map overlay in their HUDs. The terrain always differed from the maps, the actual contours never quite matching the predicted. "Looks like we'll do best this way." He plotted a course.

Kel leaned forward and adjusted his straps as he shifted his ruck higher. "Lead off, Wig."

It was still dark when they reached the first rally point for their search. A circuitous path, a hook in their trail, and they settled in a flat spot. Trails left through the jungle, no matter how subtle, were a danger. A broken blade of grass, the scuff on a mossy rock, a dropped petal. For the hunter, danger represented an opportunity. If anyone followed their trace along its hooking route, they'd walk right into a wall of fire before they ever saw the camouflaged demons that had made the trail.

Time passed. "Get sniffers out," Kel said finally. "Time to search." Each of them had a pack of the sniffer bots. Kel rolled his open, the stick-like bots coming alive in unison and scurrying into the brush like the insects they were made to resemble. He coordinated his with the rest of the team, selecting the section of terrain to search, and pulled a spare grenade off his chest to lay beside him. Sometimes the sniffers hit on a scent right off. Sometimes the doros reacted to the little bots and sent out sentries to investigate. The techs were coming up with new toys to fool the dog-men, but it was becoming harder and harder.

Hours passed. Daylight returned.

"Nothing," Kel said with disappointment. "Let's bring them home and move. What's the call—do we put out some paw-poppers, or do we save them?" The pursuit deterrents weren't big enough to kill, but that wasn't their purpose. Any doro patrol that found sign and tried to track them would regret it. The paw-poppers held enough plasma charge to burn off a foot. Not even a berserk pack of doros were anxious to follow after one or two of their mates fell howling and whimpering, one limb short of a matched set.

"Save 'em," Poul offered. "I haven't seen any indication they're in the neighborhood. Meadows says it's the same for them. We may want all of them later."

Twice more they repeated the process, patrolling deeper and deeper, slowing their pace as the light fought their concealment. It was as the sun set that a sniffer made contact.

"Got a scent," Hardball said almost musically. "And another."

Kel checked. Hardball's bots lit up on the map over a patch covering a dozen meters. "Tunnel entrance."

"Got one. Two," Wiggy said. Kel's own responded in kind on their crawl into a tiny depression.

"Freeze them and let's go seismic," Kel said. The bots were supposed to freeze on first detection. Regardless, sending out the manual command was the safest action.

"Got pings under my spread," Poul narrated as the icons changed to a pulsing blue. "Unless I miss my guess, they're over a main tunnel. Lots of activity." Poul counted softly. "I've got five distinct hits." At least five firm returns over a spread of fifty meters meant the tunnel was big.

"That's worth calling in a strike by itself," Kel said. "But if we're on so many accesses and tunnels on just this side of the range, there're probably ten times that number of doro deeper. I'd like to map the full complex before we pull out and call in the Boomers."

"If we're gonna do it, might as well do it right," Hardball said.

"Bertie, you copy this?" Kel asked into the ether.

"Yes, CCN Alpha. I'm spinning us up now. On our way." Bertie was with the Talons, monitoring everything. He would've alerted the two crews at word of the sniffers getting a scent, but with the seismic confirmations, he bet the two blackbirds were firing up to lift already.

Kel worked. "Poul, turn 'em loose and let's get ready to move out."

"Roger," Poul returned. "You heard the boss—let's get ready to beat it."

Kel made a decision. "Bertie, this is pick-up one, this is pick-up two," he said, his choice for a primary and alternate LZ for extraction bounced to their ACM as he marked them. Near the river, low and too wet for a tunnel system, both spots were unlikely to have doros waiting.

"Got it." There was a slight pause. "Alpha, Bravo is enemy contact. They're requesting CAS."

"Meadows is in contact," Poul repeated to the rest of the team.

On a side channel Meadows updated them. "We're making for our extraction. We've got a real party over here."

"This is a big one, alright." Hardball's voice came through tiny on the side channel.

"Bertie, what's the TOT?"

"Wait one." Bertie was running the air coordination and terminal guidance from the back of one of the Talons. The ACM was in communication with both the Talons and the bombers. The Navy crew were only mildly shocked when read in to his existence. To the rest of the world, he was just a DOGR. A robotic mule. A mechanical beast of burden. The air crews took to him quickly once they got over taking direction from an AI, fully supportive that he would run the air portion of the operation. If the team trusted him, why shouldn't they? Only an AI could juggle so many balls in mid-air—literally—and so deftly.

"Ten minutes, Alpha." That meant they were heading out at super cruise to reach them.

"See you soon, Bertie. Let's do it." Kel was on his feet, ruck strapped tightly. "Lead us out, Wig."

The bots had swarmed the spots with the strongest scents and tunneled. Once they hit a passage, they would release swarms of micro-drones to explore and track the underground complex. By the time they hit the extraction point, they should have a 3-D map of the tunnel system.

"Dropping paw-poppers." Kel had a handful of the green mines, tossing them onto their trail as he walked backwards. He dropped the last and faced forward. "You next, Hardball. Bottom of this draw. Let 'em have it."

Hardball paused to let Kel pass him. "Gonna git some today."

On the side channel Meadows was calm and brief. "Bertie, I'm going to bring you in for a close run. Guns only, this azimuth."

Even with audio gain enhanced to max, Kel only thought he could hear the guns in the distance. Meadows and Bravo were in a gunfight just a few klicks away, but like light itself, the jungle ate even the noise of it. Wiggy led them fast, nearly at a trot. The gurgle of the river meant they were either farther ahead than he thought, or the course of the river was greatly different from what was on the map. It had to be the latter.

A muffled buzz followed by a sharp squeal came from behind them. Paw-popper. They were definitely being pursued. Another pair of the same noises trailed a moment after.

"That'll change their minds," Hardball laughed.

Poul waited at the river. "Two at a time. Captain and I will hang back. Go."

Kel faced back next to Poul as Wiggy and Hardball hit the water. They were lucky, it was a narrow spot in the river, only a few meters to the other side. "Take a mine," he said. He felt Poul pull at his ruck.

"Your turn." Poul turned a shoulder to him and Kel pulled one from the center pouch. He laid it on a thick tree, hesitated, then released. The anti-personnel mine held.

"Set on motion. Go." Kel clicked his teeth and the arming icon in his bucket turned red.

Hardball and Wiggy were out of the water. Kel waded in a step behind Poul who, after a few strides, lost footing, sunk, and went under. He grabbed what he could find with his free hand and lifted as he plodded forward. He dragged the ruck and Poul with it back to his feet. Hornets buzzed overhead, crashing into the brush beyond with the sound of moist green, too wet to burn. Silent blasters flared back the other direction, crashing sizzles of impacts behind them. Wiggy and Hardball fired automatic streams of white hell to create a ceiling above them. A grenade buzzed in flight and exploded. At the bank, he turned to bring his weapon up and add to the death toll. The exchange of fire ceased.

"Forget it," Wiggy said as he felt a tug from above him. "We got 'em. Come on."

He let his K-17 snap back to his chest as he crawled on hands and knees up the bank.

They ran. Two explosions. Barks so high-pitched, they hurt the ear. The mines.

Bertie's voice was back. "CCN Alpha, prepping extraction site one. How copy?" The Talons must be overhead. Kel checked the map.

"Drop that daisy cutter. Now." He knew the rest of the team heard but couldn't help himself. "Daisy inbound. Get down." The unmistakable staccato hammering of a Talon's main gun rapped out a rhythm in the distance. They were near enough now to hear the other fight. Meadows was no doubt calling it in close as Bravo made for their extraction. Kel was hoping they could avoid the same.

Overhead a repulsor whined, a thousand meters above. That he heard it meant it was well past, and any second... Plasma, white-hot like the corona of a star, shot into the air as the daisy cutter ripped in the distance. A count of two and the rumble reached his chest and ears together. Water sprayed down suddenly from the leaves just like a cloudburst, then ceased.

Hardball sang. "Daisy, I love you. See you in a minute, girl." The daisy cutter burned out a section of the jungle twice as big as what a Talon needed to land, vaporizing trees to dust in a flash. Any doro within a half a grid would be just as cremated.

"Move," Kel said as he got to his feet, his ruck lighter as the diet of grenades, mines, and charge packs had fed him. The last bandolier of grenades came out and he hung it around his chest. "Bertie, we're moving to the extraction point. Beacons are on." He lit his own, joined by three more transponders bouncing on the map. A thousand meters and they should make the newly created clearing.

The jungle above was abruptly chopped apart into a rain of vines and branches. A chug-chug-chug, chug-chug-chug echoed from their left.

"They've got an auto-cannon," Hardball said. "It's working this hill." The slug thrower was very effective in static defense against light armor and dismounted troops. It denied large areas for advance. This one was just making noise.

"Keep pushing," Poul said. "Keep to that low ground."

"Like we've got a choice," Wiggy said. "We've got to take this draw anyway to reach the LZ."

The bottom was soggy and slowed them, the vines crisscrossing no differently than the beams of a prison cell. Wiggy had his torch out, using it like a sword to slice through the largest of them.

"Let me, Wig," Hardball said, igniting the plasma arc of his own torch.

"Thanks." Wiggy's voice was clipped. Strained. He'd led the way the entire patrol, and had mercilessly plowed the way for their extraction run. Kel cursed himself. He should've rotated Wig out sooner. Gabe knew Wiggy would never ask to be spelled from the duty. They broke through into an opening, a natural clearing of sharp jagged grasses its carpet, the sunlight on it too bright.

"Skirting around this," Hardball said as he led them back to thicker jungle and a path around the open area. "We've got a couple hundred meters to go."

"Captain," Bertie said. "You have pursuit at the two-seventy." The jungle was thin enough here the Talon could detect the heat signatures of advancing doros.

"Glad for the assist. How many, how far?"

"Twenty. Other side of the small clearing."

Kel loaded a hell round and sent it arcing between two trees. Plasma streams pushed tiny balls of burning phosphorous into a huge umbrella beneath its airburst.

A pitiable scream rewarded his choice and he launched another one in a new direction.

"Bertie, rake everything west of us. We're moving fast as we can."

"Stand by for rain," Bertie said.

Kel sent one hell grenade after another, as fast as he could, in a wide spread. Poul and Wiggy launched plasma grenades up through the gap of the clearing to arc far away, hoping the explosions found doros in the dark foliage beyond. The blaster cannon of the Talon did as ordered, white burning death tilling the jungle behind them as they pushed on.

Bertie's voice came through strongly. "Captain, the doros are pushing hard to intercept you at the extraction point. They're driving a crew-served weapon platform in that direction. Let us work the problem. I recommend staying put for now."

A crew-served repulsor sled? The doros must have a massive tunnel nearby.

"Roger, Bertie." He checked the map. "Hardball, find us a spot for STABO."

"Got it, boss."

"Bertie," Kel called the ACM back. "Give the pilots the option. We're keeping our transponders lit. Come find us. We're not risking bringing you down for a landing. Get the STABO ready. We'll make a clearing."

"Understood. Pilots say good on STABO. Out." Bertie could hold conversations with multiple humans simultaneously, talk to the other machines of war, work a crew-served blaster on his back, all while at a full-tilt eight-legged run. He must be very busy indeed to not carry on with his usual banter.

"Just checked the tunnel mapping progress, sir," Wiggy said. "We've got a ninety percent map. It's massive."

Kel couldn't pause to look. "Bounce it to Bertie."

Hyper rockets from the Talon screamed over the treetops, and secondary explosions told the tale of targets destroyed. Kel joined in to hack at the jungle. A rocky patch teased them through the tangle, a tiny break in the layered prison.

"Boomers en route from orbit," Bertie said. "They're ready to drop as soon as I give them the clear."

Kel broke into the clearing, the last man. Above them the downforce of the Talon's repulsors beat the green ceiling into a cyclone. The twin-tail black shape blotted out the light that had called to them only a moment before.

"Got it," Poul said. "You first, Hardball."

Kel grabbed a handful of cable and dragged it to Wiggy in front of him, who took it and locked it into his chest ascender.

"Get yourself locked on, Kel!" Poul yelled. "You're the last."

He let his carbine drop to pull slack with both hands and guide the line to his ascender. "I'm on. Bertie, let's go!"

A yellow muzzle flash broke through into the clearing, whizzing past Kel as Hardball was the first to rise off the tiny patch of mossy rocks. Kel's K-17 was back in his hands. He worked the trigger, the reticle in his HUD hovering over the tunnel they'd hacked through the jungle. *Now there's the doro I know and love. They haven't forgotten how to lose their dog-men minds when a kill is getting away.*

Doros flinched, his blasts burning holes through heads and chests. But with autopilots set to "kill," they climbed over the fallen who blocked the narrow passage, frothing and twitching, ignorant they were already dead. Their charge ended as they toppled into the rocky clearing, no longer able to rise. Blasts joined Kel's from above until suddenly he was above the forest, light as the air itself. Sunrays danced over the carpet of jungle. Flying.

"Everyone, sound off," Kel said.

"Never better, boss," Hardball said.

"Good here," came Wiggy.

"Poul?" Kel asked when he heard nothing. He strained to look overhead. Poul was suspended above him. He clicked to team status readout just as a groggy Poul replied.

"S'okay. I'm. Good."

He didn't sound good. His vitals were solid. Nano sealants hadn't deployed to cover a wound. None of his auto-tourniquets had fired.

"Poul, talk to me," Kel asked again.

"Frellin' big ass branch nailed me in the bucket. My ears are ringing. Where's Bravo?"

"Bertie, how's Meadows and Bravo?" They were gaining altitude and speed now, dangling below the Talon as it climbed away.

"They're out and safe on Talon Two, Captain."

"Meadows," Kel entered the Bravo channel. "You good?"

"We are, sir. I guess it's only fair to call it a draw."

"Steaks it is, then," Hardball said. "Hey, look."

They were flying backward below the Talon. Bombs carpeted the plain, raindrops falling in the desert, clouds of white expanding into larger patches by joining the others in the green sea. He cranked his HUD. Three Boomers in an inverted "V" formation lingered at the edge of space.

They peeled off and another trio descended into the stratosphere.

"Never a sight more beautiful—not woman, not flower, not art." Hardball's voice took on that dreamy quality again. "Mine enemy's pain delightful, the succor that feeds my heart."

"What the hell was that?" Wiggy burst out. "Terrible."

"Oba's beard, Gabe," Kel exclaimed. "Keep it inside. Ugh. At least, not until your poetry gets better. Stick with the classics when you feel inspired, man. No more originals, 'kay?"

Sims's voice came from the Bravo channel. "We all heard that, Gabe. I wish I could unhear it." Laughter followed from both team channels.

Hardball's drawl was back. "Jus' glad to be alive, brothers. And pleased as all hell to see that jungle turned to ash. And every dobie with it."

They sailed over waves of green, losing sight of the storm of falling bombs, the jungle swallowing the cataclysm just as it did the record of every past attempt to shape it into something it could never be.

28

The Talons were already loaded to take them to the new FOB in the morning. A thousand klicks north, fresh hunting grounds promised new meat for the grinder. Kel begged off joining the team for dinner. The mess on the base was excellent, but even if it was their last meal prepared by the Black Horse cooks, he wasn't hungry.

The base had grown considerably. They were there from the beginning, when it was little more than green nets shading the tents and habs, resting on red clay the daisy cutters and defoliant poisons exposed beneath the jungle. Flying over the camp, grids of bright orange still poked out between the camouflage, revealing the puerile attempts to bring order where order could not exist. Duracrete had been laid to resist the quagmires that came with the rain but even so, the daily showers turned everything to red mud. It washed over the walks like paint, a grand artist somewhere defying the attempt to civilize even this tiny patch of jungle.

Kel caught a glimpse of himself. He had no idea how much weight he'd lost. He didn't want to know. Days and weeks of patrols—eating next to nothing, constantly moving, never sleeping—had burned off too much. No matter how much he tried to make up for it when back at the compound, it was a losing battle to rebalance the scales between missions. But it didn't matter, because it seemed he no longer needed sleep or food like a mortal man. What he did need, was to move.

He took off at a trot, saw his opening, and unleashed. A burst of speed, a leap, and he was on top of the first storage container. He jumped to the next, a rolling descent to land in a springing crouch, and the race to the next series of expedient obstacles. He and the team did this run whenever they could, but tonight, Kel wanted to do it by himself. The next time he got to run wouldn't be in silkies and lightweight runners; he'd be in armor and fighting the jungle for his life. A group of Black Horse soldiers parted for him.

"Psycho dark ops," he heard one of the basics say as he pelted them with mud, the soles of his feet kicking red clods on their backs as he blasted by.

How in the name of Oba do they know about Dark Ops? Kel fumed. For a covert unit, Legion Dark Ops had somehow become known by name. Was it a group of appointed officers he'd sped by? They had the surliness. A little too clean for being in a combat zone. A little too fat. This part of the base was filled with support troops—comm, maintenance, supply. To Kel it was madness. In the Legion, everyone had two or three jobs, but when it came to time to KTF, underneath every bucket was a warrior. To his thinking, these troops were poorly disciplined and lacked self-respect. No wonder, if the points were their role models. They were a cancer.

But the army was not all populated with playactors, seeded into their ranks by politicians. The Black Horse troops returning from patrol were lean, wiry kids with sharp eyes and quiet confidence. They were soldiers he would recognize in any garb, in any setting, their eyes telling him that they knew the ultimate lessons, the wisdom that could only be learned by carrying the rifle.

"I'll write you up if you do that again, soldier..." A voice trailed off behind him. He laughed.

He followed the curving route matching the perimeter energy fence. He returned the wave from the guys in the airfield guard tower, and kicked harder onto the flat path. A burst of speed to finish the perimeter around the airfield, then a climb up the hill, over, under, and through the maze of habs to return to the main base and the start of a new lap.

What turned into two more, and some work on one of the hanging bars outside the closed mess, ended with guilt instead of accomplishment as his reward. The sun was dipping low and an orange hue was taking over. There was work yet to do, and he'd left it undone. Time for a shower, finish packing his personal items, and look over the movement plan with Braley before a few hours of sleep.

He thought he knew a shortcut to the SIG compound between the city of tents, but found himself unsure as he took a narrow trail between habs, down a set of sand bag and duracrete stairs, crooked and sinking sideways into the hillside, losing the masquerade of permanence from the many rains.

"Lost, Captain?" said a voice from the darkness of the small cul-de-sac he stumbled into. "Turner, isn't it?"

His ambusher sat on a veranda outside a single room hab, a camo net suspended over everything to recreate the same jungle canopy they'd burned away.

"If you're not hurrying off to KTF, come have a seat."

The hair on the back of his neck stood up as he realized it was the Black Horse commander, General Weyer.

Kel had stumbled into the general's quarters. The old warrior was dressed as he was, in silkies. Not exercising, but on his own front porch, just an old man having a moment of peace. You could breathe the moist air a little deeper when the temperature dropped below 40 as the sun left and the jungle choruses of buzzing insects and shrieking birds picked up.

"I beg your pardon, General. I must've gotten turned around. Please, excuse me, sir."

"Turned around, Captain? A recon man like yourself shouldn't admit to that. When I was lost, I'd always say I was investigating an alternative route."

Kel laughed uncomfortably, but when the general pointed to the empty seat next to him, he knew he had no option but to follow the polite order.

"Very kind, sir. I'm..." Kel wasn't sure what small talk to make and found himself at a loss.

The general hoisted a small glass. "Join me."

Kel knew another order when he heard one. He took the offered glass.

"Captain, that was a very impressive piece of work you and your team pulled off."

Kel briefed the combined forces after the mission but made a quick exit, and let Braley and the colonel clean up after him. Turns out they'd located and destroyed a full battalion from the Hunter Maximus Division.

"That find was every recon man's dream. I doubt you're going to locate another hive of doros as impressive up north, but here's hoping. Cheers." He made to clink glasses and Kel obliged.

"Thank you, sir. We got lucky."

He sipped. Kel was curious about the hints the general had dropped. "Sir, were you a recon man yourself?" One of

ANGLES OF ATTACK

the things he'd noticed about the general the first time he
was close to him were the wings of a skysoldier and the
three tiny gold stars. His uniform was covered with many
other insignias from the Republic Army. Just because the
Legion didn't wear skill badges or combat decorations
didn't mean he didn't recognize their significance.

"Once upon a time and a lot of miles ago. It wasn't always Pachyderms depositing us in gravtanks to roll over
rebellious potentates on the edge. I started by leading the
way on the hardest ground there ever was. Trexel Two.
That's where the first gold star on those wings came from."

"I had a commander who fought the Savages on
Trexel Two, sir." Colonel Hartenstein had once told Kel
about Trexel Two, battling one of the last groups of ul-
tra-advanced Savages.

"There were a lot of us on that insane asylum," the
general said. "And plenty of Savages to go around. A lot
of good men died there. When hordes of Savage clones
finally dropped like someone cut their strings, it wasn't a
moment too soon."

The general paused and sipped. When Kel didn't
speak, he went on. "They're out there still. They're not
gone. This is my last war, but someday you'll be fighting
them again."

"Retirement, sir?" Kel felt bold enough to ask.

"Forty-four years, and most all of it war, young captain. From two decades of Savages to what's been little
more than spanking one bad baby after another for the
House of Reason, it's been a privilege. But there's an end
to everything."

Kel felt the words hit him. The end to his life in Dark
Ops was facing him like the general's retirement.

"What's next, sir? Where to?"

The general continued as though he hadn't heard the question. "Where're you from, Turner? Not stationed. I know where that is. Where did you grow up in this big spinning bowl of stars we call a galaxy?"

Kel told him.

"They say the murria are the most beautiful species in the known galaxy. That true?"

"That's what they say, sir. I've only seen them once, on vacation as a kid. They keep to themselves in the equatorial part of Pthalo. We lived too far north to see them otherwise. They say the tourist trade's driven them farther and farther out."

"I've never been there," the general said, almost sadly. "No Savages or blaster-toting malcontents to crush, so no reason I would have. But I always thought I'd go there with Caity someday. We talked about it, she and I."

Kel understood. He guessed which of the two paths his wife had taken from him.

"She passed, sir?"

He sipped. "I'm grateful. I was there with her at the end, not in some far-flung cesspool doing the impossible for the ungrateful. But had I been, she would've understood. She was one in a billion."

Kel felt the pain for him. The pain the general didn't seem to express. He imagined the general's wife—always there for him, waiting, supporting, longing for an end to his absence, but understanding why he was gone. Eventually the separation became normal. And when the stranger who was her husband returned, he was unable to share why he was the distant man he was. She waited for the mythical day when he would dedicate his life to just her, his obligation to the Republic no longer his first priority. The promises he made, held in abeyance as the decades built, nearer and nearer to being fulfilled. *The next assignment will be better. We'll be together. And we'll finally plan our retirement. It'll be like that holo. A cottage overlooking the beach. A small garden. Mornings with the grandkids, playing in the surf. No more traveling.* Her death robbed him of his chance to make it up to her for a lifetime of neglect. Kel had to know.

"How did you make it work, sir? Being apart so much of the time?"

Mid-sip, the general glanced at him sideways. "Looking for a blueprint to follow for marital success? Hitched yet, or looking to be? I hope you know the old saw. A captain may marry. A major *should* marry."

Kel shrugged. "No immediate prospects, sir." He only revealed a partial truth about himself.

"It's all up to her, whoever she may be. A marriage will last or wither depending on her. I just got lucky, because if it were up to me, I would've ruined it within a few years. It was my wife who made our family what it was."

"Children, sir?"

"Three. Grown and gone."

"Any follow in your footsteps, sir?"

"Refill," the general ordered, not offered. "No. My absences didn't inspire them to want to be like me. They took saner paths. Only my daughter still speaks to me." Kel didn't want to know more. Here, there was more pain.

"Excuse me, General. I just wanted to drop this by."

Kel startled at the appearance of the major. The faint clicks of his prosthetics helped Kel recognize him as the briefer from the first joint planning after the invasion of Psydon.

"Major Grantham, meet our friend from the Legion, Captain Turner."

Kel rose to shake hands.

"Don," he said taking his hand.

"Kel."

"Won't you join us, Don? We're solving a lot of the galaxy's problems before Captain Turner and his team go north tomorrow."

"Very kind, sir, but miles to go and all that. Good meeting you, Kel. Best of luck."

"You, too, Don." The major strode away, the slight oddity to his gait more noticeable as he ascended the crooked stairs one at a time.

"Major Grantham lost both legs, sir?"

"He did. He was a newly minted captain, set to take a company, when the accident happened. Repulsor on a Pachyderm ramp malfunctioned and crushed him," the general explained the unasked question of how the major had come to be crippled. "He was pulling a soldier out of harm's way. Would've smashed the kid flatter than a row of atoms. Took Grantham's legs. Close to killed him."

Noncombat injuries and deaths were a part of military life. Even in what a civilian would consider peacetime, those who wore the uniform still died or were maimed. It was an inevitable truth in a life spent taming the machines of war.

"He failed regen twice. Something about a gene the medtechs couldn't suppress. So, after a year of pain and suffering, he got his prosthetics and we had him back on duty in a month. Not a moment too soon. I've known him since he was fresh out of the academy. Always a smile, always the first to volunteer, always the last to rest. He could've been one of your breed, but he grew up loving tanks.

"One time, much to his embarrassment, his mother told us she thought something was wrong with her son. Growing up, he built model after model of Magnus I, II, and III until there was no room left on his shelves. His first speeder, he modded the console to look like a Magnus IV driver compartment. Tell me a fanatic like that wouldn't have been at home in your tribe?"

Kel didn't disagree, but outsiders didn't understand. They weren't fanatics. But they were a tribe.

"You see, the accident crushed more than his legs. Once you've been a soldier for more than seven years, you'll never be worth a damn at anything else. You won't tolerate the company of lesser men. To turn him out would've killed him. But we brought him back. Even outside of a tank, he found purpose in wearing the uniform. I wanted him here with his Black Horse family, where we could help him. He'll never hold command, but an intelligence officer, I've never seen finer."

"I didn't know the Army allowed double amputees to remain serving." It was different in the Legion.

"They don't," the general said. "But I forced them to make an exemption. I may have been passed over for more stars, but that doesn't mean I don't have the ears of those who do. Or, maybe it's just because I know where the bodies are buried. I'd prefer to think they saw what I saw in Major Grantham. He's one of our sons who deserved the chance to prove he could do the job. And he has."

The general corked the bottle. "You see, my sons and daughters wear the Black Horse. And I've raised many." He checked his chrono. "It's getting late, Captain." He held the data chip up to the moonlight. "I don't want to disappoint Major Grantham by not having digested this fully before our 0500 meeting. From what we know of the doro order of battle, we have at least three full divisions unaccounted for. Do you think you'll find them north?"

Kel rose with him. "The sniffers aren't conclusive. It's the last region on the continent we haven't scoured on foot. Those infiltrator squads are coming from somewhere." The capital was mostly quiet, but small doro groups had attacked installations and were doing so with increasing frequency. Soil, contaminants in their GI tracts, pollen on their uniforms, all indicated they'd traveled to Caza-Han from well out of the area.

The general stretched. "We've been lucky in Sector A1. Your 131st and 187th have been working triple time to help the Green Knights and the Granite Division find those hidden artillery batteries. We didn't have that to contend with. If there's a pipeline of doros coming from up north and infiltrating south to reignite the war in the capital, we need to know. The Black Horse is ready to be the hammer to your anvil." The general extended his hand.

Kel took it. He mumbled a weak thanks, lightheaded from the exertion and the drink, maybe still caught at a loss for words by the surprising encounter. He was tracing his way out of the maze and back up the stairs when the words caught him, causing him to falter. They were faint, but he heard them. They carved ripples in the tissues of his heart that warmed him the rest of his life, brought to mind whenever he saw a grizzled, older man in passing.

"I hope you find your Caity someday, my son."

29

"They're not doro," Bigg said. "The Rafeer think they're better. Just like the doro think the Rafeer are inferior."

"I don't see a diff," Hardball said. "They're bigger than the average doro," he said as one of the gray-furred Rafeer strutted past paying them no mind, spear over shoulder, loincloth flapping in the slight breeze. It was as though the dog-man saw armored humans every day. Their presence was too insignificant to cause distraction from where his clan mates gathered to butcher one of the cappy that Meadows was so fond of roasting. "But they're still dog-men."

The new camp was carved out of the jungle more carefully than the base of operations they'd shared with the Black Horse. A kill zone was cut around the camp perimeter, and an LZ just big enough for two Talons sat within the compound, making it the only other spot cleared out of the surrounding jungle. Unless viewed from the edge of the clearing or directly overhead, their new forward operating base was well concealed. Dens burrowed deep beneath the roots of trees held pups and nursing mothers. Huts thatched with bushy living limbs were all but invisible. Towers and sandbagged bunkers ringed the camp, trees and vines thick around them.

Barnett chuckled. They hadn't seen much of Nether Ops since the decapitation strike on Rask and his pack mates. "Don't let them hear you say they look like doros,

Hardball. We only found out a short while ago that the doro name for them means 'jungle barbarian.' As close as we can translate, Rafeer means 'noble ones' in their own language. Or, 'the Nobles.'" The dog-men didn't look too noble squatting around the carcass, panting and growling as they carved at the rodent with flint knives.

Braley was upbeat. "However they see themselves, they practically begged to help once we told them we're here to make war on the doro. This is their territory, and they don't look too kindly on the dog-men moving in."

The "three Bs" of Barnett, Braley, and Bigg had worked together to make contact with the Rafeer and leverage the tension between them and the comparatively urbanized doro. The large dog-men lived in the remotest jungle, far away from the cities and ranches of their civilized cousins.

"They track better than our bots," Bigg said. "The first patrol, they led us right to a doro encampment like they were following a route map. Three days out, they got us to within a dozen meters of a tunnel entrance before the bots even caught a sniff of it. Got us back out again without a trace. Whereas we've been littering the planet with bots and sensors with not much to show for it, a few days after making their acquaintance, the Rafeer got us a lead on the nearest doro anthill for your first op. The Rafeer are as eager to get the doro out of their hunting grounds as the zhee are to purge the unclean."

"For the promise of blasters and some help, they're willing to commit to the cause," Braley added.

"And plenty of Republic credits," Barnett clarified. "They're not so isolated in their jungle they don't comprehend the utility of a fat bank account."

"All sounds like a very pragmatic minority for us to exploit," Kel summarized.

Poul sighed. "Now we have to see what kind of soldiers they'll make."

Meadows eyed the breakup of the butchering party. Cappy meat swung from poles as the Rafeer carried it off to different directions around the camp. "Something tells me they're going to do just fine."

Kel passed a group of Rafeer leaving the med station. JP had been implanting translators in their new troops a few at a time, fitting voders to those that were wary of the implants. Kel greeted the first one he passed. "Good day to hunt."

"Good day to kill," the Rafeer said to him in his own language of growls, showing a mouth full of teeth in response.

He found JP inside the small hut, crouched over a grav container. "How goes it?"

"Surprisingly well," JP said as he opened another box of the communication devices. "I expected more resistance, but once I got the first few implanted, most of them want one over a voder. I might run out of them at this rate."

"Tell Barnett. He'll get us another shipment on the next run." Nether Ops had been a deep well of money and gadgets on this latest endeavor. Barnett built a good relationship with the pack elders by delivering on every promise, save their request for "big forest stone walkers." The Rafeer knew of tanks, and thought they'd be a dandy thing to have against the doros. Kel and Barnett had to explain that the tanks wouldn't operate well in the thick jungle, but won them over from their initial disappointment with armor cut to fit their peaked chests. The young omega Rafeer had not yet tired of sparring, yelping delightedly with each deflected spear tip that glanced off the smooth surface.

They weren't tech savvy, but nonetheless took to blasters like schoolboys to candy. The rifles Barnett scored for the Rafeer were better than the blasters he sold to the doro. "I've been saving these for just such an opportunity. Luckily my stash in Caza-Han didn't get flattened." N-16s, anthropometry modified for the Psydon residents. Sims, Wiggy, Hardball, and Woobie took squads to the range to practice what they'd taught them in camp. It was a process, making the Rafeer believers that aimed fire was better than blasts sprayed indiscriminately like a leg lifted against a tree. Barnett had the foresight to have the export quality blasters limited to semi-automatic mode only, thank Oba!

But testing themselves against JP had been their greatest joy. In no small part he'd gained their trust early by his tireless bouts during pack PT. The Rafeer fought well, but against JP, stripped to silks, he flung them around like toys. On two legs or four, no attacker could find advantage. Surrounded by the pack, JP sent attackers flying and limping away. What the Rafeer didn't know: JP was holding back. If he hadn't, none would have risen again.

JP was the master of the two-centimeter punch. Kel knew the trick, but their medic took it to a new level. From a finger's breadth away, JP could punch from a standstill and crack one of the new armor shells in half without harming the wearer. The first time he demonstrated his controlled power, ears folded down and whimpers hummed. The Rafeer had thought the plates made them all but invincible.

"This armor will deflect a blast and save your life, but don't forget, a trained warrior can defeat even the best tech when his mind and body are united in a goal." JP's bark set off the chain reaction. Ears stood straight and howls filled the air.

As effective a lesson as it was, Kel had to insist the gimmick had been used more than enough, as the piles of fractured nano tubule plates piled up. They had hundreds of them, but enough was enough.

"Find me in the op longhouse when you're done," Kel told him. "Woobie, Hardball, you, and I will take the patrol. I want to be giving our warning order after evening meal, patrol order by 2100, rehearsals done and ready to move by 2300."

"You got it, boss. First combat patrol with the I-squared is always the most dangerous graduation exercise of any school in the galaxy, isn't it?"

Woobie and Hardball were out right now with the squad they'd selected for the mission, practicing immediate action drills for the thousandth time. The Rafeer were naturals in the jungle, demonstrating some of the best habits of a hunter without needing to be shown. But learning how to fight against a heavily armed opponent trying to kill you back, was a skill they had not yet mastered.

"But for the professor, the grading is always simple, JP. KTF or die."

Pack alphas Lupa and Bruto stood at the break in the thorn barriers, sniffing each of the squad as they passed through the camp exit. Kynar was their oldest, and she would lead the first patrol with the humans.

"Meat for the pack," Lupa growled to her pup.

"The pack needs meat for strength," Kynar growled back.

"Are the Rafeer cannibals?" Woobie asked over L-comm. "We're not going after cappy or dreex. They're not going to *eat* the doro we nab, are they?"

"I think it's a standard farewell, but I guess we'll find out," Hardball answered. "I haven't seen any shrunken doro heads or pelts since we've been here."

JP had the answer. "Those necklaces you see Lupa, Bruto, and some of the older betas wearing? Those shriveled-up mushroom things on a string? I checked. Those are the sensitive bits carved off another canus hominis."

"They cut off the doro wedding tackle post-battle?" Woobie gulped.

"I've already had the talk with Lupa and Bruto," Kel said. "Whoever we nab gets sent off to Caza-Han intact. There'll be time for trophies later."

The two senior sergeants were there to see them off.

"We're running patrols on a regular rotation," Poul said. "By the time you get back, we should have the full company ready to field." Wiggy and Sims would start training the mortar section tomorrow. Some of the Rafeer had an aptitude for math and were naturals.

Meadows had less of a difficult time with Poul as the senior CCN sergeant than Kel had anticipated. He'd taken it on himself to spend the most time with the Rafeer recruits, even bunking with them in one of the longhouses most nights. "These pups are coming along fine, sir. We'll be ready." Meadows had become something of a father to the young omegas of the pack, teaching them not just soldiery, but his own field culinary arts as well. The Rafeer didn't mind cooked meat, they just preferred it raw.

Kel traded chest thumps with the Twelve team sergeant. "Next one's yours, Top. We'll be back in seven days. I'll make contact twice daily. Holler if there's trouble. Saddle up," he said to his patrol. "I want to be klicks away by the time the sun rises."

The second day before moving into a patrol base, Kel ordered the Rafeer to suit up. Ears lay down as the team helped their Rafeer work into the mesh coveralls. Pulling the cowl over her head, Kel helped Kynar adjust her armor again.

She complained, "It is unnatural to cover ourselves."

"The nanites in the mesh will neutralize your scent. The doro won't have a clue we've been all over their den. They'll have to get very lucky on a long-range patrol to find your scent and trace it back to the camp."

The Rafeer, like the doros, could travel for two days without water. When they drank in excess, it was for the purpose of marking territory. The Rafeer hadn't swallowed a drop in a day and wouldn't be leaving any spoor.

"If you say so, Chieftain," Kynar replied. "But it would be welcome to see your airpower crush the smooth-bellies if they moved to mass on the camp." The jungle around the FOB was ringed for kilometers with sniffers and bots, and scoured by patrols.

"Better we rain steel on them in their own dens than in our front yard, Kynar."

"Agreed."

"Did you find one?" Hardball asked the pair of returning omegas. The twitching basket answered his question.

"A big one," Moon-Hunter said, hoisting the woven ball as the creature tested its cage, grumbles and sputters of frustration pouring out every so often until it gave up and went limp.

"And this will work?" JP asked with doubt. It seemed unlikely, but the Rafeer had been confident.

Pathfinder showed teeth. "We trap them all the time with the scent of the female in season. They'll burrow through stone to reach her."

Woobie shrugged. "Time to find out."

The two omegas crawled out of the perimeter. Kel had a bot positioned high in a tree. The team shared a good view of the grassy field from their hidden positions. Little disturbance registered in the tops of the swaying grass as Moon-Hunter and Pathfinder crept to the buried conduit. It wasn't long before the current of movement in the tall grass traced their return back to the thick jungle.

"Now, we wait," Kel said.

The sun was high when the first doro appeared at the edge of the clearing.

"Here they come," Kel said. "Don't shoot until I say, Kynar."

"Yes, Chieftain. We will wait."

Three uniformed doro paused in the clearing. One held a datalink and waved it back and forth over the ground. He pointed and sniffed his way ahead, testing the air as he went. The other two followed, weapons slung on backs, sniffing the air as well.

"Think they smell us?" Poul asked.

"Not a chance," Hardball said. "They're on a stroll, not a hunt. Look how they're moving. Not a bit of concern on their little dog-men snouts."

The doro holding the link stopped in the middle of the clearing. It dropped beneath the grass onto all fours, then stood on hind legs, holding up the crispy devil-digger for the others to see. Fried to a char, it had chewed through the conduit to reach the other side where the scent of its desire had been buried. The doro with the pistol on his belt put hands on hips.

Kel had their target. "Kynar, kill the other two. That's the one we want."

Silent bolts flew from the jungle. The dull thuds of impact were accompanied by puffs of burned flesh as the two doro yelped and dropped. The middle dog-man froze in surprise. He'd been sent out to investigate why one of the land lines between dens had gone dead. Getting ambushed by primitives had not been part of the day's planned activities. Pathfinder and Moon-Hunter charged on all fours. They slammed into the startled doro at full speed, toppling him effortlessly. Moon-Hunter had the stunner out and finished him off with a sharp electric pulse.

"Go," Kel ordered as they rose from the jungle and raced into the glade.

The three doro were tied to poles and carried away. Kynar and Kel supervised the squad tidying the scene. As if on cue, the afternoon rain started, sure to wash away what few traces they may have left.

"Best route to put us out of here with some haste, Woobie." The kidnapping was smooth. Escaping with their intelligence prize was another matter. They took a different course away from the ambush site.

They didn't stop until the next day when Hardball held them up. "Sir, come take a look at this."

Moon-Hunter and Kynar had snouts low to the ground. They sniffed at what appeared to be the edge of a trail. Kel eased forward.

"What do you think, Gabe?"

"We didn't cross anything this size on the way in." The trail was fully a legionnaire's shoulder-width across. A veritable speeder highway in the jungle.

"Any recent activity?"

Kynar's hackles raised with her low growl. "Smooth-bellies passed here three days ago."

"Can you tell how many?"

Moon-Hunter bared teeth. "Many scents. Perhaps a dozen."

"We cross here," Kel said. "Single file. Kynar and I will come last." He removed his ruck and dug to the bottom. He found the square vial he knew he'd remembered to stuff in the padded pocket.

"What is that for, Chieftain?" Kynar had been watching him as he searched the ruck. The Rafeer went into the jungle with only a spear. Teaching them to carry more charge packs and ammunition than they thought they might ever need was like teaching a fish to bring a raincoat. The first time they ran out of firepower though, Kel knew they'd need no more convincing.

"This," Kel said holding up the vial of gray powder. "Is taggant. After we sweep our tracks, I'm going to dust this on the trail. Anyone passing over this will leave a radioactive path we can see from orbit. It'll be like they were dragging a can of paint behind them wherever they go."

"What about dreex or stone-gizzards?"

"We'll see anything that comes in contact with it, even animals. But animals aren't going all the way to Caza-Han. I'm thinking we just stumbled across the military pipeline that's carrying doro fighters south." He sprinkled. "Let's prove it."

Another half day of slower walking, trading off the three poles between them, and Kel thought they'd come far enough. "Let's hold up and take care of our passengers."

JP had dosed the captured doro whenever he stirred, but they were ready to let him come around and walk the rest of the way. Without waiting to be told, the Rafeer stripped the two dead doro and deposited them into the jungle.

"Should we bury them?" Hardball asked.

Kynar's tongue poked between her teeth as she panted. "Nothing goes to waste in the jungle. They'll be in some beast's offal by morning."

"As for you, bare-belly," Moon-Hunter taunted, "if you don't want to be a meal for the carrion-beetles, you'll walk."

The captured doro made a whimper, the cords around its snout digging into the dark fur.

Kel hastened the patrol. "Get that scent suit and the paw covers on him and let's get moving. We want this to stay a mystery for the doro as long as possible. They've almost certainly sent out a patrol by now to find the missing repair detail. No pursuit deterrents, guys. Save the paw-poppers in case we make contact. We want the doro to think their cable tenders just disappeared."

"The Soul-Eater got them!" Moon-Hunter made the gagging bark of a laugh.

"Come to take the weak to hell," Pathfinder joined him in the raspy hack. "Even the bare-bellies understand what it means when the evil spirits eat you whole. They found you unworthy to continue the hunt. That's a doro fate, for sure."

"What will your people do with him?" Kynar asked.

"They'll interrogate him. They have drugs and brain scans to make him spill all he knows."

Kynar scoffed. "Our fires could make him talk just as fully for less trouble."

"Barnett's waiting, anxious to take your prisoner," Poul said over L-comm at the next contact. "See you tomorrow. Oh, and be expecting a party when you get back. Bruto says it's customary after a successful hunt."

"You can disabuse them of the notion that it's time to celebrate. All patrols stay out. If the doro tracked us, they'll come for us soon. We need our eyes and ears pushed out for warning. Parties come later. You and I, we're getting an op order together as soon as I get back to check out the trail we found. I'm betting we stumbled on where the trouble in the capital is coming from."

"Roger. Lupa and Bruto will see things clearly. They're a pretty savvy pair. I've seen sector commanders with less tactical knowledge. But we're not going to be able to put this off forever. You're not going to believe what they expect us to do."

30

Kel popped his lid. The humid air washed over him like stepping into a steam bath. He sucked deeply, the smell of decaying jungle filling his senses. After a nonstop week in armor without so much as a single breath of unrecycled air, it was glorious.

"Here you go, Barnett," JP said, swiping the ener-chain codes to their prisoner's new keepers. Four basics surrounded the hooded doro and whisked him away to the waiting Talon. "Be seeing you." He gave a friendly salute to the Nether-leej before turning back to Kel. "Sir, anything else?"

Kel scratched his scalp. Maybe there was time to pass a depilatory beam over his head. A sonic fresher would be great right now. He'd have to settle for a bucket of rainwater. "No, JP. Good job, man. We better check in with Poul." Save for Poul, the rest of the team were out leading patrols in anticipation of a doro probe. But it was the image of the trail that burned in his mind. The wide path, the tracks, the drag marks. A haircut and a scrub might have to wait.

Barnett crowded close to Kel. "I'll be delivering your doro and then I'm off to check on some other things. I'll get the full interrogation results and be back when I can. I'm interested in this trail you found."

"Me, too." He was tired and didn't feel like a long conversation. He was planning. At a minimum, there'd be time for a real meal before he went back out. Yes, he'd make time. His body needed real fuel. And he needed to keep his body working to get him to his next mission. *He* had to care for the machine so it didn't break down. Comfort, rest, sleep. Those things didn't matter. Getting back out there is what mattered. "I want to know what you get out of him. Nether and RI won't be going on the ground. We will. Don't even think about keeping us out of the loop."

Kel's accusation hung heavy, no differently than the fetid odor of rot.

Like the respite that came with the rains to clear the air, Barnett tried to reassure him. "That's why I said I'll be back. *Personally.* Still don't trust us, huh?"

Kel had reason, but knew he'd expressed himself badly to an old friend. "Sorry, Lev. Been a long week, you know?"

"You know I do. Gotta go. KTF, Kel."

Kel forced a grin. "You too."

"You don't have to be the one to go, you know," Poul said. He'd insisted Kel strip out of armor and get a meal. He paused between bites.

"Yeah. I do."

"Do you think Bigg would send you out like this? You look like sket, man."

Kel was already prepared to topple the stack of tiles his best friend built in a logical argument intended to get him to ease back and let Poul take out a patrol alone.

"Yup. And he wouldn't have had to ask any of us to go, or tell us how important it was. Because being slack might mean the lives of some young basics and even leejes down south. Time is critical. They're depending on us. So, it's gotta be me. That's how it is." He disregarded Poul's retort as he dug into the plate of meats and starches. He didn't know what any of it was. It didn't matter. It had a flavor. Pungent. Bitter. Strange. But much better than any vanilla-tinged protein paste.

"Well, we don't have to go right this minute. In fact, I think we're better off heading out late tonight. We've got movement on the taggants you dropped. I'm cooking something up. See what you think about where this trail is heading." Poul pushed out a new holo.

Glad the issue was settled without further discussion, Kel sat cross-legged on his mat, belly full, resisting every call to lie flat. The taggant had already produced results. The red trace meandered through the green, continuously south. Predators hunted in ranges. Routes deviated to follow the scent of prey. No animal traveled so directly and purposefully in a direction, not even when migrating. He didn't need the analyzer to tell him it was evidence of a sentient.

"I'm impressed. The doros are making good time. Thirty klicks a day is practically flying through this jungle."

Two flashing icons appeared in the corner of the holo. He moved to open them, then came fully alert, the routine response to the alerts squelched, their meaning now realized in his conscious mind. Yes, he was fully alert, the fatigue of the jungle gone as sure as if he'd taken a stim-tab. The flashing message icons meant the basics had opened up mail traffic; security was no longer a concern.

Hypercomm traffic was good for troop morale. He remembered what it was like as a young leej stationed somewhere in the far galaxy, to return from a patrol or guard to see the flashing icon waiting for him. A message from his mom. A book he'd ordered. An episode of one of his corny historical dramas. For a young troop it was small things like that which let one know there was a universe that still spun. People in it doing normal things. And maybe somewhere, someone who cared that you were in the stasis of service. The military a part of that galaxy which operated by different rules than the rest of existence. A message from someone out there who knew you as more than a last name or a number. And military life was foreign, yet exciting to them. And you tried to explain it. Maybe you shared the drudgery, or the occasional moment of panic and excitement when the two-way shooting range started. Maybe you didn't, and spared them those details, like Kel had with his mom. He didn't have to spare it for his dad. He already knew.

For him, that changed after his folks died. He stopped using the address. Because the only family he had left was his tribe. And they were right beside him.

Kel didn't get messages. Ever. He didn't hypercomm with anyone. There were only a handful of people who even knew the address. But he'd sent one of those people a message months ago. Months ago, when he'd been different. Not who he was now. Months ago, he'd felt a hole inside him. Now he couldn't remember what he'd been feeling when he composed that message. Why he'd done so. The hole that made him write that plea was now filled by something else. Something more important. Or was it? Was that why he had to take this patrol? Was it for a reason besides saving lives? Was he pushing himself to keep that hole from opening up again? His heart twisted in his chest as he knew who the reply must be from.

"Open them, man. You know who it's from." Poul was still in the longhouse.

Kel checked without opening the messages themselves. One of the messages was routed from a relay in the core, nearest Andalore. The message had been sent to the message box months ago, waiting for Kel to find it. He only knew one person on Andalore. Were they sweetening the deal to entice him away? Nothing could be sweeter than what he was doing now. He gave it no more thought.

The next was routed through dozens of relays, its origin point on the other side of the galaxy, as deep in the edge as you could get. It had taken weeks from transmission until it arrived in his box, to sit like a booby trap waiting to be sprung. His heart raced again. He closed the alerts.

"Kel! Open it!" Poul urged.

Now, Kel remembered who he had been before Psydon. What he had felt. He didn't like it. "No. It's not the right time."

Poul opened his mouth to protest, thought better of it, and closed it. Before either had to address the awkwardness, Kel focused. "Tell me what you've got cooking up."

Only a true friend knew where another's weakness lay and, rather than making the rent in the wall of his defense bigger, brought stone and mortar to repair it. Poul was that true friend. The one who would distract the Savage horde away from the faltering flank. Kel remembered General Weyer positing he was respected by his superiors because he knew where the bodies were buried. What Kel and Poul knew about each other wasn't defined by knowing each other's faults or failings, but by knowing each other's strengths.

"You've just run one successful snatch. Time for another. We know where this trail is headed." Poul pointed to the yellow squiggle that predicted the course of the trail below the red course traced by the taggant. "This spot."

He highlighted a region along the predicted path that was dense with sniffers and bots but that had no purple flashes indicating evidence of doro encampments. "We drop in here ahead of the group moving down the trail now, and prepare a welcome. I'm off to coordinate with Braley and lay-on one of the Talons. The best time to do this is tonight."

Kel considered. A quick trip by Talon to the drop-off point. A day on the ground to find the trail. Between the taggants working so well and the number of sniffers and bots they could retask to within a narrow travel corridor, it should be the easiest ambush they'd ever planned.

"JP goes with us. Woobie and Hardball stay back and run base security."

"Sure thing. They'll be disappointed, but I'll sell it to them how if the FOB gets hit while we're all gone, they'll get more kills than the rest of us combined when they call in the airstrikes."

Kel laughed. "That's just good leej psychology there."

"Get some sleep, Kel. I'll wake you in plenty of time for the patrol order. I'm running this one. You're just a patrol member. Got me?"

"Yes, Top." He knew when to admit partial defeat. "Thanks, brother."

"Don't mention it. This is going to be great."

Kel stretched out. He was fearful he would lie awake, trying to do the impossible. You couldn't tell your mind to not think about something. It was like starting a spark in a grassy field, dry and brittle from long drought. Soon, the flames of her face would burn his mind. Before he caught fire, the mercy of his snores shook the thatched roof.

A hunter's moon disappeared behind the clouds as the Talon dropped low to skim over the treetops. The pilot gave the time warning and soon the ramp lowered to reveal the night and the black of the jungle below as it sped away beneath them. The hum through the deck plating changed, the repulsor oscillations becoming slower and weaker as their forward motion ceased and they dropped below the treetops. "Touchdown," the crew chief said to coincide with Kel hopping off. He trotted out of the clearing and into the forest, the swish of grasses and footfalls at his sides telling him he was not alone as he pushed off the LZ.

The Talon was above them again, far yet near, an obedient attack dog waiting for the command to bite. When the jungle failed to explode in blaster fire, Kel sent the RTB to the pilot. "Let's do it," Poul said, and pointed. Moon-Hunter and Pathfinder moved ahead, Poul taking a spot behind. Kel was content to bring up the rear as he waited for JP and the rest of their patrol to fall in.

They kept dark, content to navigate with the Rafeer leading them through the barriers of living curtains. Their sense of smell was better warning than the best that sight could offer in this environment. Kel had little to do but follow the bobbing shape of Rafeer in front of him, so diverted some attention to the map plot. The yellow course of the trail projected along a contour line similar to what the red part of the known trail mapped many kilometers away. The Trantchatka Range, little more than a series of gentle ridges, separated the trail from the valley and river of the same name a hundred kilometers away. Sniffers were sending out a continuous ping of contacts. The spread indicated it was more than just a few doro on the trail. The program estimated fifty separate treads. Divided by two or four, it meant a bountiful harvest was on its way to them. As the approaching doros got closer, they'd have images from the bots and know for sure.

After six hours and a hint of early twilight, Poul halted them. "Pathfinder thinks the trail's ahead." A thick stand of purple flowering stalks was close, and he moved to place the densest grouping between them and where he imagined the trail led, in the unlikely case he was somehow visible. "It's as wide as a sofa and someone's cleared it recently. There's cuttings and burn marks everywhere."

"See," Kel offered. "Like I said. It's a kelhorned super-highway in the jungle."

"I didn't doubt you," Poul assured. "But until you see it for yourself, it's hard to imagine. Let's get laid in."

The sun set when the bots sent the first image. The doro were not unskilled nor oblivious to ambush. A pair of dog-men led, blasters across their chests, sniffing as they went. After a long interval, the main party appeared. Doro after doro guided a train of repulsor lift beds laden with crates, insects carrying crumbs to the nest. Blasters slung on backs, unarmored, this was a supply detail, not an assault force. They moved with alacrity and minimal security.

Poul summed it up. "These doros are moving out like they're not afraid of meeting resistance. I say we disabuse them of that assumption from now on. JP, you and your guys set?"

JP was north of them with a party of four Rafeer. "Set. This is going to be fun. The lead element is passing us now."

Kel lay next to Kynar and her pack mates. Poul relented without much protest and let Kel take the primary kill zone. Blasters were set on wide dispersion. At the range of a few meters, it wouldn't take much of a charge to roast the kill zone with each burst. Despite everything that could go wrong, every calamity that could befall them, Kel felt like giggling. It was the most ridiculous of emotions to suppress. His nervous energy made every sense tingle. His body ached to spring to life. Ambushes were the ultimate practical joke. He said a prayer. *Oba, for what we are about to receive, make us truly grateful.* He knew he was being blasphemous. There'd be time for sincere penitence later.

Many minutes passed and his eagerness dissipated, leaving him with only the grit to kill without remorse. The thrill would return afterward—when the job was well done, the bodies stacked in the kill zone, the Talon returning to take them home. It would be laughs and the high of the victory. He hoped it would be. All thoughts of what would come later left him. Kel's heart stopped as the plodding tramps of the lead dog-men ceased in front of them.

"Hold up," one said aloud. A slobbering lap of water from a canteen poured down a throat. A sniff. Two. The doro was just to their front, obscured by the jungle.

Kel whispered into L-comm, a habit impossible to break no matter how impregnable the buckets were to escaping sound. "Sket. They're on us."

"No," Poul said. "I see them on the trail bot. They're not onto you. Stay still."

The stream of urine splashed through the leaves. Kynar next to him squinted tightly until the rain ceased.

"You done?" another voice across the trail said. "We've got a day to reach the way station."

"I'm going to eat my weight in dreex when we do," the other said. The footfalls started anew.

"Headed your way, Poul," Kel told his friend farther down the trail. It wouldn't be long. He held up a single finger to Kynar, who nodded in return, white teeth so bright Kel feared they could betray their presence. He knew what she was thinking. It was going to be a sweet payback for the unknowing disrespect she'd just been shown.

The main body of the train was on the trail, the impacts of so many paws practically shaking the ground as they passed. It had to be now.

JP's voice came to them, his excitement undisguised. "I've got the trailing element in sight. Don't wait on us. Hit them."

Kel pulled the wire quickly three times in a row. The blaster team to his left opened up, the medium gun working on full auto, as was the gun to his right. He clicked teeth and thousands of needles from the beehive mines detonated as one long snake up and down the trail. Kel's K-17 tore through the greenery to his front, the impacts kicked up a rain of mud ahead. A paw-popper exploded somewhere a distance away. A doro tripped into one they'd tossed across the trail, its escape from the kill zone punished.

"Do it, Kynar," he said aloud. She blew a whistle. Kel couldn't hear the high register of the whistle, but its effect was obvious. The Rafeer rose from the jungle in response and moved across the kill zone, blasters singeing fur on the ground ahead of them as they marched forward.

"Find me a live one!" Kel yelled. He switched to L-comm. "JP, talk to me."

"Got one bound and gagged, sir," JP said. "I hit the other one too hard, I guess. Snapped his neck. They're not as tough as they look. I'm still figuring it out. Sorry, sir. We've got security set up the trail. Take your time."

"No sweat. Poul, talk to me."

"No one made it out alive. We're clean."

Kel sent the safe signal to all the paw-poppers. He'd turn it on again after they placed new ones for the investigating doros to find after they were long gone. "Keep it up while we sweep the kill zone. Out," Kel said. "Kynar, where you at?"

Kynar appeared from behind a repulsor bed, holding a knife and a bloody memento.

"Trophies later, Kynar. Find me any live doro." He prodded the assistant gunner, Swiftleg. "Come with me."

The young Rafeer smiled and put his own knife away before placing his prize into his waist sack. His Rafeer helper understood and took the opposite end of an up-ended crate to right it. Kel popped the cover with his knife, the edge of the vibro-blade humming as it tore into the crevice. He tore the lid off. Blasters and charge packs. "Poul, make your way here and help me rig these crates of rifles."

"Rog. Moving."

"We found two, chieftain," Kynar said with pride. Two uniformed doros, bloodied and bound, were dragged and tossed at Kel's feet. "Can we remove the suits?"

"Order it," Kel said. "Let the doros know we were here."

Kynar barked orders and her pack mates removed the mesh covers. Soon the Rafeer busied themselves marking the periphery of the ambush site as their territory.

"I've got a daisy cutter dropping anytime. The drone found us a good LZ one klick away. Talon's inbound."

"Then let's move." JP took Pathfinder and Moon-Hunter to lead the patrol out. Three prisoners. Two of them might not make it alive. They'd patched them up, but neither of the wounded were looking good. The one JP had cold-cocked had the red ticks of a sub-pack leader on his collar. A good haul.

Poul stayed back with Kel and Kynar to view the scene. The CCN team sergeant knelt and took a knife off one of the bodies and handed it to Kel. It had a jagged back and long edge. It looked like one of the knives displayed in the store windows of the crippled craftsman he'd met so long ago in Caza-Han. "I got one for myself already. Shame to leave it." Kel accepted the souvenir.

Kel armed the charges. Every crate was booby trapped. When more than one was activated by the motion of even slight tampering, the lot of them would detonate.

"I wish we could be here to view it," Kynar said sullenly. Like the rest of the patrol, the wet bloody prize she had carved for herself was now dangling from a cord around her neck.

"We'll see it later, Kynar," Poul tried to cheer her. "I left a trail bot to capture the show for us."

Kynar spit on the trail with contempt. "The high-jungle belongs to the Noble, smooth bellies." She howled. Her pack mates answered ahead, the mad barking echoing into the canopy. "Now you will remember."

31

Kel was sweating and felt a little dizzy. He took a deep swig from the gourd Bruto pushed into his hand. The stuff burned like fire. He gagged and fought down the rising bile.

The alpha-male panted and laughed in short barks. "Now you're a full member of my pack-family. Even your hard shell can't hide the mark of honor of a full Rafeer warrior."

Kel looked at the pattern raised on his stomach. He'd bit his lip so hard, it was swollen and the copper taste of blood still tinged his mouth. He refused the nociblock JP offered, partly not wanting to be disingenuous to the Rafeer, partly because it was a test. And he never backed down from a challenge. He'd succeeded enduring the long process well enough to receive howls and sniffs from the rest of the pack as he moved to rejoin the circle. Meadows was next to lie on the reed mat. The shaman took the flint and stone and began raising welts on Curt's stomach. He grunted at the first incision, the shaman pawing away the blood, then settled with a steeled look as sweat beaded on his forehead.

"Let's have a look, boss," JP said. The whirling five-limbed star reminded Kel of another symbol of ancient warriors he was familiar with. He felt a wave of nausea and took a few deep breaths until it went away.

"I can remove them later, guys," JP said, his wrist link voder muted to exclude the Rafeer.

"Not me," Woobie said. "Been thinking about a body mod for years. This one'll have a better story to go with it than most. I'm next."

"Curt's looks like it's gonna be one of those armor-plated grub diggers," Hardball said, a gourd in hand. He'd taken to the Rafeer brew quickly. "Looks like they got his spirit-mark figured pretty good."

"Yours will be that centipede that nests in those giant turd balls, Harding," Meadows grunted between the shaman's sharp taps on the cutter as he worked the pattern into Curt's abdomen. Curt had congratulated them on their successful ambush but had let Kel know he wasn't forgetting that Kel had earlier promised him he would have the honor of the next combat patrol against the doros. Meadows had been moody, even more so than usual as of late. Something was coming to a head for the giant leej, Kel sensed.

"Now, now, Top," Hardball said, taking a swig of the fire water. "All in a day's work serving the House of Reason."

Wiggy sighed. "Let's get this over with. I'm next, Woobie. I want a fresh design before the shaggy wizard dude runs out of ideas and I end up with something lame."

Sims pushed a hydration pouch into his hand. "We all better stay hydrated. I know where this is going."

Kynar crouched beside Kel. "Will there be word from your people soon? It's been many days. I told you, we could've had the smooth-bellies barking in much less time."

Kel wanted to refuse another swig of the foul concoction, but knew he had no choice. He took the smallest mouthful he could and feigned a neutral face as he passed the gourd back. "Soon. Tomorrow we should hear what they've learned from our prisoners." RI and the intel cells of the Legion and Republic army were undoubtedly poring over interrogation holos as they spoke. "We'll be the last to know. KITD. FODS." He was drunk.

"What is that?" Kynar puzzled, her ears curled and snout low.

"We're just like those centipedes. Kept in the dark. Fed on dreex scat."

"Nice tattoos," Barnett said. Kel, Poul, and Meadows were still in their loin cloths as the Nether Ops officer joined them in their longhouse. The rest of the team were on their mats, crashed out around them.

"Yeah. You missed a real party," Poul said. Blood-filled blisters leaked from the teeth of the dreex skull carved into his pink belly.

Kel took a drink from a hydration pouch. He'd thrown up for most of the night before he finally relented and took a dose of Postremadon to allow him to fall asleep just as the sun rose. He doubted he was out for more than an hour or two before the Talon landed and woke him. Nausea was worse than being shot.

"Don't keep us in suspense. Spill."

Barnett had retrieved the newest batch of prisoners, departed, and now returned, all without sharing word yet of what their hard work had produced for intelligence.

"You nabbed the supervisor for the communications section of the Brave Trackers Division. He mapped out their positions all the way out to the edge of where the True Warrior Division is dug in a few grids away. We still don't know the location of the Stalwart Gods, but he knows they're somewhere farther east in the Shalkot Valley. The new group, only one of them survived. He's still being worked over, but what you brought back just confirms the doro are gearing up to start an insurgency in the capital."

Kel took another sip. The nausea was returning. Maybe a ration bar would help. "What's it look like their overall game plan is?"

"The Braves and the Trues have the Trantchatka trail system completed and way stations funneling sabotage teams south to the capital until they can mass for a large-scale assault. The Stalwarts are cooking up something different we think. Our Brave Trackers prisoner wasn't privy to anything concrete, but we've got some ideas. You see, the Stalwarts are a technical division."

"Technical?" Poul asked. "What kind of technical?"

Barnett gritted teeth. "Air defense and biowarfare."

Meadows spat out his electrolyte replacement. "Holy sket!"

"I thought the Navy turned their ADA into scrap pre-invasion," Poul said. "Bombed every orbital defense station into atoms. They can't have much of an air defense capability left. Not enough to be a threat to anything in orbit."

Barnett nodded. "Nope. But they have manpads that're capable of transatmospheric trajectories."

"Who sold them starstreaks?" Meadows said. "Wait, don't tell me. Nether Ops."

Barnett grinned sheepishly. "They're not top grade. I bet two in three won't even launch."

"Point is," Poul said, "they're a delivery system."

"Don't tell me you sold them weaponized nanos and gene splitters too, Nether-dunce," Meadows growled.

"No! Of course not!" the former leej shouted defensively. "And we don't know they have them. It's just a possibility."

"Why would the doros have a bioweapon program?" Poul asked.

The Republic banned all genetic weapons programs and enforced the law vigorously. Bioweapons were almost impossible to control. Isolating just one variety of plant, such as a food source—or one variety of animal to include sentients—was impossible. The weapons could never be made as selective as their designers intended, and in the rare examples where they'd been used, had caused catastrophic unintended consequences. Worlds attacked by such weapons had to be quarantined for a hundred years. Next to Savages, bioweapons were a guaranteed way to get the Republic's attention.

"Jungle eradication," Barnett answered.

Kel picked it up from there. "Psydon is one giant jungle. The doros fought pack-clan wars for generations. The side that won used gene-deleting viruses right up until the clans united and Psydon joined the Republic."

The ability to deny territory by destroying what conceals, shelters, and even feeds an enemy makes for a decisive advantage. But bioweapons, whether used for killing people or plants, was a slippery slope. Much of the technology for making bioweapons was almost identical to that used for more benign purposes. The galaxy had collectively realized the danger of weapons designed to attack life on a genetic level. Kel was still in shock the possibility was facing them now. "I bet they still have the industry for viral-induced genetic agricultural manipulation. Anyone with vats can grow a gene-modded virus.

With the right tweaking from additional tech, it can be used to weaponize all sorts of bugs."

Barnett's face twisted as if eating something sour. The picture made Kel's stomach flip-flop anew. It reminded him of his recent retching, but knew the bitter face heralded some other bad news. "We don't know they've made that move," he lingered, "but... we do have questions." He pushed a holo out. A spine-ridged humanoid figure appeared in a background of green that made it clear the image had been captured on Psydon.

"A Hool?" Kel said. "What's a Hool doing on Psydon?"

"That's what we'd like to know," Barnett replied. The Hool weren't galactic traders. But they were known for their biotech. Black market longevity treatments, organ cloning, cybernetics. For a price, the Hool could provide body upgrades that made Kel wonder if they hadn't learned the trade from the Savages.

"Who is he?" Poul asked.

"We don't know. He's been on-planet for several months. He was documented arriving in the capital, then vanished. No record of departure. Not unusual in and of itself. There're many races represented in the free trade sector, some who stay for more than just a brief visit. But putting it together with the fact that the Stalwart Gods Division is unaccounted for, RI took a good look at what's been shipping to Psydon lately. This was sliced from the doro customs database." He added another image.

"What is it?" Meadows asked. A still hovered of an open grav container and a complex mechanism within. "Looks vaguely medical-ish."

"That's what RI thinks. Best guess, it's a gene analyzer."

"Oh boy," Kel said.

"And we think there's evidence of knock-off medical grade nano printers imported in component pieces."

Poul beat Kel to the punch. "The question's been answered to my satisfaction. No problem. Time to nuke every grid where they could be hiding. High KT, low rad nukes. No reason to give them time to stumble into a combination that'll let them unleash something nasty on the basics. The puzzle pieces are all there. They're cooking up some kind of gene weapon. We need to fry them before they can get a starstreak off the ground loaded with a gene-bomb."

Meadows picked up. "Even better. We find exactly where the Stalwarts are and jump a Mark Four on them. We've done it before. We're experts. That's what you're getting ready to tell us, right?"

"That idea's already been floated, and sunk," Barnett admitted. "The senators and delegate in joint oversight of the Psydon operation have been informed. The issue isn't settled, but the request to do just as you suggested was already turned down. The civilian command authority felt the environmental impact on the unique biosphere of Psydon would negatively impact the Republic's image in the galaxy. At least, without some kind of solid proof that a genuine threat of that nature exists."

"You gotta to be kiddin' me," Hardball said from out of their circle. He was on both feet but swayed slightly, one hand braced against the sloped roof, the other rubbing his head. "I got a hangover, my head feels like JP's been hammering at it with both fists, and the first thing I wake up to is news that a politician thinks a buncha trees is more important than divisions of troops waitin' to get melted by a nano-weapon? Please tell me I'm still drunk and just dreaming all this."

Barnett ignored him. "Umstead sent Colonel Chatsworth back to Okella to act as his direct relay to Utopion. Major Yost will be running the SIG task force on Psydon. CCN is tasked with the hunt for the Stalwart Gods."

"And we're hearing it from you?" Meadows said with a frown. "Excuse me if I don't start planning an operation just yet, Nether. I think we'll wait for Major Yost or someone in the Legion chain of command to give us our marching orders."

Barnett didn't look offended. "Major Yost and Sergeant Major Biggetti will be here soon. Things are happening quickly. They're bringing your ACM back with them. Bertie's been getting some upgrades from our tech section. He's being outfitted with detectors and a nano-killer replicator, so if you find a lab, you can deal with it on the spot, and maybe we don't have to get permission to go nuclear."

Kel grunted in disbelief and frustration. "And you just happened to have a nano-replicator ready to load Bertie with, huh? Someone was considering the possibility long before this, Lev. Tell me I'm wrong."

Barnett remained silent.

Whether they had a mission yet or not, Kel knew it wouldn't be long before they would. "Time to get spun up. Get the rest of the team animated. I don't want to wait until Braley and Bigg get here to spring this on them. Get JP moving first. Postremadon and stims for everyone, IV fluids, and a meal, in that order. Barnett and I have more to discuss."

Poul and Meadows grunted affirmatively and moved out. Hardball lost the battle to remain standing and plopped back onto his mat.

"Is that a centipede tattooed on my stomach?"

"Once you locate the Stalwarts, the rest of the operation kicks off," Braley told them. "The air campaign against the Braves, the Trues, and the way stations along the Trantchatka trail won't go until you release. We're concerned that if the Stalwarts have a weapon, a strike against the other divisions will tip our hand and force them to retaliate. Operations elsewhere on Psydon have been put on hold to keep pressure off whoever is making decisions for the doro side."

Sims was first to object. "So rather than find the site and nuke it, we're being sent in as sacrificial lambs to wipe out a gene-splitter lab, just so as not to make us look like the big-bad Rex kind of killers the galaxy fears we are."

The rest of the team grunted agreement. You could send a kill team to their deaths. That wasn't the problem. Kel saw it from Sims's perspective; the reason they were being sent to sacrifice themselves had to make sense. This was going to take some convincing. Before he could try, Bigg stepped up.

"If we get an approval, we'll pull you out immediately and let the fission bombs do the work," Bigg said. "The colonel is General Umstead's spearhead to make the imperative clear for the pols. He and the general have set up the hypercomm relays to make the process as instantaneous as possible. But if it's a hard confirmation the pols insist on before authorizing, it doesn't make sense to send you in on an evidence-gathering mission just to pull you out to drop nukes. You'll already be deep in their base of operations. That's why the techs fitted Bertie out with his new load. If you find evidence of nano weapons or any other kind of genetic reprogramming bug, kill it at the site. Otherwise, we just have to settle with killing any missile delivery system and keep on the hunt for their lab."

Kel had gone over all this with Barnett and had come around to the strategy once they'd played out all the options together. "Sims, you know even a bunker nuke isn't guaranteed to neutralize and eradicate a bioweapon. Depending on how well it's shielded and how deep it's stored, a nuke might just serve to release a bug. Close wouldn't be good enough. To use a nuke right, we'd have to walk a Mark Four into the same room to be sure. Bertie's got an analyzer and a nano-plant in his hold. He can release a self-replicating cloud of anti-nanos targeted to the bug that'll clean the place of any bioweapon. Isn't that so, Bertie?"

The ACM had been still. "I've got a full package. I can read any nano we find, determine its purpose, and write a hunter-killer program to produce counter agents."

Sims wasn't alone frowning over the heavy weight they'd just been saddled with. "I've walked the one-way path with you before," Sims said. "You know it's not that. It just seems that for a target that's potentially this critical, we're going in pretty light. It should be a full Legion hitting this place."

"Legion troops don't have nano-level resistance with their armor," Braley said. "We do. Sending them in wouldn't be much better than sending in the basics. But that's what's going to happen if you fail. The 131st is teed up to take down the Stalwarts if you don't."

Bigg jumped in. "It's not that desperate. You don't have to take out the whole division by yourselves. You have to locate and destroy any bioweapon. You do that, we'll have a Legion, an army division, an air wing, marines—you name it—standing by and ready to flatten everything and everyone still standing." He paused. "You can do this. You've done tougher."

Kel spoke to Sims but knew he was making his case to the whole team. "So, it has to be us on the ground. We're the only ones who can operate in that environment. Us and the Rafeer." Kel surveyed the team. Everyone nodded in the subtle acceptance that what they'd been told was true. Space was cold vacuum. Peace was an illusion. The only safe place was in your mind. They were the only ones who could do this.

Woobie summed it up.

"Man, it sucks being the savior of the galaxy sometimes."

"Hey." Kel got Sims's attention when they broke up. Sims hesitated but didn't come closer, his reluctance a clear message; he was wary of Kel, like a pet whose tail had been stepped on. Kel made to move closer. His friend wasn't going to make it easy on him. "You didn't need to remind me of what we've done together. And there's no one I'd rather walk the one-way path with. That's why it hasn't been one-way and we're still here."

Sims grimaced. "I was a little harsh. I know you've never forgotten what we've been through together. Sorry, Kel. But I gotta be honest. It's been different since you left Three. I know it's how it has to be, having to carry the responsibility you do now. Sometimes I just wish it were like it used to be."

"Forget it, brother. We're good."

"It's this damn jungle. Everything about this Psydon mission has worn us all down. Tempers have gotten short. We're fatigued. Even Meadows is acting irritable. He's usually a stone statue. I don't think he's taken well to being lower in the pecking order since we joined the two teams. And not being in on the action hasn't helped."

Maybe Kel had been carrying an overly optimistic view of how Meadows had adapted. "You may be right. I've got a solution for that."

32

"It's not a centipede. It's a snake. I asked Moon-Hunter. You can see the three tongues sticking out."

Meadows struck. "It's a turd-eating centipede, Harding. I know, because I told the witch doctor to put it there. He was going to give you a dreex claw or some other kind of clichéd crap, but when I explained how it was your spirit guide, he saw it my way."

That brought a chuckle from everyone as they armored up.

Gabe's voice took on a hard edge, his relaxed drawl gone. "Watch it, Curt. Don't work so hard to make me think you're serious."

"You should thank me," Meadows continued. "You can use the sad energy to fuel one of the verbal tragedies you're waiting to share the next time you ask one of us to braid your hair."

JP covered his face. Wiggy's jaw hung open. Sims's shoulders shook as he smothered his laughter. Only Woobie spoke.

"Holy sket!"

Meadows beamed. "Wolodarski gets it. Am I right?"

Gabe drew to full height, his jaw clenched. The rest of the team was misreading the situation, but Kel saw it for what it was. This wasn't the normal team bollocking. This was a personal challenge, and Hardball had responded by taking on the pall of murder, ready to duel. Kel blamed himself. It was he who'd forgotten his place as their leader and teased Gabe that he should keep his poetry in his head. He'd been the one to open up the gates to what was happening now.

Poul saw it too.

"Curt, come talk with me and the captain. We've got to get the op order going. We need to do it now."

Hardball eyed Meadows as he walked with Kel and Poul out of the longhouse. Before he left, Poul motioned at Gabe to be calm. The rest of the team had quickly attuned to the atmosphere and gotten serious. It was not the vibe Kel wanted before a mission. He had to change it.

"Curt. You're going to take the mobile guerilla strike force. Who do you want running each platoon?"

Meadows thought. "I guess I'll be taking anyone you're not."

Kel saw the logic to that. "Poul's coming with me. JP too. We may need his med knowledge dealing with anything we find inside. We're taking Kynar and her squad."

"So, what you're asking me is, can I work with Harding?"

Poul corrected. "You mean, will Harding work with you?"

Meadows sighed and slumped. "I took things too far. Gabe's a proud guy. I shouldn't have been making him the butt of my jokes."

"What's been going on with you, Top?" Kel asked.

"Sorry, sir. I've been acting more like a team member instead of a team sergeant. I know better. No excuse. I've got no beef against Gabe. How could I? He's the most solid leej in the galaxy. Just being my old self, I guess. A jerk and a bully."

"Well, find a way to make it okay with him," Poul said.

"I will. And I'll do it right. So." He returned to business. "It's time for me to do what I do best. Thanks, Captain." Meadows seemed refreshed and cheerful. "I'll take Harding, Sims, Wiggy, and Wolodarski. Each of them running a platoon. I've already thought about our insertion plan. Multiple LZs. Link-ups on the ground. Better than one marshaling area. Anyone gets hit on insertion, there's less chance of the whole mike force getting pinned down and plenty of available help. I'll run over it with you when you're ready."

"Let's get a warning order to the team, then we can get the I-squared ready," Kel said.

"Mind if I do it?" Meadows asked. Kel made a sweeping gesture and followed Meadows back into the team house.

"Hey guys, listen up." Meadows used a soft voice. Everyone stopped digging in their kit and turned to face him. "The captain and Poul have made their decision about the mission. This is what it's going to look like. I'm commanding the mobile strike force, Harding's taking a platoon with me and my headquarters element to do the recon and pathfinder the LZs to bring in the rest of the unit. The captain, Poul, and JP are taking Kynar and her squad to do the infiltration of the facility once we find it. Sims, Wolodarski, and Wiggins, you'll each have one of the remaining platoons for the supporting assault once the captain starts their penetration."

Hardball gave up nothing in his demeanor.

"Gabe," Meadows said, making no preamble. "I owe you an apology. I didn't mean all the stuff I was raking you over the coals about. I didn't mean any of it. Just being a jerk."

Hardball reacted coolly. "No need, Top. I was being a little sensitive."

"No. You weren't. You were the same professional you always are. The problem is me, and I've thought about it. I don't know if this is why, but maybe deep down, I've been kind of mad at you."

Hardball frowned. "What I'd do, Curt? I'm sorry if I..."

"Let me finish," Meadows stopped him. "You guys know I lost a whole team once. The captain and Three were there. I know Twelve hasn't gotten the full story, at least not from me. I don't ever talk about it."

For some reason, not even the insects outside made noise just then.

"After we had the service for them back on Victrix, Nail said something to me. It's all he said. Just to me. It was a poem.

We walk where they no longer can
Forward, ere we go
Our fallen brother, the better man
Our duty ever so."

Everyone waited for Meadows to continue. Not since the mission to search the Bassinus village had he spoken so many words at one sitting.

"Sometimes, when you're being serious, it dredges stuff up inside me. I fight to be the kind of operator each of the guys on Seven was. There's not a day I don't think about them. And what Nail told me. But still, I find a way to screw it up and let them down. Gabe, if you've found a way to put into words what it is that makes us who we are, don't stop. I'm probably just jealous because I can't do the same. Maybe someday you'll figure out why I'm the way I am. Then I'll understand, too."

Kel was stunned.

"There's nothing wrong with the way you are, Curt. Thanks."

"Let's get to work then." Meadows retrieved his data-pad and plopped onto his mat, opening holos and moving them around before starting to type.

Hardball relaxed, the resentment Meadows had incited, making him ready to explode into violence, dissipated like smoke in a strong wind. Poul gave Kel a wink.

"And by the way," Meadows said his last bit. "Your tat-too's a snake. I lied about talking to the shaman. I was in way too much pain after my tattoo to say anything."

"Question is, do we risk a training jump with the Rafeer, or just go for it?" Poul asked. "We can each tandem one. Bertie can take two. That's still only five of the strikers to go in with us."

"Better we risk a Talon setting us down," Kel said, re-membering the old adage about landing and walking in being the best way to arrive with all gear and personnel when the mission was critical.

"It's just a hop and pop," JP said. "I say we settle for some dry runs and take our chances."

Kel made a decision. "We have a week. We do the dry training, and if Meadows finds us the right spot, we land instead of jump." The high-altitude reconnaissance of the Shalkot Valley had been no more revealing than any oth-er. They had some good possibilities. But if the clearing they chose was right in the middle of the Stalwarts' area of operations, all Kel could think about was their sparking a response with starstreaks launching at Caza-Han and at every troop concentration around the planet.

Meadows was leaving soon, taking Harding and the first platoon on the Talons to a spot far enough away from Shalkot where they could launch their reconnaissance without alerting the doros. With any luck, they'd have the Stalwarts' location sniffed out in a week, ready to call in Kel's penetration team. Meadows and Harding would scout spots for the Navy to drop daisy cutters for the LZs. The rest of the mike force would land and surround the den, immediately launching the harassment operation while Kel and his crew worked inside. With Army artillery and the Navy standing by to support, they should be able to keep the Stalwarts bottled up and even shoot down any launches if they happened.

When the attack on the Stalwart Gods Division started, the orbital bombardment of the True Warrior and Brave Tracker Divisions would commence. When there was nothing left to bomb, the 131st and the Black Horse Division would shuttle in and sweep the remains.

Everything depended on Kel getting his force into the underground labyrinth to start the search.

"Let's break the news to Kynar and the squad," Kel said. "I bet this'll be a first in Rafeer history."

"Explain it one more time, Chieftain," Kynar said. She didn't seem perturbed by the idea of jumping out of an aircraft. At least, once he described that they wouldn't be falling from a great height like jumping implied.

JP picked up a seed pod. "Just like this." He tossed one in the air. "See how it floats down and lands softly on the ground? That'll be us."

Poul swiped a holo over them. A Goshawk dropped a hundred troops from its belly on both sides simultaneously, the troopers drifting for only seconds underneath the square canopies before touching down.

"Parachute," Pathfinder repeated. Moon-Hunter, Taskmaster, and Red-Sun had the folded ears Kel learned to interpret as a quizzical sign. "Chieftain, you say we'll be attached to you under each of the seed pods."

Bertie spoke. "Two of you will be with me, lucky blokes."

The Rafeer hadn't been surprised in any way when their DOGR was introduced. It seemed the Rafeer had become immune to any technology the humans sprang on them. Had the humans turned ordinary rocks to polished sapphires, it would cause less interest. "You'll have the softest ride of all. I get the biggest parachute."

Poul laid out one of the harnesses. "We'll show you how it's going to look and practice plenty before we do it. It's easy."

Kynar barked sharply. "Well then. It's a good day to hunt."

Kel smiled. "The pack needs meat to live."

Harding sounded enthusiastic. "It's a good DZ. I'd jump it myself with a blindfold on."

Meadows was no less upbeat. "Gabe'll be waiting with his reception committee to lead you in from the DZ. I'm staying with the main body. We're a few klicks from the main lair. We've got bots and sniffers on every trail and

LP/OPs dug in keeping eyes on the target. If there's any hint we're compromised, we'll know right off."

Kel reviewed the LZs for the mike force. "Bertie, do you have confirmation these are locked in by the Sharks?" The tactical fighter-bombers were standing by to drop the daisy cutters. The mobile strike force was at the staging area, a new mission launch site cut out of the jungle, ready to load onto SLICs and converge on the Shalkot Valley. With pride Kel imagined how they'd appear out of nowhere, as swiftly as any Legion recon company to lead the way since the original Rechs.

"The Navy is the model of attentiveness, Captain," Bertie assured. He'd continue to manage the air coordination until he was deep in the doro bunker and shut off from comms.

"Then there's nothing left to do," Kel said. "We'll see you on the ground. Turner out."

"You heard the boss," Poul said. "Time to load."

The Talon sat waiting in the grassy clearing. They were the last of the company left in their jungle FOB. Bruto, Lupa, and a group of the youngest omegas were all that was left to guard the dens.

"We wait for your return with meat and news of victory," Lupa said to them. She blessed them, Rafeer and legionnaire alike, sniffing each as they walked up the ramp of the Talon.

"This will be the end of the smooth-bellies in our valley," Bruto said. "Return home with meat for the pack." He led the howl, the omegas hoisting spear and blaster in each paw as the crew chief raised the ramp. The whine of repulsors coming to full power drowned out the barks as they lifted.

"Don't worry, Kel," Poul said on a private channel. "It's just the fate of twenty thousand human souls riding on our shoulders."

Kel scoffed. "Twenty thousand? Is that all? We've had to save more with less."

33

"My necklace is going to be so full it'll make Bruto's look as bare as a doro belly," Pathfinder boasted.

"Only if I leave you any," Red-Sun answered, his lips curling as though savoring the flavor of yesterday's kill in his mouth. Their squad were still enamored with the throat transducers and how they could sub-vocalize to each other through their implants, practicing until it was only by the gurgles and hacks of smothered laughs that Kel knew when two of their Nobles were speaking to each other. Like now, as Pathfinder and Red-Sun boasted to each other inaudibly.

The Rafeer had shown no hint of nervousness. Until the tail gate dropped. Ears laid flat and snouts closed. Kel had experienced similar scenes many times, when bluster smothered in a silent death as the moment of truth drew near. It was signaled by the freezing blast of air that filled the cabin and the tiny solid-colored light over the ramp. You didn't feel the cold in armor, but the herald of that light spoke to every jumper the same: *When the green light pops, false courage stops.*

"Good track. Hold course." Kneeling on the ramp, to Kel this was as familiar as putting fork to mouth. Another light, a faint star in the black sea below, blinked twice a second on the drop zone. It was an illusion. The marker was a simulacrum visible only in their HUDs, not an actual beacon. But Kel bet a real one wouldn't be any less invisible to a soul not viewing it from so far above the jungle floor.

They could've jumped from higher, but three kilometers was that perfect balance. High enough to be invisible to a ground observer, close enough for an accurate touchdown—laden with so much that their chutes would be sluggish to steer. From the edge of space, it was sometimes considered good enough that a team landed within an hour's walk of each other and in the same province as the target. To hit the tiny clearing where Hardball waited below, they'd need to do much better.

Bertie stepped to the ramp, Red-Sun and Taskmaster silent on either side, their previous bravado about flying like raptors to pluck out doro hearts forgotten. Their crouched hesitation did nothing to slow their advance as Bertie's mass dragged them nearer to the edge of solid reality.

"Not to worry, lads. The Talon got us here without bursting into flames and crashing horribly to render us all to nothing but greasy bits. So, the most dangerous part's over, you see? No worries. The ride up is more dangerous than what we're about to do. This is the safe part. You're going to have stories to tell about how you fell from the sky with your big brother Bertie at the helm, delivering you safe as two pups in the den to suckle at their mum's teats. Of course, the odd parachute malfunction has been known to happen, but it's a swift death. Painless, I'm told. And in this soft ground, you'll dig your own grave, you will. So you see, there's not a thing on the whole of Psydon to worry about."

If Kel didn't know better, he'd think Bertie was getting pleasure out of hazing the first-time jumpers. He intervened as it seemed Bertie was about to go on. "Head in the game, Bertie. See you on the ground."

"Right you are, sir. Happy landings, all."

"Go." Kel sent Bertie and his two reluctant passengers out into the night air. "Next pass," he told the pilots as the dual parachutes opened behind the Talon. They made a gentle circle, giving Bertie adequate lead time to land and clear out of the small drop zone before another seed pod dropped off the next leej and Rafeer pairing. Lastly, it was Kel and Kynar's turn. Against all instructions, she stiffened as he propelled them from the Talon. The lack of time to train the Rafeer didn't hamper them as their chute deployed automatically and came to life in a full spread.

"Doing okay, Kynar?" Her pants were slower now, but still loud.

"The Noble were meant to stay on the ground. We're not the masters of the world above the jungle. Your kind are truly fearless, Chieftain."

"It just takes practice, my friend. You're doing fine."

They glided down. Kel wove a zigzagging path until it was time for a pattern of gentle spirals, his course centering them over the beacon as the clearing came into actual view. He'd barely paid attention to the guide in his HUD. It was unnecessary. On a night this calm and forgiving, he couldn't have missed the drop zone if he'd wanted to. White-hot and red haloed bodies crowded around the edges of the tiny opening in the jungle. It was little more than enough room for a decent-sized swimming pool minus the sunning patio. He took a straight run over the clearing before making a sharp turn back, diving over the trees. Kynar flinched and whined as her hind legs brushed the tops. The ground rushed up and he flared hard.

He hit the release and canopy destruct sequence one after the other as fast as the program allowed. With his K-17 in hand, he didn't have but a moment before hands and paws helped him step out of his ruck straps. Hardball was at his side. "We've got to move, boss. The area's crawling with doro patrols. Good thing we didn't try to land a Talon. They'd know for sure we were on to them."

"Hardball," Meadows said on L-comm. "Are they on the ground?"

"We're down, Curt," Kel answered for Gabe.

"Good. Gabe will get you up to speed, boss. I'm holding at the patrol base. Bertie," Meadows broke to their ACM. "We're a go. Get the Navy clearing teams and the SLIC crews to phase Able Two."

"Roger, Sergeant Meadows, I'll keep you informed on channel Alpha-Three." Bertie and Meadows would keep a conversation going on the side channel as they worked together to keep all the balls in midair.

"Are we compromised?" Kel asked as they hastened into the wood line.

"Negative. But we've had to take out three of their patrols. Small two-person rovers. We didn't fire a shot, but it can't be long before the doros know something's up." Hardball's young omegas all had new keepsakes around their necks. "There's a lot of these little clearings. They were cut within the past few weeks. Still fresh toolmarks everywhere. I'm betting it's for manpads. Everything points to this being the Stalwarts' digs."

"Good job. How far to our breach point?"

Hardball pushed a route to Kel. "A few klicks and some tough jungle. We'll lead you in. I've got a surveillance team on what we still think is the best entrance." A green triangle pulsed in a tier of stepped map contours. "By what we can judge, it's peripheral to everything, and there's not another access for a half a klick. The bots read a lot of deep seismo nearby. The other entrances, too many hits. It'd be like dropping you into the center of a Savage creche. For certain, it's gonna be hairy with doros. We'll be pulling them off your backs when we hit with the mike force. Should give you the breathing room you need to work. By the time you do your thing, we'll have a platoon waiting to cover your exit and have CAS overhead to paste anything they got left to send after us. Piece o' cake."

Was there a bioweapon lab? If so, was it here? Was it deep? It was all a guess. But it was time to find out.

"Lead on."

They crawled. Bertie scooted low, the brush parting to his mass as his front legs clipped the undergrowth in a way that made Kel jealous. Hardball opened a link and a view from a bot in the trees above them opened in a new window. Enhanced, the glow of two doros stood out, their bodies red-hot against the dull rainbow of blues and greens around them.

"My boys've been beggin' for this chance," Hardball said. "We've been eavesdropping on the dog-men for days. Give the word."

Kel gave the ready signal to Kynar, the corners of her mouth raised in a way that reminded him of one of his instructors from Legion basic. The silent, evil smirk that chilled to the core. It telegraphed a world of pain about to be unleashed. "Get your masks on."

Kynar pulled out her atmomask and pushed her snout into it, the hood sealing around her neck.

"Send 'em out, Gabe."

From the darkness came a short grunt, quickly chased by a clipped bark. The two doro sentries faced the direction of the challenge, brought rifles to ready, and answered with another pair of longer, lower barks. The two Rafeer broke through the jungle, the lead waving overhead. The sentries relaxed.

"You lost?" Kel's audio gain was turned up to maximum, the chirping of insects loud enough to make him wince as he listened to the conversation.

"Not on my worst day," the lead Rafeer said as he advanced. "Dagnum is changing the roving patrol. Thinks there's something up. Been some activity near the river. Wants patrols closer to the den."

It was working. Both sentries laid their rifles down. "More likely he just wants to show the pack leader he's taking initiative by changing things up. Not even a mud-digger's been seen in days." The two Rafeer were moving up the slope along a narrow path, the nonchalant banter pouring out as steadily as the patter of the raindrops from the trees. The trailing Noble stepped from behind. Two muffled sizzles flashed brightly, then faded.

"Go," Kel said as he burst out of the brush to tear through the growth, plowing ahead as fast as he could without tripping on the tangle. Bertie pranced past him, leaping from one spot to the next, covering the distance in a dozen hops to beat him to the assassins and their kill by a full minute.

"Where is it?" he panted, as he reached the tiny plateau in the thick vegetation. The kneeling Rafeer pulled one of the doro bodies away to reveal a frame of woven vines and leaves.

"Nice work, boys," Hardball said beside him. "You two, take their place and hold tight. Alright, Captain. We'll be waiting. If you come out fast, we'll bring the hate behind you."

Kynar stood by the concealed entrance, ready to remove the gate. Kel and Poul were nearest. He checked his carbine for the hundredth time. *Suppressed*, the setting confirmed. "Bertie. Send it."

"Roger. All units, go for Super Nova. I say again, Super Nova." There was a micro pause. "Burst sent and confirmation by all units of Super Nova received, Captain."

"Breach," he said as Poul brought his weapon up. Kynar pulled to reveal the narrow tunnel mouth staring back, a curving hole into nothing and everything.

Kynar sniffed. "Pathfinder. Red-Sun. Go."

The two Rafeer dropped to all fours and crawled into the passage as if fleeing danger rather than rushing toward it. Back on solid ground, the determination had returned to make the first kills.

"It's going to be tight for Bertie," Poul said. "Tight even for us."

The tunnel entrance was little more than the burrow an animal would dig beneath a root ball to build a nest. The entrance wasn't reinforced in any way he could see. They hadn't been into any of the other underground redoubts before calling in the airstrikes, but if the deeper tunnels were so constructed, they'd collapse like a stack of tiles at the first bomb. Super Nova was rolling. Kel imagined the Sharks diving from orbit and the spread of daisy cutters they would soon drop, vaporizing huge swaths of jungle. The SLICs would already be en route, pink Rafeer tongues flapping in the breeze of the open birds as they skimmed the treetops.

He grew old as he waited for the seconds to pass before a Rafeer head poked back out.

"All quiet, Chieftain," Pathfinder said. "There's a larger space ahead. We can all fit."

"See you soon, Gabe," Poul said as he dropped low, his carbine snapping to his chest as he crawled on all fours.

"JP, bring up the rear with Bertie," Kel said. "Bye, Gabe," he said as he dropped to follow Kynar.

"The pack needs meat to survive," Hardball said. "Git you some, boss."

"Nothing more poetic for us?" Kel teased.

"I'll keep it inside for now, sir."

There was nothing to see save Kynar's hind legs as she trotted, Kel scurrying to keep pace. The tunnel sloped downward, curved, until a faint bluish light beckoned ahead. The path leveled and widened. A pair of doros lay on the dim floor where growing crimson pools fed by ebbs of pulsing blood told the story. The sentries' tawny necks were both saturated black, heads almost severed. Their weapons and uniforms lay next to them. They'd been sleeping.

"Poul, send a swarm," Kel said as he raised to a crouch to see over Poul ahead of him. The tunnel continued ahead, tall and wide enough for a single leej.

Poul tapped the small sphere and dozens of black hornets left in a hazy cloud.

"Time for gas?" JP inquired behind him.

"Not yet," Kel answered. "Let's wait until we're deeper." Pathfinder and Red-Sun had the two doro uniforms on and were putting kit on again. The atmo hoods would startle, but the doro uniforms might cause hesitation.

Sometimes, that's all it took. That extra tenth of a second of confusion to give the necessary tactical advantage. Surprise was still on their side.

"Two minutes till first daisy cutters, Captain," Bertie warned. "I dropped a repeater at the entrance. Don't know how far down it'll reach to keep us in the loop."

"The plan will roll ahead with or without us. Let's move."

The two disguised Rafeer took the lead. Side by side, the party hid behind as they crept ahead.

"One minute," Bertie alerted.

"Get ready with the gas. They won't know what to make of it at first," Kel reminded them. "By the time they get a few whiffs, it won't matter." Kel hoped the seals on the Rafeers' masks held true.

Poul was proctoring the mapping drones for them. "Three tunnels meet ahead. Two branch left and right to dens with snoring doros in each. The center passage goes deeper and joins to the complex. More detail coming now. Hold up. Kel, check it out."

Kel tapped the shoulders ahead, they paused, and he pulled up the map view. The 3D image expanded rapidly. It was very much an ant farm like the ones he'd made as a kid. Sandwiched between two panes of glass, the industrious insects burrowed in every direction, layer by layer, their trails a pattern splayed out like a nervous system. This had the very same form.

"Suddenly I miss the Nems," JP said. "Their tunnels were at least something a human would design. This is like a bad dream. We get out of this, I'm never going belowground again."

A central shaft tunneled up and down as the map revealed more with the drones' spread, the invisible artists of the developing portrait.

"That's got to be a lift," Poul said. "It goes all the way to surface. I think we found a central hub for this complex."

A subtle vibration reached them.

"Daisies are chopping," Bertie confirmed.

"It's time. Gas going out. Coming through," Kel said as he nudged between the two Rafeer. He'd given strong consideration to nerve agent, then settled for spaz. The combination of hallucinogen and retch gas would incapacitate almost instantly. It was tuned for the physiology of the canus hominis, but would spare a human only the most severe of the effects. A whiff, and the dog-men would be retching and evacuating, all while hallucinating giant dreex eating their innards as they convulsed in piles of their own excrement. It wasn't fatal, at least, not to the certainty that nerve agent was. The odd victim could aspirate and suffocate, but that would be rare. No toxin was benign or without risk.

But nerve agent—that was an entirely different calculus. It terrified him. If the seals on one of the Rafeer's masks leaked, spaz wouldn't kill them. Nerve gas absolutely would. Leejes, too. The chemistry that made nervous systems tick was universal. Dead as yesterday's dreams of riches and beauty queens with a face locked in rictus as respiratory muscles froze, the victim fully aware of the death the uncontrollable convulsions promised. As good as it was, not even Dark Ops armor was invulnerable. A minor breach in their armor and the nerve agent wouldn't care if they were friend or foe, human or dogman—a very real possibility in a firefight.

He brought up his carbine and fired, the grenade already in the tube, just waiting for a chance to fly. The grenade lobbed lazily ahead and bounced off the earthen wall, spinning off around the bend until something blocked its path and it dumped its payload in a fat cloud.

More and stronger vibrations filtered through their feet. A klaxon sounded. Someone was awake and recognized that tactical fighter-bombers dropping daisies nearby meant that the company arriving weren't coming to trade recipes.

"Perfect timing," Kel said as he loaded another grenade. "Give it a minute." The siren pulsed. Excited barks by the dozen came from beyond, quickly devolving into wet sounds of distress, whines, and chopped gags.

"Poul. With me." Kel took the lead and rolled ahead. Doros scrabbled on knees out of dens. The first chamber widened and Kel stepped to one side.

"Don't leave one alive," Poul said as he brought up his carbine. "They can still paw a grenade."

"Leave them," he countermanded. "The spaz is even more effective than the techs said it'd be. They're completely disabled and will be for a day. It's my call. Leave them for the bombs."

"Suit yourself. I'll take the other den and try to keep the Rafeer from executing the rest."

"Go." Kel sent another grenade down the central passage. Dark shapes appeared ahead through the thickening smoke. He didn't wait for a reaction before he sent blasts down the long passage into the cloud. "Contact. Doros ahead. No return fire. They're down."

JP spoke from behind. "Bertie thinks he's found a ventilation system."

"Where?" Kel asked.

"Runs next to that central lift," Bertie replied. "We fight our way forward, we'll own the bloody castle."

"Poul, with me," Kel again ordered.

"No dice. JP, up with me," Poul took his turn at countermanding. "Kel, drop back. You and Bertie find us a lab to raid."

"Grrr. Right." He let JP's extra-wide form pass. Poul was right. It was time to do what he was supposed to be doing as the leader: plan what came next, not clog his processor with attention to the menial. As fun as it was. "Bertie," he walked next to the ACM behind hooded Rafeer. "Anything stand out?"

"Not yet, Captain. The drones aren't finished, but I'm getting some images. I'll let you know as soon as I have something."

The whine of the siren continued. Kel tossed a pair of paw-poppers behind them and set them on proximity. As long as there was an operator left alive, if they came back this way, the mines would shut off on signal from their links.

"Sergeant Radd," Bertie called. "I'm pushing a route to you. Best path to the central shaft."

"Following the big arrow in the sky, gents," Poul said with way too much cheer.

They peeled off as they went to check dens and alcoves holding convulsing doros. A senior pack leader with solid red on his collar seemed oblivious to their presence, but was fumbling for a grenade on its chest when a blast from one of the Rafeer stopped his twitching. Datapads lay on desktops lashed to the walls. "Bertie. Pads." Kel had to say nothing further. An appendage hovered over a pad, then moved to another.

"Encrypted material will take some work," he said. "But there's plenty in the clear. Give me some time."

They rolled ahead. JP and Poul traded off launching gas grenades into every open way ahead. More dens.

More areas for congregation. Nothing that looked like a lab. Kel checked. They were almost to the central shaft. They had cleared one level. One level of at least ten. Most of the drones were backtracking. Having reached blind ends or surface exits, they made detailed searches of the spaces they'd already located and collected more images. Only one path was still being mapped—down the central shaft. Searching the complex for a hidden lab was going to be even slower than he'd imagined.

"Bertie, is this it?" JP asked. A gentle hum came from ahead, plasticrete walls left excavated dirt behind, a circular atrium waited beyond, the shaft of a repulsor lift at its center. "Looks more like a military installation than the rest of these dirty gouges."

"Definitely, Sergeant Pabon. I've got a trace of the whole works. Drop a grenade down one of those ducts and the whole place will be gassed in a few minutes. Four times the volume to displace all air, but needing only an effective concentration of point—"

"Bertie, the short version," Poul said. Sometimes the AI delved into minutiae at inconvenient times to make sure its reasoning was understood by the dimwitted humans.

"P for plenty, mate."

Kel crowded forward. "Kynar, keep eyes ahead."

"Yes, Chieftain." She and two of the Rafeer watched ahead.

"Sir, something of interest."

"What is it, Bertie?"

"There's a supply of succulent paste and quatrain root, as well as hundreds of kilos of a non-native beetle listed on the division supply order."

"Okay. But have you found the lab?"

"Sir, those are foodstuffs for an agnathian. They've got provisions here for a spiny. I think our Hool is here."

34

"That lift is running," JP said. He produced a torch and sliced through an access panel. "I can see the shaft. It's empty right now. This is a huge repulsor lift. Bertie, can you find a readout for it? Where's it at? At the surface or below us?"

"The lift's not linked to any central system," Bertie said with some frustration. The AI was accustomed to being the master of everything non-biologic. "The only controls are probably on the lift bed itself, bugger all!"

The Rafeer were split covering the way they'd come and the unexplored tunnel opposite the central space. It was an incongruous sight. The atrium around the central column was the first indication of something more sophisticated than what they'd been traveling through.

"This is a long-term fortification," Poul said. "They didn't dig this in response to the invasion." A fine mist was diffusing evenly through the air around them, causing the bluish tint of the artificial lighting to turn gray. Spaz was being circulated with fresh air anywhere the ventilation system reached. To Kel's thinking, that had to mean everywhere in the underground complex. In a few minutes, unless the doros had reacted by masking up, the whole of the Stalwart Gods Division should be hallucinating that carnivorous spiders and ax-wielding primates were tearing off faces and hacking off penises as they expelled from both ends simultaneously.

"Hey, guys," JP said. "It's stopped now. I'm guessing, but I think it's below us."

"Get mines set on the entrance and let's pull back for an ambush if it stops and pours out doros in vac suits." Kel wasn't sure what to expect. They'd caught the Stalwarts by total surprise, but for a military force stationed underground, the possibility of an environmental failure or a gas attack had to be a contingency. Emergency enviro suits or rebreathers had to be available, though they'd seen none yet. While the doros had been members of the Republic, perhaps they hadn't learned from their partners the need for regulations and the necessary bureaucracy to ensure a safe work environment. Did the doros have an office of safety and health? Even the Legion had regulations regarding mandatory safeguards for different operational environments. He hadn't seen any automated fire bot stations or emergency exit holos lit. If Psydon hadn't turned secessionist, the House of Reason might've invaded simply to bring their vision of civilization to the unwashed masses here.

"Meadows," Kel hailed. "You got me?"

"Roger, sir." With Bertie's repeater, they had comms with the surface. "Busy right now. SLICs are down and our company movement to contact is underway."

Kel gave him a rundown on the effectiveness of the spaz and what little resistance there'd been so far. "You may not have much resistance on the surface. Do you have the map of the installation?"

"Roger. Big sucker."

"Could be they have some air defense left. That central shaft is a repulsor lift to the surface. We're still on the hunt and going deeper. We'll likely lose all comms with you soon. If they have some surprise ready to pop out, hit anything that sticks up its head. Don't worry about us."

"Thanks for the sitrep, sir. We'll be on site within the hour, ready to bring the heat. Meadows out."

"Captain," Hardball called. "I'm aware of all. We're moving to intercept the surface access above the lift. I've got enough big booms to flatten anything that sprouts out of that hidey hole."

"Beat me to the punch, Gabe. I agree. Don't worry about anchoring our breach point. Head out where you can do some good. Your turn to get some. I'll keep you informed. Out." Kel had two courses of action to consider. Where to next and how to get there? "Bertie. What means do we have to access the lower levels?"

"Captain, I've anticipated our need to explore the lower levels. The lift is *the* access. There's a maintenance shaft but otherwise no other direct route to access the lower levels. All but the lowest two levels have their own peripheral tunnels to the surface."

"Oh, boy. So, in order to access the deepest levels, we came in by the most difficult route to get there, from the top," Poul said. "Just our luck."

"Our chosen entry point was serendipitous, Sergeant Radd," Bertie said. "We happened on the air circulation system which enabled a rapid chemical assault on the facility. Entry at any other point may have led to a fighting retreat where we would've encountered troops pouring out from the rest of the facility to cut off our escape. We could've done worse."

"Good point, Bert," Poul said. "I'm not too proud to learn optimism from a DOGR."

"Sir, I think I can streamline our search, though," Bertie continued. "The bots have sent back info on every area, save a couple of notable exceptions. One of those is what looks like a couple of small sections lost to cave-ins. Then there's the obvious finds along the way." Bertie pushed images to their buckets as he narrated. Manpads on racks and in crates occupied two subterranean store-rooms. "The intel was correct about that." The recently-cut clearings were expedient launch sites for the missiles, of which there were plenty. More levels held dens with disabled troops, food stores, a rough surgery with earthen walls, and, on the second deepest level, a huge undivided space that turned out to be a large hanger. The magnetic containment coils of a field generator sat on one platform, next to another loaded with the gimbaled armature of a mount, another carrying crate after crate of focusing rods.

JP whistled, impressed. "That particle beam cannon is as big as anything a capital class cruiser carries. It'd punch a hole through anything in orbit."

Poul, less so. "But it's too big to hide, so it has to stay underground in pieces. If they had it assembled, it might be a danger to someone. As it is, it's only a threat to anyone trying to move it, because even on lifts, it's gotta be a bear to maneuver into place up to the battery."

"It's interesting all right, but it doesn't help us with our primary mission. Bertie, what's the other notable exception you mentioned?" Kel prompted, his patience running thin for the AI's habit of not getting to the point.

A poorly lit view still showed a narrow vault door less than a meter wide, a biopad next to it. "This section is sealed. Not even a nano from one of the micro drones can penetrate it."

"Where is it?"

The map highlighted in red a blind-end tunnel below the hangar. The last stop of the repulsor lift shaft.

"No telling how big it is or what's behind that vault door, sir. But if I were the gambling sort, I'd bet the rindar farm that there's a slimy, spikey Hool down there cooking up trouble."

"Can we call the lift?" Poul asked.

"Negative," Bertie said with a hint of sadness. "You all might fit down the maintenance shaft, but I'll be left behind on the outside looking in." Bertie was necessary if what was behind the sealed vault was the lab they searched for.

Kel's decision was swift.

"Hold this intersection," he indicated to Kynar. "We're going to get that lift. Poul, JP, let's go." The Rafeers' blasters cut loose.

Moon-Hunter barked, "Smooth-bellies ahead. I hit one." He paused and sent a string of blasts. "Two. They're in suits."

"The lift is moving," JP said. The piercing buzz of a blaster bolt whizzed overhead and scorched the plasticrete wall.

"Bertie," was all Kel had to say. The light auto cannon rose from Bertie's back as he side-stepped like a show horse to where the two Rafeer lay on the deck. His head snaked around the column, then darted back only to be replaced by the autocannon, a pulse of fire scorching the gas rich air, leaving vortexes behind the lightning bolts.

"Quiet for now, boss," said Bertie. "Shall I push ahead?"

"What's up there?"

"I'm retasking the nearest micros, now, but seems we've got reinforcements coming from outside."

"No kidding," Poul said. "Thank Oba we have you here to tell us that. Didn't you kill their comms when we entered?" Bertie would've automatically penetrated and disabled any network operating in the complex.

"I did, Sergeant Radd," Bertie said like an annoyed wife telling her husband the bill went out on time, and she doesn't know why the holosuite wasn't receiving. "But it's as I noted about much of how the complex is controlled. I can't disrupt simple hard lines remotely. The Stalwarts have near zero e-band emissions. To maximize concealment, like the other installations you've found, its communications are hardline analog. We have to tap into them or cut them. Ah, here we go!" Just then an image popped up. Coming down the opposite corridor were a platoon of doro in atmosuits.

"They must be coming in from outside. Tell Meadows to get his crews on them. We need those reinforcements cut off."

JP had been working on the lift shaft with his torch, a port large enough for entry now cut into the shell. "Lift is still moving. What's coming up at us, Bertie?" The Rafeer on both sides of the lift were firing now.

"I've no drone view of the hangar level which is where the lift was stopped. I retasked everything on the lower levels to finding us a route down or a way into or out of the vault on the lowest level. We don't have infinite resources on this one, Sergeant Pabon."

"Fine," JP huffed. "I'm stopping that lift. We don't need any more hassles coming from below us." He disappeared through the hastily cut port and vanished.

"Poul, take charge here." Without soliciting permission from his senior NCO, Kel followed. The cavernous shaft ate the light of their buckets like a drop of white paint on an easel piled with black pigment. But at the bottom, the lift rose, creeping upward as slowly as a rising tide.

"Captain," JP said, "let's meet them halfway." He'd already secured a monomolecular cable to a strut and dropped the spool into the darkness. "Link behind me. We'll drop onto it and go from there."

"Go," Kel said without delay. At this point, action was better than reaction. JP rappelled down the shaft, Kel following on the same line. He looked down as he descended, pushing against the side of the shaft to create a free run for JP, who used the clearance to drop rapidly, taking a full level in a single bound.

"Your turn, boss." JP leaned out, creating some free run for Kel to take a rapid abseil down to meet him. The lift continued along its slow rising course.

"Isn't there always some kind of hatch on top of these things?" JP said. "There always is in the holos."

Kel stayed as JP took the next sailing run down the line. "If not, we'll make one."

Another level down and the lift was now just a few meters below them. JP eased onto the top, Kel eased down next to him.

"Take that end." Kel pointed as he creeped to the opposite, careful not to get pinned between the rising platform and the shaft walls. There was a central hatch, but he had another plan. "We can't disable it; we need it. What do you say we cook off ener-grenades on low dispersion and drop stunners in?"

JP had one in hand, swiping the detonator panel. "Good plan, boss. Ready when you are."

"Cook it," Kel said as he set his down. The grenade flared and a white volcano erupted. A fist-sized hole appeared in its place and Kel dropped a stunner through the smoking hole. JP beat him to the access hatch and had it open, tossed another stunner through the opening and waited a second before dropping in. The way below was crowded with twitching doro bodies.

"We've got more tricks than just gas, doggos," JP said as he blasted the paralyzed dog-men one by one. Kel joined him.

"Poul," he said as he blasted the last one, "we're on the way up. We've got a lift full of cooked critters. What's the situation up top?"

"We've got them pushed back for now. Hardball and his team are keeping more from coming in, but we've got packs of doros outside. The mike force is near."

"Tell Hardball to get inside and call air in on everything."

JP sounded pleased. "Sir, I've got the lift controls. Let's give the doros up top a real surprise."

"Got it. Poul." He switched recipients. "These doors open right into the other tunnel entrance. Stand back. We're going to finish this so we can get back to work."

"Rog," Poul said. "Make it big, but don't bring the whole place down on top of us. Please!"

The panel indicated they were approaching the top level. "Ready?"

He could hear JP's grin. "Finally. A stand-up fight with these boys. Let's do it."

Kel had an HE already in the tube and another on the holder next to it ready to load. "This thing moves like pond water," he lamented as he kicked a body aside to plant his feet firmly in the deck. A loud clank and a smooth halt came like the answer to a prayer. The double doors parted as slowly as the lift had climbed. As Kel saw the smoke and his bucket pierced the fog to show him the passage, he let loose. "Fire in the hole."

Two grenades shot through the narrow. Kel had his second loaded and launched as the first salvo exploded. They both stepped aside out of the blast in time for the second wave of overpressure, returning to them like an unwanted kitten who found his way home after a long repulsor ride.

"Poul, send it!" They hung back as more firepower launched ahead from the wings outside. Explosions and plasma flared heavily, followed by thick black smoke and a rumbling.

"Coming in!" Poul yelled out loud. "Coming in!" He was first to peer into the lift. "Looks like you had quite a party in here." Kel had tried, but there were more bodies at their feet than he cared to count.

"Wait for us," Hardball said over L-comm. "Coming in at your six." As the last of the Rafeer steeped into the lift, balancing over the bodies to find a level spot, Hardball's bucket appeared. "We're coming with you. Mined the passage behind us. Meadows is calling hell in on top of us. This is the only safe place."

"Before you lose comms with him, make sure Meadows reminds them to only use guns and AP. No heavies. This whole place will drop on us," Kel reminded.

"Rog," Hardball said as he broke to Meadows's channel.

"Join us, brothers," JP said. "Mind the rug."

Bertie's multiple legs crunched through doro chests as he stepped in. "Sorry 'bout that, boys. Hope your god accepts you in less than pristine condition. Sir, the hangar level is loaded with troops."

Kel checked the feed. Another platoon's worth of dog-men in vacsuits awaited below, staring at the elevator doors, oblivious to the drone somewhere behind them.

Hardball and his two Rafeer, still in doro uniform, stepped in. "Dang. That's more dead dog-men than I've seen in one place yet. Wiggy's right, if you want to stack bodies, make sure you're with the captain at all times."

Kel chuckled. "JP, get this boat moving. Down, please."

The doors closed at an agonizingly slow pace. "What's it look like down that corridor, Poul?"

"Success," he replied. "That tunnel is collapsed past the plasticrete. We shook the roof loose for certain. No one's coming in that way." Finally, the door closed and the sensation of movement resumed.

"Get two shooters up top and cover our descent. I don't want anyone trying the same gimmick we used on the doro." Poul snapped fingers as Taskmaster and Red-Sun let themselves be boosted high to the ceiling, pushing onto the roof of their taxi.

Kel checked the drones. The lowest level was dark and empty, the vault door and the dim biopad next to it beckoning like the door to a Lorrian trillionaire's platinum horde. "JP, straight to the bottom, yes? Express."

"It's like Bertie said, sir. This control panel seems to be basic and not linked. I'd say that guy," JP pointed at an unarmed doro heaped below the control box, "was the operator. I've got us going straight down with no sight-seeing stops along the way."

"We just dropped out of comms with the surface," Bertie said. "We've finally reached the limit of what my repeater will do."

"Hope you're a good miner," Hardball said. "'Cause first bunker buster the Navy accidentally sends down, we're going to be on our own until they bring in an excavator ray."

"Let's hope it doesn't come to that," Kel agreed. "First things first. Lock this lift when we stop, and let's get into that vault. The rest, we'll deal with when we can."

Poul sighed. "We get trapped down here only to find out that vault's holding nothing but the pack leader's virgin daughters, this is going in my memoirs as the worst mission ever."

Kel recognized it was up to him to change the mood. "I'll get us out of here."

"Yes, sir," JP said. "First let's find out what's so important they have it sealed at the bottom of this ant farm. I'll personally dig us out if there's no other way. I worked the mines on Sylar Three with my dad as a teenager. Find me a shovel and I'll make a passage big enough to get Bertie through without bending his knees. There might even be some fire crystals to find along the way for our troubles. A memento for your lady friend, sir."

Kel canted his head to Poul at the mention of Tara, who shrugged as if to say, "*I didn't say anything.*" It was probably just an offhand comment.

The lift control lit to show the next to last symbol. They tensed, expecting a storm of fire to assault the doors as they sank past, but nothing happened. The doros on the other side reacted to the sound of the passing elevator with exasperation, trying to pry the lift doors open, but failing.

"How's it look up top, guys?" Poul shouted through the hatch. A snout peered over the edge.

"Dark as a moonless night," Taskmaster's voder projected. "Doros hate heights. I doubt they'd—" Blaster fire rang out above them.

"Sket!" Hardball exclaimed. "Guys, boost me up." Gabe took a hop onto Poul and JP's locked arms, then jumped as the pair vaulted him up like a springboard.

"Another minute to go and we're there," Kel said as he checked the drone view again. It was as unchanged as it had been, dark and foreboding. The blaster fire above faded. The two Rafeer dropped down, Hardball behind them.

"Let's spot-weld that hatch. We've got them shy to try it again, but they may change their minds."

"Do it," Poul said. "Help me." Everyone joined to stack bodies beneath the access, making a ladder of dead flesh until it was high enough for Gabe to climb, sparks from his torch bouncing off his shoulders as melting beads of durasteel cooled. He climbed down the grisly step stool. "That'll keep them off us for a while."

The same clank issued, and the lift halted. "Ready!" Kel ordered as guns came up. "JP, open it." The doors slid aside as they lit the space beyond with white lights. There was no more stealth to be used, its usefulness exhausted. Now it was time for bold hate to pour forth like the storm building inside them.

"Bertie, what do you read?" Kel stood in the center, holding back the Rafeer and his teammates. He'd made the mistake of walking into a mechanical ambush before. Never again. Bertie's head stretched out on his snake-like neck, almost sniffing as the Rafeer were doing beside them.

"No active scanning. No molecular traces to indicate explosives or plasma cells charging." The DOGR's head retracted. "Seems clean."

Kel wasn't so sure. But they couldn't stay immobile from fear of what might be ahead.

"Sir, I suggest I go first. I need to slice that biopad regardless."

Bertie was critical to the mission if the lab were on the other side, but as he looked at his troops, he knew he owed them whatever protection he could conjure, even if illusory. "Go."

Bertie pranced out of the lift and onto the bare floor of the landing, stopping at the smooth black portal and the biopad a few meters opposite them. He sat on his haunches as his forelegs produced fine digits that worked the pad furiously. The silence was only broken by the sound of his tapping, one pattern after another.

"Encrypted, as suspected, but not well. It won't hold up for long. Be ready for a breach."

"Move," Kel ordered. Kynar and the Rafeer did as Poul directed, dragging doro bodies into the lift threshold and pinning the doors on both sides. JP, Poul, and Hardball rolled to the black vault door, rifles raised, ready for what lay beyond.

"Chieftain," Kynar said. "There is... there is something..." she coughed. The other Rafeer reached to their throats, the same hacking cough, a chorus of distressed yips and pants before they fell to the ground.

"Nanos detected in the environment, Captain," Bertie said. "A bioweapon's been loosed in the air."

"Dammit! Kynar!" Kel said as he dropped next to the Rafeer. He watched helplessly as she tore off her protective mask, struggling to breathe. Pink froth came out of her mouth until her body went limp, her eyes a glassy imitation of life. The gurgling noises of suffering died from the other Rafeer, now as limp and peaceful as Kynar. Kel stood. Red clouded his vision. Blood boiled in his heart.

"Get that door open. Strip charges. Full effect. Everything beyond it gets burned. KTF everything."

"Unlocking now," Bertie said.

Kel's hands found his K-17.

"They wanted a war. What we do now, the doros are going to remember for a hundred generations."

35

The glassy smooth portal reflected the image of the four operators, the black mirror capturing their leader's heart. Now he felt nothing, not even rage. Now he was a machine, built only for justice. The kind dispensed from the end of a blaster, as only a legionnaire knew how. Within the deepest part of his mind, he heard the words as if Hardball's deep voice whispered them into his bucket.

Forged in heat and fire, I do not lose myself, but find salvation by leading the charge.

"Breach," he ordered. As slowly as the lift had crawled, the door vanished, as different as hot from cold, as night from day, as joy from hurt. He was ready to kill whoever made the Rafeer perish in anguish. They would die in all the pain he could bring to them.

Kel launched a stunner deep, as two others were tossed past the threshold. Purple arcs danced, and faded. Through the door, ready to kill whatever awaited, to burn anyone in their path, the space spoke to them in shapes and voids. Wordlessly, they came together, separated, pushed, exploded, and paused.

"Are they dead?" Hardball was the first to speak.

Cells, more like displays, held slabs and bodies. Doro and human.

"On me," Kel said as he pushed through the chamber to the only avenue left to pursue. The machines and contrivances around the lab held no danger to them, so held no interest. No more important than any other obstruction to vision which could conceal a waiting attacker. The blinking lights and holos were no more essential to him than a blank wall. Observed, processed, then once cleared, forgotten. Space after space and void after void, body after unmoving body, assessed, cleared, deleted from attention as they rolled ahead.

The path ended at the entrance, the clear barrier unparted. Behind it, a spiny grinning ghoul taunted them with a mouth of tiny pointed teeth.

"Bertie, sound off," Kel prompted.

"Another nano weapon has been released into the environment. It will take some time to analyze, but it's safe to say you don't want to pop buckets."

"Breach that portal. Make it messy."

Poul removed a strip off Hardball's back and rolled it down the middle of the transparent door. The Hool on the other side stopped grinning. "What's the matter, kelhorn? We're not dropping like flies from your little bug? Don't worry, you can explain it all to us up close and personal in a second."

"Breach."

The plasma charge exploded. Poul was nearest. He kicked the shattered panels as the last barrier between him and their tormentor fell aside. Kel sped forward as the recoiling Hool protested in an undecipherable babble. Kel leaped over the table, knocking stacks of datapads and gel-filled cubes aside as he hit the alien with both feet. The sound of air escaped wet lips, the cry barely heard over the cacophony of cubes crashing from racks onto the sterile floor.

Careful to avoid its deadly venomous quills, Kel snatched the purple-skinned Hool to his feet, one hand clutching the clothing over its chest, raising it in the air, to land a gauntleted fist into its head. Blue blood flew from its mouth; a poison as deadly as any in the galaxy.

Poul yelled, "Kel, stop! He's a prisoner."

"He's a prisoner when he's in custody. There're no chains in him. Right now, he's an illegal combatant." Kel slammed the Hool against the wall, the crack of cartilage distinct from the crystal boxes it landed against.

"Kel, enough!" Poul raced ahead, chains out. "JP, help me."

Kel growled. "That Hool isn't as feeble as it's acting. I've dealt with cnidarians and agnathians before. Don't be afraid to use all the chains we have. Make sure he can't squirm a millimeter." JP and Poul wrapped chains around the Hool from shoulders to feet, the glowing binders digging into the clothing until the lights were buried and dimmed.

Poul sat the Hool up against the wall. "Want to try those spines out on us? It'll be about as effective as your little nanos, fish face."

Kel looked around. There were no exits, no additional rooms. "Bertie. I want a full scan. If this is all there is, get working on a data haul. Get us answers while I talk to our mad scientist."

"On it, Captain." Bertie moved to another table where a terminal sat, and started his examination.

"JP, check the entryway," Kel said and moved to let the wide leej pass. The Hool made guttural croaks of pain, betraying consciousness. He knelt. "Hool, you are under arrest for crimes against the galaxy. Your little nano-lab is going to bring you and anyone close to you a one-way trip to a deep mine on a prison planet for all eternity, which for you, will be mercifully short, I'm sorry to say."

The Hool was fully awake, spitting liquid words in snaps and gurgles in its own language.

"Don't feel like speaking Standard? No problem. I know you understand me. So, I'm going to ask. Why are you here?"

The Hool's lips curled inward, then it spat. Kel didn't flinch. Instead, he knelt on its knees. A trilling howl escaped the thin mouth. Kel removed his encouragement.

"Are the doros and humans next door victims of your little experiments to figure out how to program nanos for bioweapons? Might as well tell me. Murder isn't any more of a capital offense than making weapons of mass destruction." Kel applied pressure to the Hool's outstretched knees again with the same effect. It gasped.

"My property. My property. Bought. No crime."

"Property," Hardball said. "Slavery isn't legal anywhere, pin head."

Poul stood. "Gabe, check on JP."

Hardball hesitated, then nodded as if understanding. Poul wanted him out of the room. When he'd gone, Poul clicked to a private channel. "Kel, we can't torture this clown. As much as I'd like to skin the answers out of him, we need the pros to get answers out of him. We need him in one piece."

Kel stared at the Hool, who now shook. Lidless eyes rolled back into its head. Seeming to ignore Poul, he spoke in the clear. "Bertie, what've you got?"

"I haven't been listening to you torture that war criminal, if that's what you mean, sir. Heard nothing. They can't make me rat out a teammate. I'll dump my core before that happens."

"No, Bertie, that's not what I mean." Kel rose, but kept his eyes on their prisoner. *Leave it to our AI to make me see the sense of acting human.* "But thanks."

"All right then, sir. What I've found is solid evidence of nano construction and bio-nano programming. As the victims next door indicate, our evil doctor has been fashioning gene-weapons. I can't yet tell what gene loci are targeted, but we have proof there are some nasty varieties based on what happened to our poor friends. Forgive me, sir, but I'm for stringing this bastard up right here. Not sure he's got any information anyone even needs."

The Hool shuddered, as if he'd heard their conversation. "Only I know. Only I."

"Think he's bargaining for his life, Kel?" Poul asked.

"Probably." Kel remembered his promise to bring pain to the murderer of their companions. If their AI thought the prisoner had little value... he closed that line of thought. "Bertie, our job is to wipe this place clean. What about your nano replicator? How much time do you need to make a counter agent?"

On a slow day, Bertie could process a thousand pieces of data in a millisecond. The pause before answering made Kel anxious like the seconds that crawled past the moment the grenade should have already exploded, but didn't. The rumbles reaching them through the walls and ceiling only added to his feeling that bad news was coming.

"The answer is complex, sir, but I know you want the short version."

Thank Oba, Kel thought. *Finally. He gets it.*

"I can't."

Poul exploded. "Bertie. You assured us you could. What changed?"

"There's too many of them. Not by mass—by type. The prisoner has been busy. There are so many different varieties with so many gene loci encoded for both human and doro, I could be here a week knocking out one an hour, and I don't know I'd get them all."

Kel thought quickly. "Priority one. Have any been released?"

"There's no indication that any have been produced in amounts ready to load into deliverable weapons. Yet. We may have gotten here in time to prevent that."

"Thank Oba!" Poul said.

Kel likewise felt relieved. "You sure about that, Bertie? It's pretty important we're certain."

"Which is why we can't just pull out and let the techies crawl all over this place, sir. I doubt we'd get a reliable answer out of our professor here, no matter how well we doped him or tortured him. I'm forced to offer what is, I think, the only safe solution."

"What's that?" Kel asked.

Bertie turned to them. A small panel opened within his storage compartment and a container within rose into view. "The best alternative I have is to gamma this entire facility to ensure nothing escapes."

Poul slapped his bucket. "Is that a gamma bomb? How come we didn't know you had that?"

"I knew," Kel admitted. "Sorry, Poul. I hate to be the 'need to know' guy, but it was included as a last resort. The only authorization for them is against a threat like bioweapons."

Poul harrumphed. "Remind me again what you did to the last guy who gave you that same business."

"Sorry, brother. The question is, Bertie, is this a DIP or can we get out of here?" Die in place was what he was prepared to hear.

"No, sir. No Order of the Centurion for the lot of you chaps. We'd only have to DIP if these nanos were self-replicating. The swarm released on our friends was ghastly, but not capable of replicating. Any of those in the atmo outside, I'll have a counter-nano ready soon. My swarm will hunt down and eat any of that variety in a minute or so starting... now." Just then a cloud appeared from the replicator in his compartment and spread out of the lab. "Doctor Hool there has a meteor shower's worth of different buggies for both species, with all sorts of targeted effects. But none of them are replicators. Whatever gets a good dose of gamma rads here, dies."

"Us too," Poul said. "Can you remote det it?"

"I can put it on a tamperproof timer," Bertie explained. "And we can beat feet out of here. We need a solid five klicks' distance to be out of effective range or every bit of DNA in your genes and my colloidal core will be split apart like a fat man's britches."

"What about the shielding effect because the detonation's underground?" Kel asked.

"Estimates, boss. Estimates. I wouldn't wager our lives on anything less than two klicks."

Kel decided. "JP. Hardball. Get ready to move out. What's it looking like out there?"

"I retasked what drones were left to get us what views we could," JP replied. "Judging by the number of doggos come underground to hide, it looks like the Navy is giving everything a good pasting. The place is crawling with cowering pups."

"Take the lift straight to the top?" Poul offered. "If the doros are down here, let's switch places with them, call in a bird, and get the hell out of here before that gamma cooks the lot of them and the nanos."

"I like a simple plan. Gents, hear that? We're leaving," Kel said. "Bertie, plant your gamma and if you'd be so kind," he thumbed over his shoulder to the bound Hool. "Let's take the trash out with us."

"Did I miss something?" Hardball said. "What's that about a gamma?"

"Let me know as soon as you can get Meadows on the horn. Same with the air cover. Get an all stations out to check fire because friendlies are in the blast zone," Kel said as the lift crawled upward.

"On it, boss," Bertie replied. The Hool struggled ineffectively on Bertie's back. He didn't doubt the criminal was having trouble breathing. He was breathing, though. Maybe with effort, but the sounds told Kel the alien was very much alive, even if uncomfortably so. That was more than he deserved.

"Sergeant Meadows on the horn, sir," Bertie said.

"Meadows, pull the mike force back. Get everyone at least five klicks away. We're about to set off a gamma bomb."

"Holy sket! What about you guys?"

"We're fighting our way out, but it sounds like you and the Navy made us a clear path. Regardless, that bomb is going off to erase any nano in there, and we found plenty."

"I'll bring the Talons on station. If you get a spot where you can vertically extract, we'll have them on you like hair on a wobanki. I've got your L-comm channel hot, and I'll be monitoring."

"Roger, Curt. Thanks. Get the mike force out of range. That's your first priority."

"I can have two first priorities, sir. Out."

"Make this thing go faster," Hardball said. "I got a feeling as soon as the heat dies off, the dog-men are going to go back to causing trouble outside."

"Wish I could," JP said. "This thing was built to carry the thousand tons of that particle cannon, not carry impatient leejes."

"Bertie, hang back," Kel said. "Hardball, you're Bertie's battle. You two get that Hool to Barnett and the intel weenies. That is an order. Got me?"

"Understood, boss," Bertie confirmed.

Hardball was up. "Yes, sir, but I'm not turning tail on you guys to get this little fishy to market. Hell, we wuz gonna torture him to death just a little while ago."

Kel sighed. "Gabe, guys, I was wrong. Please don't ever think back on that incident and use it as an excuse to lose your cool, because you saw me do it. I want you all to be better than me. When I get carried away, I rely on you guys to pull me back. You too, Bertie. Sorry I let you down. But I'm proud of you all for always having my back. Thanks."

JP scoffed. "Pfft, the only reason I didn't pull that Hool's spine out through his waste ejection port is because you beat me to it, sir. What are we gonna tell Bruto and Lupa?" He shook his head in despair. Their friends had suffered horrific, impotent deaths. If the Nobles were to die in combat, they deserved an end more dignified than dying at the hands of an honorless micro robot.

Poul had the answer. "Kynar and her pack mates were warriors. That's what we tell them. Because that's what they were. They were our tribe, sure as if they'd been leejes." He pointed at the Hool on Bertie's back. "And that slime's going to spill it all—so we can go after his crew next. We'll bring back Hool guts on platters for them to feast on."

"Steady on," Bertie warned. "Near the end of the ride."

"Poul, JP, me. We take the battery. If it's clear, we'll bring you guys out. Then we'll make best course to friendlies. Ready?" Grunts sufficed as K-17s came to ready. A different tone of clank and a gentle rock told them the lift was locked. "Let's make it happen."

The doors parted and Kel burst out onto a duracrete pad. Revetments at one end were destroyed, one of the bombing runs had hit the mark—unintentionally and serendipitously. Revealed as well: a blanket of jungle grown over a shell. The particle gun battery was concealed under a moveable cap of forest green.

Poul called out. "I've got us a trail out of here. Should follow west to where we entered the complex, then back and away to the DZ clearing. It's big enough we can call in a Talon for a ground extraction. We can ride out in style."

"Bertie, Gabe, let's roll."

"You hear that, Hool?" Gabe said, knowing only they could hear him. "You're one step closer to the flat, dry rock they're gonna cook you on. You'll be tellin' everything you know and some of what you don't."

"Contact, front," Poul said. Kel froze. Poul led them down the slope, along the trail so narrow an insect would have to turn on its side to walk it.

"What do you have?" Kel asked.

"Two doros, sniffing. Uh oh." Poul turned loose with his blaster. Kel pushed around him and poured heat on the figures retreating down the trail. "Winged one, but he got away. I'd say the dog-men are coming out of the woodworks again."

"I'd say it's a new group of reinforcements coming from one of the other divisions," Meadows's voice came to them. "We've got word the BDA on the Braves and Trues is less than stellar, and there are a lot of small unit engagements by the Legion. I'd say the Stalwarts got the word when you hit them, and their cousins came running. We've got to get you some air support back."

"No good, Curt," Kel answered. "We'd be calling them in on top of us. If we can fight to a defendable spot, we'll give the Talons the option to try for CAS and an extraction."

Meadows sounded perturbed. "Roger. They're on station. Delta One and Delta Two. Keep them in the loop."

"Where's the mike force?" Kel hoped they were near to being out of range of the radiation wave to come.

"We're pulling back, as ordered. No one wants to get cooked by a gamma, but no one's happy about leaving you guys in the lurch, boss."

"You don't have to be happy; you just have to do it. We're busy. Quit gabbing. Turner out. Poul," he broke. "Change of direction, yes?"

"Roger, Kel. Take us back and find us another way out. I'll bring up the rear. Dropping a paw-popper on the trail behind us. Let's go."

Back on the battery top, Hardball had another trail. "Misses the tunnel entrances on the east side of the complex, but it takes us away from friendlies. Should give us a way we can make some distance happen, at least."

"Good. You can take the lead, but once we get down this slope, you and Bertie trail us, got me?"

"Grr. Yes, sir."

Down the trail they went. A sharp crack and a squelched yelp came from behind them.

"Dropping more poppers," Poul said. "We're being pursued. I'm thinking that Hool's got enough scent for them to know where we are for a hundred klicks. I'm going to keep dropping poppers till I run out, which is only a few more."

"I've got more, Top," JP said. "Then we go with AP mines."

"Agreed."

They kept pushing. After a few minutes, another popper detonated, rewarding the effort.

"We gotta get off this trail," Hardball said. "But we ain't going to make distance if we do. Bertie, how much time?"

"We need to make another kilometer in the next fifteen minutes to be safe."

Kel knew it was time for a hard decision. He made it. "Bertie. You're on your own. You can dance through this stuff. Take off. Make your best course to friendly lines. Get our prisoner delivered. Sorry, Gabe. You're stuck with us at trotting speed."

"Apologies, gents," Bertie said. "I'll link up with you as soon as I can get our package delivered. On the bounce." Kel saw Bertie's silhouette spring off, and he was gone.

"Hardball, you happy leading off?" Kel asked needlessly. Gabe's preference to stay with the team had already been registered as a complaint. "Make your best speed. We're on your tail."

"Keep up then, boys. I'll spring any ambush Bertie hasn't. Stay sharp."

"We've got ten minutes," JP reminded him. Another muffled detonation reached them. "They're not quitting."

"All the more reason to peel out," Poul said. "Push on, Gabe," he said, trotting.

Up another gradual slope, over a ridge, and into a ravine. Kel paused them. "Distance?" He had the map up but wanted someone else to check him.

"About two klicks, on the nose," Hardball answered. "Low ground. As good a place to hunker down as any."

"Hook us off this trail and into a perimeter," Kel agreed. "This is the place."

They followed Gabe and settled onto their bellies. Whether it brought them any additional shielding from the deadly burst of gamma radiation, no one knew. But it was all they could do. Like a trapped beast gnawing the leg crushed in the jaws of a trap, it was Hobson's choice. Take the only course of action available, or do nothing.

"Bertie, are you clear?" Kel asked.

"Roger, sir. Making good time. I see your squat spot. Decent. You'll be good to go. One minute, blokes. Hang in there. It'll cook any doros on your trail unless they get a lot closer to where you are in a bloody hurry."

"If we get a dose, the rad gel in our armor should deploy," JP said. "If not, then we know we're far enough away. The dosimeters are very sensitive. Here we go."

Kel knew nothing would happen, but still half expected there to be some kind of detectable effect.

Bertie spoke, joy evident as he trotted. "I'd say mission successful, Captain. Positive detonation. High order. I detect the gamma spike. Any nano and any living thing in that complex is cooked. Anything much closer than you gents, and there's not enough free-radical healing meds on the planet to heal all the DNA splits. They'll

be growing third legs and tumors and getting cata-
racts in a week, if they survive the initial radiation blast.
Congratulations, team."

"Good work, Bertie. Now get that Hool out of here and—"

The surrounding jungle exploded in white flares. Kel
initially couldn't locate the source of the blaster fire. Then
he realized it was from everywhere.

Kel was too busy firing back to give directions. The
mad minute continued. He sent blasts blindly left and
right, up the slope, then rolled to his back and launched a
grenade behind him, over the backs of JP and Gabe. Gabe
turned and did the same over Kel.

"How'd we get surrounded?" Gabe asked.

"We've got to get to better ground," Poul said. The
shooting eased, then stopped. Kel strained to listen
through the dark jungle.

"We've stumbled right into an enemy skirmish line,"
Kel said. "It's the only explanation." A doro rushed through
the jungle a meter in front of him, blaster bolts hammering into the ground around him when Kel touched off a
single shot, opening a hole in its upper chest that removed
one of its shoulders before the wild attacker dropped on
top of him.

"Where's the main body?" Hardball asked.

"We're in the frelling middle of them," Poul spat. "To
my left is a rise. It's just a few meters. I'm tossing a grenade up there. When I do, open up and let's make for it.
Ready? Now!"

Kel responded by firing to his front. There was nothing
to see through the dense foliage, but small paths opened
up behind his blasts to show bodies dropping on the jungle floor. A grenade exploded on high dispersion so close

Kel could feel the sizzle through his armor. Screams followed it.

"Go."

Kel crawled on his belly. The work going up the rise let him know he was headed in the right direction behind the man in front of him, unable to tell who it was.

"Mind the doros," Poul said. It was Poul who led the way, and it was Poul's grenade that had dispatched the dog-men just a few meters from them. He pushed a limp body out of his way as he crawled ahead.

"We found a fighting position," Poul said. "They've dug in. Lucky break for us."

No one was shooting at them for the moment. Kel checked their new surroundings. A shallow bowl was dug out of the tiny hilltop between trees, roots exposed through the thin topsoil. The excavated earth was pushed into a narrow berm around them. Three doro bodies lay between them.

Hardball coughed before he spoke. "These guys must've just laid low while the order to fire went out. That grenade you launched might've actually got these boys, Captain. Sorry, Top, I'm adding these to the captain's tally."

JP was pulling AP mines out of his ruck while on his belly. "We trotted right into their forward lines. Doro reinforcements come to bail out the Stalwarts. Maybe the Navy's knocked some of them out. Maybe it's a disrupted platoon."

Kel pulled put a mine and pushed another grenade into the tube. "Might be a battalion. No way of knowing. All they know is they've got an enemy in their lines. What would you do in their place?"

Poul answered for them all. "Keep sending small probes to find us, fix us, and finish us."

"Exactly. Let's get some help. Delta One, Delta Two, this is Boxcar Six. Request CAS, repeat, Request CAS. Troops in contact. How copy?"

A howl, a second to locate the source, a charge, a doro rushed into the pit. Hardball shot; the grenade in the dog-man's paw dropped.

"Grenade!"

Kel looked for it, saw it, just as JP shot out, palmed it, and threw it. The midair explosion peppered them with frag. It bounced off Kel's back and legs.

"Everyone okay?" he asked over his own ringing ears.

"They're doing suicide runs at us now," Poul said. He pulled a grenade off his chest, swiped it, but didn't throw. Kel counted with him, silently. *One-one thousand. Two-one thousand. Three-one thousand.* He rolled the grenade over the berm. It exploded almost immediately, raining dirt all over them. Screams came from the other side, mere meters away. "They're all over! Frag 'em. Everyone."

Kel was already cooking a grenade. He counted and tossed lightly in front of him. His audio cut out, but the blast let him know there was no doubt. A grenade exploding a meter away, only a thin pile of dirt between you and it, left no room for questions about where it was or where you were.

An explosion rang out near enough to matter, but far enough away to make them curious rather than anxious. Doros howled. Shouts followed.

"Hear that?" Poul said. "They're telling their guys not to use launchers or throw grenades. One bounced back and killed their own guys."

"Then they're going to try more rushes." Kel got his hand blaster out. Things were so close it was difficult to bring his K-17 to bear. He heard rustling and grunts nearing. "Here they come again." Kel opened up blindly into the brush. He aimed his pistol over the berm, spraying low and where he pictured crawling doros to be. Whimpers faded and died on the other side.

"Grenade!" Hardball yelled.

Kel rolled, hoping the dog-man body behind him would shield him as he worried about his three teammates. The crump and tremors rang through his armor; dirt and the wet not-dirt of bodies sprayed.

"Dammit!" Hardball said. "I'm peppered. I'm leaking from somewhere."

"Stay there," JP said as Kel felt him crawl behind him.

"Delta One, Delta Two. Boxcar Six. Troops in contact. Request CAS."

A voice came back this time. "Boxcar, we have you. On our way. We have your beacons. Five mikes TOT. How copy?"

"Five minutes," Hardball lamented with a wince.

"No big holes, Gabe," JP said. "Your auto-tourniquets didn't fire. Just small stuff through the backs of your legs. You hurt anywhere else?"

"No. I'm good. Don't even hurt now."

"Give the wound gel a minute to seal you up."

"Thanks, brother."

Kel heard the exchange while he talked to the aircrew. "Good copy, Delta. Hail when you're on station. Alright, we've got Talons inbound," Kel shared, though they all heard it. He snapped to the sound of another howl. Coming over the berm was another doro. Kel's vibro-blade was in his hand before he knew it and he stabbed, pounding with fist and burying the blade over and over.

He lost track of how many dog-men came at them. Around him, doro bodies were piling onto the berm.

"I'm out of grenades," Kel realized. "And I hear more of them. They're not quitting."

"Me too. Kel, potluck?" Poul asked.

"Potluck," he agreed.

"What the hell's that?" Hardball asked.

"Show-and-tell time, boys," Kel said. He rolled onto his back, took the AP mine at his side, and swiped the arming strip. "Get ready. Cover." He tossed the mine up as high as he could from on his back. He clicked his teeth and the mine exploded. A thousand needles flew into the jungle. Screams and howls returned.

"Holy sket!" JP yelled. "If it had been pointing at us, we'd be shredded!"

"That's why it's called potluck, son," Poul said. "Bigg's the only one we know's ever done it. Till now."

"Seemed like a similar situation." Kel explained. He and Poul had listened to Bigg's description of potluck, vowing to each other in a revolted awe that they'd avoid being in a fix so desperate, one so grave, that it would be their only option. There wasn't time now to rethink their life choices.

"Poul, your turn." Kel felt no panic. No discomfort. No worry. He was living second by second.

"Set," Poul warned. "Get ready. Cover."

Hardball let loose a string of expletives, notable only for the anatomic impossibilities they described. Needles sliced into the jungle.

"Missed me by a micron," JP said. "But there's more screaming doros, so you did good, Top."

Kel raised his K-17 to check ahead through the slaved view of his optic. Through breaks in the brush, he saw more dog-men massing. One stood at the rear of their ranks as he urged them forward, a line of them crawling on bellies, dragging weapons behind them. Kel lined up his reticle and shot the leader, his chest exploding in a satisfying spray. A hail of blaster fire whizzed over him; he jerked his carbine down—a moment too late. It was knocked from his hands.

"Boxcar, Boxcar, we are on station, how copy?"

"Bring it, Delta. Bring it down on us. We're surrounded. As close to our beacons as you can."

"Boxcar. We have no visual. We have your beacons, but we can't identify targets. We can't fire."

"Delta, if you don't try, we're dead anyway. I'm authorizing you for a gun run. You have to. Don't let these dog-men win."

The silence was as unwelcome as the sounds of the doro massing around them.

Meadows's voice broke in. "Delta, this is Boxcar Three. You heard them. You've got to believe the guy on the ground. Bring the rain."

After another pause, the distant voice returned. "Stand by, Boxcar Six. Rain inbound."

"You heard him," Kel said. "Bury yourselves. Help Gabe first." Kel grabbed a doro body and rolled it over Hardball. "Stay low, Gabe."

"You too, sir." Gabe was calm, but his voice sounded weak.

Kel tried to dig deeper into the soft earth. Reaching up he pulled the nearest body off the berm and lay in the darkness.

"It's been a pleasure, my brothers," JP said. "I'm sorry we're here, but there's no one I'd rather be with."

Poul cursed. "We ain't done yet. Incoming, stay—"

The tops of the forest exploded above them, drowning out his next. The whine of repulsors filled the air between the sounds of impacts and screams, so close Kel couldn't tell if it was from them or their enemy. He realized the loudest screams were his as the ground lifted and shook. The creation of the universe itself could be no less violent as the substance of his being was being torn asunder, the glue holding the molecules of his body together being stretched apart.

And it was over.

Silence.

"Boxcar Six, Boxcar Six, run complete. How copy?"

Kel rolled the body off him. There wasn't much of it left. "Guys, you with me?"

Poul grunted. "I caught one. My arm or my chest, I can't tell. Oh, it hurts to breathe." He coughed. Kel could hear the blood in Poul's throat. Kel felt the pain as if it was his own.

"I'm coming, Poul. Gabe, JP, sound off."

JP was standing. His carbine was in his hands. Blood covered his armor. His bucket was off. "No more!" he shouted. "I am the destroyer of worlds. I am the bringer of death. You will fail the field of battle today, whining curs!" He leaped from the pit of bodies around them.

"JP! NO!" Kel crawled over the bodies and to the berm, his hands reaching for JP to hold him back. He was gone.

Gabe's carbine lay at his side. The armored body lay as if posed by an artist, peaceful and still. Kel grabbed the K-17 and scurried to the top of the berm. A scant few meters away JP waded through fields of red, firing from both hands, pistol and carbine sending death into the advancing waves of rabid dog-men. Some were missing limbs, some more than that, as they crawled, hobbled, or limped, not from but toward the lone legionnaire. JP stood on top of a hill of dead dog-men, firing with purpose and poise while his weapons ran dry.

Kel fired, too. "More coming, Poul. Help me."

"I can't see, Kel. I'm blind. My bucket's knocked out, I think." He took a strained, wet breath. "Sorry, brother. I think I'm out of the fight."

Kel fired past JP as more doro moved out of the jungle behind him. "JP, get back here!" he yelled aloud.

"Boxcar, Boxcar, do you read?" The pilots were trying to reach him through the heavy haze of clouded perception. He pressed the trigger. Nothing happened. He pawed his chest for another charge pack, but found nothing.

"Delta, I read you. Hit us again. They're still coming." He aimed his reticle into the advancing horde and clicked. "Five-zero meters on this azimuth from my beacon. Hit us again."

"Roger, Boxcar. Stand by."

"JP!" he yelled. "Incoming. Get covered!"

JP threw down his weapons. A doro rushed him, a jagged sword raised. A smile spread across JP's face, as pure as sunlight, an aura of yellow and life radiated from him, dimming the red blood that covered him. He stepped forward to meet the rabid dog-man, his forearms swinging like scythes. The doro howled and collapsed, his arms snapping with the crunch of shattered bones, dropping the blade as JP pushed him aside and drove into the advancing pack. Swinging. Crushing. Destroying.

"You're nothing to me, not worthy to die by my hand. I pass through you like the storm over the sea."

The doros hesitated as the bloodied legionnaire waded through their ranks, turning them back like a wall holding back the rushing waters. The whine of repulsors grew louder.

"JON! GET DOWN."

Kel's world turned white. Then black. Blind, Kel felt the earth lift and he was in the air, flying. He landed on his back. In the midst of creation again, he surrendered. Limp.

"Kel, you there?" Poul said weakly. "I can't see you."

He wanted to answer. He wanted to tell Poul he was with him. That he wasn't alone. He tried. He couldn't make the sounds. What were words anyway? He no longer knew.

"Kel, it's okay. I'm with you, brother. I'll always be with you."

Kel took a breath, then heard no more.

36

"Why are you here, Kel?"

He heard the voice. It was familiar. The face, he knew, but it was different from what he remembered.

"You're not supposed to be here, though you're welcome here, brother. Man, it's been a long time. I've missed you. We all have."

Then he saw them. He recognized them in the same way he did—but didn't—the face in front of him. Around the fire were smiles and laughs. It was warm. He felt safe. Light as a feather, carefree, but strong. Whole.

"Tem?"

"Yeah, buddy. It's Tem. I'm so glad to see you, but it's not your time to be here, man."

"We've got a place for you by the fire, Kel."

It was Liu. He hadn't seen Liu since... since Q. All of Team Seven—Kim, Dari, Jaimie, Liu—sat around the fire, smiling at him like he was the toddler in the room taking his first steps.

Kel knew. "I'm dead. Aren't I?"

"Nah," Tem laughed. "But close. Listen, buddy. You gotta go back. It's gonna hurt. Sorry about that. But it just isn't your time."

Kel saw others, standing around the edge of the circle, the warm light of the flickering fire tickling their features in shadows. Men he knew. Some he didn't. All strong, fierce, yet merry.

"This isn't right," Kel realized. "I'm dreaming."

Tem shrugged. "Maybe you are at that, my brother. Maybe you are. But listen to me. It doesn't matter. We've got faith in you, even when you doubt yourself. Just keep doing your best. There'll be time to sit around the fire with us later. Right now, you've got work to do, Legionnaire. Don't stop until the job's done, you hear me?"

"Found him," a voice said. He felt rough hands. The light made his blurry eyes burn as his bucket was lifted off him. Then the pain followed. He cried out.

"Turner, do you hear me? It's Meadows. Kel, do you hear me?"

He focused. The bucket came off and the face of the man behind it was clear for a second before the pain made everything blurry again. Meadows yelled for assistance.

"Radd. Pabon. Harding." Kel coughed weakly. "Where..."

The air smelled different. Clean. The stench of jungle and blood was gone. He knew time had passed. He opened his eyes.

"Captain Turner, do you know where you are?" a soft voice asked him. "Call the doctor. He's awake," the woman said. The voice was soothing and reminded him of someone else, but he couldn't remember who, but she had long, raven-black hair. "Here. Let me help you sit up. Try a sip of this."

Something wet touched his lips and he inhaled, coughed, then felt the cool run down his chin. A second try was successful, and the dryness in his throat eased.

"Where am I? Where's my team?"

The woman had blonde hair tucked into a bun. She wasn't who he'd thought.

"You're fine, Captain. Are you in pain? I can give you something if you're hurting."

The room came into clarity. He was in a med bay, floating on a grav bed. A man in a white coat came into the room.

"Jackie, how is he?"

"He's just coming around."

"Where am I?" Kel asked again.

"You're on the *Reliance*, Captain. I'm Lieutenant Commander Deuel, your doctor. You're going to be fine. Now, follow along with me. Look at my finger."

Kel obeyed all the commands, moving arms and legs in the sequence ordered.

"Where are my teammates?" he asked again.

"Jackie, push some somnambutol. You're going to rest now, Captain. We'll talk again soon. Rest up."

"But," he tried to protest. Kel closed his eyes. Which was the dream? He didn't know. As he went under, he remembered a face around the fire he hadn't seen in years, and knew he wouldn't see again for a long time. Until he took his place by the fire again.

"Enough goldbricking, Leej."

Meadows's rough voice brought him out of sleep.

"Thought you could use some company."

The days and nights were always mixed up on a ship, but especially so in the hospital bay. He knew it had been a few days since he'd been back among the living. He'd destroyed his breakfast, cleaning his plate and asking for seconds, but before it came, he was fast asleep again. Until Meadows assaulted him with his booming voice. His stomach rumbled below the sheets.

"How you feeling, Kel?" Bigg stood on the other side of Meadows, grinning.

"Yeah. Pretty good, guys. How're you doing?" He shook himself awake. His body ached and he wanted to get out of bed, pushing himself up to try.

"Easy, man. Better stay there until the doc says it's okay." Meadows had his hands on Kel's shoulders to encourage him to stay in bed.

"Ah, that's a bunch of nonsense and you know it," he said grumpily. "If it were up to these Navy types, I'd be in bed for a month. I'm fine. Nothing a little gym time won't solve."

"Okay, hero," Bigg laughed. "Same old Kel."

He relaxed. "It's good to see you guys." Just hearing his friends say his name made him feel better. Kel. Not "Captain." He didn't remember who the captain was, but he knew who Kel was. And Kel had an obligation. Maybe he really could shake this off with a good workout.

"Say, how long have I been here?"

He suddenly realized he didn't know.

"You've been here a week, Kel," Bigg said. "We're still in orbit over Psydon, but we're heading home tomorrow. The Psydon campaign is over and the last team's boarded. We'll be on Victrix in time for you to walk off the dropship yourself."

He had so many questions. "I don't remember much after, you know, after the last. Where are the guys?"

Meadows told him what he knew he wanted to hear. "Gabe and Poul are in the next bays. Doing fine. As soon as they'll let me, I'll wheel you over there myself for a visit. They've been awake a little longer than you. You're slacking, brother. They're already walking."

Kel knew what the conspicuous deletion meant.

"JP?"

Meadows shook his head. "We searched and searched. I wanted to bring him home, but..." He didn't finish.

"Yeah," Kel said. "I understand." He remembered the last moments before the world went dark for him. "You know what he did, right? He took dozens of them down by himself. To save us." Kel felt the wetness on his cheeks.

"We know," Bigg said.

"It was the bravest thing I've ever seen. Or heard of. He deserves the OC. He's going to get it, too. I need to get on my after-action." He winced as he tried to push himself up in the bed.

"Time for that later," Bigg said, trying to soothe Kel back into comfort.

"JP deserves it, if anyone does," Meadows said. "More than that point, anyway."

"Point?" Kel asked, confused.

Meadows made a sour face. "Seems one of those new point officers the Legion got saddled with led some hairbrained mission to take out those roving artillery pieces the 187th was having so much trouble finding. Got a bunch of marines killed, but he got the job done. Got old Subs killed, too."

Subs! It was easy to be in Dark Ops and not meet up with operators on other teams when back on Victrix. With everyone deployed all over the galaxy, often the timing was never right to connect with friends between missions. He hadn't seen Subs before he'd made his departure from DO, sent down to the Legion after the injuries that made it mandatory he be exiled from their ranks.

At least, until he'd seen him by the fire.

"Yeah. I know."

"Huh? Who told you?"

He wasn't sure of what he'd seen, or where it was, but knew if he tried to explain, they'd think he was crazy. He didn't want to be bounced out of DO for that.

"I overheard the nurses talking."

"Well, don't worry, Kel," Bigg said. "The colonel will take it directly to Umstead and Barrow. JP will get the Order. Guaranteed."

"How'd it all end up?" It sounded as if the rebellion of Psydon was over.

Meadows pulled up a chair. "After we pulled you out, the Navy carpeted everything. More sorties than've been flown in decades. There's no doro resistance left. The trail you found was their last-ditch effort to keep an insurgency going in the south. We did BDAs and flooded the whole continent with sniffer bots. There isn't a dog-man left to fight, and if there is, there's not a bit of fight left in them. The 131st and 187th went back and cleaned up the rest of the planet in days."

"The Army's going to be there for a spell," Bigg added. "They'll occupy Psydon for a few generations, I'm sure. That seems to be how it always goes."

"You ought to know, Bigg," Kel said as he tried to get comfortable, not finding the position that would ease the ache in his back. "You've been everywhere to see it all before."

"True. And now, so have you two."

The next morning, Kel was irritable. He wanted to get out of the hospital ward to be with the rest of the teams in the DO section of the *Reliance*. Back with his tribe. Gabe and Poul were being discharged. They teased him mercilessly about being infirm. They laid off when he told them he didn't want to show up looking weak in front of the other operators.

"Hah! Like anyone would have the guts to say that to your face," Gabe said.

"Or behind your back," Poul added. "No worries. We'll save a bunk for you."

The grav bed was better than the bunk would be, but he felt hostile toward its comfort. He was in no pain, except when he tried to stretch his hamstrings. He'd work that out, soon enough.

"Anyone hear anything about our Rafeer?" Kel asked, trying to take his mind off his aches. He wasn't going to ask for a med. He'd refused every one offered. To ask now would seem like a big step backward.

Poul had news of their friends. "Meadows, Sims, Wiggy, Woobie—all made it to the camp and sat at the mourning fire. Sims said it was a real downer, saying goodbye to Bruto and Lupa."

Gabe touched his stomach where the raised tattoo sat. "Wish we could've been there. Maybe it's better though, so they didn't have to hear how awfully Kynar and the rest died. It would've been hard to make up a kind story about it."

"I'm sorry just the same," Kel said. "They treated us like family."

"Like members of the pack," Poul corrected. "Gabe, I'll catch up to you, okay?"

"Sure thing. See you tomorrow, sir." Gabe closed the door behind him.

Poul plopped into the lone chair. "How are you, Kel? I was pretty worried about you. You were out of it for a few days."

"I'm going to be fine, Poul. You?"

"They fixed the click in my shoulder while I was in the medcomp. Doesn't hurt anymore. Guess it pays to get an overhaul every so often, huh?"

Kel knew there was more than small talk on Poul's mind.

"What is it, brother?"

Poul looked at his lap as he spoke. "You know, Meadows told me they found you on top of me. You were shielding me with your own body, brother. Trying to protect me."

Kel thought. "Poul, all I remember was getting knocked on my ass. My bucket visor failed and I was in the dark. I didn't know where I was or even *if* I was."

"Yeah. Me too."

"Not that I wouldn't have, but if I was, it was because I got tossed there like a kitten."   Poul shrugged. Kel felt uncomfortable by the suggestion of what he'd done. He changed the mood. "Because if I'd been aware, there's no way I'd have done something like that. I mean, you are a very attractive man and all, but I just don't feel that way about you, buddy."

Poul flushed and snapped. "Hey! I'm trying to say thanks. Don't be so modest all the time." His friend was incensed. "Meadows said that's how it was, so that's how it was. Just shut up and take the thanks for being my hero. Frelling jerk."

Kel wanted to laugh but saw that Poul was very serious.

"Poul, I hope you've already known this."

Poul met his eyes, still agitated and hurt by Kel's making light of the moment. He could see Poul expected more abuse. "What?"

"Brother, you've always been my biggest hero."

"Sure. You could call me that. But it's not quite right."

On introduction, Kel had reflexively asked the doctor if he was a head shrinker. The man was too accommodating, too passive, tried too hard to be nonthreatening when he asked if he could sit with Kel and talk for a while. It was a tactic. It made Kel suspicious.

"So, what's a psychiatrist want to talk with little old me about? You're not here to ask about all my combat traumas, are you, doc? Because I'm not going to start crying for you. You're wasting your time."

The doctor shook his head. Sweetland was embroidered on the chest. "My time's pretty open for the next ten minutes, Captain. I'd like to waste it with you."

"Who am I to stop you then? Feel free. I was just going to catch up on some reports. You can watch me type until you're bored. How's that?"

Kel knew he was being rude, but didn't care. He was an officer in the Legion. An operator. He had more important things to do than lie around, and he wasn't about to give the psychiatrist any ammunition to use against him if he thought he had some influence in judging his fitness for duty. The best thing to do in an interrogation was keep your mouth shut. If the man persisted, he'd feed him some tidbit about minor combat stress and how he'd work it out on Victrix with a counselor if he felt it was affecting his performance.

"It's okay, Captain. I know who you are, or rather, what you are. I wouldn't dream of trying to crawl around in that skull, well, not like you're thinking. I may have given you the wrong impression. I'm not a head shrinker. I do more concrete work in the brain box. I'm a neuroreconstruction specialist. I was the guy piecing together the damaged axons in there." He tapped the side of his own head.

Kel blushed. "Gee, I'm sorry, sir. Here you are trying to check on me and I'm acting like an ingrate. Please." He put his datapad down and gestured to the empty chair by his bed. "What did you have to do inside my noggin?"

"Not much, I'm glad to say. Tell me, how do you feel?"

Kel shrugged. Except for the way his body felt—weak and unexercised—he felt good. "Since it's my brain healer asking, I don't mind telling you. I feel sharp. When you walked in, I was just finishing a report. It's been a while since I've felt so focused. I banged out five thousand words without a pause. Like every word was at my fingertips, ready to be typed without having to think about it. Maybe it's all the sleep, but it's been a long time since the words have flowed so easily for me. 'Spose I have you to thank for that."

The doctor nodded. "There was some damage in there. I repaired the acute shears and the damage caused by advancing edema from concussion and overpressure, but there was some chronic, underlying trauma, too. Accumulated insults that weren't completely repairable. Anyone ever tell you to get your head checked in a medcomp before? It's better to get that brain scanned and repaired after any incident, rather than let the gliosis happen. We can't do much with scars, you know."

JP had harangued him about that very thing. He felt guilty as he thought about how JP had threatened him with Meadows's overbearance. The wetness in his eyes returned. The doctor pretended not to notice.

"If it's any comfort, I don't think there's any impairment. Were anyone to ask me, your brain is fit for duty. It's more like the brain of a plasma welder who won't wear his atmomask, or a null fighter who's been punched on the ground too much. Your residuals won't cause anything much different from what many young men experience from exposure to combat. Stuff that primarily comes out in behaviors like hyperalertness, irritability—you know, the usual pluses for a legionnaire. No one will think you're any different, nor likely suspect you're better than ever."

Kel wiped his eyes and chuckled politely. "Thank you, doctor. It's a relief to hear you're not trying to downgrade me for duty."

"Far from it. But I do have some brain exercises I want you to do." The doctor stood and from within his lab coat produced a stack of flimsy. He set the pages on the tray and produced another old-fashioned device, a stylus, and set it on top.

"There's a mind-body-fine-motor connection involved in writing by hand. And rather than just copying something to improve stylus control—which is a therapy for many of my patients—I'm giving you an assignment. Just like a professor to his student. This one is going to give your conscious and subconscious mind a workout as well. I want you to write yourself an essay." He took the stylus and jotted some words at the top of the blank page, then turned it around for Kel to see. In barely legible script it said,

What I want for myself in the next ten years of my life.

"Huh?" Kel exclaimed, ashamed at the puerile sound as soon as he'd uttered it.

"I'm no head shrinker. I know how things work better than those weirdos. Don't repeat this, but some of my best friends are brain benders. The reason they went into the field is to understand why they hate their mothers. You don't need help from their kind. You don't need help from anyone but yourself, Captain. Because inside that beaten brainpan that I've slaved over are all the answers you need to heal yourself the rest of the way. I've done what medical science knows how to do. The rest is up to you. I'm telling you. It's there." He checked his chrono. "Well. I've got more axons to graft. Luck." Before Kel could respond, he was the ghost image of a flapping white coat. The doctor left Kel slack jawed, pages in hand. He read the assignment again.

"Pfft." He threw the pages in the bin. To the empty threshold he mumbled, "Nice mumbo-jumbo, brain slicer. You're a better surgeon than you are a showman. All I need is to be back in a bucket."

Braley was there at the end of the week to escort him out of the ward. "Hey there, Task Force Commander," Kel teased. "Too busy to come visit an old teammate?"

Braley dropped a fresh set of Legion silks on the bed. "Sorry, Kel. I was here when they brought you in. Been a little hectic getting things wound down before we get home."

Kel felt a new wave of guilt, imagining Braley watching over him, bruised and unconscious in the hospital. "I'm just teasing, brother. I know what it means to be in command. Your duty is to the mission and the men. In that order. I'm proud of what a terrific job you did running the show. I could never fill those kind of shoes."

Braley deflected the praise. "I'm bound for an office, and this was just the first taste of it. You went out there and did another incredible job. Once again, you were the man for the mission. It's me and the rest of the unit who are proud of you."

Kel felt the heaviness return to his heart. He couldn't say more than, "JP."

Braley nodded. "JP." There was nothing more to be said. "Come on, get out of those assless duds and let's get going. There's more than a few leejes waiting to buy you the first round."

"Easy now, Major. The docs would stroke if they thought I was going to ruin this brain with alcohol. Besides. I'm on duty."

It was good to be out of the hospital. Kel didn't want to take the slider, and insisted they walk the length of the massive ship, out to the decks above the hangers where DO was billeted separately from the rest of the passengers. The ache was better in all his muscles. He'd hit the gym tonight. He'd promised the nurses he wouldn't do anything strenuous too soon. Maybe just a short stint of calisthenics at a couple of Gs in the heavy room. He'd see how he felt after that before he planned his path back to peak fitness.

"Legion! Legion! Legion!"

Kel had no sooner passed through the bulkhead door than the roar shocked him.

"Legion! Legion! Legion!"

The passage and companionways were stacked with operators. Poul, Hardball, Meadows, Wiggy, Sims, and Woobie stood closest.

Kel snapped to attention.

Braley shouted. "Attention. A legionnaire presents himself to his tribe. How say we?"

"Legion! Legion! Legion! We are the Legion!" the crowd shouted.

Braley shouted again. "Welcome home, Captain Turner. Legionnaires, welcome this leej back into the fold!"

The moistness in his eyes was soon replaced by laughs and winces as everyone took their turn hammering his chest from a line that disappeared around the next bulkhead. Poul hammered him lightly. "Gabe and I got ours yesterday. I'm still sore."

Meadows was last after Bigg. He hammered Kel so hard, he had to take a step back to absorb the blow.

"Easy, Curt," Hardball yelled. "Don't put the captain back in the hospital! Dang, you're dense sometimes. If JP were here, he'd knock you silly."

Meadows shrunk. "Sorry, sir," he said softly. "Just glad the team's back together. It wouldn't be the same without you."

Kel laughed. "Nowhere I'd rather be, men. Thank you all for the honor. PT at 0500, Top. Sound good?"

"Never better, boss."

Kel lay on the bunk in the small stateroom, alone again. He'd taken a single sip of the offered spirit to be polite, but it made him dizzy. He'd never been a drinker to begin with, but after almost ten days in the hospital, it was like he'd gulped a full tumbler of the brown liquid.

It wasn't just the hospital. He examined himself in the mirror. His ribs showed. His thick cords of muscles were now stringy ropes that twitched beneath thin skin, the layer of fat missing between them. The jungle had taken its toll on him. The time in the hospital hadn't helped either.

He stretched out, ready to dim the lights. 0500 was going to come early. On the floor, something had fallen out of his kit bag. He recognized it and picked it up. It was the flimsy the doctor had given him. He'd pulled it out of the garbage and stuffed it in his personal bag out of shame. He stared at the words again.

What I want for myself in the next ten years of my life.

He laid the paper down. He knew he couldn't avoid it any longer. He pulled out the brand-new datapad and keyed his bio-sig. The flashing icons of the messages were there on the new screen. He opened the first one, the one from the hypercomm relay near Andalore. As he expected, the face of Grant Odom, the Lanthanum executive smiled at him. He let it play.

"Captain Turner, I hope this message finds you well. We don't need an immediate response. Quite the opposite. With your operational demands, a reply any time you're able would be welcome. I just wanted you to know. The matter has gone before the board. It's unanimous. We have an offer to make that we think will interest you. I can promise you the latitude to work how you see fit, for a compensation well deserved. Please think about it. The offer stands in perpetuity. All our best." The link closed.

It wasn't a shock. The man had said as much on Haemus. But, Kel thought it was more than just his perception when Odom emphasized the parts about "latitude" and "compensation." He played it again. No. The man had definitely changed intonation on those words.

What I want for myself in the next ten years of my life stared at him from his elbow.

The next, he knew as well who it must be from. His hand quavered as he touched the icon. There was no image. It was a text page. It began with his own words. He'd written them so long ago he'd forgotten them. Reading them, it seemed like they'd been written by someone else, as though he was intruding on a stranger's missive, the worst kind of voyeur—a spy.

Dear Tara.

Kel gulped down his butterflies.

I've tried a thousand times to find the right words. The only ones I can bring myself to tell you are just these.

I'm so sorry. I'm sorry for hurting you. I'm sorry for leaving. I think back on that day when I last saw you. It was the worst day of my life. If I could have done anything differently, please know that I would have. I would do anything to see you and your family safe.

All I know is, if there's a galaxy where you're safe and happy, then I'm happy. But if you think there could ever be room in your part of the galaxy for me again, if you call me, I will come. And I won't leave.

Kel

He swiped up. The words were so few, he blocked them from his eyes. His heart pounded and his ears rang. The message had to be a terse dismissal. Hatred. Anger. Worse than that, apathy, or indifference. He couldn't bear not knowing.

He read the single sentence over and over. So few words, so much forgiveness.

If you don't come, I'll just die!

37

The team room was the same. Kel had already adapted to the new insignia on the doors and on the PT shirts some of the guys wore. So much for the days of "Silver" and the covert unit that didn't exist and had no name. He'd lived long enough to have seen a change that now made him "one of the old guys." He'd just turned twenty-nine.

JP's ceremony was draining. Bigg was right, as always. There'd be no moving forward as a tribe until they laid Jon to rest. Why hadn't JP been in his vision, around the fire with the others? The more he thought about the vision, the more he convinced himself it had been less than that: just a mad dream. It hadn't been a visit to the ethereal plane where a bearded all-father waited to reward him. Nor a taste of the afterlife they were told awaited an operator, to be joined with his kill team for all eternity like the colonel promised them, repeating the too familiar words with JP's face floating behind him on the dais. Like the holo of their friend, it was just a representation. A dream. But a good one.

But he'd learned, some dreams could be made real.

"Your link's going off, sir," Meadows said. Kel was in his gear cage. He'd been putting to order every item, as though Rex himself would be inspecting. "It's the head shed."

"Moving, Top. Thanks." Kel checked the message. "I'll be back late. Close up shop and take the rest of the day off, guys. Is that okay, Top?"

"Sure, sir. Thanks for asking my permission after you've released the troops and made me the bad guy if I say no. You are truly an officer now."

Kel laughed. "Sorry, Top. Don't wait for me to start PT in the morning. I may have to run an errand for the colonel."

"Oh?" Hardball stuck his head out of his gear cage. "Anything we should know about?"

Wiggy wandered into the office from out of his own cage. "Maybe cooking up a new mission, sir? A little meeting with your Nether friend to get the straight intel for us?"

Kel grinned. "Nothing like that. Yet." He found himself held in place as his three teammates waited for him to speak. The moment had almost come.

"Something else, boss?" Meadows asked him, puzzled.

"Guys. Whatever happens, if you haven't heard it from me enough, you're not just my teammates. You're my brothers. Always."

Where Meadows's mouth failed, open and mute, his face betrayed his feelings to them all, the permanent frown and wrinkled forehead relaxed, shoulders slumped forward. But only for a second. The huge chest expanded and a great guffaw escaped. "Well, that makes it official then, sir. Because if we're all brothers, then I don't have to worry about Hardball trying to date my sister when she comes for a visit. But then again, isn't that what you ranchers prefer? Keeping it in the family."

"Dang it, Curt!" Hardball yelled. "I'm gonna pin your ears back for you at morning PT. And Wiggy's gonna laugh when I do, ain't you, Wiggy? He sees my side in this. Top's still got it in for me."

"Take me with you, Captain," Wiggy begged. "These two are always so loud."

"Who you calling loud, Wiggins?" Meadows feigned offense. "Not everybody's as stiff and dull as a plank like you. We used to have fun on this team! Your trouble is, nobody's given you a good bollocking in a while. That stops NOW."

Kel slid out. The door closed behind him, but the shouts disregarded it. A ballistic door could muffle a grenade, but it couldn't drown out Meadows in full character. Kel's heart felt full. The team was going to be fine.

Around the corner, Poul was coming out of the Three team room. "Going to see the colonel?"

Kel gulped. "Yeah, it's my turn."

"Braley's over there now." Poul matched pace with him as they left the floor.

"You on your way to see Bigg?"

"It's time, Kel. No putting it off any longer."

Kel had already spoken to Bigg and to Braley. He owed them that. For many reasons, not just because they were Primus Pilus Society, too. Even without that connection, there was no one closer to him. Them and Poul. And Tara. But he hardly knew her. That was going to change.

They parted at the headquarters. Kel moved to the commander's anteroom, where Braley was closing the door to the colonel's office behind him.

"What's the word, Braley?"

"Not what I expected, exactly. I'm headed to Tiberius and Legion training command. Colonel tells me I can expect to take a training regiment. It's a short colonel billet, but since I'm on the list, I've been accelerated to command it. He thinks once I get my promotion, I'll be off to the regular Legion to take a combat command."

"On the list! Braley! Congrats! From major to short colonel in less than a year. That's great."

"I'm on the list, Kel. It could be a couple of years before I'm wearing silver."

"Well, still, I'm happy for you. You're going to be sitting in that office someday." Kel thumbed at the oak door. It opened and the adjutant stepped out.

"Captain, the colonel's ready for you."

"You still doing this?" Braley whispered. Kel nodded back before he stepped off. Braley watched him go. He shook his head. "How will we survive if we eat our young so cruelly?"

He stood at attention in front of the desk and rendered a salute. "Captain Turner, reporting as ordered, sir."

The colonel gestured him to sit without returning the salute. "Be at ease, Turner." Kel sat rigidly.

"I know I've only been your commander a short time, but I hope my evaluation of your performance will carry the weight it deserves. A job well done, Captain."

Kel felt like a heel for what was coming. "Thank you, sir. That means a great deal to me."

"I've got your assignment. You're off to the Wolfhounds. You're granted a ninety-day leave en route, not including the additional thirty days' travel to the Cygnus arm. I have to say, I'm envious. The Wolfhounds are one helluva Legion. You're going to get to do things most legionnaires only dream about. It's going to prepare you for a role at the head of our Legion someday. Congratulations."

Kel pursed his lips as he considered the assignment. Maybe he'd be commanding a heavy tank company, or even get to be a pilot finally, eventually commanding an aviation wing. It'd probably be the recon company or an assault unit. That'd be fine too. But he had something else waiting for him.

"Sir. If the Legion says it's time for me to leave Dark Ops, I've decided I'm going to have to take my other option."

"Wonder when the captain's coming back?" Hardball said to Meadows as he bounced into the team room. "He made it sound like he wasn't sure himself."

"Come see this," Wiggy said from the gear locker.

"See what?" Meadows said from behind the holo over his desk. He joined them, and saw it too. The captain's gear cage was unlocked, the door open. Everything within was stacked, lids open, ready for inspection. Clean, neat, orderly. In the middle of the cage, suspended on its rack, was the armor. Polished, gleaming, bright. Missing only the human inside to animate it. The visor stared, not able to answer when its master would return.

"Something's off, for sure," Meadows said. He looked into the cage. "The captain's personal weapons and containers are gone."

"What does it mean?" Hardball's disbelief was heavy.

"Captain Turner has left the Legion," Colonel Chatsworth said behind them. They hadn't heard the door. Bigg was with him.

"Sergeant Major," Wiggy's voice pleaded understanding, "he just... left? The captain left us? Left the Legion?"

It was impossible to believe.

Bigg nodded. "He didn't resign his commission. He went inactive. With more than ten years in, it's his option."

"Inactive?" Hardball exclaimed. "I've heard about leejes doing that, but, why?"

The door slid open again. Sims burst in. "Hey guys, Radd's gone." Sims saw the colonel and stopped. "Apologies, sir. But..."

Bigg intervened.

"I know, Sims. Sergeant Radd has left the unit. And the Legion. So's Captain Turner."

"Kel Turner! Left the Legion?" Sims exclaimed.

Behind him, Braley and Woobie filed in.

"Don't stand on ceremony, Three," Meadows said. "Come in and seal the door behind you. We better get a head count and make sure we're not missing anyone else."

"Where'd they go?"

"Did they go together?"

"Why didn't they tell anybody?"

Questions flew around the room. The colonel moved out of the fracas to the empty team leader's chair. He sat silently as Bigg calmed the room.

"Guys, listen up," Bigg said, a tiredness in his voice. "Turner and Radd left last night. They didn't sneak out. They told Major Yost and I about their decision. And the colonel. It's not meant as a slight to anyone. Those are the two best leejes I've ever known, and I've known them all. I've known them both since they were barely shaving. They didn't want to make a big deal about it."

"Not make a big deal about it!" Sims said. "This feels like a pretty big deal to me."

"What I meant to say, Sims, is they didn't want to make it harder than it had to be. They didn't want to answer a lot of questions. Maybe you can understand how painful it was for them."

Woobie frowned. "So, how long had they been planning this?"

Braley shrugged. "I'm not sure. For Poul, maybe not until after Psydon. For Kel, well, he's been torn between two possible futures for a while."

"Where'd he go?" Wiggy asked.

Bigg answered. "He's got a home and a family waiting for him. They're good people. They'll take care of him."

"It's really about her, isn't it?" Meadows said, more a statement than a question.

"And Radd?" Sims asked. "He went with him? But why? Why would Poul leave?"

"I know."

From the room adjacent, Hardball stared at the armor Kel had left behind. Without turning to face them, Hardball spoke. Without the drawl he'd hidden behind, without accent, with a voice clear and strong, he said, "I saw it all, and now I understand." He took a deep breath and recited:

> *From the pinnacle top, the legionnaire looked*
> *At the mountain of bodies, and lives that he took*
> *There he saw Savage and doro and donk*
> *And the mixed blood of humans with whom they*
> *had fought.*
> *He cried, 'Oba, forgive me for all left undone*
> *For my blaster is silenced, like a cold long-dead sun*
> *From bright clustered stars, to the galaxy's edge*
> *For the honor of Rex, I've followed, I've led.'*
> *So tall was the mountain of enemies stacked*
> *'Twas nearer to heaven than earth at his back.*
> *A doorway appeared as heavens did part*
> *And a sweet siren beckoned, spoke to his heart.*
> *A peace promised long, so rare and so dear*

Waited ahead, with fine souls gone from here.
He placed gauntlet firm on the pearly façade;
He pushed with all might, but his way it was barred.
In armor so heavy, in armor so light,
A soldier's heart pierced, weighed darker than night.
Then below called a leej in familiar refrains,
Coated in scarlet and earthly remains,
'The Legion's eternal, and then so are you.
Forget not the trust and the honor you knew.'
The legionnaire looked to the ether and clouds
And yelled with new courage the truth he had found:
'I searched for my soul, but my soul I could not see.
I sought my God, but my God eluded me.
I looked to my brother, and I found all three.

THE END

Explore over 30+ Galaxy's Edge books and counting from the minds of Jason Anspach, Nick Cole, Doc Spears, Jonathan Yanez, Karen Traviss, and more.

HISTORY OF THE GALAXY

1ST ERA BOOKS

THE FALL OF EARTH

1ST ERA SUMMARY

The West has been devastated by epidemics, bio-terrorism, war, and famine. Asia has shut its borders to keep the threats at bay, and some with power and influence have already abandoned Earth. Now an escape route a century in the making – the Nomad mission – finally offers hope to a small town and a secret research centre hidden in a rural American backwater. Shrouded in lies and concealed even from the research centre's staff, Nomad is about to fulfil its long-dead founder's vision of preserving the best of humanity to forge a new future.

2ND ERA SUMMARY

They were the Savages. Raiders from our distant past. Elites who left Earth to create tailor-made utopias aboard the massive lighthuggers that crawled through the darkness between the stars. But the people they left behind on a dying planet didn't perish in the dystopian nightmare the Savages had themselves created: they thrived, discovering faster-than-light technology and using it to colonize the galaxy ahead of the Savages, forming fantastic new civilizations that surpassed the wildest dreams of Old Earth.

HISTORY OF THE GALAXY

3RD **ERA** SUMMARY

The Savage Wars are over but the struggle for power continues. Backed by the might of the Legion, the Republic seeks to establish a dominion of peace and prosperity amid a galaxy still reeling from over a millennia of war. Brushfire conflicts erupt across the edge as vicious warlords and craven demagogues seek to carve out their own kingdoms in the vacuum left by the defeated Savages. But the greatest threat to peace may be those in the House of Reason and Republic Senate seeking to reshape the galaxy in their own image.

4ᵀᴴ ERA SUMMARY

As the Legion fights wars on several fronts, the Republic that dispatches them to the edge of the galaxy also actively seeks to undermine them as political ambitions prove more important than lives. Tired and jaded legionnaires suffer the consequences of government appointed officers and their ruinous leadership. The fighting is never enough and soon a rebellion breaks out among the Mid-Core planets, consuming more souls and treasure. A far greater threat to the Republic hegemony comes from the shadowy edges of the galaxy as a man determined to become an emperor emerges from a long and secretive absence. It will take the sacrifice of the Legion to maintain freedom in a galaxy gone mad.

HISTORY OF THE GALAXY

5TH **ERA** SUMMARY

An empire defeated and with it the rot of corruption scoured from the Republic. Fighting a revolution to restore the order promised at the founding of the Republic was the easy part. Now the newly rebuilt Legion must deal with factions no less treacherous than the House of Reason while preparing itself for war against a foe no one could have imagined.

HONOR ROLL

We would like to give our most sincere thanks and recognition to those who supported the creation of *Galaxy's Edge: Angles of Attack* by supporting us at GalaxysEdge.us.

Artis Aboltins

Guido Abreu

Chancellor Adams

Myron Adams

Garion Adkins

Elias Aguilar

Bill Allen

Justin Altman

Jake Altman

Tony Alvarez

Galen Anderson

Jarad Anderson

Robert Anspach

Jonathan Auerbach

Fritz Ausman

Sean Averill

Nicholas Avila

Matthew Bagwell

Marvin Bailey

Joseph Bailey

Kevin Bangert

John Barber

Logan Barker

Brian Barrows

Robert Battles

Eric Batzdorfer

John Baudoin

Antonio Becerra

Mike Beeker

Randall Beem

Matt Beers

John Bell

Daniel Bendele

Edward Benson

David Bernatski

Justin Bielefeld

Trevor Blasius

WJ Blood

Evan Boldt

Rodney Bonner

Thomas Seth Bouchard

William Boucher

Brandon Bowles

Alex Bowling

Jordan Brann

Ernest Brant

Geoff Brisco

Raymond Brooks

James Brown

Jeremy Bruzdzinski

Marion Buehring

Matthew Buzek

Daniel Cadwell

Brian Callahan

Van Cammack

Chris Campbell

Danny Cannon

Zachary Cantwell

Brian Cave

Shawn Cavitt

Kris (Joryl) Chambers

David Chor

Tyrone Chow

Jonathan Clews

Beau Clifton

Robert Collins Sr.

Alex Collins-Gauweiler

Jerry Conard

Michael Conn

James Connolly

James Conyers

Robert Cosler

Ryan Coulston

Andrew Craig

Adam Craig

Phil Culpepper

Ben Curcio

Thomas Cutler

Tommy Cutler

David Danz

Brendon Darling

Alister Davidson

Peter Davies

Walter Davila

Ivy Davis

Nathan Davis

Ashton Davis	Mark Franceschini
Ron Deage	Elizabeth Gafford
Tod Delaricheliere	David Gaither
Anerio Deorma	Christopher Gallo
Isaac Diamond	Richard Gallo
Christopher DiNote	Kyle Gannon
Matthew Dippel	Michael Gardner
Ellis Dobbins	Nick Gerlach
Gerald Donovan	John Giorgis
Ray Duck	Johnny Glazebrooks
Christopher Durrant	Justin Godfrey
Cami Dutton	Luis Gomez
Virgil Dwyer	Justin Gottwaltz
William Ely	Gordon Green
Andrew English	Shawn Greene
Stephane Escrig	Preston Groogan
Steven Feily	Brandon Handy
Meagan Ference	Erik Hansen
Adolfo Fernandez	Greg Hanson
Ashley Finnigan	Ian Harper
Matthew Fiveson	Jason Harris
Kath Flohrs	Jordan Harris
Steve Forrester	Revan Harris
Skyla Forster	Matthew Hartmann
Timothy Foster	Adam Hartswick
Bryant Fox	Ronald Haulman

Joshua Hayes	James Jeffers
Adam Hazen	Tedman Jess
Richard Heard	Eric Jett
Colin Heavens	James Johnson
Brenton Held	Randolph Johnson
Jason Henderson	Scott Johnson
Jason Henderson	Josh Johnson
Jonathan Herbst	Tyler Jones
Kyle Hetzer	Paul Jones
Korrey Heyder	John Josendale
Aaron Holden	Wyatt Justice
Clint Holmes	Ron Karroll
Jacob Honeter	Timothy Keane
Charles Hood	Cody Keaton
Tyson Hopkins	Brian Keeter
Ian House	Noah Kelly
Ken Houseal	Jacob Kelly
Nathan Housley	Caleb Kenner
Jeff Howard	Daniel Kimm
Nicholas Howser	Zachary Kinsman
Kristie Hudson	Rhet Klaahsen
Mike Hull	Jesse Klein
Donald Humpal	Kyle Klincko
Bradley Huntoon	William Knapp
Wendy Jacobson	Marc Knapp
Paul Jarman	Travis Knight

Steven Konecni	Jacob Margheim
Ethan Koska	Deven Marincovich
Evan Kowalski	Cory Marko
Byl Kravetz	Lucas Martin
Brian Lambert	Pawel Martin
Clay Lambert	Trevor Martin
Jeremy Lambert	Phillip Martinez
Andrew Langler	Tao Mason
Dave Lawrence	Ashley Mateo
Alexander Le	Mark Maurice
Paul Lizer	Simon Mayeski
Gary Locken	Kyle McCarley
Richard Long	Quinn McCusker
Oliver Longchamps	Alan McDonald
Joseph Lopez	Caleb McDonald
Kyle Lorenzi	Hans McIlveen
David Losey	Rachel McIntosh
Ronnie Loven	Jason McMarrow
Steven Ludtke	Joshua McMaster
Brooke Lyons	Colin McPherson
John M	Christopher Menkhaus
Patrick Maclary	Jim Mern
Richard Maier	Robert Mertz
Chris Malone	Pete Micale
Brian Mansur	Mike Mieszcak
Robert Marchi	Ted Milker

Jacob Montagne	Eric Pastorek
Mitchell Moore	Zac Petersen
Matteo Morelli	Corey Pfleiger
William Morris	Dupres Pina
Alex Morstadt	Pete Plum
Nicholas Mukanos	Matthew Pommerening
Vinesh Narayan	Nathan Poplawski
James Needham	Jeremiah Popp
Travis Nichols	Chancey Porter
Bennett Nickels	Chris Pourteau
Trevor Nielsen	Chris Prats
Andrew Niesent	Aleksander Purcell
Sean Noble	Joshua Purvis
Otto Noda	Max Quezada
Brett Noll-Emmick	T.J. Recio
Greg Nugent	Jacob Reynolds
Christina Nymeyer	Eric Ritenour
Timothy O'Connor	Walt Robillard
Grant Odom	Joshua Robinson
Colin O'neill	Brian Robinson
Ryan O'neill	Daniel Robitaille
Max Oosten	Paul Roder
Tyler Ornelas	Chris Rollini
Jonathan Over	Thomas Roman
James Owens	Joyce Roth
David Parker	Andrew Ruiz

Sterling Rutherford	Michael Smith
Lawrence Sanchez	Tyler Smith
David Sanford	Sharroll Smith
Chris Sapero	Michael Smith
Jaysn Schaener	Alexander Snyder
Landon Schaule	John Spears
Shayne Schettler	Thomas Spencer
Brian Schmidt	Peter Spitzer
Andrew Schmidt	Dustin Sprick
Kurt Schneider	Cooper Stafford
William Schweisthal	Graham Stanton
Anthony Scimeca	Paul Starck
Preston Scott	Ethan Step
Rylee Scott	John Stephenson
Aaron Seaman	Seaver Sterling
Phillip Seek	Maggie Stewart-Grant
Christopher Shaw	John Stockley
Charles Sheehan	Rob Strachan
Wendell Shelton	William Strickler
Brett Shilton	Shayla Striffler
Vernetta Shipley	Kevin Summers
Glenn Shotton	Ernest Sumner
Joshua Sipin	Aaron Sweeney
Christopher Slater	Carol Szpara
Scott Sloan	Travis TadeWaldt
Daniel Smith	Daniel Tanner

Lawrence Tate

Tim Taylor

Robert Taylor

Justin Taylor

Daniel Thomas

Steven Thompson

Chris Thompson

William Joseph Thorpe

Beverly Tierney

Kayla Todd

Matthew Townsend

Jameson Trauger

Scott Tucker

Eric Turnbull

Brandon Turton

Dylan Tuxhorn

Jalen Underwood

Barrett Utz

Paul Van Dop

Paden VanBuskirk

Patrick Varrassi

Daniel Vatamaniuck

Jose Vazquez

Josiah Velazquez

Anthony Wagnon

Humberto Waldheim

Christopher Walker

David Wall

Justin Wang

Andrew Ward

Scot Washam

Tyler Washburn

John Watson

Bill Webb

Hiram Wells

Ben Wheeler

Greg Wiggins

Jack Williams

Scott Winters

Jason Wright

John Wurtz

Ethan Yerigan

Phillip Zaragoza

Brandt Zeeh

Nathan Zoss

ABOUT GALAXY'S EDGE

Galaxy's Edge is an expansive, interconnected military science fiction series. Galaxy's Edge Season One, which begins with *Legionnaire* by Jason Anspach and Nick Cole, has sold over one million copies.

For news about upcoming Galaxy's Edge audio books, merchandise, lore, and events, visit www.galaxysedge.us and sign up for the KTF newsletter.

To connect with other Galaxy's Edge readers as well as the authors, join one or all of the Galaxy's Edge Fan Clubs on Facebook, Reddit, or Discord.

ABOUT THE MAKERS

Doc Spears is a United States Army veteran.

Jason Anspach is the co-creator of Galaxy's Edge. He lives in the Pacific Northwest.

Nick Cole is the other co-creator of Galaxy's Edge. He lives in southern California with his wife, Nicole.

CPSIA information can be obtained
at www.ICGtesting.com
Printed in the USA
FSHW021302210221
78812FS

9 781949 731460